Praise for *The Officer Says "I Do"*

"Murray, a Marine's wife, puts plenty of authentic flavor in this sensual tale of loving and life in the military. Issues of patriotism, commitment, capitalism, abstinence, abuse of power, and conformity entwine with eroticism and romance for an exciting read."

—*Publishers Weekly*

"Fun to read… entertaining, thanks to Murray's insights into the attraction of opposites."

—*Booklist*

"Charming… a fun and spunky romance. Anyone who enjoys a great romantic comedy with some hot bedroom action will definitely enjoy this one. Especially those who like a man in uniform!"

—*Minding Spot*

"One of the best I have ever read… You cannot put the book down."

—*Night Owl Romance*, 5 stars, Reviewer Top Pick

"Totally hilarious, with a loving twist of opposites who do attract… If you love an uplifting romance this is one you'll enjoy… it sure put a smile on my face."

—*BookLoons*

"Funny, charming, and sexy… a ridiculously fun novel with fabulous characters that will you leave you smiling and writing that will leave you wanting more. It's all a girl could want and then some!"

—*The Romance Reviews*

"Great characters, smooth writing, sensual love scenes, and heartwarming romance, the whole package was wonderful! I can't wait to read more of this series."

—*Book Lovers Inc.*

THE OFFICER
Breaks the Rules

JEANETTE MURRAY

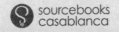

sourcebooks
casablanca

Published by Sourcebooks Casablanca, an imprint of Sourcebooks, Inc.
P.O. Box 4410, Naperville, Illinois 60567-4410
(630) 961-3900
FAX: (630) 961-2168
www.sourcebooks.com

Printed and bound in Canada
WC 10 9 8 7 6 5 4 3 2 1

Chapter 1

JEREMY PHILLIPS SETTLED THE PROTECTORS OVER HIS ears, adjusted his glasses more comfortably on the bridge of his nose, and took a relaxed stance. Then, at the signal, he picked up his Beretta, clicked off the safety, and fired fifteen rounds. As the smell of black powder and CPL agent filled his nostrils, he checked his gun, set the safety, then slapped a hand over the switch to draw the paper target forward.

His best friend, and today's shooting partner, Timothy O'Shay ducked his head around the divider and mouthed something.

"What?" Jeremy yelled back.

Tim cocked one eyebrow and tapped a finger to his ear, pointing out the obvious.

Oh. Shit. Right. Jeremy took the protectors off and set them on the ledge in front of him, next to his Beretta. "What?"

"I asked how long you were going to waste bullets when your head's not in the game."

Jeremy gave him a withering look. "I'm not wasting bullets."

Tim's answer was a glance between the two targets—his and Jeremy's—now only a few feet away. Jeremy took a look also.

Tim's dummy showed two tight clusters of bullet holes, so close together they'd ripped large chunks from the paper. Several in the head, the other in the chest. Not a stray hole at all.

His dummy, by comparison, looked like a constellation of wrongness. Half the bullets sprayed over the outline's shoulders, the other half catching the figure in the arm or some other undesirable area.

"You'll have to remind me how you shot expert at the last firearms qual," Tim said casually as he stripped the target down and replaced it with a fresh one.

"Just having an off day." When Tim said nothing, Jeremy glanced over his shoulder. His friend smirked and shook his head. "Bite me, O'Shay."

"You know what Dwayne would say to that." Tim straightened his shoulders in an effort to look taller. "If you were a female, I just might take you up on that one," he said with an exaggerated drawl.

Though he tried to fight it, Jeremy cracked a smile. Their deployed friend, Dwayne Robertson, always did let his natural drawl thicken up to an almost obscene level when he was telling a joke. Tim nailed it perfectly. Jeremy clipped on his own fresh target and sent it back. "Yeah, yeah. When's that big lug coming home, anyway?"

"He just left not that long ago. For all we know, he might get delayed past the original seven. Stuff's shifting over there. Makes for interesting deployments." As he thumbed the last few bullets into his clip, he pushed it in and locked it. "Seriously, what's going on? You've shot for shit all day, and I know you could do better than this blindfolded. What's up?"

Because Tim was holding a loaded weapon, now was absolutely not the time for the truth. So instead he lifted a shoulder and dismissed his friend's concern. "If marriage is gonna turn you into some walking therapy session, I'm not so sure we can be friends anymore."

Tim just laughed and flipped the switch to send his target flying back. "It's not the prison sentence you make it out to be."

"Right."

"No, really. I guess it could be if you were unhappy. But when you've got the right partner, it works out. Pretty damn well, I think." A self-satisfied smile crossed Tim's face as he watched his target settle into place. But the preoccupied look in his eye behind his protective glasses said he wasn't actually seeing the target at all. He was thinking about Skye, his wife.

Jeremy gave a grunt and rolled his shoulders. Tim might be blissful in love and all that, but it wasn't for everyone. At least, not for him. Not right now. He had shit to do before he thought about settling down. And his mind wasn't in the dating game. Not when he was too hung up on one irritating, annoying, always-in-the-way female who made his teeth grind and his blood boil.

In all the right ways... and wrong ones.

He waited for his own target to settle before readjusting the mufflers over his ears and reloading his weapon. Deep breath in, then back out. This time he wasn't going to rush it. Wasn't going to just punch holes through the paper for the satisfaction of the hit. Conciseness, precision, accuracy.

He sighted the target, then took a calm breath in. Waited until his heartbeats slowed enough to time the trigger squeeze between them. And on a slow breath out, he fired one shot.

And his brain exploded in color and sound, light and movement. Voices. Action. Motivation and intrigue.

Before he even glanced at the target to check his shot, Jeremy clicked on the safety, set the gun down, and started patting his pockets for a pen. Where the hell did he put it? Aggravated, he turned in a tight circle around his cubicle before spotting his pen on the ground by the bag he used for his ammo. He sifted through the bag but came up with no paper. Terrified he was about to lose the scene playing out in his mind, he pushed up the sleeve of his Henley and started to write across the underside of his arm, from biceps to elbow to wrist. Black ink smudged, but he kept going, knowing he'd have an interesting time deciphering it later but not caring in the moment. He had to get the idea down or he'd lose it.

Writer's block was a bitch in heat. And he wasn't about to let the perfect solution to the corner he'd written himself into last week slip through his fingers because of a lack of paper.

Distantly, he realized he no longer heard the muffled pops of Tim's gun. Quickly, before his friend could realize what he was doing, he jotted the last few words down across the inside of his wrist and pulled his shirt down.

"Hey, what stopped you?" When Tim glanced around the divide and saw Jeremy squatting on the floor, his brows rose in question. "You okay?"

"Yeah." Standing, stuffing the pen back in his pocket, he shrugged. "Decided you were right. My head's not in the game. No point in wasting bullets."

"I was planning to go a few more, if you don't mind waiting."

Jeremy smiled, feeling more relaxed now than he had in a week. "Sure, maybe I'll go one more round." He waited until Tim was settled, then lined up his own fourteen remaining shots. With a more relaxed breathing rhythm, and a looser stance, he fired until he came up empty. And when he recalled his paper target this time, he couldn't hold back the satisfied smirk.

Fourteen head shots, one through the chest—the chest shot being his first before he'd started jotting notes. Not a single stray in the bunch. "Not bad," he mumbled to himself.

Then everything in his brain stalled as he caught a whiff of something feminine, something that climbed over the scent of black powder and CLR and made its presence known. A scent he knew too damn well.

"Not bad at all."

And with that light, airy voice from over his shoulder, his mood dipped dangerously low once more.

"Mad, hey." Tim leaned over to give her a hug. Madison hugged back tightly.

"Thanks for letting me know you were out here." She hefted her bag from over her shoulder, taking the stall on the other side of Jeremy. "Empty for a Saturday."

"It's early yet. Lazy people are still in bed." Tim peeked around her arm. "What'd you bring?"

She held up her .22, brand new and ready to be tested.

"Ah. See you broke out the Desert Eagle for this one," he said solemnly, then laughed when she punched him in the arm. Her brother's face twisted in comedic dismay. "Well, hell, Mad. That's a girl gun."

"I *am* a girl, you ass." She kicked at his feet and he shuffled back, laughing all the way to his stall. "And this little sucker fits in almost any purse," she added, then felt stupid for justifying the completely frivolous purchase of the small handgun. It really was a girly gun. But it was so cute…

Not able to avoid it any longer, she glanced at Jeremy's face for the first time since she got to the range.

Thunderclouds would have been a friendlier welcome. His face was a mask of annoyance and frustration. Well, that made two of them. Though God only knew what he was so frustrated about. If he thought she was stalking him, he had a more self-inflated ego than she thought.

But either way, she'd play it cool. "Morning Jeremy," she said, keeping her voice light and casual.

"Morning." His own voice was tense. With stiff motions, he turned back to his target to set up a fresh paper outline.

She watched him for just a moment, taking in the rigid line of his spine, the hard set of his shoulders. The way his head looked so tightly screwed to his neck he might as well have been in a brace.

She'd been the one to initiate their kiss months ago. She'd been the one to keep trying, keep showing him there was nothing wrong with them trying each other out for size. And he was the one who'd retreated. And she knew it was her fault he'd lost that loose gait, that easy stance, that distant, dreamy set to his eyes he'd had when she walked up.

Well, not her fault. Not quite. It wasn't like she walked up and punched him or something.

Now that she thought about it, the idea had merit…

No. Madison snapped her ear protectors on and slipped on the glasses before loading up. She wasn't going to do anything to tick him off or give him ammo— pun intended—to ignore her further. He was doing a damn fine job of it all on his own.

Lining up her shot, she took the breath she knew she needed to calm her down, then fired until she ran empty.

Not her best, but she'd never been the marksman her brother was. Every Marine was a rifleman first. She was more of a healer, really. Though it didn't hurt to kick a little ass on occasion. Which made her job as a Navy nurse a near perfect fit for her.

She ejected the clip and peeked around the corner of the partition to see Jeremy packing up his things.

"Leaving already?"

He didn't glance up. "Yeah. I have stuff to get done today."

It was a lie, she knew that much. He probably would have stayed another hour or two if she'd not shown up. But she refused to feel any guilt about it. That was his choice. All of it—the entire situation—was his choice. There was one very simple solution, and he refused to take it.

"Have a good day, then. Make sure to tell Tim bye before you leave." From the sounds of it, Tim had just started a new round and would be a minute.

"Right. Got it." Hefting his bag over one shoulder, he straightened and finally looked her in the eye.

Jeremy sucked at hiding anything from her. He might just seem sullen or closed off to her brother and Dwayne, his two best friends. But men weren't the most perceptive, and Madison could always see the little wounds he hid with his quiet nature. They called to the healer in her, even as she wanted to strangle him for being so damn stubborn about letting her inside his emotional walls.

"Jeremy," she started, not sure where to take it. Not that she had the chance.

He shook his head once. "Not now, Mad." And he turned on his heel and pushed through the door leading to the lobby.

Not now. That was a first. Normally he said *No. Never*. Was it a slip of the tongue? Or a hint there was hope?

"Where'd Jeremy go?"

Madison snapped from her zoned-out stare at the door and looked at her brother. He wore the confused puppy face she always teased him about when they were kids.

"Said he had things to do. Guess he forgot to say good-bye," she said lightly.

"Oh. Huh." Tim shrugged then flipped the switch, waiting for his target to zoom in.

Men, she thought with affectionate irritation. Undercurrents were lost on them. To fill the silence, she asked, "How's Veronica settling in?" Veronica Gibson, Skye's cousin, had moved into the area a month ago from… well, she wasn't entirely sure where she originated. She was currently taking up residence in her brother's extra bedroom.

"Good. Great, actually." Tim rubbed the back of his neck. "She and Skye are constantly talking or hanging out. She's coming out of her shell more now, thank God. You should come by later, have lunch. They both have the afternoon off."

"You just want me to drag Veronica away so you

have your wife and your house to yourself," she joked. And when a flush crept up his neck, she laughed.

It did funny things to her heart to see her brother find the woman he loved more than anything. And what an unlikely combination. But love didn't always ask for opinions, as Madison clearly learned the hard way. Otherwise she wouldn't have fallen for the one guy determined never to be with her.

Dammit, Jeremy. Why are you so stubborn?

———

"Dammit, son. Why are you so stubborn?"

Jeremy sighed and let his head hit the back of the couch. "Sir, I—"

"No. You listen to me, Marine."

Jeremy rolled his eyes, though it was only for his own benefit, given his father was across the country at the moment and his phone didn't have a "smartass" alert system.

"You've put ten good years into the Corps. And you want to piss it away now?"

"No, sir. I don't think anything about my time in the Corps is wasted if I put it to good use in the civilian sector. From my understanding, a military background on a resume can—"

His father huffed out a breath. "Don't give me any of that wishy-washy civilian crap."

Right. Anything not Marine-related was absolute crap. How could Jeremy possibly have forgotten?

"You've got ten more years, then you can retire. Pick up pension, become a contractor. Do consulting work. Damn good living."

Your living, Dad. Your choice.

Jeremy made a noncommittal noise.

"I know I'm repeating myself." His father sighed. "And I'd prefer not to have this conversation over again myself. But I'm saying this because I believe it's the best for you. Stay the course. Stick to the plan. I didn't raise you to be a quitter."

Why, oh God, why had Jeremy even thought that hinting about wanting to get out when his contract was up was a good idea? It always led to this. An old-fashioned standoff at the OK Corral.

Because you needed a distraction, and even a lecture from Dad is better than sitting around thinking about… her.

If he hadn't known that his father's pushing came from a place of caring, if he didn't respect his father, it would have been so much easier to simply hang up and not deal with it. But Jeremy waited until his father's bluster wore down, then he told his dad he'd call again next weekend. Reluctantly, his father hung up, apparently satisfied that at least Jeremy wasn't going to run out and sign his separation papers first thing Monday morning.

No. He wouldn't do that. Though the thought occurred to him more and more every week that he was done, through, completely finished with the Corps. But the actual act of leaving? Jeremy wasn't an idiot. That would never happen. Not to mention, he had no clue what the hell he would do after ten years in the Marines. Maybe that was crazy, even contemplating leaving the Corps without a settled plan. But he couldn't help the direction of his thoughts.

As if on cue, his mind drifted back to Madison.

Watching her—though she wouldn't have realized he was—at the gun range today had sparked a heavy, undeniable pressure in his chest. There was something ridiculously sexual about watching slim, delicate fingers that he knew were soft and smooth load a gun without hesitation, take aim, and fire like it was all business.

And didn't that say something about how far gone he was, if watching her shoot turned him on? The way he'd acted around her the last time they'd been alone, he was shocked she didn't use him for target practice.

He forced his mind back to the current clusterfuck of problems... life after the Marines. If there was such a thing. His father would disagree. And at the core of it, Jeremy knew defying his father's life plan for him just wasn't going to happen.

Jeremy pushed off the couch and wandered to his computer desk a mere fifteen feet away. That was the beauty of a small apartment... nothing was far out of reach. He sucked in a breath and prayed as he lifted the sleeve of his left arm, then breathed out with relief when he found none of the ink on his arm had smeared beyond recognition. Opening up a new Word document, he typed furiously, doing his best to make out the notes he had scribbled on his arm so quickly at the firing range.

A brand-new villain to add to the mix. A new set of problems for his characters. Challenges to overcome. The core of his book started to reformulate and reassemble in his mind, like gears locking into place and cranking the machine to life.

Finally spent, he sat back and stared at the cursor blinking on the screen. Why the hell couldn't he do this after he got out? Write. At least part-time.

It's a pansy-ass excuse for a career.

Jeremy blew out a breath and rolled his chair over to the miniature kitchen area—which the landlord had sworn was a "kitchenette," though Jeremy was sure that was just to make it sound less like a hole in the wall. He grabbed a bottle of water and shut the fridge door again before he could be reminded there was likely something—or several somethings—in there that should have been tossed out who knows how long ago. Maybe if he gave it another week they'd grow legs and walk themselves out.

If he could just finish the damn manuscript, maybe send it out to a few places, that would give him an idea about whether his efforts were even worth it. Nobody had to know, he rationalized, taking a drink to wash away the dry mouth that took over every time he thought about letting someone read his work.

His eyes swung back to his cell phone, his father's words still echoing in his ears. Could he actually walk away? Sad that a man in his thirties just couldn't answer that question for himself. But his father's respect meant more to him than he could explain.

He had a while yet. If nothing looked promising, he could sign for another three years. It wouldn't kill him.

What might kill him, though, was keeping his hands off his best friend's little sister for as long as they were both stationed together.

—◆◆◆—

Madison knocked once then pushed the front door open. The knock was just a polite show of respect, now that Tim wasn't alone in the home. His wife, Skye, didn't care if she came and went as she pleased. But Veronica was still a little skittish, and Madison tried her best not to scare the poor girl.

"Skye? Veronica?" Madison dropped her bag on the entry table and kicked off her shoes, letting them land next to the pile of Skye's sandals by the door. "Anyone here?"

Skye's voice drifted from the living room. "In here!"

Madison turned the corner to see Skye and Veronica with their heads bent over what looked like an old issue of some women's magazine. "What's up? Taking one of those 'Is he hot for you?' quizzes?"

Skye laughed, and to Madison's surprise, Veronica smiled as well. The girl was quiet, reserved in a way Madison could never identify with. But slowly, as the second month closed on her visit with her cousin Skye, the girl came out of her shell a little more. Encouraged, Madison sat on the other side of Veronica and peered over her shoulder.

But before she could see what they were looking at, Skye smoothly closed the magazine and slid it to the coffee table. "Just passing time. Tim went into the office for a while after the range, and we both have the day off so we're doing the girl-time thing."

Curious, but not willing to pry, Madison let the idea of asking about the magazine go. She shifted back until she was propped against the arm of the couch. "Cool. What's on the agenda?"

"You have a full day off?" Veronica asked.

"Today and tomorrow. I actually have a weekend off, on a weekend."

Skye gave a shocked face. "Imagine that!"

Her work hours were the definition of awkward, being a nurse at the naval hospital on base. But she loved the job too much to ever care. Midnight, four in the morning, high noon... if she was at work, it was a good day—most of the time. But still, everyone needed a break.

"How's the restaurant thing coming along, Veronica?"

The woman ducked her head but forced it back up and gave her a smile. "It's good. I'm lucky Skye gave me the serving job."

"No luck at all. You're a natural. Very detail-oriented, quick, responsible." Skye smiled reassuringly. "I didn't give it to you; you earned it."

There was a story there, Madison mused. She'd known it since the day Veronica was introduced to the group. But as Skye told them all, it wasn't their place to pry into people's lives.

She heard the faint rumble of her brother's engine, the whine of the garage door being lifted, and she smiled.

"I actually came over to see if Veronica wanted to get some lunch with me," she said, and watched the other woman's eyes light up. Veronica was good for the ego, that much was for sure. She relished any chance to hang out or be invited somewhere.

"Yes!" She jumped up, then sat back down quickly. "Wait. I mean, Skye and I were going to hang out this afternoon. So maybe—"

She stopped as the door opened and Tim walked in, surveying the trio of females.

"It's like an Oprah book club in here."

Madison flipped him the bird. "Oprah this. I was just asking Veronica to lunch with me," Madison said, then gave her brother an evil glance. "But I could always invite Skye as well…"

"No, no." Tim dropped his bag and headed to the kitchen. "Thanks a lot anyway, squirt. But you two have fun. I'll keep Skye company."

"I'll just bet you will," Madison murmured with a smile.

Veronica looked less convinced, glancing between her and Skye. "Are you sure?"

Skye smiled and gave her cousin a friendly shove. "Yes, absolutely. Go! Have fun. Get something sinfully delicious for dessert. Enjoy the day off."

"Yes, ma'am," Madison quipped, then bent down to give her sister-in-law a kiss on the cheek before grabbing Veronica's hand and dragging her toward the front door.

As Veronica climbed in the passenger seat of Madison's car, she bit her lip. "I hate the thought of leaving Skye behind."

"Left behind, but not left alone," Madison said as she backed out of the driveway. "Trust me, Tim will keep her busy."

"Oh." Veronica's eyes widened almost comically. "Oh."

"Uh-huh." Enjoying the woman's naïveté, Madison winked. "We should all be so lucky to score a nooner."

"Nooner?"

Madison laughed. "We have so much to talk about, you and I."

Chapter 2

MADISON CHECKED THE WHITEBOARD FOR HER NEXT patient. Working the ER wasn't her favorite rotation, but it was never a boring one.

"Here." Her coworker, Matthew, shoved a clipboard in her stomach. She grabbed on before it could clatter to the ground. "Curtain three. You'll want this one."

Madison screwed her eyes shut and held the chart to her chest. "Please tell me it's not another extraction. The last one almost did me in."

Matthew snorted. "How that kid got so many dimes up his nose—"

"Among other places."

"—is beyond me. But no, not an extraction. Road rash. Motorcyclist came in himself."

"Just walked in? No other injuries? No ambulance?"

Matthew shook his head. "Nope, just the rash. Walked in, no limping. He was the only vehicle involved, no crash. Just says he can't reach the area to clean it himself, doesn't want to chance it." He grimaced. "Despite the lack of injury, he was pretty annoyed, though I think mostly at himself and the guy he had to swerve for. I think your nice, soothing personality might do the trick."

"Soothing personality, my ass. You just don't want another patient. Smart guy, though, coming in instead of trying to tough it out." She grabbed the supplies she'd need and tossed them on a small wheeled cart. She gave a quick *coming in* warning and backed through the curtain.

"Okay. So, looks like we've got a case of road… rash…" She trailed off as she glanced over her shoulder and saw a pissed off Jeremy slouched in the chair next to the exam table. He was in cammies still, his black helmet sitting on the exam table.

"Hey." He nodded as if she were just sliding into the booth across from him in a restaurant.

"Jeremy." She looked at the chart in her hand to double-check. Sure enough, Jeremy Phillips.

I have got to start reading the names on the charts before introducing myself to patients.

Smoothing her flyaway hair back behind her ear, she smiled. "Hi. Are you my rash?"

He cocked an eyebrow.

Shit. She just called him a freaking rash. "I mean road rash. Are you… do you…" She turned around and gripped the cart, breathing in and out before facing him again. And in a calm voice, she managed to say, "It says here you laid down your bike, took some skin off." *Wow, that sounded almost intelligent, Madison. Nice work.*

The corner of his mouth twitched, but he managed to hold it together. "Yeah. Some jackass pulled out in front of me and I didn't have enough time to slow down. Went sliding." He patted one hand on his helmet. "Glad my bike's still in running shape. Though it's gonna need a little TLC after that."

His bike? His freaking bike? That's what he was so worried about? Her heart nearly stopped at the image of Jeremy and his motorcycle sliding across asphalt, her throat closing at the thought of him not skidding to a halt in time…

"Hey." Jeremy was up and grabbing her elbow. "You just went white as a sheet. Sit down." With a hand that left no chance to argue, he pushed her down into the chair he'd vacated. Then, squatting down on his haunches, he grimaced a little, then grabbed her hand and chafed.

"I feel like my nurse needs a nurse. What's up? Low blood sugar?"

She shook her head, not trusting her voice quite yet.

"Do I need to call someone?" His soulful brown eyes were trying to read her. She felt it as clearly as if he turned the page of a book. Only the pages were in her heart.

"No," she managed to get out. "I'm fine. Just been a long shift." Injecting some much-needed steel into her backbone, she stood up, Jeremy standing alongside her with another grimace. "Are you sore?"

"A little. I'll feel it tomorrow for sure."

"Take the day off from work; use heat on the sore areas. And don't lie around. Walk, as long as it's just sore and not painful. Keep the muscles limber." She went back to her cart and started organizing her supplies. "Were you wearing your leather jacket?"

"Yup."

"Good. That probably saved you the worst of it." She motioned to his blouse before turning around to start setting up her supplies. "Go ahead and expose the area so I can get a good look at it."

As she opened some gauze packets, she heard the rustle of clothing from behind.

"I had lunch with Veronica the other day," she said,

mostly to fill the silence without turning around. Silence always freaked her out just a little, though she had no clue why.

"She's an odd one."

"That's not very nice," she chided gently. "New place, new people, naturally shy personality. Just give her some more time to get used to things before you make judgments, please?"

A pause, then he gave a gruff, "Yeah. You're right. Sorry."

She tugged at her ear. "I might need to see the hearing specialist. I thought I just heard you apologize, but that can't be right."

"Can it."

She held up a syringe packet over her shoulder. "Be nice, or I'll give you a shot just because I can." Turning, she braced herself to fight her body's reaction to his bare torso, wondering how bad the abrasions were. Did they cover his back? Arms? Chest?

Instead, she saw his olive green undershirt was still on, the short sleeves tight against his biceps. But his pants... that was another story.

Letting her eyes roam down from his still-covered torso to his shredded red plaid boxers, she couldn't stop looking at his muscular thighs, dusted with dark hair and flexed, she assumed, against the pain. Now those were thighs she wouldn't mind straddling. Then she drifted down to his cammie bottoms, now pooled down around his boots, and let her eyes roam back up again to his face. He gave her a wry smile and a shrug.

Oh, Jesus.

"It had to be your ass, didn't it?"

—⁓—

Jeremy bit back a laugh when Madison gasped and covered her mouth with one hand, as if she couldn't believe that flew out of her mouth.

He could easily believe it, though. Madison was always one to say something first, think about it later. Her bold honesty caught him off guard sometimes, but he liked that about her. She said what she meant and didn't try to hide it behind polite, worthless conversation.

He did his best to make light of it so she didn't freak out and leave him with another nurse he didn't know. "Sorry. I know it's a pain in the ass…"

She groaned, then her lips quirked in a reluctant smile, just like he planned.

Jeremy shrugged. "If I could reach it myself, I would have just gone home. But—"

"Thank God you didn't. There's no way you could have cleaned this yourself." All business now, Madison finished arranging the tools of her trade on the little silver cart she'd wheeled in. Then turning a professional eye to the many places his boxers were torn, she glanced at the table before shaking her head. "It'll be easier if you stand, I think. But if you get lightheaded, let me know and we can change things up."

"Lightheaded? From a scratch?" Did she have to make it sound so pathetic?

"It's not a scratch, it's road rash. And it's not going to be fun when I'm cleaning the dirt and grit out of there. God only knows what's stuck in your skin right now."

"Thanks, Nurse Ratchet. Could you try not to sound so happy about the idea?"

She grinned then cracked her knuckles, covered with purple latex gloves. "This might be fun, actually."

He bit back a groan. Talk about payback. He knew she was pissed about his decision to keep their friendship where it was. Not to act on the attraction they each felt. But he couldn't go there. It wasn't right. And if that pissed her off… it couldn't be helped.

Only now she had the perfect revenge in the palm of her hand. Did he actually want Madison scrubbing dirt from his abrasion?

Thoughts of some random male corpsman getting anywhere near his ass with a syringe made him shudder in horror.

Okay, yeah. Lesser of two evils here.

She squatted down on her haunches, using feather-light touches with her fingertips to scoot the fabric of his boxers—thank God he was wearing them today, rather than the more embarrassing option of a pair of old briefs—over to inspect the area. From his hip down the side of his thigh to his knee was a raw mess. His right shoulder and arm had been protected by the thick leather of his jacket. But his uniform pants had provided very little protection from the road. Which just taught him a fantastic lesson about remembering to change back into his jeans before heading home.

"I hate to say it," she said in a voice that told him she was anything but remorseful, "but you'll have to take these off. It's likely there are some fabric bits in there I need to get to. And they're in my way."

He sighed, then glared down at her when she made a squeak that sounded mysteriously like she swallowed a laugh. "This really isn't funny, you know."

"Actually…" She snorted. "It's pretty damn hilarious."

Rather than argue over the merits of how amusing his situation was, he simply hooked his thumbs in his boxers and pushed them down, hissing a little as some fabric peeled away from the injury.

And then she wasn't laughing anymore. Belatedly, he realized that he'd just bared his ass, literally, to the one woman who he never meant to get naked with. The same woman he dreamed about rolling around in bed with for days. Hell of a conundrum there. The fact that there was a constant hum of activity right outside their curtain did nothing to alleviate the intense intimacy of the moment. Almost as if they were cocooned inside their own little box, and nobody was going to intrude.

And she was on her knees, eye level with his barely covered junk. For the love of Christ.

He kept his back rigid and put his hands at his sides. If there was a God, He would prevent her from noticing he was fighting an erection.

"Just hurry up," he growled, hating how sharp his tone had to be. But now wasn't the time to fuck around.

Fuck around. Bad choice of words. Impossible-to-erase mental image.

Madison, scooting herself around. Lifting his shirt up. Wrapping small, delicate hands around his cock while she smiled that mysterious, *I'm thinking of a delicious secret* smile of hers just before she—

"Holy Jesus!" He jerked forward and out of her reach, his delicious daydream plowed to smithereens by the burning, scraping sensation over the sensitive, raw flesh. "God, Mad. What the fuck?"

She just smiled serenely—which was not nearly as

hot as her delicious secret smile—and held up a pad of gauze. "I'm trying to clean the area. And the more I think about it, this would be easier if you get up on the table. It's not as easy to reach as I thought it would be."

He stared at the table, then back to her. "Could you…" He circled his finger.

She rolled her eyes but stood and gave him her back.

Jeremy hopped on the table, lying down on his stomach to hide his serious boner. Damn, that hurt. He didn't have any false modesty, and nudity didn't bother him. But letting Mad know he was rock hard even despite the pain wasn't in either of their best interests.

And there he went again, thinking things he really shouldn't be thinking.

Tim's baby sister. Tim's baby sister. Tim's baby sister.

That helped. Watching her gather more gauze and slip into her professional mode helped a little more. But when she stepped behind him and began gently scraping with the gauze pad, lust took a backseat in his mind to fighting against the pain. It took every ounce of concentration not to squeal like a little girl when she grazed over the raw skin, removing the dirt and grit collected from his meet-and-greet with the asphalt.

"Sorry," she said, voice quiet. Very un-Madison like. "Do you want a local to numb the area? It might be best."

"No," he said, teeth gritted.

"This is never fun. I'm trying to be quick without rushing."

"I know." He hissed in another breath, then let it out slowly. As she poured some liquid with a fat syringe over the area, he felt a moment of cool relief—like rubbing aloe from the fridge over a sunburn—before she went back at it.

And although he knew he shouldn't, he watched her work over his shoulder.

Madison's nose scrunched a little, her tongue planted between her lips, as if she were in total concentration, in some nursing zone where only she and her task existed. Her right hand was firm but not harsh as it wiped and worked to clean the abrasion. Her left rested right above the abrasion, which happened to be over the curve of his ass, ready with the syringe. Warm, soft, totally inviting. All she had to do was slide that hand a few inches lower, over his hip and…

And nothing. Because he couldn't go there. Despite his previous slips, getting involved with his best friend's sister was a line, an invisible boundary that guys didn't cross. It seemed beyond wrong. Like he couldn't go out and get his own girl, so he picked from the most easily accessible pool.

Easy. A word that would never apply to Madison O'Shay. Being with Mad would be like trying to hold on for dear life while you were being tossed around the eye of a hurricane. The guy that finally managed to nail her down for keeps had his work cut out for him.

And annoyingly, the thought of some other guy winning Madison over made his back teeth ache with frustration.

"You need to relax a little more."

"Huh?" He glanced at her face again.

She blew out a breath, stirring the few hairs that escaped her regulation bun. "Your body, you're all tense." As if to prove a point, she reached for his hand and curled her fingers around his tight fist, squeezing.

"If it hurts too much, I'll just go get that local now. It won't take me more than a minute."

"No. No, I'm fine." With effort, he unclenched his fists, closed his eyes, and tried to take his mind elsewhere, willing his muscles to relax enough to finish the job. "Sorry."

"It's fine. I know it's uncomfortable." Her voice was all business again, as if he could have been any random Marine in here getting worked on.

He knew that was best. But he hated it anyway.

"I'm having people over next weekend to break in the new place. I know I've lived there for a while now, but I haven't had any guests over. I'm always at Tim and Skye's place. So I wanted to play hostess for a change. I didn't know if Tim had mentioned it."

He had. But Jeremy gave a noncommittal answer, as usual. "Not sure if I can go," he mumbled.

"Oh. Okay. That's fine."

But it wasn't. He could hear the hurt in her voice, knew there would be just a hint of sadness in her eyes if he dared open his own to look.

He didn't dare.

She continued on in silence. Which seemed heavier than the conversation before it.

"Okay. I think you're good. Do you have something else to change into, or will you need a pair of scrub pants?"

"I've got jeans in my bag." He waited for her to step away and turn her back to him before hopping down and pulling up his now-ruined cammie pants. He couldn't walk out the door in them. But for the moment, until she stepped past the curtain, they were his best chance of coverage.

Madison stood still, watching as he belted the pants. She bit her lip—a sign he recognized now as meaning she was holding back something.

"What, Mad?"

"I hate how things are between us," she blurted out, then blushed furiously.

"How things are…" he said, waiting for more information before he stepped in it.

"I just… Yeah. After that whole thing with you and me outside Dwayne's apartment, I don't know. I don't like that we can't seem to be friends anymore."

"That's not true." Was it? He couldn't deny he was always watching where he stepped with her now. "You'll always be a friend."

She chewed her lip a little more and stared over his shoulder instead of at him, but she shrugged as if she were done with the convo. "All right."

"Madison." He croaked her name, unable to hold it in.

She met his eyes then, and he could see the pain there. "I'm sorry."

"It's fine." She turned away, fiddling with instruments on the cart. "Seriously. I'm a little embarrassed that I was throwing myself at someone who didn't want me back."

"I never said that." The words were out before he could stop them. But they were no less than the truth.

Her hands froze, but she stayed facing away. "But you won't give us a chance."

"Madison." She wouldn't turn around. He touched her shoulder. "I can't."

Her shoulder jerked under his hand, and he dropped

it. "Keep the area dry for a few days, and change out the dressing tomorrow morning with this." She tossed an individually wrapped gauze pad large enough to cover the bulk of his abrasion onto the table. "If it looks worse, or the skin around it starts turning red, come back in."

And with that, she pushed through the curtain. The flap closed behind her, and he was alone in the cubicle, suddenly swamped with sound from outside. As if Madison's presence had been a mute button, locking them in a soundproof room, and when she left, the world and all its sounds intruded once more.

Dammit. He sat down heavily in the chair next to the exam table and opened his bag to hunt for his jeans. Jeans he should have put on before heading home but he was too stubborn to bother with.

What the hell was he going to do with Madison?

Nothing, a voice that sounded suspiciously like his father told him. *A career in the Corps requires a wife who can be with you, be flexible, be supportive. What kind of parents could you be if you were a dual-military couple?*

Nothing, a more reasonable voice echoed. *Madison is Tim's sister. A real friend wouldn't go there. Not ever.*

He prayed he was friend enough to remember that in moments of weakness.

———※———

Madison slammed into her apartment with enough force to scare a SWAT team. The man was so infuriating, she couldn't even begin to unravel the ways he made her want to scream.

Actually, screaming sounded pretty good. She

debated for a moment, then decided her neighbors wouldn't be as pleased with the result as she would.

She flopped down on the couch, then rolled enough to reach around and untie her bun. It annoyed the hell out of her, how tight she had to keep her hair back. Talk about a headache. But when she thought about cutting it, she just remembered all over again how annoying it was to grow back out when she wanted to change. And the regulation length for short hair for females really didn't flatter her face all that much either.

The silence of her home pressed around her, choking her. For the first time ever, she lived alone. In college, she had roommates. During OCS, she had several roommates. And at her first duty station, yup, a roommate. Even moving here, she originally planned to live with her brother Tim while he was deployed. Though she would have been the only one there, his things and his emotional presence would have made her feel better.

But then it turned out he was, um, married, and Skye wanted to live with her husband. Go figure, she thought with a smile. So she did the mature thing and found a place for herself on the fly, giving the newlyweds some time to get to know each other without a sister underfoot.

Maybe she could get a dog. No, too much work and her hours were too unpredictable. The poor thing would be home alone way too much.

A cat, maybe. They were more self-reliant and didn't need to be taken out for walks all the time.

Too bad she hated cats. Too pissy and selfish. She was selfish enough.

Something else she hated… the way Jeremy was dodging all chances to see her, to be alone with her.

She snorted a little as she remembered the look on his face when she asked him to drop his boxers in the hospital. Priceless didn't begin to describe it. But, God, that hadn't been easy for either of them.

Her professionalism kicked in, thank the good Lord, and she managed to work without trembling hands. But while he kept his eyes closed, trying to relax his muscles, she couldn't help but notice his body. And when she'd finished and bandaged the area, she took just one self-serving moment to look her fill.

He was cut, that was for sure. Not as bulky as Dwayne, but he had his fair share of muscle. Lean and sculpted, that would be how she described him. It wasn't an obvious strength. Someone could easily overlook him when taking bets on a fight. But Jeremy had a body that was quick and sharp and made her mouth water.

The first time Jeremy dropped trou in front of her, she didn't imagine it'd be in this capacity. But she'd take it.

And he fought her. He as much as admitted there was an attraction on both sides. She wanted him, and she'd made it beyond clear. The way he responded to her, it was clear he felt the same. But he held back and refused to get involved. She knew he wasn't dating someone else, so what was his issue?

Madison stood, body aching just a little from the twelve hours on her feet, and shuffled back to the bedroom where she tossed her scrubs on the floor and hopped in the shower for a quick rinse off. After drying, she grabbed an oversized pair of sweatpants and a sweatshirt she'd liberated from her brother's closet when she moved out. Despite the fact that she was bone-tired, she knew she wouldn't fall asleep. Crawling in bed now would only lead to aggravation, she'd learned over the years. After a long shift in the ER, her body needed an hour to decompress before any sort of sleep was an option.

So she grabbed a magazine and headed back for her couch. Except, she passed by the second bedroom and couldn't help but peek in.

She had no need for an office, and the only bedroom furniture she owned was in her own room. The two-bedroom apartment had seemed like such a waste, but she liked the complex and no one-bedroom units had been available. All that sat in there now was a lonely looking—and sadly underused—elliptical machine and a few stray boxes that she had yet to put in the outside storage unit her apartment came equipped with.

Maybe another roommate was the ticket. Her mind immediately flashed to Jeremy.

Easy, girl. That's not going to help at all.

Being more practical, she scanned the room again. She had the space. But she was past the idea of putting an ad in the base paper. No, she'd need to choose a roommate more carefully this time around. She wasn't twenty-two anymore. Didn't want a party animal or a complete slob. She was bad enough on the slob front.

Something else to think about. After she plopped back down on the cushions and started flipping mindlessly through the fluff magazine, her mind wandered once more to Jeremy and the haunted look in his eyes as he told her that yeah, despite the fact that he wanted her too, he wasn't going to make that move—ever.

But at least she knew he wanted her. It wasn't lack of desire that held him back.

A crinkling sound had her looking down to see her hands clenched around the magazine pages. She smoothed them out. It wasn't fair to either of them, really. They wanted each other. They were both single, healthy adults. So why couldn't they give it a shot? Whatever his reasons were, it didn't seem fair to put them ahead of their own desires.

So maybe she would try again. Bump up the campaign to get Jeremy to set aside his silly reservations about the two of them in a relationship and see if things could go somewhere.

Feeling a little lighter now than she had before, Madison flipped again through the pages, smiling to herself as she started forming a much more subtle, simple plan of attack.

Chapter 3

JEREMY LAY BACK, HISSING AGAIN AS HE BUMPED HIS hip. Damn thing hurt like hell. All day his leg had been on fire at work. Like hell would he ever admit that to anyone. But damn, the thing was painful. Not to mention the numerous other bumps and bruises his body took on from the minor crash. He'd been avoiding changing the bandage all day, mostly because he just didn't want to know what it looked like. Seemed easier that way. Denial was always healthy, right? Soon he'd have to get to it.

But first, a beer.

With his hip cocked up, he stretched out on the couch to watch *Seinfeld* reruns when someone knocked on his door.

Tim ran straight home to his wife after the workday was done, and Dwayne was deployed. Which only left...

He had no clue. But he grunted, called out a gruff, "Hold on," and leveraged himself up as easily as he could. Thankfully he'd changed into mesh workout shorts when he came home, or his pants would be rubbing against his road rash like a son of a bitch.

He hobbled only a little on stiff legs to the door and yanked it open without bothering to check. "What?"

Madison stood on his doorstep, eyes narrowed at his pissed tone. "That's a fine thanks I get for coming over here to check up on you and see if you need help with your bandage."

As usual, his body fought a losing battle to ignore what she did to him physically. Rather than say no, he gave in and stepped back, letting her into his apartment.

She spun around once and shuddered. "Seriously, you need a new place."

"It works for me."

"It screams pitiful bachelor."

"Then there's no false advertising." He hobbled the first step, then sucked it up and walked without the limp to the mini-kitchen area. "Want something to drink?"

"No." Her eyes took another lap around his apartment—which took about seven seconds—and she shook her head. "It doesn't even have a kitchen."

"Yes it does." He knocked a hand against the two-burner stove. "See?"

"That's a kitchenette. Not a kitchen."

He made a face. "Kitchenette is a girl word. It's a mini-kitchen. So, therefore, I've got a kitchen."

"I know you can do better. Why don't you?"

"Leave it alone, Madison." He sat down on the rolling desk chair, giving her the whole couch. The less their bodies touched, the better off he was.

But she didn't sit down. "Did you change the bandage this morning?"

He wiped a hand down his face and mumbled something under his breath.

"Jeremy Phillips!"

Jesus, it was like his mother came back to life just to give him hell. "I said no. I forgot about it." Total lie.

"What a lie."

He never could bullshit with Madison.

"Let me guess. Didn't want to do it because it would

hurt too much." She blew out a breath and dropped her book bag on the steamer trunk that doubled as a coffee table. "Figures. Men. They act so tough and rough, but the moment they have a boo-boo, they turn into the biggest wusses possible."

"That's not a scientifically proven fact," he pointed out, grabbing a bottle of water from the fridge.

"It's enough of a fact for me. Don't forget, I see people in pain all day. The women grit their teeth and apologize for being an inconvenience. The men are all, 'Don't you have a shot for that?'"

He chuckled, because it was the exact thing he'd been thinking while she cleaned the wound. "Yeah, well, it hurt."

Madison patted the sofa cushion. "Come on over, tough guy. Lie down and let's get that bandage changed."

He'd rather chew glass, but that wasn't going to add to the macho image she mocked. So he went for stoic silence as he dragged himself across the few feet to the couch. Doing a controlled fall, he landed on his stomach, face in one of the throw pillows that came free with the couch. Actually, it was a pretty comfortable position. He could settle in for a nap quite easily. "You're not going to turn Evil Nurse on me and make me cry, are you?"

"It hadn't occurred to me," she said sweetly. But the glint in her eyes told him the thought very much occurred to her, and she was giving it a lot of consideration.

He groaned but held still.

"Uh. Earth to Jeremy. I need those off."

"Hmm?" he mumbled into the pillow. This was actually a pretty comfortable position. Maybe he should look into napping like this more often.

Something tugged on the cuff of his shorts… presumably Madison. "These. They need to come off. Let's go. Pants off, big boy."

And just like that, his comfortable position became severely uncomfortable as his dick swelled and pressed hard against the couch cushions.

Jesus, he had it bad when even the knowledge that their encounter would bring pain didn't detract from his boner. There was something extremely wrong with him.

"Turn around," he growled. But when he looked up, she sat on the steamer trunk, arms crossed over her chest, one brow raised in the *you have got to be kidding me* face.

"Seriously?"

"Yes, seriously. Turn around."

"I can assure you, Jeremy, I've seen enough of the male form in my day not to swoon with excitement." Her voice was dry, sarcastic, and totally typical Madison.

The thought of her watching more than one dude get undressed—even for her job—made his fists clench. But he just lay there, waiting.

And she sat, also waiting.

Showdown. High noon.

"Fuck it," he mumbled, then turned to face the back of the couch, more to hide his erection than anything, and shimmied out of the shorts as best he could. Thank you, God, for elastic waistbands.

"Don't do that!" she shrieked. "You're going to hurt yourself!"

Too late. His eyes stung as the side of his leg against the couch cushion burned like hellfire. But he refused to let her see that, so fast as he could, he flopped back down on his stomach, hiked the leg of his boxer shorts up as far as he could, and did his best to cover his ears with his arms.

Too bad it didn't drown out Madison's lecturing.

"…stupid, ignorant, moronic man! You can't be serious. Why is it always men who make the worst patients?"

"I assume all of this is rhetorical?" he asked, voice muffled against the pillow.

"Bite me."

More unnecessary, completely unwanted images popped into his head. Madison stretched out below him, whispering "bite me" in his ear while her knees raised up. His teeth grazing the extended tendons in her neck, making her moan with delight. Making her want more. Making him…

"Christ!" A burning pain streaked from his leg out to the tips of his fingers, raising the hair on the back of his neck.

Madison peeled away the pad without an ounce of fanfare and tsked mockingly. "I'd say I'm sorry, but lying to patients is something I try to avoid."

"How about lying to a friend?"

"That too," she said cheerfully. "This wouldn't be so bad if you hadn't just rubbed your leg into the cushion. Or if you'd changed this when you were supposed to."

"Thanks for the memo."

Despite her warning about the pain, despite the fact that he knew he would deserve her harsh treatment, her hands were gentle. Soothing as they rubbed on some cream. As they checked the area. Almost caressing at times, it felt good. Would have felt better without the sting of pain. But her touch soothed out the rough edges of the sting.

"Where's your bike?"

He dragged his mind from the faraway place he'd let it drift. "Took it to the shop last night. Wanted it checked on after all the skidding it did. Plus the paint's jacked up, so they'll fix that for me."

"I hope it's okay." Silence reigned for a minute, then she said, "I've never ridden on one. What's it like?"

"You? Never been on a motorcycle?" He raised his head at that, a little surprised. With the number of military guys who rode, and having been surrounded by Marines since she was born, he was shocked she'd never been taken for a ride.

"Please," she scoffed. "Like Daddy would have let me go off on some corporal's bike when I was growing up."

True enough. Madison and Tim's father was extremely protective of his little girl. Not that Jeremy could blame him.

"And I've just never been on one as an adult." She tore off a piece of tape to drape over the new pad covering his wound. "Would you take me out sometime? Just for a short ride?"

Rock, meet Hard Place. He grunted, hoping that would suffice as a noncommittal answer.

Of course it didn't. "Was that a yes?"

He cracked one eye open to see her smiling at him innocently. She must practice that look in the mirror. "Yeah. Sure." His voice sounded rusty. But just the thought of having Madison behind him on his motorcycle, arms wrapped around his waist, thighs squeezing his hips as he leaned into a turn, breasts pressed against his back…

And hello, Mr. Boner. It's been about five minutes since you were here last.

Madison sat back and nodded. "You're all set. Am I going to have to come back tomorrow, or will you be able to do this yourself like a big boy?"

"I've got it," he answered quickly. Making the ritual of taking off his pants in front of Madison a daily thing was his idea of a certain level of hell. He'd pass if at all possible.

Madison blinked a moment, as if surprised—or even disappointed?—in his answer. But she nodded and quirked into a smile. "Well, good. You need to take care of yourself."

She stood and gathered her things, shoving them into her book bag randomly. He stood as well, yanking his boxer leg down when her gaze was averted for a moment, then grabbing a roll of tape that had fallen to the floor and passing it to her.

"Thanks." She zipped the bag and hefted it over her shoulder. Then her eyes dropped for a moment and she looked back up. "I'm really glad you're not worse off, Jeremy."

"Yeah, me too."

"I won't bother you again, coming over."

"You're not a bother, Madison." His own desire for her, that was the bother. The circumstance, that was a bother. Never her.

She gave him a smile. "Good. Then I hope this won't bother you either."

--m--

Madison dropped her book bag down to the coffee table trunk thing. But he didn't move. When she put her hands on his shoulders, he didn't budge. And when she raised up on her toes, he didn't even blink. So she decided to go for the gold and pressed her lips to his.

Nothing. He didn't step away, didn't step forward. Didn't participate, but didn't pull back.

What the hell? She angled her head a little, pressed her body to his more tightly, but no dice.

Finally, with the feeling of foolishness racing up her spine, she tried one more thing.

Her hands drifted up his shoulders, around his neck, and she let her fingernails scratch lightly at the back of his scalp. Meanwhile, her tongue darted out and licked the seam of his lips.

There. If that didn't do it, then nothing—

"Dammit." The growl was the only warning she had before Jeremy's arms locked around her back and he pulled her so tightly against him, she couldn't tell where her front ended and his began. His mouth slanted further over hers, giving the perfect angle to open more fully for the kiss. One hand lowered more, cupped under her butt, and lifted so that she was barely standing on her own any longer.

And she felt it. The unmistakable proof that he wanted her as much as she wanted him. His erection straining the front of his boxers—which she would bet dollars to donuts he'd forgotten he was wearing.

That she—Madison O'Shay—had enough feminine power to make a man so confident in his own ways forget his restraint gave her a thrill. But mostly the thrill came from Jeremy. It was him. Always him. Since she was sixteen, it'd been Jeremy Phillips for Madison.

Too bad he still wasn't in on the long-term program. Yet.

He tasted like butterscotch, she realized belatedly, and chuckled. As if trying to reprimand her for losing track, his teeth nipped her bottom lip and she stopped laughing entirely. He was serious, as usual. Everything was serious for Jeremy, and this was no different.

Woo-hoo!

When his mouth left hers to graze down her cheek, under her jaw, and scrape against her neck, she whispered his name. As if she couldn't hold it back any longer, and needed to be reminded this was what it felt like when dreams came true.

Tactical error.

Hearing her voice flipped some sort of switch in him, and he jerked back, away from her, away from even being close enough to reach out and touch.

His breath came in hard pants, like he'd run a marathon but hadn't trained for it. And his eyes were glassy, as if seeing something he shouldn't be.

"Jeremy?" The nurse in her came out, and she wondered for a moment what was wrong. His detached look scared her just a little. "Jeremy?"

"No." He shook his head once, eyes clearing. "No. Madison, we can't."

"Why can't we?" she insisted. "You haven't given me one good reason why we can't. I accepted it, thought it meant you weren't interested in me, and I left it alone. But now I know. I know you want me too. So why are we fighting something, putting the effort into avoiding it, when we could just *have it*?"

"I never said I wanted it," he argued. But when Madison's eyes trailed down to the clear erection he was sporting, Jeremy grabbed his mesh shorts and stepped into them, a scowl on his face. "Leave it alone. It's not supposed to happen."

"Still not a reason," she pointed out, which only made his scowl darken.

"It's all the reason we need." He adjusted the waistband on his shorts and crossed his arms over his chest. The message couldn't be more clear if he wrote it on a Post-it note and slapped it on her forehead. Discussion closed. "Thanks for stopping by. My leg feels better already."

She stared, willing him to change his mind, to back down, say he was sorry and beg her to please give him another shot. But she knew he wouldn't. A man's pride only stretched so far, and Jeremy's had been given a workout the last two days.

Tactical retreat time, as her father would say.

"Fine." Picking up her book bag, as if nothing had happened and she was just paying a friendly call, she waved to him over her shoulder. She couldn't help but notice the confused look on his face when she sent him a pleasant smile.

Good. Let him guess. Let him try to figure out what the hell was going on. Let him stay on his toes for once.

"See ya around!"

"Probably not," he finally managed to get out. "I've got a lot of work going on right now."

"Ah." She stood with the door wide open. "Then I guess I'll see you Saturday for the get-together at my place."

Awareness of his previous promise washed over him, and she smiled again. "Bye!" And she shut the door behind her as she left.

Yeah. Tactical retreat was one thing. But as her daddy also said… she wasn't really retreating. She was just advancing from another direction.

—⁓—

"This was fun. Yes, we'll talk again soon. Bye!"

Veronica waved once more to Skye's parents and hit *end call* on the screen. Then she hit the red X and watched as the Skype program minimized down to the dock at the bottom of the screen.

Technology was amazing. She'd missed out on so many unbelievable advances. Just one more reason she'd made the ultimate choice she finally had to make, coming back to America for good.

She missed her aunt and uncle desperately. But thanks to modern technology—which seemed much more amazing to her than anyone else—she could talk to them face to face. At least as much as one video camera was to another. It helped, more than she could say, when she felt the loneliness creeping in. If only she'd had this sort of thing available to her a few years ago.

And wasn't it a shame that she didn't miss her parents with the same ferocity as her aunt and uncle? Though her parents had barely even acknowledged her moving back to the United States with anything other than disappointment. And guilt.

But she didn't share their passion for missionary work, for finding the most destitute, barren places on the globe and making a difference. She wanted a life of her own. At twenty-six, it wasn't unkind or selfish of her to branch out and start a life of her own— even if her parents tried to make her feel that way.

And she was blessed that her cousin had embraced her so willingly.

More than once, she doubted her choice to leave her aunt and uncle's home in Texas and move in with her cousin, even temporarily. But there were so many more opportunities for her here in California. And she intended to grab at as many of them as she could, while she could. She might be naïve and still working to catch up with other people her age, but she wasn't stupid. This opportunity wouldn't last forever.

A little bubble sound came from the speakers, and then a face popped up on the screen.

Her eyes widened and she jerked back in the computer chair, completely taken off guard.

"Hey there. You're not Tim. Or Skye," the man on the screen drawled.

She glanced toward the door, listening to see if either one had come home while she was speaking with her aunt and uncle. But no, she was still alone.

"Do you talk? Or are you taking a mime class?"

"What?" Her eyes snapped back to the screen to watch the stranger tilt his head to the side and chuckle in a deep-throated sound that sent chills up her arms. Combined with his easy smile and eyes that held more than a little bit of humor, her gut didn't clench in the normal way it did when she met new people.

Or maybe that was just the added benefit of being two computer monitors away.

"Just checking. I assume you're a friend of Skye's?"

"I'm her cousin." Before he got any ideas, she added, "I'm staying here. I didn't break in or anything."

He laughed now, full-out body spasms included, to

the point where she wondered if he would tip back in his chair and fall over. But it gave her the chance to look at him better.

He wore an olive undershirt and camouflage pants, just like Tim did when he worked. But the lighting in the room behind him was somewhat poor. She could barely make out a bunk-style bed and shiny walls, but little else.

"Well, that's one I haven't heard before. No, I didn't think you broke in. If you stopped to Skype on your way out the door, you'd be a poor excuse for a burglar."

She cracked a smile at that. "Probably." Then, realizing he called her cousin's computer, she scrambled for a pad of paper in the desk. "I'm sorry, I should have asked. Do you want me to take a message?"

"Nah, no message. Just thought one of them might be home and I could catch them at the computer. We didn't have a date or anything." His voice, which had been so full of laughter before, suddenly sounded tinged with disappointment.

It finally clicked, and she felt awful for not having picked up on it sooner. "Are you deployed?"

He grimaced. "Yes, ma'am. Unfortunately, I am."

"What's your name?"

He raised one eyebrow and stared at her long enough that she flushed. "It's on the screen, darlin'."

"Oh! Oh, of course." She glanced at the top and saw Dwayne Robertson. The mysterious, missing Dwayne. Of course. The other best friend who recently deployed. Why hadn't she put that together sooner? "I apologize; I'm still learning the ropes of this program, it seems."

Learning the ropes of modern life in general. Skye taught her to Google just two weeks ago. Not much need for computers and search engines in the jungles of South America.

"Not a problem." He sat back and laced his fingers over his stomach. From the angle, his biceps strained a little at the edge of his T-shirt. Veronica felt a stirring in her belly she hadn't felt before. Ever. It wasn't nerves. And it wasn't excitement. So what was it?

"How long you stayin' with them?"

"For a while," she hedged. Truthfully, she had no clue. She didn't make enough working as a waitress to afford her own apartment. And Skye and Tim never treated her as if she were a burden. But she felt it all the same. Just a little more of the guilt she was raised with rearing its ugly head. She could have been Catholic, for all her parents' love of guilt as discipline.

To change the subject, she asked, "Are you doing well over there?"

He smiled. "Well as can be, I'm sure. Bored is more like it."

"Bored?" That sounded almost ideal, given where he currently was.

"It's not exactly a fighting deployment. Our mission here isn't to run out and catch bad guys. We're here to build, not tear down."

"Oh. That sounds… nice, actually." She'd always thought of militaries in the terms she knew of them. The South American militias she'd witnessed, been warned by, avoided at all costs. They were never ones to rebuild. Destruction was their game.

"It's never one hundred percent safe. But I'm little

more than a desk jockey this time around. No real action for me."

"Isn't that what you'd want?" she blurted out. It was war! How could he not want to be safe with a nice, easy job?

He shook his head. "You don't typically join the military hoping for an easy ride. Not that I'm dying to see a lot of action or anything. No death wishes here. Just a nice scrap now and then to mix it up wouldn't be out of order."

"I'm sure," she murmured. What must his life be like? She could easily imagine less-than-stellar accommodations, as she'd lived in third world countries most of her life. But despite that, her parents and the other missionaries had managed to shelter her from the more unseemly side of life. Sterile. It's the only way she could explain her first twenty-six years of life.

He leaned forward and gave her a slow smile that started little birds doing gymnastics in her stomach. "So, Ronnie—"

"It's Veronica," she said automatically.

He nodded. "What's your story, Ms. Veronica?"

"My story?" she squeaked out. That was absolutely not something she was willing to share. Not with a stranger. Even Skye only knew the important bits—the CliffsNotes version, her cousin had called it—to her pre-U.S. days. She certainly wasn't about to spill the entire sob story to someone she'd never met. "I'm as boring as they come."

His eyes tracked around, and she could easily imagine he was taking all of her in. Her skin prickled as if he'd actually touched her. "Boring? I doubt that's true."

She swallowed and rubbed a hand over her arm to soothe the goose bumps away. "It's very true. No story here."

He chuckled again and leaned back. "Everyone's got a story. I hate to call you a liar, darlin'. So I'll just sit here and you can imagine I said it."

What? Of all the… She grabbed the pen and pad of paper. "Are you sure there's no message I can take for you to pass along to Tim or Skye when they get back?"

The smile dropped just a little, and she instantly regretted the tone of her voice. "Nah. Just that I said hi, and they can try me anytime on here if they're in the mood."

"All right." She had to say something more. Make amends for being so upset earlier. "I hope you stay safe, Mr. Robertson."

"Dwayne." He perked up at that. "Do you, now?"

"Do I what?"

His voice lowered to a purr. "Hope I stay safe."

"Of course. I hope everyone stays safe."

He winked at her. Winked! Then in a slow, smooth voice that had the hair on her arms standing straight up again, he looked dead at her. As if there weren't two computer screens and thousands of miles between them. As if he could actually see right through her, into her, know all her secrets. "You know, you really are a pretty one, aren't you?"

She gasped and clicked the end call button.

Of all the… Veronica watched as her hand tapped the pen against the desk in rapid-fire motions. Then the pen slowed, stopped, and rolled away.

What an arrogant example of the male species,

thinking she needed to hear he found her attractive and that he could sucker her in with that honey-coated Southern drawl. He probably wasn't even from the south, just developed the accent to lure in unsuspecting females.

Or maybe she was being overdramatic. He was being nice. It was a compliment. She had to stop turning everything people said into an inquisition, dissecting their reasoning behind their words. He'd been kind. And it's not like she had to speak to him often anyway. That's the absolute truth. She could just put Dwayne Robertson and his wandering eyes out of her mind completely. The conversation meant nothing. Nothing at all.

But she couldn't help the smile that crept over her face as she stood up and turned the computer off.

Chapter 4

SATURDAY NIGHT, AND MADISON WAS A WOMAN ON A mission. Mission Jeremy.

Too bad her brother didn't get the memo and was unconsciously doing everything in his power to ruin said mission. Or maybe he did get the memo and was on a mission of his own. How else could she explain why Tim insisted on playing yet another game, rather than heading home to hang out with his wife? It was sabotage, obviously.

Mission Make Madison a Pure Spinster.

Sorry, bro… that's not gonna happen. She grinned at the thought of her brother's imagined outrage. Men could be such hypocrites. Always thinking they had to defend the virtue of their womenfolk while they didn't have a problem taking a lover or two before marriage themselves.

She watched from behind lowered lashes as Jeremy poured himself an iced tea in her apartment's kitchen. A real kitchen, not a dinky kitchenette. She knew he had some misguided thought that going after her would break the bonds of brotherhood or some such crap. And maybe there really was a secret guy code that you didn't date your friend's sister or whatever.

But why? Why was that even an issue? If Tim dated her best friend… Okay, that didn't work, since her best friend was Matthew, and he was gay. The thought gave her a serious chuckle, which she swallowed. But that was all beside the point. Then again, she lacked the Y chromosome, which carried the stupid gene as far as she was concerned.

Jeremy took the slow route back to the coffee table with his tea. And since he'd played his card early in the round and wasn't needed again until the next one, he took his time.

He paused by a picture of her from graduation, and she got another good look at him.

If his one hang-up was that he didn't want to offend or piss off Tim, that might be a tricky one to overcome. They were best friends, had been since TBS ten years ago.

But to her mind, that meant Tim should be happy they were together. If the guy was good enough to be Tim's best friend, wasn't he good enough to date Tim's sister?

It was a logical thought process.

Too bad men were born without a logic gene. That one, she reasoned, must be connected to the second X chromosome.

"Madison." Veronica nudged her and pointed to the deck. "It's your turn."

"Oh, whoops! Mind drifted," she said easily. Playing Apples to Apples might have been a bad idea, as the downtime between rounds gave her mind way too much time to wander.

Madison drew a green card and laid it down. "Disturbing."

A quick hush filled the room as everyone else glanced at their cards. Madison watched as Jeremy continued to stare at her pictures. "Are you going to play this round, Jeremy?"

He took a side step over, grabbed the top card from his stack, and tossed it down without even giving it a glance before resuming his study of her photos.

Madison rolled her eyes. Nice.

Finally, Veronica laid down her own card, chewing her lip as she did. Madison shuffled them on the table without looking, then sorted them into a pile and picked them up. "Drumroll please."

Tim beat his fingers on the coffee table.

"What is disturbing? We have… mold." She laid down the first card. "Pretty gross. Next one is conspiracy theories. Definitely something to play with your mind. The third card is…" She rolled her eyes. "A little on the nose. But it's the morgue." She'd be willing to bet that was Jeremy's. "And then lastly we have our winner." She snorted with laughter as she laid the card down face up. "Beanie Babies."

"What?" Veronica shrieked in surprise, then immediately shrank an inch as if she wanted to take it back.

Tim pumped his fist. "Yeah, that's right! That one was mine."

"I don't get it." Veronica took the red cards and stuffed them on the bottom of the stack, grabbing a fresh card from the top for herself. "How are Beanie Babies more disturbing than the morgue?"

"It's not always about the best match," Madison reminded her. "It's whatever the judge thinks is the best, period. Best funny card, best serious card, best whatever. I happen to find the game works best when I play for laughter. Plus, those things always creep me out. Their eyes… it's like they are just staring at you."

"Know your audience," Tim crowed as he snatched the green card and set it to the side with his other greens.

Veronica looked confused but didn't ask further.

Skye came next and laid down her green card with a wicked smile. "Charming. What's charming in your cards?"

As Madison glanced through her cards, she couldn't concentrate on her best pick. Jeremy finally sat down next to her on the floor, his knee brushing hers as he settled into a spot and picked up his own hand.

Did he feel the same chest-tightening thing she did when they were close by? She hoped so. The world wouldn't be fair if she suffered alone in silence. Realizing she was last to go and everyone was waiting on her, she tossed down the first card she glanced at, then immediately wished she hadn't.

Skye picked up the red cards and started to giggle immediately. Madison bit the inside of her cheek. At least her sister-in-law got the point of the game.

"What is charming? You guys said... Republicans?" Skye raised a brow at that. "Uh-huh. Moving on. Bonbons, yum. Diamonds, which are naturally any girl's best friend. And last but not least..." Skye looked right at Madison with a huge grin. "Festering wounds? Seriously? There's a card for that?"

Madison shrugged innocently. "Apparently. *Somebody* played it."

Eventually, after a minute of debate, Skye chose diamonds.

"They're just all sparkly and fantastic," she said when the rest of them groaned and Tim smirked.

"Thank you, baby." He leaned over and kissed her, sliding the green card to his ever-growing pile.

"No fair. Nepotism at work," Madison grumbled.

"I don't think it works that way when you don't know whose card belongs to who," Skye pointed out. Then she glanced at her cousin. "Oh, I'm sorry, sweetie."

Veronica looked down in front of her, no green cards in sight, indicating she'd yet to win a round, and shrugged. "I don't have very good cards."

Jeremy straightened his red cards and set them aside. Then he drew the top green card and laid it down. "Sexy."

A pleasant buzz hummed through Madison's bloodstream as she contemplated which card to put down. There was the safe bet, *kilts*. Totally effective, completely true. Or there was the more amusing choice, *cabbage*. Nonsensical, but funny.

She'd never liked playing it safe. And she wasn't in the mood to laugh right now. Biting the inside of her cheek, she laid down her choice.

Jeremy grabbed the four cards and shuffled them with his eyes closed, then picked them up.

"Being in love."

There was a chorus of aws, and everyone knew it was Veronica's card.

"Then we have recycling."

Clearly Skye's.

"French wine?" Jeremy asked with a skeptical look for everyone. "What's wrong with a good, cold beer?"

Skye motioned him to keep going.

"And then we have... my body."

Tim and Skye erupted into laughter. Veronica blushed furiously and grabbed her empty water bottle as if she were going to take it to throw it away. But Jeremy said nothing, only stared right at Madison.

He knew it was her card, no question about it.

Her brother and Skye said something, but she didn't hear. The world blocked out, and nothing existed but Jeremy. His eyes were like melted chocolate, pools she wanted to fall into.

"Jeremy."

He broke the connection to glance at Skye. "Sorry, yeah?"

"Pick a winner."

"Ah, right." He gave the cards another glance and pushed forward the card reading *being in love*.

"That's mine!" Veronica bounced back to her seat and grabbed the card. "I won one!"

Everyone clapped to jokingly celebrate her victory and she smiled.

But Madison was too busy trying to figure out if Jeremy realized he was rubbing his knee against hers under the table, or if it was just a coincidence.

She never was a big believer in coincidences.

―᠁―

Madison stood and stretched her legs. "That was fun, you guys. Thanks for coming over to help me break the place in."

Veronica curled up in the recliner. "Do you need help cleaning up?"

Skye stood and grabbed the chip bowl, now full of crumbs, and walked it over to the kitchen. "Of course she does. We'll—"

"We'll get out of her hair so Madison can clean," Tim finished for her.

"Timothy," Skye scolded.

"No, he's right. I'm sort of specific on how I like to clean. Thanks though, Skye." She gave her brother a look from the corner of her eye. He so owed her. "Veronica, you wanna stay and help, maybe watch a movie afterward?"

"Yes!" She jumped up and started grabbing every cup in sight as if her life depended on a clean house. "You don't mind driving me back to the house afterward, do you?"

"Of course not." She shoved Tim and Skye toward the door.

After Skye headed out to the parking lot, Tim turned back around and kissed her on the cheek. "Thanks, squirt."

"Uh-huh," she said, smiling when he all but skipped after his wife.

Madison closed the door and shook her head. The man was a giddy idiot for his wife. Which wasn't a bad thing... unless it left her on full-time KP for the rest of their lives.

Then again, if she kept racking up the IOUs from her brother, maybe she could parlay those into not giving her grief about a new relationship she was hoping would start up soon...

As she leaned against the door, Jeremy walked up, hands in his pockets, caught in quiet contemplation as always. "Sure you don't need any help?"

Madison was sorely tempted to say yes, just to keep him with her. But Veronica was there. And that just wasn't going to do. So instead, she went along with her Mission Jeremy plan and said, "Thanks, but no."

He looked almost relieved, like the thought of sticking

around in close quarters with her might have killed him. Flattering, really. But as he walked by her to open the door, she slid her arm around his waist and gave him a side hug. Completely platonic, non-threatening.

Everything in his body stiffened, from his shoulders down to his hips. She could feel the muscles on the side of his torso clench under her hand. But she didn't linger, much as she really wanted to lift his shirt and feel that skin with her bare hands.

"Thanks," she said as if nothing happened, and stepped out of reach. He stared at her a moment, very much a deer in the headlights. So she planted a hand on his back and gently pushed until he stood on her doorstep, then waggled her fingers in a sassy good-bye wave and closed the door with a quiet click.

"He likes you."

"Ah!" Madison jumped and held a hand to her heart as she spun around. Veronica stood behind her, dishcloth in hand, staring at her as if Madison were one of those optical illusion posters that you could make change shapes if you just concentrated hard enough.

"Scare a girl to death, why doncha?" As her breathing returned to normal, Madison walked toward the kitchen.

"He does, doesn't he?" Veronica followed along on her heels, determined, it seemed, to get an answer. "And you like him."

"That's not exactly it." *Like* was too tepid a word for what they had going on. It seemed so bland, so… mashed potatoes, hold the gravy.

"I think I'm right." Her voice stronger now, buoyed by confidence, Veronica grabbed a plate from the drainer and started wiping it down. "I think you both like each other. And you're doing a little mating dance to see who might make the first move."

"Now there, I can say with one hundred percent honesty, you're wrong," Madison said smugly. *Because I already made the first move.*

"Oh." A little crestfallen, Veronica put the dish away in the cabinet and grabbed another. "I'm sorry then. I hope I didn't make you feel uncomfortable."

Madison waved that away and turned on the water, waiting for it to get hot. "Not at all."

They worked in silence, making a nice wash-and-dry team. As Veronica settled the last glass back in the cabinet and shut the door, she said, "Thanks for letting me hang out here this evening. I always feel a little in the way at their house. I mean, when both of them are home."

Madison hopped up on the counter and let her feet dangle. Her heels fell into a comfortable *thud-thud* pattern against the cabinet below. "I know what you mean. It's why I got this place as fast as I could once Skye showed up. They never kicked me out, never said I had to go. But I knew it's what they needed."

She thought back to her empty second bedroom, and the light finally went on. "I'm such an idiot. Why didn't I think about that before?"

"Think about what?" Veronica hung the dishtowel neatly over the handle of the oven.

"You need a place, right? You want to get out of Tim and Skye's townhouse."

"Hmm," Veronica said, looking a little sad. "I can't really afford my own apartment right now."

"Which makes what I'm about to say so perfect!"

Madison hopped down and grabbed Veronica's shoulders. "Move in with me. I've got a spare bedroom. And I sort of really hate how quiet this place is."

Her friend's eyes widened. "Are you serious?"

"Of course I'm serious!" Picking up steam, Madison jumped in place a little. "I always have roommates, and this is my first time living alone. Frankly, I hate it. And the bedroom is a good size. Plus, since I have a bathroom in the master, you'd get your own bath, even though it's out in the hallway. Come on." She grabbed Veronica's hand and tugged her down the hallway and into the nearly empty second bedroom.

Veronica stood in the middle, spinning slowly, Then she ran a hand over the screen of the elliptical machine.

"We'll move that out of here, of course," Madison said. "Frankly, I should just sell the thing. I run outside or on the treadmill in the weight room anyway."

Veronica said nothing, just continued to turn, staring at the ceiling, the walls, the closet.

"It's not the Taj Mahal or anything, but it's a safe complex and I've never had problems with the neighbors."

Still nothing from Veronica, only wide-eyed staring around the room and her lips slightly working, as if speaking to herself.

"Uh, you okay?" Madison wondered if she'd spoken too soon. "If you're not interested, I promise I won't be offended."

Finally, she stopped spinning and faced Madison. She could see tears gathering in the other woman's eyes. "No. I mean, yes, I'm interested. I'm very interested." She sniffed, then gave a quick laugh. "I don't know if I can afford half the rent."

"Whatever. We'll say a third, since my room is bigger and has a private bath." Frankly, she'd have let Veronica move in for free, but Madison had a feeling saying so would hurt her feelings. Or her pride, which Mad could relate to. "It's not the money that I care about. We can work that out so you're comfortable. I just want someone else here. Living alone doesn't really work for me."

"And you won't mind someone else in here, taking up your space?"

"It'd be our space." She stepped forward and held out a hand. "Roomies?"

Veronica stared at the offered hand for a long moment before a smile broke out on her face and she wrapped her fingers around Madison's. "Roomies."

⁓

Jeremy did his best to occupy himself. He tried going for a run, but the POS gym at his complex already closed for the evening and there was no safe path to take at night in the area. Such was the problem with living in a crappy apartment in a not-great area. Next came writing, though that was a wash since his mind wasn't in the game. He hated spending time putting down words he knew he'd delete later. It never worked out for him.

In the end, the only thing he could do was sit there and think about Madison. That hug. The way she glanced at him through the afternoon. Her subtle flirtation using game cards.

Apples to freaking Apples, for the love of God. Who flirted using a card game?

And why the hell was it so effective?

He even went so far as to clean his kitchen sink,

which somehow morphed into scrubbing down the entire kitchenette, even removing the two burners and wiping under them, though he'd probably cooked on his stove a total of three times. When he was finished, the entire area sparkled, cleaner than the day he moved in. But there was zero satisfaction.

No, the only satisfaction he wanted right now came in the package of a five-foot-five Navy nurse who drove him insane. Which basically equaled no satisfaction at all. And thanks to his own stupidity, he had only himself to blame. What the heck was he thinking, brushing up against her under the table? Right in front of Tim, no less.

Clearly, Jeremy had a case of the stupids and it was Madison-induced. Nothing else could explain exactly how he could totally lose his mind and his resolve when it came to avoiding Madison O'Shay the minute he saw her in person.

His phone rang, and he resisted picking up. But it could always be work—a Marine was never truly off duty—and he glanced at the caller ID just to make sure it wasn't the OOD calling with an issue.

His father.

Jeremy felt zero guilt hitting the ignore button. Now was really not the time for another lecture on whether he'd filled out recommitment papers or if he'd been thinking which duty station he'd like to try next. Or if he'd talked to his monitor about career options from here.

No. No. And no.

Quick convo from his end. Long argument from his father's. Easiest to just pass, at least for now. Next weekend he couldn't avoid the old man.

Jeremy fell to the rickety couch and grunted as his back hit the support wood below the cushions. Time to get another cheap couch. Surely some Marine was moving or something soon. He'd just keep an eye on bulletin boards and yard sale sites. Fastest, cheapest way to acquire new furniture.

What would his father say if he mentioned he was dating someone? Probably jump for joy. Just another piece of the career Marine puzzle in place. A nice, simple girl who would love to follow along in his footsteps as he moved from one side of the country to the other. One duty station to the next. Keep the kids in order while he deployed.

Someone like his mother. Or at least how his mother would have been, had she lived long enough. A mom he barely knew. Did anyone really remember anything before they were four?

He pictured telling his father he was dating a Navy nurse. And watched as the mental picture of his father's face turned purple, steam rolling out from his imaginary ears like the smokestack of a train.

Yup. Ignore was the best option for now.

He glanced around once more at the apartment, then knew he couldn't stay here any longer. Time to get back on his bike and go for a ride. He needed to clear his head, and stewing wasn't going to do it. Plus, having just gotten his bike back from the shop, he couldn't deny the need for a little speed, test her out. Get back on the horse—or rather, the hog.

Twenty minutes later, he was at the one place he never thought he would be. Madison's apartment complex. How the hell did he end up here? This wasn't the plan. It wasn't even remotely where he'd intended to go.

"Stupid bike," he mumbled as he kicked out the kickstand and stood, shaking out his legs. He had two options. Either go knock on her door—which would be the wrong choice—or head back home without telling anyone he'd been here—the smart one.

Clearly, Jeremy was done being smart. Intelligence was overrated anyway.

He knocked on the door, and Madison answered almost immediately, shock in her eyes.

"Jeremy. Hey…"

She had her sweatshirt on and a bag in her hand, like she was about to go somewhere. "Where you headed?"

"Where am I… oh." She tossed her bag toward the couch, not caring when it fell to the floor instead with a clash of keys and change and who knew what else a woman's purse could contain. "No, I just got back from dropping Veronica at the townhouse. Walked in the door five seconds before you knocked."

"I see." *Yes. That's right. Impress her with your awesome verbal skills. Woo her with your…*

No. No wooing. None of that. "We need to talk."

"Oh. So serious." She smiled but stepped back and let him in. "Want a water?" she called as she left him in the living room and went to the kitchen.

"No, I won't be here long." *I hope.* He listened while she rummaged around in the fridge and walked back, carrying a bottle of water. "Thought Skye gave you one of those filter pitcher things."

She glanced ruefully at the bottle of water. "I know. I'm addicted to the convenience though. Don't tell her.

It was sweet, and I use it when she's over. And I try to use it when I think about it."

His lips quirked. She was, at the end of the day, fiercely loyal to her family and friends. "I won't say a word."

"So, what's up?" She cracked the seal and took a long drink. He watched her throat work as she swallowed twice, and his own mouth watered in response. "Jeremy?"

That snapped him out of it. "Yeah. Right." He cleared his throat. "I just wanted to clarify something. I know what you're up to."

"Up to?" An innocent *who, me?* look crossed her face. So very unnatural for Madison. "You'll have to be more specific." She set the water bottle on the end table and unzipped her zip-up hoodie.

"Ah." His eyes tracked the zipper's progress, like Pavlov's freaking dog. "Specific."

The metal rasp filled the silence until it popped free. "Yeah. You said I'm up to something. What?"

Her hands crept back up to her shoulders and pushed the sweatshirt off, letting it droop down to her elbows, shoulders covered in thin jersey T-shirt material.

When was the last time a thick, old, battered college sweatshirt and worn T-shirt had been so sexy?

"Jeremy."

Her voice sounded hoarse, like she'd been running outside and the cold got to her throat.

He couldn't look at her, not like this. Turning, he made a big deal out of inspecting her couch. "This is nice. I need a new couch. Where'd you get it?"

"Seriously?"

"Yeah. No." He rubbed the back of his neck. This was not how he planned the conversation. Actually, he hadn't planned it at all. Time to put the cards on the table. "Are you coming on to me?"

She chuckled behind him. "You came over here, not the other way around." He thought she mumbled something that sounded like "this time," but he wasn't sure so he ignored it.

"I meant earlier. With the game." This was stupid; he couldn't stare at her couch the whole time. Bracing himself, he turned and took the full punch of Madison, in just her T-shirt and shorts, bare feet, arms raised while she shook out her ponytail.

"That was a game. Apples to Apples. You play the cards you have."

He blinked twice. "What about now?"

Arms frozen overhead, she stared at him as if he'd suggested she were an alien. "Now…"

"Right now. Look at you. You're undressing in front of me." Heat crept up the back of his neck, but he wasn't going to give in, not now. He started, so he had to finish. Damn his pride. "You're doing that sex thing with your hair and you're taking your clothes off right in front of me and I'm not stupid."

Her arms dropped to her sides and her eyes widened, then narrowed in a way that told him he was in deep shit.

Chapter 5

MADISON CROSSED HER ARMS OVER HER CHEST AND took a warrior stance. "Let me recap, if you don't mind."

"Go right ahead." He was safe with a recap... as long as she stood on her side of the living room. If she got within lunging distance, he seriously wouldn't give himself the benefit of the doubt.

Whether he'd be lunging to strangle her or to kiss her, he wasn't even sure.

"You came over here. All on your own." She grabbed her sweatshirt that she'd draped over the arm of the couch and walked to the hallway closet to hang it up. "I didn't invite you over, and I had no clue you were coming over."

All true. And, despite his earlier claim, stupid on his part.

"I take off my sweatshirt because it's warm in my apartment, and I'm still fully clothed underneath."

Maybe in the most technical sense. But her old T-shirt, from high school he would bet, might as well have been missing for all it hid. The soft, well-worn material curved around her breasts, the screen print job long since cracked and faded across her chest, only drawing the eye to places it shouldn't go. The ragged hem stopped an inch or so before her jean shorts, revealing a pale strip of skin that he'd guess was as soft as the shirt she wore.

Fully clothed, sure. But in his mind... she might as well be naked. Since that's how he was picturing her anyway.

But Madison clearly wasn't aware of where his mind had drifted—thank God—because she kept going. She started to pace behind the back of the couch, making sharp turns as if she were in a parade, full uniform, rather than in the comfort of her own home. Once Mad got her steam on, you didn't have any choice but to ride it out. "Then I take down my hair because I'm sick of having it up and it's giving me a headache, and suddenly I'm some sex-nymph?"

"Well, I never said nymph," he argued, then wished he'd kept his mouth shut when she turned hot eyes to his.

Damn, she was something to watch when she was pissed. He shifted his stance just a little, hoping to ease the ill-timed rising pressure in the general vicinity of his crotch.

No, no, no. That was definitely not what he needed.

"You never said nymph," she repeated, expression stunned. "Jeremy, I think you owe me an apology."

So did he. But that didn't mean he was going to feel good about it. "I'm sorry. I don't know what got into me. I'm gonna go."

She met him at the door and put a hand on his arm. "Jeremy, we're friends. Right?"

Friends. What a pale word to describe what he wished they could be. He swallowed that down. "Friends, yeah. Of course."

"Don't go away mad, please? I'll forget it; we'll just go on from here, okay?" She smiled so genuinely that he ached, knowing he was walking out the door instead of getting to touch her again.

"Sounds good." And though it took way more effort than it should have, he stepped outside and closed the door behind him.

His duty to his father wasn't something he could shrug off. And Madison… God love her, but she just didn't fit into that plan.

Not to mention he had a duty to his friend—his best friend—not to screw things up with his friend's sister. Hell, what would happen if they dated and it ended badly? Nobody would be happy.

No, he couldn't risk that. His friends were everything to him. And Madison was a friend, as she said. He couldn't risk losing one of his friends over something he could control.

He had enough issues in his life without pushing away people who supported him. No. He and Madison, much as he wished, were never going to work.

This is so working.

Madison propped her back against the door and slid down to the floor, butt plopping on the carpet, grin spreading over her face. The timing of his visit was a little ahead of her schedule, but who cared? She hadn't expected to see Jeremy again tonight after dropping Veronica off at Tim and Skye's place. Still high on excitement from the plans they made for the apartment while watching a movie, Madison was prepared to come home and crash.

But Jeremy showed up. And apparently had something crawling under his skin, since he came ready for a fight. Or confrontation. Or something.

Madison could think of several better uses for all that energy, but he wouldn't be ready to hear them. Not quite yet.

But his reaction to her normal, everyday actions, like taking off her freaking sweatshirt, was the real triumph. She hadn't planned it, hadn't even meant for that to happen. Who the hell could predict a guy would drool over a freaking sweatshirt? But he clearly couldn't help himself. And she wasn't going to argue with that. If he got *sex-nymph* from her unzipping a hoodie and shaking out her ponytail, who was she to say no?

He wasn't ready yet, she reminded herself as she stood and walked back to the bedroom to get ready for bed. Still battling some unseen demons. That was just like Jeremy, to be in his own head and not able to separate what he imagined and what was real. The man was so internal compared to the other guys it threw her off.

But she'd work that out with him if it killed them both. Which, God knew, it just might. He wasn't one to give up once he dug his heels in. But she wasn't one to give up a fight once she picked the battle.

It was war. And all was fair game.

--~~~--

Jeremy waited for his supply guy to call back. And waited. And waited. After calling the office and getting the Marine's voice mail, he let the phone drop back to the cradle with a small clash.

"Damn. He knows I can't move forward without his say-so." Jeremy doodled on the notebook in front of him, then let his wrist go lax and sketched a little, free form, letting the pen move as it wanted.

Nonsense shapes started taking form, connected and interlocked somehow. And then he saw a profile. Profile of a dead woman. Trying his best to stay zoned out—something he'd never done before—he let his hand work, let the scene take shape. Let the pen capture as many details as possible before he couldn't stand it any longer. He ripped the drawing out, set it aside, turned to a fresh page, and started scribbling down as many notes as possible.

Her hair. Her eye color. The expression on her face as she'd died. Body placement. Who killed her? He didn't know yet. He'd figure that out when he got back to his apartment. But he wasn't about to let this moment pass him by. This subconscious, glorious moment that gave him the perfect idea for a murder.

Who found her? He wasn't quite sure.

Where was she? That much he knew, without a doubt. And he grimaced as he wrote.

In the shadows, the unlit areas behind the O Club. The place where he and Madison first kissed, so many months ago. Where he got his first taste of the forbidden fruit and realized it was sweeter than he'd ever imagined. And now that he knew, he would crave the one thing he couldn't have like it was oxygen.

Finally, his hand started to cramp and he sat back to shake it out. Writing at the office wasn't something he made a habit of. But with nothing to do and nowhere to go until the supply guy called, he didn't feel guilty for taking five minutes to jot down some plotline notes.

He checked his watch.

Okay, fifteen minutes.

He stood and walked to the kitchen area down the

hall to grab a bottle of water from the main refrigerator. As he walked back down, he saw someone slip into his office. Walking up, he watched as Tim circled the desk for a minute and started to shift through papers.

"Looking for something?"

Tim jolted at the sound of his voice, startled rather than guilty. "Yeah, I wanted to see if your supply guy got back to you yet."

"No, I'm still waiting for the..." Jeremy's throat closed up as Tim's hand hovered over his notebook with his plot notes. Shit. What the hell...

"If you wanna head back to your office," he said casually, pausing to take a sip of water and wash the dust from his throat, "I'll call down at you when I get word."

"I can wait here. Nothing going on back there." Tim walked back around and fell into one of the chairs opposite his desk. "I hate feeling useless. The longer this year goes on, the more I feel like a desk jockey and not a real Marine."

As his friend settled into the seat, Jeremy breathed his first full gulp of air in minutes.

"Yeah, I know what you mean. No action and all paperwork makes Jeremy a—"

"Crab ass?"

He lifted a brow at that. "Close enough."

"Then what's the difference when you are getting some action?" Tim laughed a little. "That came out wrong, but I guess it amounts to the same."

Jeremy's hands shook a little and he balled his fingers into fists. Keeping his steps calm and unassuming, he went to his own desk chair and sat down. Then, as if just now noticing how messy his desk was, he started collecting papers seemingly at random, piling them all together.

Naturally, the notebook ended up on the bottom of the pile, well hidden by the rest of the forms. Funny how that happened.

Tim grimaced. "How the hell you get any work done around here when your desk looks like that, I'll never know."

"Easy there, Mr. Clean. Your stick is showing."

Tim just rolled his eyes as Jeremy laughed, the last of the tension seeping out of his shoulders and gut.

Tim was known for being anal, even earning the nickname Lieutenant Stick in TBS—for having a stick up his ass about regulations and rules. He'd relaxed considerably since his marriage to Skye, but he still had his moments of compulsive organization and super-cleanliness. But his wife usually eased those rough moments, and he'd become even more easygoing in the last few months.

"Are you all ready for your week out in the field?"

Tim grunted. "It's action, at least. A little notice would have been nice, though. I feel like we're always playing catch-up around here."

"Nature of the beast."

"Hurry up and wait," they both intoned at the same time, then chuckled together.

"I'm ready," Tim went on. "I just hate not having a warning. Forty-eight hours isn't much."

"That's not exactly uncommon. We rarely have that much notice before heading out to the field. Plus, you're only gone for eight days," Jeremy pointed out.

"Yeah, but I like to let Skye know as soon as possible if I'm gonna be gone."

He resisted the urge to roll his eyes. A year ago, heading out to the field at the last minute wouldn't have given Tim a second thought. As organized as he was by nature, he could have been set and ready to roll in an hour. Shit changed when you added a wife to the mix.

"Can I ask you a favor for while I'm gone?"

Jeremy sat up straighter but smiled. "Only if it's not paperwork," he joked.

Tim smiled and shook his head. "Nah. It's easier than paperwork. I promised to help Veronica set up a new bedroom set for her over the weekend, but now I'll be gone. I don't think she wants to wait a second longer, but she's too polite to say so."

New furniture? Piece of cake. "Sure. No problem. Do you need help dismantling what you've got set up now?"

Tim shook his head. "No, the furniture in the guest bedroom stays there. We would have let her have it, but she's got new stuff coming in. Skye's parents bought her a new bedroom set... something about making up for years without her own. No clue what that means, but whatever. She's moving into Madison's guest room. They'll be roommates now."

"Madison's place. Roommates. Really?" Jeremy's throat did that uncomfortable closing-in thing again. Damn, could he just not catch a break? He made mental plans to avoid her whenever possible for the near future, and suddenly he's right back at square one.

"Yeah. I think Madison works all weekend, but

Veronica has keys now. So if I give her your number, can she text you to come over when she's ready?"

"Absolutely." He'd scoot in, assemble in record time, and scoot back out again. Like a thief in the night… only during the day. And without stealing anything.

"Great." Tim slapped his palms on his knees, then pushed to stand up. "I'll let them know you're able to help. Thanks." And before he left, he leaned back and said, "And keep an eye out for my girls while I'm gone. All three of them. Yeah?"

Jeremy scoffed. "Corny, dude."

Tim smiled lazily. "Probably. But I'm not used to leaving someone behind. Just in case, you know. Makes me feel better knowing they have someone to call if something comes up."

"Sure. No problem." Yeah, he'd keep an eye out… for ways to not act like an idiot. Prime example, the other night.

Impressive, really, when a guy managed to insult a woman by claiming she was seducing him, when all she was doing was taking off a sweatshirt.

But she wants me.

He knew it as sure as he knew the Marine Corps Hymn. And he had no clue what to do with the information, other than ignore it.

Because he'd been doing such a fantastic job of that so far.

But this time he had no more chances to screw up. He and Madison were flammable together. Lighter fluid and a spark. He couldn't afford to go after her, and she wouldn't give up coming after him.

Just like in battle, he'd play it by ear. Planning only

took you so far. After that, instincts kicked in. He'd pre-
pare, steel himself against the effect she had on him, and
hope for a good show of resolve.

The only thing worse than being alone with your own
thoughts was being alone with your own thoughts for
days at a time.

And therein lay the problem with Madison's three
days on, two days off shift schedule at the moment.
If she didn't make the effort, she'd spend way too
much time with herself. God knew that was a recipe
for disaster.

She stared at the clock, calculated how long it would
take her to grab a shower and get dressed, and reached
for her cell phone on the nightstand.

"Hey, Veronica. It's Madison."

"Hello," Veronica's smooth, cultured voice answered.
"How are you?"

Madison smiled. Veronica always sounded so proper
at first, like she'd been raised by nuns in a convent.
Luckily she loosened up as conversations went on.
"I'm free for the day and I don't want to spend it alone.
Wanna grab some lunch?"

"Yes!" Veronica squealed, then coughed. "I'm sorry.
Yeah. That would be wonderful."

"Cool. I'll pick you up in forty-five minutes, okay?"

Veronica agreed and they hung up. Madison trudged
out of bed—the payment for making the phone call—
and snatched a towel from the cupboard before turning
the water on ultra hot.

An hour later, she sat with Veronica in a local bistro,

ordering a diet soda and watching as her friend ordered a smoothie with glee.

"It's just crushed ice and fruit stuff," Madison commented as Veronica handed her menu back to the server.

"But they're delicious." Veronica closed her eyes as if already savoring the flavors. "I can't believe I missed out on these for so long."

"Neither can I," Madison murmured. "Ready to spill your beans yet?"

Her friend's eyes snapped open like window shades pulled too hard. "What beans?"

Madison laughed. "Your backstory. Everyone's got one. Yours is pretty unknown. You know, where you grew up, what you did before you got here, your parents, siblings."

"Only child," Veronica said, eyes growing distant, as if she lost where she was in the conversation. "I'm an only child. No brothers or sisters."

Madison watched her friend for a moment, then sat back in her chair. "Normally I'd joke and say you could have mine, but even when my brother's a pain in the ass, I still love him. I take it you wished you had one or two?"

"Oh, I would have loved a dozen siblings. But that just wasn't in the cards." Veronica graced their server with a sunny smile as he set the smoothie in a parfait glass in front of her. "Thank you so much. This looks great."

Madison nodded as her own soda was placed in front. She toyed with the straw, waiting for Veronica to go on, elaborate more. But she didn't. "So it was just you and your folks?"

"Yes, just us three."

Awkward silence.

Madison tried again. "Where did you grow up?"

"We moved around quite a lot. This really is very good. Would you like a sip?" Veronica held the glass out in offering, eyes silently pleading for the conversation to end.

"I'm good, thanks." *And that brings us to the end of the fishing expedition. For the day, anyway.* "I can relate to the moving part. Thanks to Dad being in the Marines, we moved around a ton. Every few years, a new base. Or a new country."

"Were you lonely?"

"Nah. I mean, I had Tim no matter where we were. And as much as I give him crap about being annoying— mostly because he is—he's a good brother too. When we moved to an area where there weren't many kids, he didn't ditch me. He let me hang out with him and his friends, even though they were older and I'm sure I slowed them down." Madison smiled at the memory of a young Tim lecturing her all the way to the park about not being a dork or a dweeb or embarrassing him. And then kicking the ass of another boy who dared call her a dork himself. Name-calling was a right and privilege reserved for siblings.

"And your father, is he the reason you decided to join the military?"

"Ha!" Madison laughed, then laughed harder and doubled over, clutching her stomach, letting the chuckles roll out unchecked.

Veronica quickly grabbed her soda and moved it to the side. "Are you okay? Because if you are, people are staring."

"Oh my… Oh my God. Ha. Whew." Madison wiped her eyes and straightened. "Sorry. That just hit me as so funny. Somewhere across America, wherever my parents are on their road trip of a lifetime, my dad just got a huge pain in his side and he doesn't know why. No, he wasn't the reason. For Tim, I'm sure the legacy played a big part. But he had his own desires, and the military was a good fit for him, with or without Dad's experience."

She traced a fingertip over the glass sweating on the table, drawing a pattern in the drops of water. "I wanted to be a nurse, for sure. I went to college. Did my thing. Knew I would walk away with student loans and hated that thought. So I figured, hey, why not do Navy ROTC? Get a few years of experience and then get out, take my degree, and live where I wanted to as a civilian."

"I'm sorry, I am a little confused." Veronica held up her hands in question. "Why not the Marines? Why Navy?"

Madison smiled. "Ah, there's the wrench, isn't it? The Marine Corps doesn't have medical personnel. All medical staff are Navy."

Veronica looked confused again, which Madison couldn't blame her. "I don't understand. Why?"

"Long story short, the Marines are a department of the Navy." Madison lowered her voice and leaned in, grabbing her drink back as she did. "But don't say that to a Marine. It's true, but they'll hate hearing it." And she gave her friend a wink.

Veronica nodded, but Madison could tell she was still confused.

"Anyway, despite his bluster and grief he gives me over being in the Navy, Dad's still proud. He knows

I'm doing what I love, and that matters most with my parents."

A shadow crossed over Veronica's face, but her tone of voice didn't change when she asked, "And you'll be getting out soon, right?"

"Nope. That's the thing. I thought it would be a good way to get some experience and have college paid for. But now that I'm in, I love it." She shrugged. What could a girl do? "I love the Navy. I have no plans to leave."

"And the thought of seeing action doesn't frighten you?"

Madison thought about that for a moment, then waited while their server placed lunch in front of them. She cut into her quesadilla, watched steam rise out, and put her knife down to let it cool. "I think I'd be a fool to say that the thought of action doesn't worry me. Not being afraid doesn't make you brave. Having no fear makes you foolish, in my book, if there's a real threat. But it's accepting and recognizing the fear and doing something to work around it." She picked up one of the tortilla wedges and pointed it at Veronica. "That's bravery. So says my father, anyway."

Veronica sighed and stabbed a piece of chicken in her salad. "You make it sound so… easy. Dwayne just made it sound like a big game. Though, now that I think about it, that was probably his way of coping."

"Dwayne?" Madison's eyes shot over to her. "When did you meet him? Wasn't he already deployed when you got here?"

"He was." She was staring at her salad, but Madison would have sworn the other woman blushed a little. Though it was hard to tell, since she was so shy, what the rising color was in response to. "He and I actually crossed paths over Skype the other day. I finished up with my aunt and uncle, and he called in to see if Tim or Skye were home. I was the only one there, so he got me instead."

Madison nodded. "And you guys talked?"

"Just a little. I know I wasn't who he'd hoped to reach so I didn't want to take up much of his time."

Madison laughed at that. "I'm sure he wasn't at all displeased with having someone—anyone—to talk to. You probably made his day. Dwayne's a social creature."

"I could tell." Veronica went back to her salad.

Madison dug in to her quesadilla. After polishing off a wedge, she asked, "Are you ready to move this weekend?"

Veronica's eyes lit up like a plugged-in Christmas tree. "Oh, yes! All my things are in boxes. I mean, it's not much. But the furniture is in Tim and Skye's garage and it's all ready to be assembled. I'm so glad Jeremy could help."

Madison set down her Diet Coke, glad she hadn't taken a sip yet. Otherwise, she would have choked and made an ass out of herself. "Why is Jeremy coming over to help?" That wasn't in the plans. She had no clue yet what to do with him. Too soon!

Veronica shrugged. "Tim was called into the field for the week, so he asked if Jeremy would mind terribly coming over to set up the furniture. Tim said he knew I was looking forward to the move, and he didn't want to hold things up." She smiled so widely, Madison did her best to fight off the massive bad mood that threatened to take over lunch.

It was important to her friend, and so she would be happy for her. She could manage that much. It wouldn't kill her to figure out a plan of action in a few days. Just like nursing, you tackled one issue at a time.

"This really is a lovely smoothie." Veronica sighed. "Are you sure you don't want a sip?"

"Does it have any rum?" Madison asked, eyeing it hopefully.

Veronica laughed, as if that was the best joke she'd ever heard. "Of course not!"

"Now that's too damn bad."

Chapter 6

MATTHEW BENT OVER TO GRAB EXTRA SUPPLIES FROM the lower cabinet, his scrubs lifting up his back to reveal a few inches of tan skin. Madison slapped a hand over his back with a loud snap that had him straightening and jumping a few feet.

"What the… ah. Madison. Shoulda known it was you," he said with a grin as he reached out to pinch her arm.

Madison ducked away just in time. "You need to keep your clothes on. Or wear something under that scrub shirt."

"Aw, look. If you can't resist me and my sexy body…" Matthew wiggled his eyebrows at her in a comical way and flexed one of his rather impressive biceps at her. "I know this is just a temptation too sweet for the ladies."

"Uh-huh." She slammed the top cabinet shut and reached in a drawer for packs of empty syringes. "Too bad you aren't out for the ladies."

"Well." He winked at her and pushed the cart they were loading with supplies to refill after their shift closer. "The guys don't mind it either."

She laughed, glad he was starting to feel more comfortable mentioning it, even in jest. Though he was a civilian, not a military member, and Don't Ask, Don't Tell was a thing of the past, Matthew had always been of the mind to keep it all to himself. He felt as if his job depended on him being closeted rather than out. Madison was one of the few people he let know.

She could understand the hesitation on his part, though she didn't agree with how strict he felt he needed to be. But it was his choice, not hers, who he shared the info with. So she kept it to herself.

"So, how is road rash man?"

"Hmm?" She counted the gauze pad packets. "We're a few short on these. Remind me to make a note on inventory."

"Sure. And don't stall. The hottie from the other day. The motorcycle Marine with the bad case of ass-meets-asphalt? Jeremy something. I thought you two knew each other."

"Oh, he's fine, just… wait." She spun slowly on her heels to stare at Matthew's back. "How did you know we knew each other?"

He glanced over her shoulder, his sarcastic face obvious even in the low light of the supply closet. "Come on, Mad. You walked out of that exam room like your scrubs were on fire. Plus, you've mentioned his name like a billion times since we first met. Hard not to remember. I knew something was up."

"I have not mentioned him a billion times." She paused a moment, hand hovering over a pile of freshly laundered gowns, mind rewinding over the past year. "Have I?"

"Uh-huh. You have," Matthew answered cheerfully. "It was always in passing, always a simple *Jeremy this* or *Jeremy said that*. I doubt anyone else would have noticed. But as your official not-so-stereotypical gay best friend, it's my duty to tell you that you were a tad obsessive about it. In a cute way," he hurried to add before she clocked him one.

Madison huffed. "See if I ever listen to you obsess over your latest crush again." But though her voice jested, her mind whirled. She mentioned Jeremy, sub-consciously, more often than she could remember. Damn. It was worse than she thought.

"So what are you doing about it?"

"Doing?"

Matthew checked the door, made sure it was closed, then hopped up on the counter. "Yeah, hi. Hot guy, single, and you're semi-obsessed. So what's the plan?"

"Not obsessed," she murmured, mostly out of habit to deny, deny, deny. "But there's a plan."

"Yes. I knew it. That's my girl. Spill."

The door swung open, shining light on the dim room like a floodlight in a police raid. Nurse Henley, one of the supervising floor nurses, poked her head in, lips pursing in disapproval.

"You two shouldn't be in here with the door closed for so long. People are gonna talk," she said.

"Talk?" Madison asked innocently, biting the inside of her cheek to keep from laughing. "What do you mean?"

Nurse Henley gave her the beady eye, then Matthew, who slowly slithered down to the floor from the counter-top and began recounting the sterile cup packs. "No hanky-panky in the supply closet. You wanna do some-thing dirty, you take it home." With that short—and completely unnecessary—lecture complete, she let the door swing shut behind her.

Madison and Matthew waited to the count of ten by silent agreement, then burst out laughing.

"That never gets old," she said, wiping her eyes. "Do you think everyone in this place just assumes we're secretly humping in every dark corner?"

Matthew straightened from holding his gut with laughter. "You know, if I had to choose a beard, you'd be my number one pick."

"Aw, that's sweet." She gave him the finger and started counting all over, having lost her place.

"Well, tell me. Wouldn't you use me?"

Madison didn't look up from her counting. "For what?"

"A beard."

"I'm straight."

"Not the point. It's hypothetical."

Madison sighed and stretched her neck, realizing she lost count again. "Fine. In theory if I needed a beard for something…" She trailed off as her mind drifted into plan-making mode.

"For something," Matthew prompted.

"Shh," she shushed him, staring blankly at the wall next to the door.

A minute passed, then two. And then she smiled, a large smile. "You know… I might need a beard after all."

One of Matthew's brows rose. "Going girl on us, are we?"

She snorted. "Not even close. No offense."

"None taken. I don't wanna go girl either."

"Ha. Clever. But no. I might borrow you and your… muscles. Just for a little bit, if you're not opposed."

He shrugged a shoulder. "What for?"

Madison headed for the door, cart trailing behind her. "Are you free on Saturday? I've got a friend who needs help putting together some furniture."

—∿∿—

Skye bound in to Madison's apartment, arms full of bags. "I'm sorry I'm so late!"

Madison just laughed. As usual, her sister-in-law was moving to her own schedule of life. "It's fine. Jeremy just got here a few minutes ago. Veronica's in the bedroom with him, helping him figure out where the best place for all the furniture is before they start building. Which I think takes some of the fun out of it, but they didn't ask me."

"Oh. Good." Skye let the bags drop to the floor where she stood. "I was running a few minutes behind from my shift at work, but then I realized I hadn't gotten her anything as a housewarming gift."

"The house is already warm. I've lived here for months," Madison pointed out as she started to dig through the bags.

"You have, but she hasn't. I thought just a token or two would be a good sign of support, now that she has her own place—so to speak."

"Thoughtful, anyway." That was Skye. Always looking out for others.

"Is Veronica okay back there with Jeremy?"

Madison glanced up at Skye, confused about the worried tone in her friend's voice. "I assume so, since she was the one who suggested he help her figure out the placement before he set the stuff up. Why?"

Skye waved it off, as if she hadn't just asked a strange

question. "No reason. I just thought since they hadn't been around each other as often, she might be nervous." When Madison cocked a brow at her, she added, "Because she's so shy."

"Hmm." Madison moved some of the bags to the couch to clear the path for when they brought over boxes later. "I don't know if she's shy so much as just unsure. I think sometimes I don't give her enough credit. She's soft-spoken, but she's no pushover."

Skye thought it over for a moment. "You're right. I need to stop playing mother hen. She's a big girl."

Veronica walked in at that moment. "Do you want to come see the placement, Madison? I told Jeremy to wait until you gave the okay to set it all up."

Madison blew out a breath and shoved a strand of hair behind her ear. "Sweetie, we've been over this. It's your apartment too now. So you don't need me to give you the okay before you go ahead and pick where your furniture goes in your own bedroom."

Veronica's eyes went a little dreamy. Madison imagined some women might look that way when they were thinking of their wedding day, or staring at their newborn baby. For Veronica, all it took was a room of her own. Very strange. And a little sad, though Madison struggled not to think of it that way.

"Well, I'd like your input anyway, if you don't mind."

"Sure. Why the hell not?" She dusted off her hands on her jeans and headed back to the bedroom where Jeremy was surrounded by posts and metal framing and little bags of screws. The furniture, a nice oak color, was laying in pieces on top of the cardboard boxes they were packed in. And teeny tiny little white flecks that flaked off of the Styrofoam padding for the furniture were currently littering the carpet. Damn. She'd have to get the vacuum out later. She hated vacuuming.

No, she wouldn't. This was Veronica's room now. She smiled slowly, positively gleeful that she was now responsible for cleaning much less square footage.

"Wow, looks like the IKEA fairy landed."

Jeremy huffed out a laugh. "Yeah. She's got a lot of stuff. I wasn't sure it'd all fit, actually."

"Oh." Veronica's face fell. "Do you think it won't? Well, if it's not—"

"I was kidding." Jeremy gave Veronica a gentle smile. "Of course it'll all fit. Remember? We just measured it. You picked great spots."

Veronica melted a little at that. Not in the *hot guy complimented me, I'm so into him* sort of way, but more like, *I don't hear compliments far enough in my life* sort of way. Madison felt that same wave of sadness curl up her throat, but she battled it back down. There was a positive side to this… Jeremy's soft treatment and understanding.

"Thanks. You've been working so hard at this. I'll get you a bottle of water. You want a bottle of water, right? How about something to eat, like a granola bar? Or a bowl of cereal? I can't cook well, but I could make you an omelet."

Madison watched from another angle as Jeremy reached behind him nonchalantly and rolled the almost-full bottle of water sitting behind him under a piece of paper. "You know, a bottle of water would be fantastic. I'd appreciate that."

Eager to help, Veronica scooted out of the way, calling, "Be right back!" over her shoulder.

Madison smiled a little to herself.

Jeremy cocked his head to the side. "What's so amusing?"

She held up three fingers and ticked them down one by one. "Cue the blowup in three... two... one..."

"*Bottled water?* What in the world does she have bottled water in here for?" Skye's voice was clear as day all the way from the kitchen as she huffed and started lecturing Veronica on the evils of plastic.

Jeremy gave her a grin. "Looks like you're busted."

"It happens. I forgot she was coming over or I would have put out the filter pitcher. I'll get the lecture later, for which I will appear duly chastised. And then we both walk away knowing I'll end up doing what I want to anyway and we'll be repeating the process in another month. At least I recycle." She grinned when Jeremy chuckled, then toed a bag of screws to the side. "This looks like the world's most annoying craft project. Need any help?"

"Yeah, if you don't mind." Jeremy patted the carpet by him and she sat down, legs crossed beneath her. "Veronica's a sweetheart, but she's really not much help with this. Too nervous, her hands shake. Not that it's rocket science, but a second pair of hands to hold stuff steady is always welcome. Plus, my arms are getting tired. One piece of furniture is one thing. But an entire bedroom set, damn."

"No problem. Steady hands, aye."

He laughed and bumped her shoulder with his, then went back to reading the instructions.

She resisted the urge to glance over his shoulder, using the guise of checking the directions for a chance to press her body against his. Not in her plan. Not today.

Jeremy's voice cut through her mental scheming. He held the instructions out, turning them one way and another, as if not sure he was even looking at them right side up. "Okay, grab post A and slide it around so it's ready for screw three and the spring thing to connect it to post F."

Madison stared at the available pieces of wood and metal. "That wasn't English."

"It was IKEA English. Which is recognized in at least twenty states." Jeremy reached over her lap and grabbed a mini wrenchlike object, his arm brushing against her breasts as he pulled back.

Madison's nipples hardened automatically, as they usually did when he touched her. Jeremy, on the other hand, didn't even seem to realize they'd touched, let alone where. He had eyes for IKEA only.

The furniture floozy.

There was a knock at the door, and Madison was reminded of her master plan. Or, well, at least the next step of the ever-evolving master plan. Though, now that Matthew was there, she almost regretted having started it. No going back now, though.

She heard Skye's confused greeting, then Matthew's more lively hello.

Jeremy cocked his head to one side. "Who's that?"

"Oh, I invited another friend over. Wasn't sure how involved this process might get. Thought the help might be welcome," she said, like it was no big deal.

In theory, it wasn't.

In practice, it was a big deal. A big fucking deal.

Suddenly, she second-guessed her choice of involving Matthew in the plan. He'd agreed to be a willing participant, so it wasn't as if she tricked him into coming. But still…

As Matthew's obviously male voice grew louder, following Skye down the hallway toward the bedroom, Jeremy's eyes shifted a little. "Friend, huh?"

"Yup. Guy I work with at the hospital. He's great; you'll like him." All true. She was positive that Matthew and Jeremy would be great friends, if they met under the right circumstances.

These, however, weren't such.

"Mad, hey!" Matthew walked into the room, picked her up under the armpits, and hauled her up for a big hug, spinning her around once.

Over his shoulder, she couldn't help but notice Jeremy staring holes through Matthew's head before directing his intense focus down to the paper clenched in his hands.

Okay. She started it, so she had to go with it. Plan Matthew Makes Moves was now in action.

―――

Who the hell was this dude?

A tall guy with a tight graphic T-shirt and shaggy blond hair stepped into the room. Without hesitation, the new guy greeted Madison, picked her up, and spun her around like a toy.

Jeremy watched as the guy's hand slid down to support her body from her thighs, just under the curve of her ass.

Friend from work, he mentally scoffed. Like fucking hell.

The other man set her down and grinned. "So how goes it? You said you needed help with furniture?"

Jeremy stood up, and the other man's eyes widened, as if he hadn't realized anyone else was even in the room. "Yeah, sorry you got dragged away from… whatever you were doing. I've got it, though."

"Oh. Well, I'm already here to lend a hand. Maybe it'll go faster this way." The guy shrugged, then held out a hand. The sleeve of his shirt cut into the muscle in his arm. The guy looked like he lifted weights and surfed for a living. A beach bum with a gym membership. "Matt McCormick. Call me Matthew."

Jeremy shook his hand, doing his best to not squeeze too hard like a douchebag. "Jeremy Phillips." He took his hand back and wiped it on his pants before he could help it. "So you guys work together?"

"Yup." Matthew slung an arm around Madison's shoulders, to which she rolled her eyes in response. What did that mean? Did she not want the guy putting the moves on her? "We work the same nursing rotation. Hey, wait. Jeremy Phillips. Yeah, I remember you. You came in the other week after laying down your bike, right?"

He held back a wince. Not a finer moment he wanted to remember. "That's me."

"Cool. Glad you're okay, man." Matthew surveyed the room with everything laid out, then swiped the hair out of his eyes with one hand.

Get a haircut, hippie. Jeremy shook off the negative thought. He had no right to feel this… jealous? Was that what this burning, pinching feeling in his chest was all about?

"So, just putting together some furniture, right?" He bent over to pick up one of the instruction sheets. "I actually have this dresser at my place. I've had to take it apart and move it twice already. I could put it together in my sleep now."

"Great!" Madison said, eyes lighting up.

"I got it," Jeremy insisted, pulling the paper out of the other guy's hand. "They asked me to do this as a favor, so I'm working on it."

"Two heads are better than one and all that," Matthew said easily, taking the paper back.

"Too many cooks," Jeremy replied, grabbing the paper and stepping away. And then he felt about three feet tall… the average height of a five-year-old. Exactly how he was acting.

Madison glared at him. Without removing her all-too-knowing gaze, she patted Matthew's arm. "How about you help us load some of Veronica's boxes over at Skye's place? So when the furniture is done, Veronica has something to put away."

Matthew stared at him too, and there was no mistaking the tone of this gaze. Primitive, all the way. One male taking measure of another. Though how he measured up, Jeremy had no idea. "Sure. No prob." He turned and headed back to the living room by himself, calling out to Skye along the way as if they were already best friends.

There was a beat of silence. Then Madison nudged a metal bar with the toe of her running shoe. "I might need to go help him."

"Sure." Jeremy realized, as she was turning to go, he didn't want her to leave. Not with Matthew. But really, not at all. Her sitting with him, surrounded by puzzle pieces claiming to be furniture parts, was the most relaxed he'd been in who knew how long. And he wanted more. Stupid as it was, dangerous as it was, he wanted more of it.

"Will you be okay here?" She stared at him, as if this were a serious question. Like there was a definite right or wrong answer.

He always hated these types of questions in school. Give him an essay any day.

"Yeah. I'll be fine. I'm a guy; we build shit. It's what we do. Hammer, saw, screwdriver." He sat back down, refusing to look at her face for his own safety. He didn't want to know if he chose right or wrong.

It felt wrong. It felt really wrong to him. But that didn't matter.

"Okay." Her voice sounded small for once, rather than the larger-than-life quality it usually had. "I'll be— we'll be back later, then."

He waved over his shoulder, as if it didn't matter where she was or what she did or who she did it with.

But it mattered. It shouldn't. But it mattered so fucking much.

Chapter 7

MADISON SAT IN THE CAR, FOLDING AND UNFOLDING her fingers together, not sure at all that she'd played this hand well.

"Being a beard is fun."

She slapped at Matthew's arm without looking at him. "You're not a real beard. I'm not pretending to be straight."

"You're pretending. Isn't that the major point of the beard? Being something you're not?"

"What am I pretending to be?"

She slid her eyes over to Matthew's in the driver's seat, only to catch a hell of a look from him.

"You're pretending not to be in the mush with that guy."

"In. The. Mush." Madison shook her head and laughed, albeit hollowly. "There's a new one."

"It'll catch on. Face it, Mad. You've got it, and you've got it bad." He stopped for a moment, then chuckled. "Just call me Usher."

Madison groaned. "Awful. I'm going to call you awful if you keep this up."

"I say this with all the platonic love in my heart, but you are the world's worst person at hiding shit. It's written all over your face. He might not see it, because guys tend to wear blinders at the most inappropriate times. Mostly when it concerns themselves."

"So what am I pretending to not be again?"

Matthew reached over and squeezed her knee. "Not completely in love with him. And totally okay with the fact that he isn't going to be asking you over tonight to watch the game."

"What game?" As far as she knew, no games were playing that anyone would care about.

Matthew shrugged. "Isn't that what all guys use as code for 'Come over for some beer and sex?' No? Just me then, huh?"

She slugged him again.

He laughed, pretended to veer the car off the road at her abuse, then straightened. "Be nice, or I won't share the bright sunny side to this whole tragic thing."

Madison perked a little. "There's a bright side?"

"Oh yeah." Matthew made the turn, following Skye back to the townhouse where Veronica had left all the boxes full of her possessions. "And it's really very simple. Funny how women tend to wear blinders right back."

"Speak English please, Usher," she said through her teeth.

"He's dying about it. The whole 'I want you but I think I can't have you' thing is killing him. He wanted to rip my head off, stuff it down the garbage disposal, and toss a few lemons in after it."

"He looked fine." Madison reached for the door handle as he put the car in park, but Matthew's hand covered hers.

"Trust me, he's not. That guy back there? Dying on the inside. Something holds him back from going after you balls-out. No clue what it is; I can only see so far into the situation. But there's something holding him from going after you like some wild animal stalking its prey."

Madison absorbed that fact for a minute. "Was I childish, inviting you over?"

"Maybe a little." Matthew opened his door and grinned at her. "But there's a bright side to that too. I'm a fantastic pack mule."

———

Jeremy attacked the furniture project like the hounds of hell were nipping at his feet. Like hell was he going to let that surf bum come back and see him only halfway done with the project and think he was struggling or some shit. No. He wouldn't be able to get it all done— effing screws and bolts and forty-seven different ways to assemble a bed frame—but he could make a huge dent in the project. And not look like a jackass when the crew returned.

The front door opened and Skye's voice rang out in the empty apartment. "Jeremy, we're back!"

"Still back here," he called back, focusing on the teeny, tiny screw that the instructions swore was critical to the entire construction.

Whatever happened to wood? Real wood, from one tree. Carved out, sanded down, nailed together. Jesus Frankenstein Christ, this thing was a mess and a half. You needed a master's degree and two doctorates in aeronautical engineering to put the damn thing together.

Skye came in and stepped gingerly around the grave-yard of scrap parts. Her eyes ping-ponged between the floor and the mostly constructed bed frame. "Should this much still be left over?"

He glanced around the floor and let his eyes widen. "Oh shit. That's all still left over?" He laughed when Skye looked horrified. "Yes, they're all extra parts, in case something happens, so you can replace them. I'm not building Veronica a faulty bed." *God, I hope*.

"Oh." Skye looked relieved. "She'll be glad to hear it. And she's extremely grateful."

"Yeah. I know." The gratitude that girl put off was almost uncomfortable. As if he was curing cancer in her bedroom or something. But it came from a good place, and he wasn't about to mock her for it. He just didn't think he could handle someone as sweet and gentle as Veronica on a daily basis.

"Screw you, McCormick!"

Madison burst into the bedroom, delicate flower that she was. As if the heavens above wanted to provide him with an example of the reverse of *sweet and gentle*. "See, I told you he'd be more than halfway done."

Pride bloomed through his chest, even though he mentally realized it was pathetic, as far as compliments went. He—wait.

"Who said I wouldn't be more than halfway done?"

She grinned. "Matthew thought you'd need a second pair of hands. I bet him you'd be more than halfway done all by yourself, so thanks. He's buying pizza."

Pizza. Bet. Yeah, okay then. He nodded and concentrated on the world's tiniest screw again, trying to get the damn thing to align properly with the—

"Nice work."

The man's deep baritone had him clenching his fingers, dropping the screw in the thick carpet. "Fuck." Just what he needed.

"Uh-oh." Skye stepped out of his light so he could look closer between the carpet fibers. "I think we might be distracting Jeremy. How about we step out for a bit and order that pizza? If he needs us, he can call."

"Yeah. Sure. Hey, I bet you'll be on my side, Skye. Madison here likes all that greasy pepperoni on her pizza. I'm more of a veggie lover myself."

Skye bounced in place. "Me too!"

Matthew slung an arm around Skye, all buddy-buddy, and they headed out the door. Jeremy wondered what Tim might have to say about that sort of close contact. Not that he thought for a second Skye was tempted by the surfer boy. Skye and Tim were so into each other it was almost embarrassing.

In an enviable sort of way.

Not that he'd ever admit that out loud. Hell no. Matter of pride, that one.

Someone cleared their throat and he glanced back up. Madison gave him a small smile. "Are you sure you don't want help?"

He wanted things to go back the way they were an hour ago. Madison sitting next to him, joking with him, being his second pair of hands, another set of eyes. Being a friend.

A friend that might just crawl into his lap, snug her ass against his raging erection, loop her arms around his neck, and—

"Jeremy."

He shook his head and realized he'd been staring at the blank wall by Madison's arm. "Sorry, what?"

She shook her head and snorted. "Sure you don't need to take a break? You zoned out there for a bit."

"No," he bit off. "I'm good."

She waited another beat, as if giving him a chance to change his mind. Then she shrugged and walked out the door.

And he zoned out again, only this time watching her fine, heart-shaped ass sway down the short hallway before hooking a right to go to the living room. And he was forced to shift, then give up and crawl to his knees to readjust his shorts around the straining erection tenting the zipper.

He really had to get a grip on this hard-on for his best friend's sister. Tim asked him to watch over her... and the others. Not think about them naked.

Of course, thinking of Skye and Veronica naked wasn't even possible. Not even a minor threat. Madison, on the other hand...

God, she'd look fantastic naked. All those toned muscles, slick skin... She'd go all out. He knew it. In bed she'd be an active participant, fighting for dominance all the way. And when she lost, she'd lose without grace, but damn that would be a sweet submission as he—

"Triple meat okay?"

"Jesus!" Jeremy lost hold on the two metal rods of the bed frame—currently rivaling the rod in his pants on a scale of one to fucking hard—and they clattered down in a ringing peal that had him wincing.

Matthew whistled low. "Sorry, didn't mean to startle you."

"You didn't startle me," he said through gritted teeth, picking up the metal again. What the hell was he doing with this piece, anyway? "You just... whatever. What did you want?"

The other man propped a shoulder against the door-frame, then changed his mind and walked in to sit down on the floor a decent distance away. Smart guy. "Madison said you'd want the triple meat pizza. I was just double-checking for her."

"Oh. Yeah. She's right." He stared at the instructions intently until the words blurred in front of his eyes. *Blink. Blink, dammit.*

There was a long silence, to the point that Jeremy wondered if the other guy had fallen asleep, or somehow teleported out of the room. But he wasn't going to look up. Not if it killed him. It was like some silent, unspoken showdown, and he'd be damned if he was going to lose to a gym rat hippie surfer.

"She's right about a lot of things."

Okay, so he looked up. Matthew the surf bum was giving him a too-knowing glance that sort of freaked him out. The sort of look he imagined therapists gave their patients right before they called them on their bullshit.

"Who, Madison?" He snorted. "Squirt's not right about much."

"I thought only her brother called her that."

The man knew way more intimate details than he wanted him to. "I'm his best friend. We hang out enough in a group. It all comes out to the same thing."

It was Matthew's turn to snort. "I'm going to bet the way you think about her is nothing close to brotherly."

Who was this guy—Jesus? "Yeah, sorry, but you're way off. I don't really have time to think about Madison. She's a friend, but I don't spend my downtime thinking about friends." Lies double-battered in lies then deep-fried in more lies.

Matthew shrugged. "Fine. Works for me. If she's free and clear, then it's not poaching, right?"

Poaching? Like Madison was a fucking animal and he was a weekend safari hunter. A screw dug into Jeremy's palm, and he realized he'd been clenching his hand too tightly. He loosened his fingers, rubbed at the red mark on his palm, and sighed. "Sure. Whatever."

Matthew laughed, a big roaring laugh that had Madison poking her head in.

"What's going on in here?"

Matthew fell to his side, curling up into a semi-fetal position, and laughed harder.

Jeremy waved her off. "It's fine. Your boyfriend here is just having a mild seizure. Nothing to worry about."

She glared at him. "He's not my boyfriend." Then, as if to prove it, she walked in and kicked Matthew in the thigh, which only had him laughing harder. "Get up, weirdo, and tell me what's going on."

He shook his head and rolled the other direction, facing away, still laughing his weirdo head off.

He's not my boyfriend.

Four words had never sounded more sweet. And that was seriously fucked up. "I think maybe he's been out in the sun too long or something."

"Or something," Madison mumbled, agreeing with him.

Finally the subject of their conversation seemed to calm down enough to sit up and rub at his damp eyes. "Madison, babe, could you run to my car and see if you can find my cell phone? I think it fell out of my pocket in there, but if not then I'll have to run back to Skye's townhouse to look."

She raised an eyebrow at that but shrugged and left the room.

As she left, Matthew's goofy grin morphed in front of Jeremy's eyes to a hard, grim line.

"Look, here's the deal. You want her. You don't want to want her, but you do all the same."

"I don't—"

Matthew cut him off. "Six of one, half-dozen of the other. You're about to say you don't want her. Which is half of what I just said, if you were listening." He reached out and grabbed the knob for a dresser drawer and twirled it in his palm, taking his sweet time getting to the point. "I love Mad."

And apparently, when the man had a point, he had a big one.

Jeremy's blood boiled until he saw red. Another reaction he had no right to feel. But feel, he did.

"Yeah," Matthew smirked, as if reading Jeremy's mind. "I thought that would be your reaction. You couldn't look more pissed off if you tried for it. Looks like someone just shot your dog in front of you."

God dammit. He wasn't just going to sit here and take shit from this guy because he was Madison's friend. The muscles in his neck screamed, he was clenched so hard against the urge to throw himself across the room and beat the guy into dust.

He held up a hand. "I love her, as a friend. She's my *best friend*. That's the end of it, lucky her. I would make her a terrible boyfriend." He smiled, almost to himself, as if enjoying a private joke about something. Though what he could have to smile about when he just admitted he loved her but would never be with her, Jeremy couldn't say.

The thought of never being with Madison definitely didn't leave him with a smile.

"So what's your main excuse?"

Jeremy looked up to see Matt holding out the next piece he needed for the bedpost. He reached out to grab it. "Excuse for what?"

"Not going after the girl. Mine is we're best friends. Well, among other things," he added, almost under his breath. "You're a single guy, I'm sure girls are something you enjoy on a regular basis." He laughed at Jeremy's snarl. "Maybe not recently, then. So what is it? Guilt? Misplaced duty? Got a girl on the side nobody knows about? Think she's not good enough?"

"Of course she's good enough," he snapped, then grumbled to himself.

Matthew nodded. "More than good enough, that's for damn sure. Here's the thing. I'm not moving in, so you can stop staring at me like you want to rip my arms off and beat me to death with them. But I'm not the only male on this base, in this city, or in this state. And one of these days, someone else will see her, want her, and not just as a friend, like I do."

Jeremy stared for a moment. Was he really having this conversation? "Anyone tell you you talk too much?"

Matthew laughed, not at all offended. "Madison does, on an almost daily basis. And here she is." He stood as Madison poked her head back in.

"I do what?" Madison asked, confusion written all over her face.

"Tell me I talk too much," he replied easily. None of the heavy subject they'd just discussed was evident in his posture or tone. The guy was good.

"Oh. Well, it's true. Your cell wasn't in the car. Skye says we can have her key to go run back over and check."

He gave her a sheepish grin that Jeremy saw right through, then dug in his pocket and held up his phone. "Sorry, babe. I forgot I put it in a different pocket. My bad."

She blew him a raspberry and disappeared again.

Matthew stood and clapped a hand over Jeremy's shoulder. Clearly, the past five minutes had done a lot to help out Jeremy's feeling about the guy because he didn't immediately want to punch him for it.

"Just think about what I said. I know she's important to you. But you gotta work your own shit out, it seems, and figure that out on your own."

And then he walked out of the room, leaving Jeremy to wonder how long he had before another guy just like Matthew walked into her life and didn't hold back.

———

Madison stretched and rolled her neck to one side. Lord, the crick in her neck was unreal.

"Are you sure glasses should go here?" Skye asked.

"Yes, by the fridge makes the most sense." Veronica nodded firmly.

"I just think over by the sink would be so much easier for you. Why don't we—"

"Skye," Madison murmured.

Skye looked up from collecting glasses and into Veronica's resolute face. "Whoops. I'm doing it again, aren't I?" She set the glasses back down and held up her hands. "Your place, your choice."

Veronica gave her a quick hug. "I know you just want to help. I'm not upset."

Skye smiled as Veronica went to work shelving the cups. "That's definitely new. When you moved in here, you didn't care what I did with your kitchen."

Madison shrugged and hopped up on the counter. "Long as everything is in here somehow, I don't really care." But Veronica did. Which was why she'd asked for permission to rearrange a few things, just to make sure it all fit, she insisted. What Madison knew she was leaving out was the part where the kitchen was a disorganized clusterfuck. But Veronica was way too polite to point that out.

"Is Jeremy still setting up the bed?" Skye asked a moment later. "I thought he would be done by now."

Madison shrugged, but she didn't want to admit it made her nervous, how long he and Matthew had been back there together. No sounds of breaking furniture or death screams, so she assumed everyone was still alive. But Matthew had a big mouth. God only knew what he was saying.

Skye reached in a big shopping bag and brought out some sort of appliance and set it on the counter. "And here's the panini maker you bought. Where should it go?"

Veronica beamed and grabbed the appliance. "I know exactly where."

"Do we seriously need a panini maker? Isn't that why God invented Panera and those awesome people who slice your bagels and make the sandwiches?"

Skye and Veronica stared at her like she'd just insisted they all strip off their clothes and go skinny-dipping in the complex pool.

"It's a panini maker," Skye said slowly. "They're delicious."

"Uh-huh." If she couldn't put boxed brownie batter in it and bake it, or scramble eggs in it, she didn't really see the point. But she was saved from admitting so when someone knocked on the door. She hurried over to get it, using the cash Matthew had left her to pay the delivery boy, and brought the pizza back to the kitchen.

At least this was something she could do. Using a pizza cutter—the most well-used item in her kitchen—she separated the slices onto a plate.

"Madison." Skye sighed. "Paper plates?"

"Putting takeout on real plates is like a crime against nature. Boys!" she called. "Pizza's here!"

Matthew showed up a moment later, as if already sensing the food was in the general vicinity. Which he likely did. The man ate more than a Holstein heifer and never gained an ounce.

Madison, on the other hand, would be out running tonight to combat the calories. Damn men and their metabolisms.

"Cool." He grabbed a hot slice from the box before she'd had a chance to cut through it completely and stuffed it in his mouth. Then Madison watched as the pleasure morphed into pain and he grabbed a bottle of water and chugged. "Hot. Fucking hot!"

She shrugged and patted his chest. "If you weren't such a pig, I'd have told you that before you bit in. But there you went, following your stomach again like Toucan Sam."

"That's follow your nose," he shot back, but with a grin.

"Who is Toucan Sam?" Veronica asked as she brought over plates.

They both stared at her in openmouthed shock. Finally, Madison said, "The bird guy from the Froot Loops commercial when we were kids?"

She blinked a few times like an owl, then laughed. "Oh. Right. The commercial. Of course. I just had one of those..." She snapped her fingers and waved by her head. "You know, where your brain blanks."

"Brain fart?" Matthew offered helpfully.

She smiled. "That. Only if there's a less gross version, then that's what I had."

Matthew laughed. "You're a riot." He leaned over to give her a kiss on the cheek. Veronica danced away easily, keeping the plates between them, eyes focused on the fridge as if she hadn't noticed him bending over. Anyone else catching the movement out of the corner of their eye wouldn't have noticed at all. But Madison did. It hadn't been lost on her that men in general seemed to make her roommate wary, even one as harmless as Matthew. At least until she came to know them better.

Jeremy walked in at that moment, staring between all of them. "So, what's the deal?"

Madison handed him a plate with green veggies coating the slice of pizza. "Got your favorite."

He stared down and sneered at it. "It's got vegetables on it."

"It's healthy."

"It's a salad."

"It's mine." Skye nipped between them and stole the plate. Then she threaded her arm through Veronica's and walked her back over to the living room couch. "Let's sit down and relax. We've earned it."

Jeremy reached around Madison, his arm brushing hers for just a moment. And she held her breath, too afraid to relax and fall into him just a little more and startle him off.

That just about summed up her life perfectly. Afraid to breathe and scare Jeremy away.

Jeremy gave Matthew a look. "Staying for pizza?"

Matthew smiled back. "Sure am."

Jeremy nodded and followed in Skye and Veronica's wake.

"Well." Madison lifted out a piece of pizza for herself and put it on a plate. No sense in giving Matthew one. He was raised by wolves, after all. "You two seem chummy all of a sudden."

"Isn't that why you invited me over?" Matthew blinked innocently at her.

"Shut up," she mumbled. But he didn't take offense. Just leaned over and gave her the kiss Veronica shied away from.

"I know, I know. Look, we're cool. He's a good guy. And he didn't offer to rearrange my teeth, which I appreciate greatly. So I think my work here is done. Leave him guessing."

"You're leaving? You just said you were staying." Sure, her intentions might not have been pure in having Matthew over to begin with, but she did love hanging out with him outside of work. "We don't see each other much anymore, I feel like."

"I know. But I was just messin' with him." He winked at her. "Got a hot date."

"Ah, anyone I know?"

"Nope. He's new." He gave her another kiss, then headed out of the kitchen. Calling a brief good-bye to the rest of the gang, he let himself out.

Madison took her pizza into the living room and sat on the floor next to Skye.

"He left so soon," Skye said, disappointed.

"Yeah, he had things to do." Madison took a bite and let the delicious melty-cheese goodness engulf her taste buds. Then fought with a stringy bit that hung off her lip. As her tongue worked to get the rogue string of cheese into her mouth, she glanced up and saw Jeremy watching her.

Or, rather, her mouth. And not in the horrified, *can't you eat pizza correctly?* sort of way. But the hungry, *I want to eat more than pizza* sort of way.

The way that had her entire body reacting until she crossed her arms over her chest to hide her hardening nipples.

And she realized the time for playing coy had reached its end. She gave him her best look right back.

The one that said *you're invited to dine anytime*.

Chapter 8

HE LEFT. HE JUST LEFT. MADISON TOSSED THE LAST plate into the garbage can with flourish.

She'd given him her best version of come hither and he'd still balked. Stumbled out the door and off on his motorcycle into the night.

Damn him.

She was losing ground, it felt like. And it couldn't continue. But first, she knew she had some ground to make up... in the gym.

With no better way to expend the pent up frustration clenching her muscles—plus the memory of the pizza she'd inhaled—she changed into a moisture-wicking tank, and her running shorts and running shoes, and slipped her apartment key into the hidden mesh pocket on the inside of the waistband of her shorts. Veronica was off to a movie, and she wasn't going to leave the door unlocked. Then, feeling a little better already, she popped her iPod earbuds in her ears and skipped down her apartment steps and two buildings over to the twenty-four-hour gym. Yet another amenity that made her choose this complex.

It was almost empty, minus one guy using the rowing machine. Most people had better things to do on a Saturday night than work out. Madison couldn't blame them. She'd prefer a different sort of cardio workout herself. A more horizontal one, one that included a partner. But alas, not tonight. She turned on her iPod and clicked for the songs to shuffle. After a quick stretch, she hopped on the treadmill and set a comfortable pace for three miles. Checking the time at a mile and a half—the distance she had to run for her semi-annual Physical Readiness Test, or PRT—she smiled at her good pace and kept pushing, working off the pizza before it had a chance to take residence on her butt.

Calories were sneaky that way.

As she completed her third mile, she grabbed one of the towels by the door and patted her face and chest dry, then lay down on the bench used for weights and lowered the volume on her iPod. From the corner of her eye, she caught her fellow Saturday night gym user walking toward the door, dropping his used towel in the basket. Finally, the place to herself. Using the overhead bar, she stretched out her arms and then relaxed, concentrating on her breathing pattern.

She sensed more than saw someone new in the gym, and she lowered the sound on her iPod in response. At least until she saw who it was and judged them.

"We need to talk."

Oh, hell. She fought the urge to turn the sound back up—childish, she knew—and sat up slowly, engaging her ab muscles along the way. "How did you get in here, Jeremy? The door shut behind me and it's keypad locked."

He rounded the bench and stood in front of her, black leather jacket still on, helmet tucked under one arm. Aw, damn. Why did he have to still be wearing the jacket? And carrying the helmet? Her instincts struggled hardcore against the desire rolling low in her belly. Some people looked flat-out ridiculous when they rode a bike or wore the clothes, like posers trying to play James Dean. Jeremy just looked… right.

Jeremy pointed to his ears. "You wanna take those out?"

She held up the iPod. "The sound's off." But habit had her removing the earbuds anyway. "So you got in here how, again?"

"The guy who just left held the door for me. Nice security. You should warn the managers to send a notice to the residents not to let people in behind them like that. It's begging for something to happen."

She shrugged and pulled the material of her tank away from her stomach to air out the hot skin a little. Not that it did much good. The heat she was feeling was definitely coming from inside. "You have a point. I can always mention it to management. So that answers how you got in here. Now for the why."

He laughed harshly and dropped down to the incline bench in front of her, legs splayed out wide, helmet in his lap. "Fuck if I know." He stared out the large window of the door, as if the inky black night sky was going to give him the secret to his thought process.

She dragged the towel back over her face once more and then tossed it on the ground before standing up to shift weights. "If you're just going to stand there, could you at least spot me on some bench presses before going?"

His eyes widened a little before he shrugged and stood to help her remove the forty-five-pound plates some inconsiderate jerk had left on before she got there and replaced them with twenty-fives, one on each side. "Can you handle this much?"

She could. Relatively comfortably. But because she was annoyed at his tone, she added another five-pounder on her side, watching him skeptically add one to his as well. "Just spot. It doesn't require you to talk. Lucky for you, since you never seem to do it well."

She sat down, adjusted where her butt hit, and then stretched out under the bar. Thanks to her short arms, she needed help unracking the bar, but from there, she gave him credit. He didn't try to hold on longer than necessary to ensure she had her grip. Which would have really sucked if she'd added another fifteen on each side, rather than the five she stuck with.

Controlling her breathing, she looked up only for a moment and realized that at this angle, Jeremy's crotch was right next to her face. A hip-thrust away from touching. And there was no mistaking, even upside down, the fact that he had a major pop-up tent going behind that zipper.

The weights shifted ever so slightly, and she knew if she didn't pull her head out of her ass and concentrate on the task at hand, she'd hurt someone. Likely herself.

Sensing the shift, Jeremy's hand went next to hers to stabilize. "You okay? You got it?"

"Yeah." She blew out a breath, blanked her mind, and went for twelve reps, struggling a little on the last push. But she did it, and when he lifted to help her rack the bar, she managed to keep her arms from wavering.

"Not too bad, squirt."

She sat up, forgetting for a moment she wasn't even close to done with her normal three sets. "Why do you call me that?"

"Squirt?" He shrugged and propped one booted foot

on the supporting bar below the bench, arms draped casually over the weights. "Tim does."

"Tim's my brother."

His face darkened a little. "Yeah. He is. And maybe the reminder's good for both of us."

"For you," she shot back. "I don't give a damn about him being my brother." Okay, that came out wrong, but in the context it made sense so she didn't take it back.

Clearly, Jeremy knew what she meant. "Mad, it matters. It just does."

"Uh-huh. I can see that." She didn't look down, but even from the corner of her eye, she could tell his tent was still popped. Big time. No hiding it.

He did glance down, and then shrugged. "So? You're female; I'm a guy. You're in skintight clothes. It happens." The way his mouth pulled tight told a completely different story.

"Right. Okay then. You sure told me. My mistake." Madison lay back down, but facing the opposite direction, so her feet were under the bar. "I guess if that's just the end of it, then there's not much more I can do about the whole thing, is there?"

"No."

"You can go; you don't have to stay." When he didn't move, she said something she wished she could take back immediately after she said it.

"I can always call Matthew for company."

Quick as lightning, so fast she never had a chance to anticipate his intentions, Jeremy was over her in an instant. Covering her body from chest to knee. His torso rested heavily on hers, pressing into her breasts. One knee was propped between her thighs on the bench, his other leg down on the ground to keep him balanced.

"Call Matthew? You have to be shitting me."

She said it. Now she had to own it. "He's a good friend. And we have fun hanging out. Plus, he likes working out, and he'd be fine spotting me." All true. Though once again, context mattered.

"He doesn't want you. He told me himself."

Matthew. What the hell? Worst. Beard. Ever.

"So what?" She thrust her chin out, defiant even in her vulnerable physical—and emotional—position. "I'm used to it by now. Men not wanting me."

Pressing his hips down, there was no mistaking the hard erection nudging against her hip. "This. Does this feel like not wanting you?"

"I—I don't know." God, how was she supposed to think when he did that?

His mouth found her pulse below her jaw. One hand skimmed up her ribs to cup her tank-covered breast. "How about this?"

"Not sure." Her voice was unsteady. "Maybe you should try it again."

Jeremy's knee brushed right against her core, now damp with longing and an inability to deny how much she lusted after the man right on top of her. "And that?"

"I…" All thoughts of even trying to come up with something to say fled when he dragged his mouth over hers and stole her breath with a kiss that rocked her.

Rocked her to the core.

Without hesitation, as if they'd been doing this for years, her arms wrapped around him, bringing him even closer, if it was possible. Keeping him there. Not letting him go. Not giving him the chance to put anything more between them.

"Jer... Jeremy." Her breath was coming too fast. Too hard. She was going to black out if she didn't get herself under control.

As if sensing she needed a minute to breathe, he skimmed his lips up over her nose, brushing lightly against her eyelids, over her brows, down her cheek to rest below her ear while his leg met her center in a rhythm that would have been way more fun without all the denim and nylon and spandex between them.

His knee and thigh rubbed against her, making her shudder without even trying. The man didn't even have to freaking try and she was melting for him. Some small part of her brain was a little ashamed of that.

But not ashamed enough to stop what felt so freaking good.

"Madison. God. God dammit." His teeth scraped against her lobe, breath hot on her neck. "Don't tell me I don't want you."

She couldn't answer, just hummed in response.

"That's never been the problem. Never."

Don't talk about problems. Not now. Not ever. Just keep doing that thing with your—

She gasped, shuddered. But she didn't want her first climax with Jeremy to end like this. Not by herself, not without him even making the effort. It was almost like cheating the moment. As if realizing she was on the edge of some cliff she couldn't push herself over, Jeremy reached down with one hand and rubbed, just briefly, against the front of her shorts.

And she spiraled down the dark cavern into a pool of

bliss, not even caring that she was coming in a public gym, where anyone could walk in at any time.

While her heartbeat returned to something that didn't resemble cardiac arrest, she shifted just a little to let him know he was heavy. But she didn't speak. Didn't want to burst the bubble of intimacy—however fleeting it might be—that surrounded them in the quiet, dark gym.

The door opened, and a guy in his twenties walked in, only to freeze and stare at them with mild horror. "Dudes. That's gross. Get a room, but wipe down the bench first."

One bubble bursting, coming right up.

Madison gasped and turned to hide her face in Jeremy's shoulder. But he took that moment to launch himself off of her body, and she went rolling from the bench to landing on the floor mat instead with a thud. Her shoulder jarred, and it took two tries to get her breath back, but it didn't hurt.

"Jesus Christ." Jeremy kneeled down beside her and shoved until she was on her back. "Mad, talk to me. You okay?"

The sound of the door closing filled her with relief.

Madison groaned and covered her eyes with one forearm. "I might die of embarrassment. But yes, I'm fine." Sort of.

Did the word "fine" include instances where she just climaxed from dry humping like a fifteen-year-old?

Jeremy took her shoulders and helped her sit up until her back rested against the bench. "Sure you're okay?"

She waved off his hands. "Yup. Not one of my finest moments, but I'll live."

Jeremy seemed to believe her this time and flopped

down to sit in front of her. Silence surrounded them again, now that their bubble-bursting friend had left for less intimate pastures. Finally she caught glimpse of his helmet and grabbed it.

"I always thought you looked kinda hot on the bike." She let her fingers trace over the lines of the thick plastic, over the visor, and around the jagged design that so seemed to define Jeremy's personality.

"Really?"

"Yeah. I had all these awesome fantasies about you and me and the motorcycle and vibrations…" She realized she said all of that out loud and she flushed, glad the light was too low to see for sure.

But Jeremy just laughed. "Sounds close to what I've been dealing with."

Almost by silent agreement, they stood. Madison handed him his helmet back. Screw preamble. He just gave her an orgasm through her gym shorts. They were sort of past playing coy. "Do you want to come over?"

He took the helmet, rotated it in his hands, then shook his head. "I can't seem to stay away from you."

"So how about you not stay away from me in my apartment? Where there's a bed? You know, the slightly more comfortable version of a workout bench?" she added as she nudged the aforementioned bench with her knee.

He smiled but shook his head again. "Just give me some time, okay, Mad? I need to think."

Oh, no. No, no. No, no, no, no… "No."

"No?" He took her arm and directed her toward the door. "What do you mean *no*?"

"Hold on." She shook him off for just a moment to

take the weights off her bar, wipe down the bench—smiling just a little at the memory—and toss her towel in the hamper by the door. Once they were out into the crisp night air, they aimed toward her apartment. Apparently he was walking her home.

"I don't like the things you come up with when you think. You go too deep, make too much out of small things." She turned and faced him, reaching her hand down low, feeling the outline of his still-hard cock in his jeans. "This isn't complicated. I mean, it could be." She grinned at him. "But we'll save the gymnastics for another night. It's sex. We both want it—and we want it with each other. Why make it more difficult than that?"

"Because what we do in the bed—or on a bench—might be just sex. But it never stays that way. There are other people to consider, other feelings. Other... issues." He stepped out of her reach. "So give me time, Mad."

Madison sighed. He'd already retreated into his own little world again, where everyone was against them and he could please nobody. She'd learned quickly that when this happened, there was no fighting it. Best to just give up for the day, reboot overnight, and start all over the next morning. "Fine. Walk me the rest of the way?"

"Of course." He continued on, and when she reached for his hand, he didn't pull away. The feel of their fingers laced, his slightly rougher skin between hers, brightened the moment. It was progress, however small.

And she felt zero guilt about pulling the waistband of her shorts down a little lower than necessary to dig her apartment key out of the inside pocket. Tit for tat, and all that.

He growled, but she already straightened the shorts before he could do anything more. Laughing, she opened the door and gave him a smile.

"Thanks for walking me home, Marine." She patted him on the cheek in a sarcastic move meant to keep the moment light. But he shocked her by grabbing her wrist in a loose grip, two fingers over her pulse. Against the light pressure of his touch, she felt her beat thud in a too-fast rhythm. Then he turned, pressed a soft kiss to her palm, stepped back, and left without a word.

Madison stepped into the apartment on wobbly legs, shut the door, and sank down to the carpet.

Veronica popped her head around the wall that separated the entry from the kitchen. "Hey. You're back. When I came home from the movie I wondered where you were, since your car was still here. Oh, you worked out. Was it a good one?"

Madison shook her head, then nodded. "Yeah. It was pretty freaking great."

———※———

He was an idiot. Certifiable, undeniable, incompetent moron. He deserved to have his ass kicked. By anyone willing to stand in line.

Jeremy let himself into his own apartment and wondered what in the name of Hades had possessed him to act like that. Humping against Madison on a fucking workout bench, in the middle of an open gym where anyone could walk in.

Where someone did walk in.

And not shutting down the entire idea of sleeping with her once some blood managed to migrate its way back up above his belt buckle. He'd let her think there was a chance they'd sleep together. That he would ever let it happen. That he could…

He was a moron.

And thanks to that one taste, that one moment of pure Madison-infused passion, he was never going to sleep again. That one moment—and the fact that he couldn't follow through—would keep him awake for life. God dammit. He tossed his helmet on the couch, debated falling into bed fully dressed, then decided he needed a cold shower after all.

The bathroom was as tiny and pathetic as the rest of the apartment. But it had running water, and most days the water actually looked clean. So he wasn't going to complain. After a quick rinse off, he grabbed a pair of shorts and slipped them on, not bothering with a shirt. Then he took a turn around the apartment. Too wired to sleep now, but not quite done with Madison.

He grabbed his jacket from the couch, unzipped his pocket, grabbed his cell from the zippered chest pocket, and flipped it open. One text. From Tim.

Speaking of a cold shower…

How did it go with V's furniture?

Oh, Veronica's furniture was just fine. All set up and ready for her to start moving things in. Not a single problem there.

The rest of the day was the definition of the word SNAFU.

Between best friends and bar benches, nothing had gone exactly how he'd expected it. His emotions had run the gauntlet from jealousy to anger, lust, and fear. And he'd left Madison's apartment—the second time—with the most painful case of blue balls he'd experienced since his teen years.

All in all…

Great. Everything went great.

There. Vague enough to answer the question. Not a lie, at least when applied to putting together the jigsaw puzzle that was Veronica's bedroom set. The rest of it, well, Tim didn't ask how the day went.

He sat on the couch and waited, then flipped his phone open again as it buzzed with an incoming text message.

Thanks for watching over my girls.

His girls. All three of them. He was fucked.

No, not fucked. Not yet. They managed to avoid that, at least so far. But God, he'd been tempted beyond belief in the gym—the gym, of all fucking places—to just tear down those tiny little shorts she wore, yank up her tight tank top, and go to town like a starving man at an all-you-can-eat buffet.

And yet, it almost seemed like he was fighting an uphill battle with no weapons and only a half-assed motivation. Telling himself he didn't want her was just straight-up lying. Who was going to benefit from that? Nobody.

He sighed, stood up, and went to grab a bottle of water from the fridge. His eyes spotted the notebook he brought home with him every weekend from the office. The one with notes both on work and on writing in it. Stretching his neck to one side, then the other, he realized only one thing was going to get rid of the tension bunching his muscles.

He had to kill someone.

Chapter 9

JEREMY WAITED UNTIL HE WAS FINISHED KILLING OFF his next victim before surfacing enough to grab a water and a power bar. Hunger gnawed at his belly, a reminder that he'd been writing through the night and well past his normal breakfast time. He really needed to stop doing this to his body. Too little sleep and not enough fuel made him a cranky bastard, even he knew that.

Well, crankier than usual, anyway.

And despite the bloodshed and the gore of his latest murder, the uncertainty of his hero, and the devastation of the victim's family, he still couldn't get his mind off Madison.

Time to resort to a fail-proof way of forgetting anything in his life besides pain and torture.

Time to call Dad.

He dialed, knowing the old man would be up even though it was before nine on a Sunday morning. The guy kept time better than ten Swiss watches averaged out.

"Hello?" His father's gruff, no-bullshit voice came through the speaker loud and clear.

Jeremy smiled and shook his head. "Morning, Dad."

"Morning, son. Weekly report?"

He sighed. "Or we could just call it our weekly catch-up phone call. Or our bonding time. Or—"

"There a point buried here under all the extra words?"

"No, Dad. No point at all." He stretched his legs, then

wandered out to the postage stamp–sized patio off his living room for some fresh air. The cool morning air slapped at his bare chest, his tired eyes, jolting him to alert status better than three cups of coffee. "Just trying to say hey, see how you were."

"Nothing unusual to report. Work as usual. Seems like they come up with more idiots to work under me every month. Don't make quality employees like they used to, that's for damn sure."

Which, as Jeremy knew, was code for *these aren't retired Marines, so they mean spit*. His father's love of the Corps rose to levels Chesty Puller couldn't understand. "Sounds frustrating."

"Damn straight. Seen your monitor yet about your next assignment? Lejeune? Quantico? Okinawa?"

"Not yet. It's been pretty busy at the battalion right now," he hedged. Naturally his father would ask about the only other annoying thing in his life. So why not make it two for two? Hell, maybe his father could talk some sense into him. "I've been... seeing someone." Sort of.

His father's voice perked up immediately. Jeremy could easily picture him sitting up a little straighter—if it was possible—and leaning forward expectantly. Pleasure bloomed in his voice. "Is that right? Tell me about her."

"She's a nurse at the hospital here on base."

"Good, good. Nice career for a Marine's wife. Easy to move around. What else?"

Ha. Marine's wife. Madison would just love to hear that. As if she didn't have her own life and identity. Jeremy smiled just thinking about what it would be like, watching his father and Madison square off in a battle of wits. God only knew who would come out the victor. But it'd be something to watch. "She's actually military herself, sir. Navy nurse. I think—"

"Christ Jesus," his father muttered, cutting him off. "You can't be serious."

He'd spent months trying to talk himself out of being serious with Madison. He did his best to avoid what was quickly becoming almost inevitable between them. Pulling back, resisting lighting that spark between them that would most likely send them both up in flames. And he'd started this route specifically for his father to talk some sense into him.

But the way his father said it just made the hair on the back of his neck stand up. Made him want to push back against the censure.

"I don't know how serious I am yet. But I don't see a problem right now." Minus the whole best friend's sister thing. Not that his father knew that part. Now he was going purely on principle.

"She's in the Navy. Is this just a phase for her? She going to be getting out soon?"

Jeremy scoffed. "I don't think anyone joins the military on a whim. Sort of an important decision. But if you're asking if she's a lifer or if she's only staying in for a few, no idea yet."

"Get your head out of your ass, boy. You can't get serious with someone in the military. What kind of life is that? You need a woman by your side. Playing her role. Supporting your career."

And hello, nineteen fifties. Nice to see you again. "Dad. Come on."

"No." The word was like a blade, cutting through Jeremy's argument. "There is no 'come on' here. Your spouse is a big decision. The mother of your children is a big fucking decision. Do you think I didn't take my time and consider the ramifications, consider if she was cut out for the job before I asked your mother to marry me?"

A sliver of ice slid through his veins as the one subject he never wanted to talk about was once again mentioned. "I wouldn't know, Dad. I was only four when she died." His voice was cold, even to his own ears. But he wouldn't apologize for it.

"I know it. And I did my damn best by you. But you better believe when your mother and I met, it was in the front of my mind, seeing how she would handle my career, be there for me, stand beside me, support me. There's a certain kind of woman who can do that, and a certain kind who can't. Your mother was one who could, God rest her soul."

God rest her soul, indeed. Seems like she had enough of a hard time here on earth. She could use a little peace in the afterlife. "Dad—"

"Much as I wanted to be there all the time for you," his father went on, voice softening a little, "the military made that impossible. If your mother had been here, she would have been your constant. That's important, in my mind, to kids."

And Jeremy agreed, at least with that much. Having his mom home while his father was gone would have made his life a hell of a lot less complicated, rather than being shuttled to his grandparents or whatever relative could take him that month.

Though he was in a contrary mood, that was one

undeniable fact he couldn't escape. He wouldn't—couldn't—do that to any kids of his own. Letting them drift while he was deployed or on a TAD, or just in the field for a week at a time. His childhood had been anything but ideal. And he wouldn't repeat that cycle.

"Dad…" He stopped, wondering if he should wade in further. Then he figured he already was waist-high, so he might as well go for it. "If having someone by your side was so important, why didn't you remarry?"

His father coughed a little, cleared his throat, then hummed. "That's, well, that's not something…" His voice faded away, and Jeremy regretted asking.

Then, quick as lightning, his gruff, unemotional father was back. "Pull your head out, son. Don't pussyfoot around with this woman. She's nothing but trouble, no matter how good she might look on paper. You need more. You need something stable. And you won't get that in a dual-military marriage."

Jeremy sighed. "Roger." He hung up a few minutes later, not sure if the phone call had served its purpose or not.

Well, he wanted something to take his mind off of Madison. But this wasn't exactly how he'd expected to do it.

A shrink could take three minutes and know exactly what his problem was. Jeremy was split into two parts. The half that wanted—with almost naïve hope—to keep pleasing his father. The man, the only parent he knew, who raised him as best he could. To thank him for not simply awarding custody to his grandparents and moving on after his wife died, though that might have been easier in his position.

Naturally, the other half—the less naïve half—wanted to chafe against the guidelines passed down to him by the man who looked at life as a sort of battleground to navigate, with military precision and no consideration for emotions.

Hell of a thing, when your own adult mind couldn't decide whether to honor your father or give him the figurative middle finger.

Jeremy stepped back into his apartment and glanced toward his bed. He could take a nice, long nap. That would clear the cobwebs out. Sundays were for napping, really. And the fact that he didn't sleep the night before basically meant he was due some shut-eye. But something pulled him back to his jacket and helmet. Something that said he needed peace as much as—if not more than—rest. And though it might cause him a world of hurt later, he knew exactly where to get it.

Madison kicked her foot in a hypnotic rhythm over the back of the couch as she tried to find something—anything—on television that wouldn't make her weep with boredom.

No. *Click*. No. *Click*. No.

"Um. Do you want to watch a movie?" Veronica asked from the love seat.

"Oh, crap. I'm sorry, I still forget I'm not the only one here." Madison sat up and tossed the remote on the cushion next to Veronica. "Here, you take it for a spin. See what looks good to you."

Veronica grabbed the remote and immediately turned it to MTV, where a *Jersey Shore* marathon was playing.

She sat forward, popcorn bowl balanced precariously on her lap.

Madison's eyes widened with shock. "Oh my God. You have got to be kidding me. You, of all people, watch this crap?"

"What?" Veronica asked, not taking her eyes off the screen as someone who appeared to have been painted Oompa Loompa orange fell off a bar stool and her supposed "friends" cackled with laughter.

"You seriously like this show?"

"It's interesting," she said, still not looking in Madison's direction. Whatever was on the screen held her captive, and Veronica tilted her head to one side as if trying to make out exactly what was going on.

Madison watched for a minute, trying to see the appeal. No wonder Veronica was concentrating so hard. These people didn't speak any version of English Madison knew. When the show had to use subtitles for English, she knew it was nothing she could ever watch.

Her phone vibrated next to her on the couch and she grabbed at the lifeline. It was a text. From Jeremy.

She checked from the corner of her eyes to see if Veronica was paying attention. As if it mattered, since she couldn't possibly read the text from the love seat at that angle. But something about him contacting her made the entire thing feel more sneaky.

Grab a jacket, wear boots. Come downstairs.

She desperately wanted to sprint to the window to see if he was outside or if it was all some cruel trick. But she would play it cool if it killed her.

And it just might.

And why would I want to do that?

There. That sounded somewhat nonchalant. Which was the total opposite of how she felt. Her hands shook as she set the phone back down beside her, like it didn't matter if it buzzed again anytime soon.

And then she grabbed at it like a dying man grabs a lifeline when it buzzed once more.

Just trust me.

Three short, relatively simple words. And yet, they held a wealth of meaning behind them. And she was going to do it. Time to fling herself off the cliff and see what happened.

Standing, she stretched and stuffed the cell in the pocket of her jeans. "I think I'm gonna take a walk or something. Get some air."

"Do you want some company?" Veronica tore her eyes away—reluctantly—from the TV and gave her a look that said *I'll go with you if you want, but please don't want me to.*

"Nah," she said with a smile. "Go back to your weird orange people and their bizarre shore." She wandered back to her room, grabbed a jacket, and slipped on a pair of simple boots with low heels, and walked back out the door, all without Veronica so much as blinking.

Walking down the steps, she paused as she saw Jeremy leaning against the side of her car, his motorcycle parked next to her. His eyes were shaded by aviator-style sunglasses, and he wore his leather jacket, arms crossed over his chest. His snug jeans and thick black boots only added to the whole picture. A picture she salivated over.

Damn, the man made it look good.

She hopped down the last step and strolled over

to him, running one finger over the handlebars of his motorcycle. "So, what was so important you couldn't come up to the front door?"

He smiled. "Just thought you might wanna take a ride with me."

"A ride? I get to ride the bike?" she asked, all but clapping in her excitement. Then she stepped back, laced her fingers behind her back, and coughed a little. "I mean… eh. I wasn't doing anything. So I guess if you're bored and need someone to hang out with…"

"Uh-huh." His mouth twitched at the corners, but he kept the poker face otherwise. "Here." He tossed her something that hit her in the stomach before she could react. Glancing down, she grimaced and held up the simple black helmet.

"What?" He looked at the helmet too. "It's never been used, if you're worried about cooties. My bike came with that one."

"And you never used it?"

"Nah, already bought this one." He patted his own personalized one under his arm. "So put it on."

"This is it? You don't have anything cooler?"

He slid his shades off, slipped them in the pocket of his jacket, and positioned his own helmet over his head. "Sorry, no. I didn't realize we were attending a headgear fashion show. It's the only spare I have. And you don't ride without a helmet." When she just stared at it, he reached for it. "If you don't want to ride, I can just take it—"

"No." She held the helmet out of reach. "I want to." Then she sighed but smiled as she turned her back toward him to put it on. He brought an extra helmet just for her. It might be such a simple act, but it meant a great deal that he'd come specifically to get her for a ride. Not just passing by and stopping in on a whim. Not killing time and only popping over for a few minutes. He left his apartment specifically with her in mind.

And her heart swelled just a little at the thought.

Helmet on, she fumbled a minute with the chinstrap until he stepped around her and pushed her fingers away. "You'll make a mess out of it. Let me do it."

She tilted her head to the side so he could see what he was doing. His fingers, not yet in gloves, brushed the sensitive skin under her chin and down her throat. If she didn't know better—and she wasn't sure what she knew anymore—she would have said he was doing it on purpose. Stroking her, feeling her skin, making her nerve endings stand up at attention all under the guise of helping her with her chinstrap. But that wasn't really Jeremy's style.

Was it?

She gave him a glance, but his eyes remained on his fingers as they snapped the strap in place. Then he gave her a grin and a quick pat on the top of the helmet. "All secure. Let's ride."

She'd been waiting for just such an invitation for longer than he knew.

———

Jeremy waited until she climbed up behind him, chuckling under his breath at the effort it took. She was athletic, and not a wuss, but she was short and unaccustomed to the motion. Her leg hitched up and she almost toppled over before he grabbed her and pulled her up.

"They really should think of the short people," she grumbled, voice muffled through the helmets.

"Just hold on tight, and stay aware until you pick up the rhythm. Don't zone out." Which was all too easy to do, he knew, when you weren't the one driving. But just his luck, she'd veer left when he was turning right… He started the bike, any idea of conversation lost under the roar of the engine.

The feel of Madison behind him on his bike was one of the most erotic things he'd ever experienced. Her thighs clenched around the outside of his. Her arms wrapped around his waist like a big hug, hands splayed over his stomach. They twitched ever so slightly against his muscles when he leaned into a turn or made a stop, making him want them to creep lower. Her breasts pressed into his back like soft pillows.

But her head. Damn it, her head. Despite the helmet protecting her, he felt her lower her cheek to his back, between his shoulder blades, resting comfortably against him, almost like she was ready to take a nap. Completely trusting him with her safety and well-being. Submitting to his protection.

God dammit. The whole ride was undoing him. And he put himself in the position on purpose, of all things. Because try as he might—and oh, he'd tried—he couldn't stay away. Couldn't deny himself these little moments of Madison. Of her total attention. Of pretending, even for a few minutes, that there was something more between them.

He leaned into a turn as they exited, heading for a park he knew was nearby. One that would be empty now, as people were still at church or just waking up from sleeping in. Then her hands clenched around his shirt again, and he groaned. Because she couldn't hear him anyway, so why hold in the sounds of pleasant torture?

They slowed as he approached the semi-hidden park that was often neglected by the city. Every few months, someone would come in and do a half-ass job of mowing the area, taking a weed whacker to the areas just around the playground equipment and leaving the rest virtually untouched. Rare was the time he'd come here and find someone else around. And, as he predicted, the area was completely empty as he guided his motorcycle down the narrow dirt lane that led to the playground area, along with a few picnic benches.

Perfect place for his own fictional detective to come when he needed a little quiet reflection to work through the clues leading up to the first of what he hoped to be many successful cases.

Her hands clutched in his shirt once more as he pulled to a complete stop and cut the engine. She held on a moment longer than necessary before letting go.

It was sinful, just feeling it over the cotton of his T-shirt and his jacket. What those hands would be like on his own bare skin...

Madison slid off the back of the motorcycle and unsnapped her helmet, leaning over to shake out her hair that had flattened down. Jeremy enjoyed the backside view in her jeans before she stood straight again and handed him the helmet.

"What is this place?"

He removed his own helmet and set them on the seat, leaving his jacket draped over the seat, and walked behind her into the playground area. It'd been a few weeks since the last mowing, and thanks to the recent rains, the grass was tall. They high-stepped over to the first picnic bench where Madison hopped up and sat on the table, feet resting on the bench below.

"Just a playground. Doesn't get much use."

She eyed the grass warily. "No kidding. You could lose a toddler in the landscape. Why are we here?"

He shrugged, not entirely sure why he brought her to his thinking spot. "Just some place I go when I need a little time away."

"You live by yourself; you could have time away in the comfort of your own apartment," she pointed out as he sat down next to her.

He smiled. Whereas he liked his space, Madison was one who loved people, loved being surrounded by noise and activity and friendship and conversation. Hell, she had her own nice apartment all to herself, and she went and ruined it—to his mind—by getting a roommate. To her, the idea of needing time alone to recharge some mental battery would be absurd. "Yeah, that's true. But sometimes you just need to step outside of your own area and get a better look at things. You know?"

"Things like what?"

To share or not to share… That was more than just a question. It was a possible life-changing decision. If he told her about his writing, it would seem more real. More serious. More like something he could fail at, rather than just a hobby that didn't matter much.

Not to mention, it would possibly put up one last barrier between them. What if she mocked his ideas? Thought it was a worthless idea, like his father. Told him to give it up, get his head out of his ass and concentrate on his career in the Marines…

But what if she wouldn't? No, he decided. She wouldn't. He knew that. And he trusted her. "I like to write."

She bumped his shoulder with hers. "I know that."

"You do?" he asked, surprised. Glancing at her, he took in the way she lounged back on her hands, heels kicking out in a childlike arc that made him want to smile.

"Yeah. Of course. You were always jotting stuff down somewhere. Thinking hard. Making notes. Your notebook is never far away. I sort of put two and two together."

If she was able to put it together… had Dwayne? Tim? The thought of them knowing, of them possibly joking about it even in a friendly way, made him want to throw up.

As if she could read his mind, she rubbed a hand over his knee. "No. They can't add up. I don't think Tim or Dwayne would know anything unless it was right in front of their faces, God love them. I'm sure they haven't noticed."

He breathed a sigh of relief. "It's just personal. At least now."

"What do you write?"

"Mysteries. Detective stuff. Nothing much." He shrugged, but when she frowned he asked, "What?"

"I wish you wouldn't do that. It's obviously important to you. So why do you put it down like it's nothing? It matters to you, so it's something."

Nailed him. "Habit, I guess. You don't want people

to know what you're writing in case it sucks or you never make anything of it. Easier than having to relive rejection over again with your friends."

She nodded, then stared into the distance. "Thanks for telling me. I always wondered how long you would keep it a secret."

"Forever," he joked, and she laughed. Before he could think of what else to say, she jumped down and raced across the small field toward the playground equipment, her short legs looking five kinds of ridiculous the way she kept her knees up high to wade through the grass.

He followed at an easy lope, his longer legs not having nearly as much trouble as she did with the terrain. By the time he caught up to her, she was halfway to the top of the dome-shaped climbing bars. He followed without a word, smiling the whole time. And when he reached the top he sat next to her, hooking his knees through the bars and letting his feet in their heavy boots dangle.

She watched the clouds float by in silence, as if that was the only plan for the entire day. And she took his hand, lacing her fingers between his, and simply sat. Not making a move, not trying to play hard to get. Existing. As if this was just how they spent every Sunday morning. Being lazy at the playground, being with each other, soaking in the other's presence.

It was something he could get used to. Not that he should.

Her phone buzzed in her pocket and she reached for it automatically. He wasn't offended; he'd have done the same thing. In their line of work, not checking a message could mean serious problems.

When she sighed and flipped the phone closed again, he squeezed her hand. "Something wrong?"

"Yeah. I totally forgot to make Veronica a set of keys for the storage unit, and she needs to leave soon for work. I guess some of her work clothes got put in the storage by accident. So I need to be there to unlock the door." She gave him a wistful look, eyes full of emotion and zero guile. "I don't want to leave yet."

He smoothed a few strands behind her ears. "I know. Neither do I."

Taking the risk to his heart, he leaned in and brushed a kiss over her lips. Just one, as light as possible. But enough to let her know where his head was.

She smiled, eyes darkening just a little, lids lowering a fraction. "Damn keys." Then, with one more sigh, she started to climb back down. "Can you run me by a hardware store to get a second copy made? I can't believe I forgot to make the storage key duplicate when I made the apartment and mailbox key."

"No problem." He walked with her back to the motorcycle, laughing silently as she hopped around the taller weeds like a doe. The woman had more energy and spunk than anyone he knew. And she invigorated him, just by being near her. Like an emotional battery charger.

Soon enough, it would work the opposite way. Being near her, around her, beside her without sleeping with her… it would drain him. How much longer could he keep this up?

Chapter 10

MADISON RELUCTANTLY UNCLENCHED HER HANDS from around Jeremy's waist as the motorcycle slowed to a stop in her parking lot. Damn, that was over way too soon. Not just having an excuse to wrap her arms around Jeremy, press against him, feel him move over and around her. But the actual thrill of riding on the back of the bike itself. She'd never been on one, though God knows how, since every third Marine owned one, and she was friends with dozens of them.

Just another first she shared with Jeremy. Maybe that's why she'd never been on one before. More special this way.

"Shit," he muttered under his breath.

Okay, that wasn't special talk. "What?"

"Your brother's here. That's his car."

She hopped off the bike, nearly pitched forward when her foot caught on the seat, and righted herself against the SUV next to her. Dammit. They really didn't think about the short people when they made these things. "Where?" She turned, her peripheral vision hampered by the clunky helmet. But Jeremy quickly leaned over and unsnapped the helmet, pulling it off so she could see on the other side of the parking lot where her brother's car sat, empty.

"Yeah. That's his. The guy has fantastic timing." She shook her head and ran her fingers through her hair in a vain attempt to fluff up the flat strands. Not that it worked. Stupid hair.

"If it's all the same to you, I'm just gonna head out. You okay to go up by yourself?" Jeremy looked uncomfortable, though she couldn't tell if it was because of her brother being there, or because this felt almost like the end of a casual date and he had no clue how to close the deal.

Probably a combination of the two, which made him twice the fool.

"I'm fine. I came down myself, I'll go back up." Before he could get any ideas about making a smooth getaway, she leaned over and gave him a kiss to curl both their toes. Shockingly, he didn't pull away. But he didn't lean in either, didn't give back. That was fine. He was exempt from PDA. This time.

She waited as he backed his bike away from the curb and pulled out of the parking lot. Just as she was about to turn away, she noticed him lift one hand up in a backwards wave before turning the corner out of sight. That one wave, though it might seem pathetic to some, made her feel almost as mushy and happy as the kiss did. With light feet and a lighter heart, she skipped up the apartment steps until she reached her apartment door and walked through.

"Hey, squirt." Right on cue, Tim stood from her couch and gave her a once-over. "Where've you been?"

"Oh you know, hot date with a guy on a motorcycle," she said airily as she walked into the kitchen.

"What?" Tim's voice sharpened, then he chuckled. "Ah, yeah. One of Hell's Angels, right?"

"Sure," she played along as she grabbed a bottle of

water. "You know me. I live to be someone's old lady on the back of a chopper. Thinking of getting Bubba's name tattooed on my arm."

"Nice." He looked at her once again. "You look different." Then he shook his head and shrugged. "Anyway, I was just coming over to apologize again to Veronica for not being around to help out with the furniture and see how it went. Jeremy said it all went okay."

"Yup. Furniture's good to go. It was easy construction, once we figured out the whole garbled instructions. I swear, it looks like English but it reads like some dead language."

Veronica breezed past like a cartoon puff of smoke. "Hey, Madison. Thanks for coming back. Totally forgot I didn't have a key to the storage locker."

"Wait! Here." She held the brand-new copy out before the puff of smoke formally known as her roommate walked out the door. "My fault I didn't have that one ready for you. That should take care of it."

Veronica snatched the key from her hand and walked out the door, closing it hastily behind her.

Tim's mouth gaped open. "Was that actually Veronica? I think that's the first time she's ever used so many contractions at one time. And she was completely rushed. Didn't even say—"

The door cracked open and Veronica's head poked back in. She gave them both a shy smile and softly said, "Thank you," before closing the door behind her once more, only softer this time.

Madison smirked at her brother. "You were saying?"

Tim shrugged. "She's changing, but for the better."

"I totally agree." Taking her water, she headed back

into the living room, unzipping her jacket and letting it
fall to the floor behind her as she walked.

Tim scoffed and picked it up, draping it over the back
of the couch as she plopped down on the love seat. He
was changing for the better too… but small glimpses of
the neat freak still shone through on occasion.

She gestured to the cushion next to her. "Gonna sit
down for a bit?"

"Nah, I haven't seen Skye today. She was at work this
afternoon when I got home, so I just showered and ran
over here quickly. Wanted to make sure there wasn't any
leftover stuff you needed help with after the big move."

"Jeremy took care of it all," she assured him.

"Good guy." Tim toyed with the zipper of her jacket
for a minute, as if lost in thought.

"Something on your mind, bro?"

He sighed and smoothed the jacket back down. "Just
Jeremy. Something's going on with him lately, and I
can't figure it out. He's moping around more than his
usual delightfully sullen self."

Caution, swimmers. Choppy waters ahead. "Maybe
he just worries about D. It's weird not being over there
to watch your buddy's back."

"Maybe." But he didn't look convinced. "Anyway,
thanks for not caring about the change in plans on
Jeremy helping instead of me."

"No problem. Glad he could make time for us."

"He'll always have time for you. Dwayne, too. You're
their little sister as much as mine. They'd do anything for
you." With that, Tim leaned over to give her a quick, absent
kiss on the cheek before walking out, giving a cursory,
"Lock this behind me," as he went. Always the big brother.

"Little sister, my ass," she mumbled as she stood to go lock the door. "That is not how he kisses me, bro."

And with that smug smile, Madison went to go take a nap before her week of late-night shifts began.

———～～———

"Spill the beans, oh satisfied one." Matthew nudged her as she stood by the main desk on the OB floor.

Madison scoffed. "Satisfied? Hardly. I think confused is more like it. He wants me. And I feel like we're making headway. But it's one of those two steps forward, one step back sort of things. Every time I think we're getting somewhere, we stumble."

"Ah, *amore*," Matthew said with a phony French accent that had Madison giggling. "Dude totally wants you. And man, I can't blame you for wanting him." When Madison raised a brow, he grinned. "He might not be for sale, but I can still window shop."

Madison smiled and shook her head. "You're incorrigible."

"It's all a part of my charm." He reached over and grabbed a chart. "Williams in room 302 needs another IV drip in about fifteen."

"I'll get it." She sighed and rolled her neck, working out the kinks. Though OB was her favorite in all the rotations, it was hard on the body. Moms needed what they needed as soon as they needed it, and Madison was the one responsible for getting it. But who could resist the cute little babies? Once they were all cleaned up, naturally. The best part, though, were the fathers, who always looked so mystified and poleaxed when they were handed their little bundle for the first time, almost as if they were afraid they might break it. Then that look of pure love would cross their faces and—

"You're going gooey."

"Hmm?" She glanced up to see Matthew grinning down at her. "I am not."

"You were thinking about him again, weren't you?"

"No. I was not," she said with total honesty. The look on Matthew's face said he didn't believe her one bit. Her phone buzzed in her sweatshirt pocket and she grabbed at it like a lifeline. "Hold on. Text message."

"Is it from lover boy?"

She nudged him with her foot, a silent threat that she could kick if he kept it up. "No. Veronica. Just wanting to know if she can borrow my computer to get some stuff done." Madison typed a quick affirmative back, letting her know she could use whatever she needed, along with the password to unlock the screen from sleep mode, then shut the phone.

"You know what you need to do?"

"Please tell me, oh wise one." This would be good.

Matthew walked around the desk and reached under to the mini-fridge stashed by the chair, grabbing the Coke he was addicted to. "You need to make one big push. Subtly is not your friend with this one, it seems. He's a hard nut to crack—pun intended—so you need to do something big to push him over the edge. The little stuff's been good so far. Cute, even. But right now you need something that he can't ignore. The now-or-never moment."

"The now-or-never moment?" She stared at him, not even sure if he was speaking her language any longer.

Matthew rolled his eyes like she just asked him how to start a basic IV. "In the movies, there's always that one moment where the main character has the choice. Do I take this road or that one?"

"Sounds like the guy's lost," she said idly.

"More or less," Matthew agreed. "But the point is, the main character in every movie is staring at two choices. The comfortable choice, or the road less traveled."

"I think you're mixing metaphors and media now. That was Robert Frost."

"Whatever." He waved that away, nearly spilling his precious Coke in the process. "The point is, you've laid the groundwork. Everyone's on even levels now. The field is wide open."

"Movies, poetry, and now sports," she murmured as she reached over him to grab a water.

"So go do something he can't ignore. One big, fantastic push to have him say yes, yes, yes. Grab you, kiss you senseless, and make you scream with passion…" Matthew's eyes glazed over just a little, and she poked him in the chest with one finger. "Sorry. Got lost. Had a moment of jealousy. I'm better now. Where was I?"

She raised a brow. "I believe I was screaming with passion."

"Right. Or, he turns you down and loses you forever."

"Forever? That's a little drastic." And terrifying. She laid a hand over her racing heart.

Matthew shrugged. "You can't turn back after the now-or-never. It'd be too weird." He glanced at his watch. "Williams needs that drip. Do you want me to—"

"No, I've got it." She stowed her water back in the fridge and headed to grab the bag. But she held a hand to her pounding heart as she walked and thought for a moment about Matthew's words.

The big push made sense. They were tiptoeing around the idea of being together. Well, she was tiptoeing. He was pretending to ignore the whole subject entirely. And the thought that it might just take one big choice to finish the dance and get them into a relationship was thrilling.

And terrifying. What if Jeremy wasn't ready? If he said no, and she lost the only opportunity she had to connect with him…

Not the way to think about that. Madison pulled out the saline bag and walked with renewed purpose to 302, determined to make the now-or-never be a now.

Because never wasn't an option.

—⁂—

Dwayne sat back and rubbed a hand over his face. Skype was a beautiful invention for deployments, but Jeremy was making the video chat an almost painful experience. "Jer, dude, it's pulling teeth with you, man. What's going on?"

Jeremy shook his head. "Sorry, man. Just a lot to deal with right now. Work and stuff."

Uh-huh. Dwayne didn't buy that sorry excuse for a minute. "Any new chicks in the picture? Been over to Slider's recently? Right before I left there was that one hot girl we kept running into. The blonde. What was her name? Talia? Tina? Them—"

"No," Jeremy cut in. "No new… chicks."

"Maybe there should be," Dwayne muttered.

"I heard that." Jeremy scowled back at him.

"Well, good. You should get laid, for the love of Chesty."

"No," his friend repeated through clenched teeth.

This would be yet another issue with deployments. No way to tell what the hell was bugging a friend, and no way to fix it. "Fine. If you're going to be an ass, I'll just call Madison."

"Madison? Why?" Jeremy sat up straighter.

Dwayne raised a brow. "Because she's my friend, and I call her sometimes to talk."

"We're talking." Jeremy waved a finger between the screen and his chest, somewhat needlessly.

"No, I'm talking, and you're doing a whole lot of scowling and mumbling and spreading your bad attitude. Plus, Madison's fun to chat with. She works weird hours. So our schedules mesh up better some weeks thanks to the time difference." Dwayne looked forward to his Skype calls with the squirt. She had funny stories, and she was always enthusiastic to see him. He loved her like a little sister, and she managed to make him smile. Which was definitely something to grab onto out in the middle of Bumfuck, Afghanistan. Any smiles were a blessing.

"You've talked to her recently?"

Now he was getting closer. Something was up with Jeremy, and Madison might know a part of it. Or maybe all. "Yeah, not too long ago. She just switched rotations, so it's been a little longer than usual." Dwayne sat forward and smiled as wickedly as he could manage. "She promised if I was a good boy, next time she'd show me something… interesting."

"Like hell she did!" Even through the screen, Dwayne could see Jeremy's jaw clench, his fists bunch, his muscles tighten. This wasn't the stance of someone in disbelief, or laughing off a joke. He was pissed at the mere hint of Madison being naughty on a webcam.

Interesting. Very interesting. Dwayne shrugged and sat back further, settling into his desk chair the best he could. Nothing was more uncomfortable than the cheap plastic and metal the Marine Corps called furniture. Especially for a man his size. "So maybe she didn't. A boy can hope, yeah?"

"Fuck off," Jeremy growled and disconnected the call.

Dwayne was still shaking with laughter five minutes later when he double-clicked to call Madison's laptop. She should have had enough time to get home and shower by now after her shift. He knew she liked to check email and surf online a little bit before crawling into bed. And since he still had a good thirty minutes before he had to report to his office, he could see what was going on at her end of the stick. Just a little friendly fishing expedition between friends, to see what was going on with Jeremy.

The program rang once, then twice, and then she answered. But the *she* who answered wasn't Madison.

It was that cute little thing from a few weeks ago at Tim and Skye's place. What was her name… Victoria? No. Veronica. That was it.

"Well, hey there." Though unexpected, he wasn't displeased with the turn of events. "You making a habit of breaking into people's homes and using their laptops?"

The little blonde's eyes widened and her mouth formed an adorable O of shock. Then she shook it off and glared at him. "I didn't break in. I live here."

"I thought you lived with Tim and Skye."

"Only temporarily. Now I'm Madison's roommate. As of last week," she added quickly, like he was going to check to see if her story added up.

She was something new and interesting, that was for sure. "I think I believe you." Her brows lowered at the words and he chuckled. "I thought I'd give Madison a call before I went in to work. But she's not there, huh?"

"No. I think one of her patients was ready to deliver right as she was going to leave. So she got caught up a little longer than expected." Folding her hands in front of her, prim as a schoolteacher from two centuries before, she asked, "Can I take a message for her?"

Lord, he liked the way she talked. All proper and dignified, until something sparked her up, and then she could spit fire with those eyes like nobody's business. "Nah, just looking for some conversation, as usual. Nice to see a friendly face sometimes."

Immediately, Veronica's face softened. "I'm sure it would be. I'm sorry she isn't here at the moment. I assume your time is limited for contact."

"You assume correctly." He thought for a moment, checked his watch, then made a decision. "How about you talk to me instead?"

"Me?" she squeaked. "You wanted Madison."

"I did," he conceded. "But she's not available and you are. And as we've already been introduced—"

"Hardly," she cut in, but she smiled as she said it.

"As we've already been introduced," he repeated, "I consider you a friendly face as well. So. Care to make a Marine a happy man and give him a touch of home?"

She bit her bottom lip and looked around, as if scared someone would catch her being friendly and punish her. Then she sat up a little straighter and nodded stiffly. "Of course."

Good girl. "Tell me about yourself."

She blinked twice, owl-like, and tilted her head to one side. "What do you want to know?"

"Anything you want to tell me."

"I love the color yellow," she said with a smile.

That genuine smile, without artifice, without guile, without any sort of agenda attached to it, warmed something deep in him that he'd thought permanently frozen a long time ago. "I could see that about you. And yet, you're wearing blue."

She quirked her mouth. "I don't think yellow looks good with my hair," she said, voice dropping as if imparting a secret.

"I happen to think yellow would look very nice on you. But I'm partial to blue myself." He stared at the prim little button-down shirt, thinking how odd it was that she had every button—even the one at her throat—done up. Most women at least left the top, if not a few more, undone in a casual setting. But the image somehow seemed naughty while also nice. Like it was a temptation set there to make him want to undo a button or two. "Tell me something else," he urged, enjoying the little game they seemed to be caught in.

She did the lip-biting thing again, eyes drifting to the side in thought. Then she smiled. "I hate tofu."

He smothered a laugh behind his hand, disguising it as a cough. "That doesn't tell me much. I think everyone does."

She made a face. "Not Skye. She loves the stuff, though I don't know why. But I tried not to complain. I was a guest, after all."

Veronica had good ole Southern manners written all

over her. But she didn't carry the accent. "Where are you from?"

It was as if someone flipped some internal switch inside her, cutting out all the light that made her glow inside. "Nowhere special."

"Everyone's from somewhere special."

"I disagree." One hand crept up and started playing with the golden braid that hung over her shoulder, the end swinging in front of her breasts like a pendulum. The braid looked thicker than his wrist, and when she let it go, he'd bet it swung down close to her waist. He hadn't seen hair that long in… ever.

"Dwayne?"

"Huh?" Smart. Real smart answer. He shook out of his mental, almost hypnotic, daze and blinked. "Yeah?"

She frowned a little and tilted her head. "Are you sure you don't want to leave a message for Madison?"

He checked his watch once more and sighed. "Yeah, if you wouldn't mind asking her to run over to my apartment when she has a chance and just do a once-over?"

"Your apartment? You have one here?" Veronica looked utterly confused again.

"Yup. I don't live out of my truck while I'm stateside. It's locked up, but I do like someone to run by every so often just to check. Madison has a spare key."

"Of course." Veronica nodded again, her neck so tight he wondered how her head didn't pop off and roll away. "I'll pass along the message."

She reached in front, and he realized she was going to click off. So he said, "Ronnie."

She looked up. "Hmm?"

He liked that she didn't even seem to realize he'd

called her Ronnie this time. "You'd look good in yellow." He closed out before she had a chance to. But even
as the screen went black, he saw a small smile creep
onto her lips.

Dwayne stood, stretched, and grabbed his travel mug
he loaded with coffee once he got to his office area. But
even as he walked out into the smothering Afghan heat
and immediately felt sweat pooling in the small of his
back, he couldn't keep the grin from spreading across
his face. Getting to talk to Miss Veronica again was
unexpected, but as it turned out, it was one hell of a nice
way to start the day.

—∾∾—

Madison opened the door to Dwayne's apartment and
coughed once at the smell. Not a bad smell, but definitely an apartment that hadn't been opened in a while.
Though he'd been careful to empty his kitchen of all
food and make sure his trash was gone, being closed up
for months on end gave the apartment a musty smell that
any home would suffer from.

Guilt hit her as she opened a window to air the place
out. She made a mental note to come back more often
and do the check. She should have thought of this
before. And a week before he was due home she'd run
over to air the place out better and give it a good scrubbing. Though she was no neat freak herself—the same
couldn't be said for her brother—she liked things clean.
And though he wasn't a slob, Dwayne was, at the heart
of it, a bachelor. He didn't notice streaked mirrors or
dust on shelves.

At least his place wasn't as bad as Jeremy's. Dwayne

had a nice two-bedroom apartment that, while not perfect, was adequate for having people over to watch a game or order pizza and hang out. Jeremy lived in little more than a shoebox, though who knew why.

Madison made a quick run through all the rooms, checking windows to make sure they were still secure and keeping an eye out in case anything looked off. But all was well with Dwayne's little apartment, and she felt better knowing she'd given it a little chance to breathe and double-check the security. She'd come back again in a month to do so again.

She sat down on his armchair, smiling when she sank in to the well-worn, well-loved leather. D and his big body certainly made a dent in the cushion. She missed him. Missed having that brotherly connection with someone not actually related. The guy was fantastic with advice, and she never worried about him being too protective like she did with Tim. She curled in just a little, tucking her feet under her. He'd have known what to do with Jeremy. And he would have kept his mouth shut about it, too.

Too bad she'd missed their chance to Skype the other day. Luckily Veronica had been there to take the message and talk to him. Though oddly, now that Madison thought back, her roommate had blushed fiercely while giving her the message. Veronica was shy; maybe the encounter had startled her.

No. She threw that thought away. D was sweet as a kitten and could charm any woman into thinking he was harmless. No way would he scare even the sometimes-timid Veronica.

She slapped her palms on the armrest and pushed

up. Time to get back to her own apartment and do a little cleaning. She'd been neglecting that chore the past few weeks.

As Madison walked to the door, something swinging in the breeze of the open window reminded her she needed to close and lock it. Good thing, too. She did so, then looked back to see what caught her eye.

Keys, a few different sets, swung from a post by the door. One would be for Tim's townhouse, naturally. Tim had a key to Dwayne's place as well. Just a piece of security for the guys who lived alone. Or, well, alone until Skye showed up.

She took a step toward the door, then stopped.

If Dwayne had a key to Tim's place, then he likely had a key to Jeremy's as well…

No. That was wrong. It would be a complete invasion of privacy.

But instead of her feet pointing toward the door, somehow she found herself walking to the key rack instead.

One key ring had smaller keys, like for a mailbox. Likely one to his apartment, and one to his PO Box. The second key ring had spare keys to his truck, which she knew was stored safely. But the third ring had two house keys. One with a piece of tape with a T written on it in marker. The other, a J.

Bingo.

As if watching someone else's hand, she reached up and snagged Jeremy's key from the ring and slipped it in her pocket.

Chapter 11

JEREMY WALKED INTO HIS OFFICE AND SHUT THE DOOR, his eyes heavy with exhaustion. The sight of the unfinished paperwork still piled up on his desk made him close his eyes the rest of the way in defeat. He had to stop beating himself up, writing so late into the night. It was killing him. For one moment, he leaned his back against the closed office door and sighed, just savoring the quiet.

"Son."

His head snapped back and cracked against the door frame. "Jesus Christ!" He rubbed a hand over the already-tender place that would likely have a goose egg tomorrow. "Dad. What the he—I mean, what are you doing here?" His father lived on the east coast now. Not quite the same thing as having your parents walk across the street for dinner three nights a week.

Stan Phillips stood from his chair in the corner to his full, imposing six-foot-three inches. "Saving your ass, that's what." When Jeremy just stared at him, his father shook his head. "Not even going to say hello?"

He straightened and held out a hand. "Good to see you, sir." His father gave a firm shake back, then motioned for Jeremy to grab a seat behind his own desk.

"Don't mind if I do," he muttered as he sat down in his own chair. His father had a way of making Jeremy feel about seven years old again. "What's going on, Dad?"

His father sat as well, ramrod straight in the chair, like he had a steel rod instead of a spine. In some sort of ridiculous moment of defiance, Jeremy found himself slouching just a little, crossing one boot over his other knee, totally relaxed.

It was his damn office, anyway. He had the right to slouch if he wanted to.

And if that made him childish, he was going to pretend it didn't.

"This place is still as pathetic as it was last time I was here." As if to make an example, Stan took a long glance around the office, its bare walls, the lack of anything moto in the entire office.

Yeah, so he kept the walls a little sparse. Tim's office had his Academy diploma and commissioning papers hung up, along with a few pictures of him and Skye now. Dwayne's walls consisted of pics of battle buddies and moto-style quotes that he claimed help push him through the tough shit. Both had framed awards they'd won over the years. They both loved that stuff.

Jeremy preferred to just keep the place clean. Sterile. This wasn't his home, he didn't need to decorate it to get work done.

"Anyway, I had a trip to Twenty-Nine Palms set up already. Flew out from JFK yesterday morning, got some work done. Since Palms is only three hours from here, figured now was a good time to come over and kick your ass for motivation." He raised one silver brow. "You should be coming up in the boards for Major soon, right?"

Leave it to his father to not warn him about a visit. No, not a visit. Surprise inspection was more like it.

"Tim is," Jeremy said instead. "Should see the promotion in the next two to six months, I think. At least from word around here."

"And you?"

He sighed again and let his head drop back, the chair swiveling from side to side. Mostly because he knew it annoyed the hell out of his father. "No, Dad. I would have mentioned it." Something he wouldn't have mentioned... not pushing for the promotion. And not being disappointed that his name was left off this round of the Major boards.

There was always next round... which he also hoped to avoid like guys avoided the draft. Ironic, given he was already *in* the military.

"They're going to phase you out if you keep getting passed up," his father warned.

Jeremy scoffed. "Hardly. It was the first possible round." *I couldn't be so lucky.* Having the decision taken out of his hands completely? Heaven.

His father nodded and steepled his fingers by his chin. "That's true. So, plans on how to approach things so you are definitely in on the next round?"

Jeremy made a big show of shuffling papers together on his desk. Papers he'd just have to reorganize later because he screwed them all up shuffling what didn't need it. "Hey, why don't we go grab some dinner?"

His father checked his watch and frowned. "It's not even seventeen hundred yet. You always bug out this early in the day? No wonder—"

"It's a slow week. And I've done everything I can for today." Jeremy stood, waiting for his father to stand as well. "We can go grab some Mexican."

At that, his father smiled a little. "Is the best place to eat still that hole in the wall—"

"Off of Seventh Street."

"That made the whole block smell like nacho cheese and tequila?" His dad slapped him on the shoulder. "Sounds good. Let's go."

——∿——

Twenty minutes later, Jeremy realized dinner had been the worst idea of his life. Sure, he had something to do with his hands now, and the change of scenery was nice. Not to mention the homemade guac and salsa went a long way to filling the hole in his gut skipping lunch had provided.

But now he was trapped, waiting for his meal, with nowhere to run, no excuse to leave, and no way to quit the conversation if he didn't like how things were heading. There was no "end call" button when you were face to face.

"Tell me about this girl you were thinking of seeing." His father frowned as he picked up a chip. "You're not still thinking of that one. Right? The Navy nurse?"

Thinking of seeing. Right. Exactly how he'd put it. "Dad. My dating life—or lack thereof—is really not on the table for discussion. Can we talk about something else?" To prove his point, he shoved a chip piled with guac in his mouth, eyes burning just a little as the spices filled his tongue.

Stan shook his head. "No can do, son. I'm worried about you. Think you might be hitting the ten-year slump."

"The ten-year slump. Is that anything like the seven-year itch?"

"Smart-ass." But his father's lip twitched. "You know exactly what I mean. Marines come up on that ten years in, and doubt starts creeping in. It's piss or get off the pot time. Where it makes no sense to go another three years if you won't go the full twenty. So they start asking themselves… 'Am I tired of all this shit?'"

Yes.

"'Is this the career for me?'"

No.

"'Will I get out?'"

Fuck if I know.

Stan pointed at him with a chip. "Don't get sucked into it. Keep your eye on the ball. Your head in the game."

"Your nose to the grindstone?"

Stan scowled.

"Sorry, were we not listing as many clichés as we could think of?"

His father sighed, the sort of sound that signaled disappointment more than anger and made any child wary of their parents. "Insolent. You always were insolent. Do you know how many nannies I went through over the years thanks to your ability to run them off?"

Jeremy sat a little straighter. This was the first time his father initiated any sort of comment in regards to his childhood. Most of the time, their tone was not up for discussion. Ever. "No. How many?"

His father barked a laugh, eyes glazing a little with memories, a chip dangling from his fingers, forgotten. "Dozens. Too many to count. I swear, I couldn't keep a good nanny for you more than a month when you were younger. You'd hatch some scheme to scare them to death, and they'd take off screaming. Smart-ass that you

were." He said it with pride though, removing any sting
the insult might have carried.

Jeremy remembered that much. He'd scared them all
off because, in his young, innocent mind, if there wasn't
a nanny around, his father would have to spend more
time with him.

Never worked. There was always a new nanny.

"Why did you stay in then after Mom died and your
current commitment was up? Why stay in?"

His father sighed and stared out the window to the
street. His eyes stared at something, but Jeremy knew
that something wasn't out the window. It was in the past.
"The Corps was my life."

Why not me? Why couldn't I be your life? But he
couldn't bring himself to ask. Not now, not twenty
years ago.

"It's all I knew. I had a plan. We had plans together,
Samantha and I. Twenty years in, retire, start working
as a contractor. Good life, solid plan. Your mother, God
love her, was with me for the long haul."

A heavy silence hung between them. He didn't need
to say it.

And then she died.

Jeremy wasn't sure what to say to that. So he figured,
given they'd already strayed to depressing waters, keep
going. "Why didn't you remarry?"

"Hmm." His father thought that through a little while,
taking the time to scoop some salsa and chew thoroughly.
"You were young at first, and it was all I could do to
figure out how to survive with a child and a demanding
career. Then I was gone more than I was here. And I
think, in the end, I just…" He shrugged. "I'm not sure.

I couldn't wrap my mind around taking the plan I'd created with your mother and putting another woman in there. Details changed. But the plan remained the same." The distant look evaporated and the hardened hazel gaze swept back to Jeremy. "And I did the best I could with you. You had a good childhood. Right?"

"Right." Because it would break his father's heart to hear otherwise.

As if reading his mind, Stan shook his head. "I know I wasn't there as much as I should have been. But you had your grandma and grandpa—my parents—when I was gone on training trips." Which was often. "And it was hard. You should have had your mom there with you, every time I deployed."

Agreed. But life wasn't fair. Jeremy took a swig of his warming beer to wash the unfortunate taste of regret away. His childhood, in retrospect, had mostly sucked. Being bounced around from house to house based on his father's training plans or deployment schedules. Having to switch schools even more than the average military brat because his grandparents lived somewhere else.

And yet, his father had done his best, provided with what he had, what he knew. And though he was heavy-handed and a stubborn pusher about it, Stan had wanted what he thought was best for his own son.

Stan leaned back and relaxed a bit. "That's the problem with this woman you mentioned. This active duty nurse."

Ah, shit. So this was where it was leading. "Dad, I told you—"

"No, no. Hear me out now. You're both in the military. Might seem convenient. Even appropriate. You know what the other one is going through. You can commiserate about the shitty hours, the time away from home, the training. The works."

All true, so far. And even something Jeremy hadn't thought of yet. There really were benefits to Madison's career. Huh.

"But then you start having a family. She gets put on shore duty while she's pregnant, and for a while after that. It's nice, yeah? She's home a lot, got the tight little family unit. Then *bam!*" Stan's slapped a hand on the table, rattling the salsa dish, tipping over the chip basket. "She's back on regular duty and you're split up. She gets sent somewhere else entirely. You're stationed in opposite ends of the country. Or hell, different countries entirely. One of you deploys. The other's out on a mission somewhere. And what happens to the kids?"

Jeremy sat, frozen. It was like another fucked-up version of his life all over again. Getting shuttled around to whatever relative had time to care for him when his dad's number was up to head out somewhere again. No stability, even within the already-unstable military lifestyle.

Even if he got out, there was uncertainty in that. Would he find a job soon enough? Would he be any happier getting out than having stayed in?

Would his father still respect him?

One thing was true. Though the military had its own sense of uncertainty, there was a certain sort of peace knowing you would be paid every month, that you had health care. And it was only for another ten years…

Shit. When did he start agreeing with his father? "Dad—"

"I care about you. I want the best for you."

That stopped Jeremy in his tracks. Raw, true emotion, without all of the military BS to tone it down.

Stan stared at the table for a moment, then coughed and straightened. "So. Where do you think your monitor will send you next?"

Jeremy sighed and grabbed his beer and signaled with his hand for another. Yup. Dinner was a mistake.

Now or never. Now or never.

Matthew's words echoed through Madison's head as she sat on the couch, then stood, then paced, and finally sat down again.

Where the hell was he? She'd entered Jeremy's apartment—if you could call it that; she preferred to refer to it as the Gateway to Hell—more than an hour ago. Sure, she'd given herself some time to beat him home and was relieved when his bike wasn't out front. But now it was starting to feel like this wasn't her best laid plan. In fact, not a great idea at all.

Was she the crazy lady who broke into a man's home to seduce him? Would this end up on the ten o'clock news? *Desperate female arrested, suspected mental disorder.*

Oh, Jesus. She was spinning. It wasn't as if she was digging through his underwear drawer or spraying her perfume over his pillow or anything. She was a friend who happened to have a key—whether through ill-gotten gains or not—and was coming over for a friendly visit.

Nothing creepy about that, right?

Looking for a way to distract herself, Madison took

the three steps over to his desk chair and sat down, determined to separate all the loose papers into piles. Or at least wipe away the five decades of dust covering his monitor. Lord. She sneezed just looking at it. Grabbing a tissue, she wiped until the screen was no longer covered with some sort of filmy gray. She took a second tissue and started carefully wiping down the keyboard. She even flipped it upside down, trying to shake out the crumbs from who knew how many meals eaten while he sat in front of the computer. Since he didn't have a kitchen table… probably all of them. The man seriously made Skye look like a neat freak.

Her elbow bumped the mouse and the screen popped to life, startling her when the bright white of a document flashed instead of the generic landscape screensaver. It was none of her business, and her main focus was on bending a paperclip to the right size so she could scrape the—oh Lord, was that a piece of lettuce?—out from between the W and E key. But the top of the page caught her eye, and before Madison even realized, she was reading on.

Chapter Nine? What the hell? She started to read a few sentences, then pulled her eyes away. This was so not okay. Breaking and entering was one thing. But going through his private stuff? That was too far.

Wow, that sounded crazy… even to her.

The roar of a motorcycle pulling into the parking lot jerked her from worries about what the color orange would do to her figure and she raced back to the couch, as if she hadn't been doing anything but minding her own business on someone else's couch.

Still sounded crazy. She'd have to work on that.

At the last moment, she looked back at the computer and realized the obvious white of the document was highly noticeable, versus the black of the screensaver. *Please come back on soon. Please.*

She heard Jeremy's key in the lock, and the deadbolt scraped over before the door swung open. He didn't even glance at the couch as he tossed his helmet and backpack over her direction. On instinct, she caught the helmet before it hit her in the face, letting the backpack slap her in the side. She might as well have been a throw pillow, for all the notice he gave her. Walking straight to the kitchen area, he grabbed a bottle of water from the fridge and a couple of pills—ibuprofen or something similar, she could guess from the shape of the container—and tossed them back with a gulp. Then, almost as if some invisible shift of atmosphere alerted him to a difference in the room, his head slowly turned in her direction.

His eyes widened, and the hand holding the bottle slipped down until it knocked against the handle of the fridge. "What the hell are you doing here?"

She placed the helmet on the couch next to her and smiled, like nothing was out of the ordinary. "I came over to see you. How are things?"

He shook his head slowly, like he wanted to clear a fog from his mind. "You came over—how did you get in here?"

She held up a hand, key between her fingers. "Dwayne asked me to run by his place sometime to make sure that everything was okay, nothing being bothered. And while I was there, I realized he had a set of your keys."

"Which you stole."

"Reconned," she clarified with a grin. "Just borrowing. I'll replace them later. Which leads me to ask, why did you never give me a spare key to your place? I have Dwayne's and Tim's."

He just lifted a brow, his expression saying *maybe because of something like this?*

"Okay, forget I asked." She took a moment to evaluate him from head to toe. His eyes were slightly unfocused, his mouth pulled into a grim line. His shoulders were close to around his ears, like he couldn't relax them even if he tried. And his stance was battle-ready… though that might be her fault as much as anything else. "What's wrong?"

He laughed, but it was harsh and she winced at the sound. After one more swig of water, he recapped the bottle. "What isn't wrong?" He plopped down on the office chair and glanced idly at his computer. Then, realizing the screen was activated, he pushed a button to turn the monitor off.

Madison sniffed delicately. "Did you go to that place on Seventh? You smell like nacho cheese."

"Yeah."

Pulling teeth with this one. Well, she was no dentist, but she'd give it a go. "Did you go with friends?"

"Quite the opposite. My father. The most stubborn person I know." He eyed her suspiciously. "You two have quite a lot in common, ironically. Madison, what are you doing here?"

She stood then, watched as his eyes took her in full length now. She was glad she'd come dressed for battle. Not quite the battle he might expect. But a fight all the same. She'd slipped into her tightest jeans, tossed on a

men's white undershirt tank top that she knew showed
the outline of her bra, and tied up the end in a knot in the
back so that a sliver of her midriff showed.

Battle. Hell. It was an all-out war. And Jeremy was
a worthy opponent. But he was about to surrender, if it
was the last thing either of them did.

Now or never.

He was going to die. Plain and simple. Today was the
day Jeremy Phillips died.

First, the dinner with his father. Not even his two
beers could eliminate the off-center feeling the constant
haranguing from his father about his military career—or
lack thereof—gave him. And of course, the constant
reminder that dating a woman in the military would just
never work out.

Naturally. Because doing anything to keep his old
man proud for more than a week at a time was clearly
beyond him. The ability to stop caring if his father was
proud was also, apparently, beyond him. Catch-22.

And now, in the sanctuary of his own apartment,
where he could pound away at his keyboard if he wanted
to for hours of stress relief, or watch a game in his underwear, or just pass out in bed because it'd already been a
pisser of a day… stood the ultimate temptation. Madison
O'Shay, sexy as sin in some see-through tank top and
jeans that he was pretty sure would require industrial-
strength scissors to get off, staring at him like she wasn't
sure which body part to start nibbling on first.

And not a single one of his defenses leapt to the fore-
front to save him. No, not one. It was as if the entire day

had been carefully constructed to beat him down so hard that the moment he truly needed the ability to resist, he was broken.

"Jeremy?" Her voice was soft, uncertain. "Are you feeling okay?"

He rubbed his eyes with his finger and thumb, bore in just a little too hard, hoping the pain would snap him out of imagining what that tank would look like tossed over his chair. "No. Not really. It's been a hell of a day, Mad. Could we do this another time?"

She smiled, and he just realized he'd all but suggested they have sex some other day. He scowled. "That's not what I meant."

"I think you don't know what you mean." She took another step forward. "Are you drunk?"

"No," he said, completely honest. He never would have ridden his bike drunk or even remotely buzzed. He was just suffering from an acute case of Life Sucks.

Her smile widened. "Good. Then you have no excuse for this later."

He set the bottle of water down on his desk, making sure the cap was tightly screwed on, and stood up. "Excuse for wh—"

But he couldn't finish. Who could, when his arms were full of warm, soft woman and his mouth was being expertly manipulated by lips intent on seduction?

Not many men. Definitely not him. That's for damn sure.

Automatically his hands went around to bring her closer, pull her against him. Let her feel the ridge beneath his jeans and show her exactly what she'd walked herself into.

If he'd hoped for a maidenly gasp of horror and a quick exit, he'd have been sorely disappointed. Feeling his own arousal only seemed to spur Madison on. As if she needed any sort of encouragement. Whatever she was doing was just damn fine with him.

No. No, wait. Not fine. Damnit, no. He pulled back, but she managed to step with him. "Madison. No."

"I hate that word," she murmured, pressing her lips to the pulse hammering below his jaw. God, he was going to pass out at this rate. "I think you hate it too. Let's not use it tonight."

He was on the brink of agreeing. Of telling her sure, what the hell. But he knew better. This wasn't a what-the-hell. It was his best friend's sister. A woman he could never be involved with and get out unscathed. A disaster in the making.

"God, you think loudly." She pulled her head back just enough to look at him and raise a brow. "Jeremy. We're adults. And I'm here because I want you. You clearly want me back. And I think it hurts you to say no. Can we stop making this more complicated than a couple of hot hours between the sheets?"

He stepped back once more but stumbled and sat down hard at his desk chair. Madison, who never let go of her hold of him, fell with him, straddling his lap.

She laughed, the sound filling his sterile apartment, filling his mind, filling in holes that had nothing to do with physical hunger and everything to do with his soul. "That was actually convenient, though I don't think it was your main purpose."

Yeah. Feeling her core press against his erection was

exactly the purpose. Pure torture—what red-blooded male didn't want some of that? "Madison."

She bit on his earlobe, then licked the stinging spot with the top of her tongue. Then she whispered, "Your day sucked, didn't it?"

"Yeah," he breathed. "It really did."

"I want you so bad I can barely breathe. You want me. And you need to put the day behind you. Decompress. Let's decompress together."

And he lost it. Every reason, every good thought, every piece of common sense he'd ever had about the two of them fled his brain. God, he needed her. Needed the feeling she brought to him. The fire through his blood he hadn't felt in so long. The sense of living for something other than the daily grind and someone else's dream.

He needed Madison. Even if just for the night. Even if there was a shelf life of twelve hours in the relief, on the pleasure. He'd take it, and God help him tomorrow.

He gripped her thighs from behind and stood. Instinctively her legs wrapped around his torso and she laughed with glee.

"Nice choice, Marine."

It might be. Or it could be the worst decision of his life. He'd find out tomorrow. Tonight he just needed her.

Chapter 12

SOMETHING CHANGED. AND NOT JUST HIS CONCESSION to give them a chance in the bedroom. Madison felt his entire body posture, the stiffness in his muscles, even the way he breathed change the moment he gave himself permission to let go and have a little fun with her. As if some massive weight, or some important burden was lifted from him, even temporarily.

It was a huge deal, she knew. And she wouldn't let him down. He might be thinking this was only for the night. Might not be able to see past that for his own sanity. But she'd show him the truth of the matter later. No worries.

One night wouldn't be enough for him. And it damn sure wouldn't be enough for her.

As he walked her backward toward the bed area, she unwrapped her arms from his neck, leaned back just a little, reached down, and pulled the tank up and over her head. The material slid from her lax fingers as Jeremy's eyes immediately drifted down to where her bra covered her breasts. Barely. It was the prettiest underwear she owned. The only pretty underwear, really. And thank God she'd had the foresight to put it on before she came over. Somehow she didn't think plain cotton Hanes panties and a ragged sports bra screamed *do me, hot stuff*.

"Mad." He set her down on her feet next to the unmade bed, eyes still at her chest. With what she could only describe as reverence, he traced his thumbs over the scalloped edge of the cups, where her breasts filled the material and threatened to spill over just a little. So maybe she needed a better fit. Pretty bras weren't her thing… she'd guessed on the size. Like hell was she going to let some stranger cop a feel with a measuring tape to get a better idea on her size.

Jeremy didn't seem to mind.

Just the pass of his thumbs over her skin made her shiver. But when he reached around to undo the clasp, she stopped him. "Not yet. Let's work on you a little first."

Maybe it was a cop-out. But the momentous occasion was starting to weigh on her, and she wanted it to last. Any shield to protect her she'd keep up as long as physically possible. Not that the lace was doing a great job of protection, given her pebbled nipples were clearly outlined through the thin material.

But Jeremy didn't argue. Instead he just reached behind him, grabbed a hunk of shirt between his shoulder blades, and pulled the polo up and over his head in one swoop. His olive undershirt clung for a moment, drifting up before falling back to cover his torso. Damn. Unable to stop herself, she pushed it back up and over his head as best she could. He bent down obligingly to give her a hand as she struggled to pop the neckline over his head. His dog tags made cheerful clinking sounds as they fell back against his chest. She'd caught a glimpse; no way was she letting him cover back up.

She breathed a little sigh of… what? Relief? No, more a sigh of contentment as his upper body was bared to her completely. She'd seen him without a shirt on before, working out or at the beach when the whole gang had gone. But here, in his apartment, just the two of them, the soft glow of the overhead lights and their hard breathing the only things surrounding them, the whole thing was more decadent. Delicious. And she had the opportunity to touch rather than just look. Skimming her hands up from his abs, she covered the lean muscle there, the cut ridges and planes of his chest up to his sculpted shoulders. Bulky, he was not. But built, oh yes. Enough to have everything feminine in her silently giggling with anticipation.

"That's better."

The corner of his mouth quirked. "If that's all you wanted, then…" He reached for his shirts on the floor.

She laughed and grabbed his wrist. "No way, bucko."

He raised a brow. "Your turn." And before she could stop him again, he reached around her and flicked open the clasp of her bra. The material gave immediately and she wanted to cover herself out of instinct. But she wasn't exactly a virgin, and this wasn't her first trip down peek-a-boo lane. So why the modesty?

The enormity. As the lace fell away, she knew they were hitting the point of no return. And it was scary. But when the look in his eyes turned from interested to downright predatory, she knew there was nothing to worry about.

"God, Madison." He reached out and cupped one in each hand, testing the weight, lightly rubbing his thumbs over her tight peaks. "You've always had these, right?"

She swatted his arm, biting back another laugh. "They're under lock and key in my scrubs or uniform."

"Thank God," he muttered, then before she could say a word he nudged her down on her back across his bed. Habit had her smoothing the sheets out as she slid down. She had no time to guess his next move as he unbuttoned her jeans and tugged them and her panties off in one fell swoop.

Well. The matching panties were a bit of a bust. Glad she hadn't expected a huge reveal there.

Her flip-flops fell to the floor along with the denim and lace, and she was completely naked. But this time, the frank lust on Jeremy's face had her squirming with excitement rather than embarrassment. He looked his fill, not moving over her quickly to continue. But savoring the moment, as if he was taking mental pictures so he could think back on the moment repeatedly.

Talk about an ego booster.

She stretched just a little to the side, knowing it'd push out her booty and breasts in a more flattering way. She wasn't as long and lean as Skye, but she kept her body in shape and hoped that would be good enough.

His eyes flashed, and she was grateful he hadn't suddenly expected her to morph into a five-foot-ten Amazon sex goddess.

"Are you waiting for something?"

"My heart to start back up," he answered honestly, then unbuttoned his own pants before shucking them, his boxers, and boots all as fast as he could. When he almost plunged to the floor nose-first with one boot caught in the hem of his jeans, she laughed. When was the last time she'd laughed, honestly enjoyed herself so much during sex?

He shot her a look that promised revenge, so she smothered the sound in a pillow.

"Just for that," he crawled over the side of her,

skimming a hand up from thigh to breast, "I'll have to punish you."

He tweaked one nipple a little harder than she expected, and she gasped, arching into the touch. "Sounds serious."

"Very. I would've loved nothing more than crawling over you and getting deep inside. God, I would have wanted nothing more. But I think that might be too easy."

"Easy my ass," she mumbled, thinking of how long it'd taken her to get them to this point. But she bit her lip when he pulled at her other nipple in silent command.

And the laughter suddenly evaporated. The atmosphere shifted, morphed, grew into something completely different. Not playful any longer, but almost desperate with need. Not just wanted it. But needed. To be in control. To lead in bed, have the ability to make the choices.

She wasn't about to say no. Not when his hands were doing fantastic things to her skin as they brushed up and down her body, barely missing all the good parts. She struggled a little when his fingers skimmed over her thigh, hoping to bump him to where she wanted.

"Uh-huh." As if to emphasize his control, Jeremy took his hand away completely. So not what she wanted. Her entire body stilled, barely breathing, and he resumed his torturous exploration.

"That's right, Mad. Let's just take this nice and slow."

She looked up at him, not at all shocked to see the depths in his eyes. He'd always been quiet, his conscious a little deeper than most men she'd known. But now, it was like he was on some other plane even she couldn't reach. But it was what he needed, apparently. And she wasn't going to deny him.

His lips feathered out over her brow, down her cheek, by her ear. He whispered things she couldn't understand, wasn't even sure if they were words. But they sounded beautiful anyway. Finally, as his hand crept around her thigh and between them, dipping in to skim over her center, she breathed with combined relief and anxiety.

"Jeremy. Please kiss me."

He sat back and stared at her. Too far? Had she pushed too far? Maybe she'd snapped him out of whatever place his mind had retreated to.

But he smiled, a sort of smile she'd imagine a pirate giving just before he conquered an opposing ship. He bent over, his dog tags landing against her sternum, the metal warmed from his skin. And he gave her what she wanted. A kiss, yes. But also reassurance that it wasn't just her body he was making love to.

Whether he realized it or not, his lips told the story as they carefully, gently brushed over hers. His heart was engaged too.

Goddammit. How was he supposed to ignore her breathless request for a kiss?

He wasn't, that's how. There was no way he could feel how wet she was for him, hear her little pants of breath, and then know she wanted to be kissed and deny it. Even if it was going to make turning away from this night that much harder.

So, because he was a masochist, he kissed her. Or maybe just because it felt right.

But he knew, even as her thighs tightened around his wrist, her breasts pushing into his chest with every breath, her tongue flicking out to meet his... No. One night wasn't going to be enough.

She opened for him more, giving him the chance to slip in one testing finger, then two. Stretching her, testing her, driving her closer to the brink. She had to be close to gone before he got inside her, or he'd embarrass himself and come before she even got out of the starting gate.

He wanted her too damn much. Not just any woman. Madison. God, it was Madison beneath him.

She gasped as his fingers curved around and found a particularly interesting spot. Nails bit into his arms and her head tilted back. The pulse in her neck beat double-time. And he gave in to the temptation to slide down and give some attention to her nipples.

Sweet little marbles, just begging for some tender loving care. He had it in spades, and he was willing to share. Taking one into his mouth, he sucked deep, smiling against her skin when her breath hitched in her chest. Fingers drifted up from his arms into his hair that he kept just this side of regulation length. And she scratched lightly.

Aw, hell. Almost forgetting for a moment about her pleasure, he nuzzled into her hands, wanting more of the scalp-tingling delight. Then she vised around his fingers once more. *Dammit, asshole, concentrate. You're not number one here, she is.*

He pumped his fingers in, letting his thumb graze her clit only intermittently, though she wanted it more. He grinned at the tightening of her muscles, reading all too well she was getting frustrated, annoyed, and if he kept it up… pissed. *Too bad. I know what you need.*

I know what we need.

The thought hit him like an arrow. And immediately, regret followed that this would never last.

But for now, he had her.

He used one forearm to shift her body over until she was completely on the bed, then reached with his other for a condom in his drawer. Damn almost-full box. He'd seen scary little action since Madison PCSed to his base. But that was his fault.

And he was damn well about to end the dry spell.

He finished covering himself in the fastest job he'd done since he learned how to use a rubber and used one knee to spread her legs wider. "Madison."

"Hmm." She smiled almost blissfully as she lifted her hips up to meet him. But he wasn't ready. Not quite yet. Although it killed him to hold off, it was important.

"Open up."

One side of her mouth quirked. "I'm open, Jeremy." To emphasize, she lifted her pelvis again, wet heat brushing against his cock.

"Your eyes, babe." He kissed the corner of one closed eyelid. "Open up."

He needed to see her. If nothing else, he needed to take this one memory with him when it was all over.

She blinked a few times, then caught his gaze and smiled. "Hey."

"Hi." And he pushed in. Slow, steady, no force necessary. But he could see every inch of progression reflected in the dreamy look her eyes took on. As if there were nothing in the world more complete than the moment they joined together. He couldn't disagree. Gritting his teeth, he continued until he was completely in. Dammit, heaven and hell were a fine line apart. And he straddled it.

"Jeremy." She sighed, her eyes drifting closed again, hands coming to scratch lightly at his back. And he lost it. Just lost it. Any hope of control completely gone.

"Swear… next time… better." It was the only thing he could say before pulling back and pushing ahead again, repeatedly, until his body took on the pattern all on its own. Like a machine, working under its own steam so he could relax and enjoy the ride.

God, what a ride. She met him thrust for thrust, actively seeking her own pleasure. And when she reached down between their bodies for just a moment to tease herself, the fight to prolong the pleasure was over.

"Mad. Madison." He bent down and pressed a kiss to her neck where it met her shoulder and felt her— thank you, God—start to clench around him in her own orgasm. And with that final knowledge that she'd reached her pleasure, he finally took his own.

Wow.

Holy wow.

She didn't have better words for it. None existed in the English language. That much she was sure of.

Madison rolled over just a little to watch Jeremy sleep. Shockingly, after a quick clean-up, he'd curled around her in bed and held on tight. She'd assumed he would make some bullshit excuse about why she had to go, to give them both space and time. Time for him to shore up his defenses and come up with some logical explanation why they should never do that again. Blah blah blah.

But the old adage about assuming was true.

Instead, she'd been able to feel him around her, his breath on her neck, one hand resting just below her breast, his arm heavy on her stomach. Nothing could ever match the feel of his chest rising and falling behind her in a slow, steady rhythm that said he was completely at peace.

And she'd helped give him that.

Oh God, she was getting completely emotional and weird about this. She'd given him peace? She grimaced into the darkness. Even she knew that was corny as hell.

So maybe he just brought out the best and the worst in her in equal measures. Not that she didn't already know that much. They'd always bickered like barnyard cats going after the same mouse.

Even before she knew what it meant. At sixteen, she thought it was just some weird feeling that she'd constantly wanted to swipe at her brother's new best friend. They sniped at each other, and everyone got a kick out of it. Said that was how they knew Jeremy was a part of the family, when he fought with Madison like another brother.

But when she wasn't within sniping distance, there was nothing sisterly about how she'd felt. No, she kept her distance, but the crush her sixteen-year-old heart had developed on Second Lieutenant Jeremy Phillips had nothing to do with sibling love. Not that she'd have admitted it then. Hell, no. He was just starting off in the Marines, a shiny new lieutenant. And she'd had a boyfriend of her own. One still in high school with her.

She could have forgotten about Jeremy entirely, really. At sixteen, nothing is true love. She'd even convinced herself it was just a symptom of her wanting to break up with her boyfriend. Any new guy would have caught her immature interest. But when she saw him again at twenty-two, there was no denying she'd wanted him. Wanted him with a maturity and intensity that couldn't be explained away on youth. And he'd still acted like she was a kid sister.

At least, around her brother. But there'd been those moments that he'd looked at her, when everyone else was busy. Those heated looks that said she wasn't crazy to be attracted, to want. To desire. That knowledge had fed into her need for him for years to come. Even when they were separated, even when she dated other men. Even when she'd been close to getting engaged. She knew there was a reason no other man made her feel the way Jeremy Phillips did.

And now here they were. Sharing a bed after the best sex of her life. Curled up around each other like they did this every night, as if there was no reason to think they wouldn't do this again for many nights to come.

But she knew better. Even as he slept, she was sure his subconscious was trying to rationalize their night together. Why he'd done it, how he could explain it away.

Oh, he'd have some fantastic bullshit excuse for why they had to back off, cool down, forget it ever happened.

Too. Damn. Bad. She grinned as she snuggled back against him. If he thought she'd accept his "It was fun, but now it's over" speech in the morning, he was an idiot. She drifted off, her lips quirking as she envisioned the lovely argument they'd have over it when they woke up.

But if she was going to argue, it'd have to be with herself. Because in the morning, when she woke up, she was alone.

───⁓───

Canada. Canada would be good. Canada was constantly overrun with people on the lam, right? Surely one more person wouldn't be a big deal. Of course, most people fleeing to Canada were likely either convicts or deserters… He was neither. Just trying to escape a well-deserved ass whipping from his best friend.

No, that definitely wasn't the right answer. Running away to Canada had been a knee-jerk idea. Clearly, Canada wasn't far enough. Afghanistan. That's where he needed to be. Government-sponsored vacation to the deserts of Afghanistan. Seven months of riding around in bone-jarring Humvees, eating crap food, and sleeping on a paper-thin mattress. That would help.

Help erase the feeling of Madison under him. Of the satiny feel of her skin beneath his palms. The sweet cushion of her body pressed against his. The sound of her breathy little moans and sighs that told him exactly how much she enjoyed whatever he was doing.

No. Afghanistan wasn't far enough. The moon. Were they sending deployments to the moon yet?

"Hey."

Jeremy jolted and nearly tipped his rolling office chair over. He spun around, facing the door, heart still pounding in his ears. "Jesus, O'Shay. Give a guy a warning before you pull that sneaky shit."

Tim grinned. "What? Not my fault you were somewhere completely different. I'm taking off for home." He glanced around the office for a moment. "Your dad still in town?"

"Nah." Jeremy shook his head. "That was a one-day-only event. Just in the state on business. He's already gone back east." And with him, his judgment and pressure.

"Ah, okay." Tim tilted his head and studied him with an intensity that made Jeremy want to squirm. "You need to talk? Grab a beer or something first?"

Just what he needed. Some alcohol to loosen his tongue so the first thing he did was blurt out "I had sex with your sister."

Jeremy shook his head. "Nope. I'm fine. Just tired." The last part was the truth, at least. The first part, complete lie. He'd never be fine again.

Tim shrugged and slapped a hand on the door frame. "If you're sure. Come over for dinner sometime soon. Skye misses having people around constantly, now that Veronica's out of the house."

"Sure. Just say when," he said absently as Tim walked down the hall.

He waited for another five-count after the sound of bootsteps faded. Then picked up his cell phone. Then he set it back down again. What the hell was he going to do? Text her and say… what?

Hope you got home okay.

No. That would only bring in the reminder that he hadn't stayed around to see her off in the morning.

Wish I could have said good morning.

An untruth. He booked it out of there to avoid the morning-after talk like he was about to fail a PFT. Nerves, combined with his own inability to separate his emotions from the reality of the serious situation, meant he wasn't ready to have that conversation yet.

I miss you.

Truth. But not going to help the situation any.

I'm an ass.

Also true. But she probably knew that. He left her alone at his place, after all.

He gripped the cell phone with his thumb and finger, then gave it a spin, watching the hard case swirl over the top of his desk. Then he remembered. She was working nights this week. So she wouldn't likely be able to answer him right away anyway. No point in texting if she can't answer.

Reprieve. He breathed a little deeper and settled back in his chair. He closed his eyes, let the silence of the office soak in. In the mornings, the absolute chaos almost killed him. In the afternoons, the rush to get stuff done and get out as soon as possible was annoying. But now, when almost everyone was gone, he liked this best. The quiet, the solitude, the ability to work without fourteen people needing his input right that second.

God, he really was a loner cave dweller.

But was that such a bad thing? Even in the Marines, it takes all kinds.

Jeremy reached for his pen, eyes still closed, using his other hand to search for his notebook. Free writing, when he didn't even let himself look at the paper, sometimes yielded the most amazing and complex plot points, character references, or backstories. He let his pen flow without watching, just rambling, letting his own mind drift along with the soothing sound of scratching.

Drawing. He was drawing something. Not the best artist in the world, but he'd come up with more than one physical character description from doing this. He let it go on, trying hard not to focus, which was an oxymoron in itself. The pen halted, stunted, he knew, by the fact that he was concentrating too hard. Time to let his mind wander elsewhere, completely uncensored, to keep it preoccupied and away from the paper.

And as always, when allowed to, his thoughts drifted back to Madison. But now he didn't have to fantasize about what she was like in bed. He had the full-blown picture in his mind. What she looked like flushed from an orgasm. What she tasted like in the middle of the night. What her hair looked like in the morning after a long night of making love. The way her warm body molded against his in the dark.

"Phillips."

His hand jerked, sliding a long, thick black mark across the paper. His eyes popped open to see Colonel Blackwater standing in his doorway, a bemused expression tilting his lips.

Well, hell.

Chapter 13

JEREMY STOOD AND FACED THE CO, DOING HIS BEST TO slide a folder over his notebook casually without looking down. In a long list of people Jeremy didn't want to see, the colonel was at the top. All this afternoon needed was for his dad to show back up and he'd have the trifecta of people he preferred to avoid. "Sir. What can I do for you?"

Blackwater edged into the room and wandered around, taking in the bare walls. "Did you leave your diploma back at home with your father?"

"Hmm? Oh, no, sir. I have it. Just never felt the need to bring it in."

Blackwater's mouth tightened a little, then relaxed. "How are things in your neck of the woods?"

Warning yellow lights flashed *Caution* in his mind. The CO was a man of authority over his career. And Jeremy's duty was to follow his orders. But Jeremy also knew the man was a sneak and had no problems prying into the personal lives of his Marines. Not with friendly concern, but out of some odd sense of satisfaction when he could shape the Marine's life. Like some weird omnipotent puppeteer, wanting control over everything.

Tim ran into the same problem last year but handled it with much more diplomacy than Jeremy would ever be able to manage. "Things are fine."

"I notice you're always one of the last to leave the

office for the day." Blackwater started staring, unapologetically, at the papers covering Jeremy's desk. As if he had the right. "No family to run home to, correct?"

"That's correct, sir," he replied through clenched teeth. He fought the urge to yank everything away from the man's gaze. Thank God he didn't have anything personal…

His notebook. Fuck. Waiting until the man's eyes were averted to a far corner of the desk, he glanced down to make sure it was fully covered by a file.

It was. Barely.

The CO picked up a form and started reading without another word.

Go right ahead, sir. What's mine is yours, apparently.

"I'll admit I probably stayed at the office a little later than I do now, back in my young, pre-family days." Blackwater set the sheet back down and walked to the other corner of his desk to pick up something else. "No thoughts of settling down?"

And how is this any of your business? "No. No thoughts at all," he lied. No practical thoughts anyway. Just a fantasy that would stay just that. Fantasy.

"A good Marine has something back home worth fighting for. I believe your father knew that."

"My father…" Had his dad actually gone to the CO with his concerns? No. He wouldn't have. Despite his own concern, even Jeremy knew his father wouldn't go that far.

"I knew him, once upon a time. We crossed paths at a few points in our careers, though we never served directly together. Had his work cut out for him, raising you alone after his sweet wife died."

Sweet wife. That's my mother you're talking about.
Jeremy bit his tongue to keep from cursing.

"Someone who understands, even supports, the cause
is important. My own Patricia is irreplaceable." The CO
set the paper down and looked him in the eye. "Now.
Have you given any consideration to your next contract,
where you might ask your monitor to send you?"

How the hell did Tim keep from knocking this guy's
teeth out when he was pulling this shit with his marriage
to Skye? "No, sir, I haven't."

He nodded and headed back toward the door, one
hand gripping the frame. "Time to get a move on with
that, son. Re-up will be here before you know it, and you
don't want to be caught with your pants down." He patted
the frame of the desk once, wedding ring dinging harshly
as it struck the metal, then nodded and walked out in the
hallway, turning toward the direction of his own office.

"I'm not your son," Jeremy muttered quietly once he
heard the CO's door shut. He flopped down, covered his
eyes with one hand, and sighed. Damn, that man was
draining. Thank God he was heading out soon, to be
replaced by, hopefully, a more understanding CO.

Jeremy glanced down at his desk and started shuffling
papers into neater piles. The thought of Blackwater's
hands all over his things just made him that much more
determined to have everything out of sight and away
from the man's prying eyes.

His fingers bumped the file, and he remembered the
notebook, his free-form thoughts he'd been working on
before interrupted. He pushed the rest of the papers into
his top desk drawer, determined to go through them in
the morning, and shifted the file to the side.

And stared, equal parts horrified and stunned, as he was faced with a rather decent drawing of Madison's face. Head tilted back, eyes tightly shut, lips slightly parted. Just like she'd been the night before in the middle of her own climax.

Holy fuck. This was what he got for letting his mind wander to Madison while trying to work on free-form.

He tore the page out of the notebook—something he rarely did, as he thought even bad ideas deserved their moment—and wadded it up. But just as he was ready to toss it in the trash, he pulled back. This wasn't something he wanted some janitor to see. He'd get rid of it at home. Burn it or shred it or something. Destroy it in some way to make sure nobody else would see it.

Too bad his own mind couldn't unsee the image. Now he had a raging hard-on and no fix in sight.

"Stupid jarhead." Madison slammed the clipboard on the desk hard enough to have the desk nurse jump and glare at her. "Sorry," she muttered.

"Trouble in paradise?" Matthew sailed by her with a cart of supplies, and she turned on her heel to follow, wincing a little at the squeak her rubber-soled shoes made on the tile floor.

"Paradise. Right." She snorted. "Hardly." Okay, so in the heat of the moment, the whole thing had seemed better than paradise, if that was even possible. But the morning after had totally popped that dream bubble. Because there had *been* no morning after. Just a morning alone. Embarrassing, really.

"What happened, toots?" Matthew stopped the cart

and grabbed a few supplies, slipping into a room quietly
to restock the cabinet while the new mother slept the
sleep of the drugged. Lucky lady. Madison waited for
him to come back out before following along once more
like a puppy on a leash.

"He left. In the morning. No note, no explanation, no
promise of talking later. He just left."

"Hmm." Matthew wheeled the cart back toward the
supply closet and took out the key to unlock the door.
"Why do you think he left?"

"Because he's a chickenshit?" she asked sweetly.

"Try again."

"Okay, fine. A stupid jarhead?" She sighed and
pushed a hand over her slicked-back bun. "I don't know.
He probably wanted some time to think about what he
had to say."

"Was the sex good?"

"Matthew!" she hissed then looked around. They
were alone, as usual, on the floor. Unless someone was
in active labor, nights on the OB floor were relatively
quiet. No hustle of family constantly coming in to see,
no flower delivery services. A smaller staff, though no
less capable and with extras on call at all times. Even the
mothers in labor seemed to somehow calm down more.
She relished the nights.

"Oh, I see." He gave her a sad smile and tsked. "The
sex was that bad, huh? I mean, I can see—"

"It. Was. Not. Bad," she whispered harshly, then realized what she'd all but admitted. Though why she was
censoring herself with her best friend, she had no clue.
It wasn't like she hadn't been honest about her sexual
encounters before.

Matthew rolled his eyes, then shoved her arm until she stumbled into an empty room.

Madison stared at the flat-screen TV and the over-sized armchair that pulled out into a couch for the expectant fathers to sleep over on. "You're not going to take a nap in here again, are you?"

He shot her a look that would wither plants. "Stuff it, O'Shay. That was once. And I was just resting between double shifts." He rolled his shoulders. "Go ahead and tell Uncle Matthew all about it."

She made a face. "Don't be gross." But she cocked her head to one side, noted it was dead silent on the floor, and plopped down on the armchair. A minute or two wouldn't hurt. "I went over there last night with a spare key. He came home in a horrible mood. Then we, you know…"

"Madison. You're a nurse. Last month you pulled an iPod out of somewhere an iPod should never be. You can say the word 'sex.'" Matthew looked too amused at her embarrassment.

She flipped him off instead. "After, we fell asleep—"

"That boring?"

She smirked. "That exhausting. Then he woke me up like two hours later for another round—"

"Well played, sir."

"—and then when I woke up again, it was morning. He was already gone. Didn't even try to say good-bye, the bastard."

"You're not the most friendly of people when woken up," he reminded her. "Could he have tried, and you bit his arm off so he didn't bother?"

"No. Trust me. I woke up just fine the first time he did it."

"Damn you," Matthew muttered. Poor sad, sexually frustrated male.

"Right back at ya," she said cheerfully, then frowned. "So I don't really know where that leaves us. Is he regretting it? Did he really just not have time to stick around and wait for me to get out of bed? Is he planning his move to Canada?"

"Likely all of the above." Matthew held out a hand and pulled her up from the chair. "You could drive a man to drink, O'Shay. And I do mean that in the best possible way."

She elbowed him in the ribs.

"Watch that," he said with a wince. "I'm not one of your big, tough, unbreakable Marines."

She glanced at Matthew fully, shaking her head. If he kept his hair a little shorter, you wouldn't even know he wasn't in the service himself. The man liked to work out. He joked that the dating scene on his side of the road was more competitive, and he had to keep up. But the results were fine to look at for anyone.

"So now what's the plan?"

She shrugged. "He didn't call or text all day. But he's got a life so I didn't really expect it. I figured he might send me something after he got off work, but now that I'm the one at work, he might not want to bug me. So I guess when he calls, we'll just… talk. We were friends first, before this happened."

"And if he wants to pretend it didn't happen?" Matthew asked gently as they approached the station desk.

Her heart clenched at the thought. But she shook her head. "He won't. I won't let him."

Madison kicked off her scrub pants and watched them sail halfway to the hamper before dying a slow death on the carpet. She could relate. If she had her own choice, she'd fall to the floor and not get up until someone more well-intentioned than she was came by to pick her up, too.

Sadly, she didn't have that option. She needed a shower and a bed, stat. She rinsed off quickly in her small bathroom, doing her best to stay upright and not fall over and drown. But she knew, as she toweled off, this wasn't the worst part of a long shift at the hospital that ended early in the morning.

Nope. The worst part was when she crawled into bed, closed her eyes, breathed a deep sigh of relief… and nothing happened.

Her eyes popped back open; she was going to have to resign herself to the fact that she was still too strung up from her shift to fall asleep. She glanced at the nightstand and her phone and rolled her eyes. She would not—repeat *not*—check her phone again. For the forty-ninth time. Slow shift meant she had that much more time to think about what it meant that Jeremy didn't even try to get a hold of her. The only text she'd received had been from her mother at 0530, asking her to call when she had time.

Mostly she was just glad to be able to walk quietly into the apartment and back to her own room without running into Veronica. She loved the girl, but now was definitely not the moment for chitchat. She was too tired for chatter. But this time of the morning, even Veronica was still sound asleep. Most people were.

Well, she wasn't going to be able to sleep anytime soon. Might as well call Mom.

With tired eyes, she hit the right speed dial number and let it ring, using the moment to grab the towel she let drop by her bed to scrub at her wet hair a little more.

"Hello?"

"Hey, Mom."

"Madison! Sweetheart, how are you? It's so early."

Just the sound of her mother's voice slowed down her mind considerably. Like a drug-induced calm, it was as if her body recognized comfort through the phone and responded. "Just got off shift, can't sleep yet. Where are you guys?"

"Heading over to Louisiana now. It's my turn to pick, and your father's grumbling profusely."

"I am not," came her father's gruff voice, slightly distant sounding.

"What's in Louisiana?"

"New Orleans, of course," her mother said, like it was completely obvious.

Timothy Senior and Susie were taking to retirement like ducks to water. After spending a lifetime of moving around from coast to coast—sometimes country to country—Madison and Tim had both assumed their parents would relish the ability to spend the rest of their lives in one spot, with the chance to plant some roots and grow in a community.

More fool them. They'd barely lasted a year before the nomad fever grabbed hold and wouldn't let go. Shocking them all, her parents bought an RV and were making a go of touring across the country, taking turns on who picked what attraction they would see next. Often this handing-off of choice meant their pattern over the country was more of a zigzag with a few loops thrown in for good measure rather than a normal, logical sweep. But, as their mother laughingly pointed out, they had nothing but time. Time she got to spend with her sweetheart.

It was crazy, it was unexpected, and it was beyond adorable. Madison prayed she'd still be so in love with her own husband in forty years. You know, if she ever found one in the first place.

"It's not even Mardi Gras time," Madison pointed out, snuggling deeper in the bed, pulling the covers up to her ears.

"That's not the point. I haven't seen the city yet, and so we're going. Now, tell me what is going on in your life. How are things at work?"

"Work's good. I'm on the OB floor again."

"Oh, your favorite! Are you still working with Matthew?"

She smiled. The first time her mother met Matthew, she'd been assured Madison would marry him. *Best friends make the best husbands,* she'd advised Madison wisely. But on the second visit, she clearly figured out Matthew was not the man for her. "You know, I do believe he's attracted to other men," she'd said, slightly mystified at the idea, though not put off by it.

Mothers. Intuitive only when they wanted to be.

"Yes, we're still working together. I can't shake him."

"Good. I spoke to Tim the other day and he gave me Dwayne's update, so I won't keep you awake any longer for that. We sent him a card the other day… I hope it doesn't get lost in the mail."

"You know how things go over there. He'll either get it in about five days or five months."

Her mother laughed softly. "True enough." There was a pause, and Madison could hear the whine of the RV engine, the sound of some country song playing, and her father humming along. "Madison, sweetheart. Are you okay?"

She straightened a little in bed, then shifted to stare at the ceiling. One hand crept up to nervously twirl the end of a damp lock of hair. "I'm fine. Why?"

"You just sound a little… out of sorts. That's all. Do you want us to swing over? It's a bit of a drive, but I can always change my choice from New Orleans to—"

"No." She said it a little sharper than necessary and winced. "No," she tried again, more calmly. "I'm fine; please don't derail plans for me. I'm just really tired. Long shift, you know. And I didn't sleep well the night before." *What with all that sex I was having. Really cuts into a girl's beauty sleep.*

"All right, then," her mother said, sounding less than convinced. "But you know we're always willing to come for a visit. Always."

Madison's body relaxed a little again. "I know. Thanks, Mommy."

Her mother chuckled. "You haven't called me that in a long time."

"I'm in bed, I'm sleepy, and my mom's voice is in my ear. I think I regressed momentarily."

"I miss it sometimes. Of course, these days I'm more looking forward to the Nana stage. When do you think Tim and Skye will—"

Madison yawned loudly and exaggeratedly. "Oh wow, Mom. I think I just hit a wall. I should probably turn in now while I have the chance."

"Oh. Well, okay then. I love you."

Only a little guilty for cutting their convo short, Madison said, "I love you too, Mom." They hung up, and Madison let her phone drop to the bed beside her. Then she smoothed a hand over the extra pillow next to hers.

Cool. Unused. Unneeded.

Not for long. She'd had a taste of what nights with Jeremy could be like, and she'd be damned if she would give it up so quickly. Even if Jeremy thought he would get away with it.

———

Jeremy sat back, rubbed tired eyes, and stared at the clock on the wall. Calculated. And realized he had approximately seven minutes to slip into his cammies, grab breakfast, and head to the office if he was going to show up at a respectable time.

And he hadn't slept at all. Not even an extended blink. Something, a singularly fantastic plot idea, grabbed him by the throat the moment he'd walked through the door, and he barely moved from his computer since. He'd meant to just make a quick note for later. Instead, he'd kept going, and going and going, until the real world drifted away and the only thing that existed for him was the fictional world, the characters, their plights.

On the plus side, he was nearly done with the rough draft of the book. On the negative… he was about to fall on his face with exhaustion.

Debating for a few moments, he realized he had a choice. And for once, he was going to do what made him more happy. He might not get the chance often, and it might be a small step, but today, he was going to indulge it. He picked up the phone and called Tim.

"Hey, what's up?"

"Not coming in today." He sighed, hoping to sound sorry. "Just not feeling great."

"Ah." Tim was silent for a moment. "Yeah, no problem. It's Friday anyway; most people are going to be leaving early. You didn't have anything on your calendar, did you?"

"Nope." He coughed once, then realized that was taking it a little too far. "The only thing I had left for the week is a Fit Rep, but I can finish that up here and email it in."

"Sounds good. I'll let Blackwater know."

"I'll shoot him an email too, but thanks for telling him in person." Jeremy hung up, then quickly dashed off an email to the CO explaining he wouldn't be in that day and a note about the Fit Rep, so the man didn't think he'd forgotten.

After another fifteen minutes to concentrate on finishing the last Fit Rep he'd started the day before, he sent that off as well, then stumbled to bed. The moment his head hit the pillow, he was inundated with Madison.

Her smell still clung to the sheets, which his lazy ass hadn't changed yet. Or maybe not lazy so much as reluctant to remove the memory. And even though he was to-the-bone tired, even though he wanted to curl up and die for a good eight hours, he did something he knew he'd regret later.

He picked up the phone and called her.

"'Lo?" her raspy voice answered. It was thick with sleep, and completely sexy. He hardened instantly.

"Hey. You sleeping?"

"Jeremy?" There was a pause, and he imagined her pulling the phone away to check the screen. "What are you doing calling? Are you at the office?"

"I'm playing hooky. What are you doing?"

"Catching up on shut-eye. I got home around six in the morning." Her voice was tinged with irony, since she likely knew he was well aware what she'd be doing at this time.

Jeremy checked the clock. She'd been sleeping for a good two hours. "I'm taking the day off. Need to get some rest myself. But I can't sleep."

"Did you call for a bedtime story? I gotta tell you, I'm rusty on my Mother Goose." He heard rustling and a creak, as if she were shifting around in bed.

"I was hoping for some company for the day. That is, if you're free and don't have any plans." *Say you have plans. No, don't say that. Say you're coming over. Oh, fuck it. I don't even know what I want.*

A long pause. Long enough for him to check the phone to make sure they weren't disconnected.

"Jeremy, are you asking me to come over there for a nap?"

Well, eventually he wouldn't mind a more physical way to pass the time, but for the moment... "Yeah. I guess I am."

She was quiet again, then a soft, "Okay," was her only reply before she hung up.

He set the phone down on his nightstand. *Getting in deep, Phillips.*

He could swim. It would be fine. Simple. Casual. Completely nonchalant.

Complete bullshit.

Madison drove up to the apartment complex and killed the engine. After only two hours of sleep, when Jeremy had called the thought of not coming over had been a very strong one. Damn, she was tired, and even the momentary thought of amazing, sweaty, burning up the sheets sex with Jeremy couldn't rouse her from bed. But the moment he asked her to come over specifically for a nap, she knew she was a goner. How could she turn that down?

So she drove over carefully, taking as many back roads as she could. She was relieved when she reached her destination. It was almost like driving with a hangover. Not drunk, but definitely not at her peak either. Grabbing her tote bag, she stumbled out of the car, up the stairs, and knocked on the door. When she heard nothing on the other side of the door to indicate he was on his way, she tried the knob. Unlocked. She shook her head at the lack of precaution, then slipped inside and shut the door behind her. And this time, she locked the dang thing.

He wasn't on the couch, or at his computer desk. Which meant there was only one other place he could be. She turned the corner and found him facedown in bed, still fully dressed in a polo shirt, jeans, and his tan combat boots. Likely the exact same thing he wore on his way home from work the night before. She sighed, shook her head again in disbelief, and started unlacing his boots.

"Bedtime story my ass," she grumbled as she jerked at the laces. "Needs a keeper, that's what he needs. Probably stayed up all night doing God knows what."

Jeremy's only response was a light snore. She couldn't hold back the chuckle. One boot, then the other fell to the floor. She stepped back, hands on her hips, and estimated how hard it would be to at least get his jeans off.

"Nope. Not even going to try. That's your problem." She shoved at his shoulders until he rolled to his side, then crawled in beside him. Without her holding him up, he slumped back over against her, his chest heavy behind her back.

The dead weight of his body forced air from her lungs. But she wiggled just a little and made it work. Much as she hated to admit it, independent female such as she was, the simple fact that his warm body was next to her made her smile. Not that she'd enjoyed having to play nursemaid first. But when he shifted, mumbled something completely incoherent, and draped one heavy arm around her waist, she closed her eyes on a happy sigh.

He might not know it, might not want to admit it. But Madison was sure that at least subconsciously he wanted to make room for her. And not just in his bed.

Chapter 14

THE THUNDERING DRUMS OF A PULSING HEADACHE were Jeremy's first link to the world of the conscious. Then came the lights, much too bright for the middle of the night, burning his eyes through his closed eyelids. Who the hell was shining a goddamn light in his face?

Jeremy shifted, moaned, and covered his face with one hand. The other hand, it seemed, was stuck somehow. He took the chance and peeked with one eye to see what situation he'd gotten himself into.

First he noticed a very delicious pair of breasts pressing into his chest. Hard to miss those. Not to mention the rest of the body they were attached to, suctioned to the side of his body, his arm tucked under her. Turning his head to the side just a tad, he saw a mop of brown hair and realized it was Madison.

Of course it's Madison, dipshit. Who the hell else would it be?

He angled his head just a little farther and checked the clock. Almost noon. Damn, so not the middle of the night. More like middle of the day. Right. He took the day off, and Madison was working nights.

It came back to him then, his pitiful phone call to her hours earlier. He shook his head gently, trying to clear the last of the sleep from his mind. What was his point of calling her again? Come take a nap with him? How childish could he be? What, should he wake her up and offer her a juice box and a snack?

Madison groaned and snuggled deeper into the covers and his own warmth.

Okay. So napping wasn't such a bad idea after all. Except for the fact that he was hard as a rock and she looked like she had another four hours of sleep left in her. Not the best situation ever, but he'd survive.

Or did he have to? She came over here on her own. Maybe she wouldn't mind a gentle wake-up call.

Slowly, he rubbed his hand over her back, smiling when she arched and made what sounded like a purr in the back of her throat. Taking the risk, he smoothed the other hand down her ribs, brushing the sides of her breast, over her hip.

Instinctively her body moved into his, following his movements, not wanting to lose contact. Yeah. She wouldn't mind the post-nap activity he planned at all.

He inched the sweatshirt up her stomach, pausing at the band of a sports bra. Not your easy front-clasp dainty number. But he'd work on it. She shivered as the cool air of the room hit her torso and went to grab for the covers to yank them up. He stayed her hand, rolling and pulling her under him. She smiled, a dreamy tilt of her lips, and he hardened all over again. Damn, she was beautiful. Even with the faint shadows under her eyes, her hair in some messy top knot, her face completely free of makeup. She'd always been perfect to him.

"Madison," he whispered.

She didn't respond.

He inched the sweatshirt up and over her head, not

an easy feat when working with dead weight. But she didn't even blink. Just snuggled back into the pillow and looked like she would slip back down into another nice, deep REM cycle.

"Madison," he tried again softly.

This time, he skimmed a hand down her rib cage until he hit the waistband of the sweats she wore. A little wiggling, some more maneuvers, and he slid them down her legs until they disappeared off the end of the bed. Clad in the gray sports bra and simple white cotton panties, completely lax in sleep, she revved his blood more than lace lingerie and a practiced pose ever could have done. That wouldn't be Madison. She was simple, unaffected. Beautiful.

And God, he wanted her.

Kissing his way up her leg, pausing at her knee where he knew she was ticklish, she shifted but didn't say a word. "Mad. Wake up, honey."

Nothing. Guilt started to chew at him. Maybe she needed the sleep more than he realized. Was he being a selfish asshole to wake her up so soon after asking her to drive over on two hours of sleep?

Maybe. But he was accustomed to being an asshole. Par for the course. And he needed her now like he couldn't believe.

"I seriously hope you aren't stopping there."

His head snapped up, eyes finding hers in the harsh noon light. She smiled slightly. "Yes. I'm awake. I have been for a while. You're like the eighth dwarf, Clumsy. You really think you could have gotten that sweatshirt over my head without some help? Please."

He rolled his eyes and gave her a healthy bite on the

inner thigh. She squealed and tried to wriggle away, but he pinned her. "Brat. You could have made it easier."

"Where's the fun in that?" she teased. Then with a more serious light in her eyes, she reached down to frame his face with her hands. "It was nice, waking up to you." Something stern entered her gaze. "I wouldn't have minded waking up with you the other day either. But someone made a quick escape."

To distract as much as to please, he hooked a finger under the edge of her panties and stroked her once. "I'm here now. You up for some fun?"

"Aren't I always? Fun is my middle name."

"I thought your middle name was Ann." He grinned at her, and she started to open her mouth—likely to give him another sassy answer—but he flicked his fingers up and through her wet heat, and she snapped it shut again.

"Ah. Maybe fun is your middle name. Madison Fun O'Shay. Has a nice ring to it." He did it again, finding that one bundle of nerves and massaging it the way he knew she liked. She squirmed under him, unable to stay still, unable to do much of anything but give in to him.

His favorite.

"Take them off," she moaned, one hand coming down to push at the elastic of her underwear. "Off now."

"No." She gave him a mutinous look and tried again to push them down herself, but he caught her wrist with his hand. "My show. I'm running it. Lie back and enjoy it."

If looks could shoot, he'd have a chest full of lead.

She needed to hear it more often. The word no. She was too strong, too used to doing things her way.

He could handle that. Handle her. And it stung to

realize just how badly he wanted to handle her… for as long as he could.

Which wouldn't happen. So he had to focus on the moment and enjoy it while he could.

Using his thumb to keep tight circles going, he slid two fingers into her, curling around to hit the right spot. She hissed and raised her hips, and he knew he'd struck gold.

"Jer—please, Jeremy," she panted, moving her hips in the opposite direction of his hand, as if strengthening the connection.

Because he knew she needed it—and hell, he needed it too—he quickened the pace until she imploded around him, clawing at the sheets, screwing her eyes tight, and parting her lips on a silent cry.

God, there was nothing sexier than Madison Ann O'Shay in the middle of an orgasm. Nothing. He quickly removed her panties and kissed his way up her stomach, over her ribs until he got to the utilitarian gray sports bra.

"Sexy," he murmured, toying with the elastic band that rode just under her breasts.

"Shut up. I fell asleep naked after work and grabbed the first things to put on before driving here," she grumbled but smiled. Her eyes were still shut, as if it took too much effort to open them.

"You sleep naked at home?" He placed a hand over his heart. "Thank God I didn't know about this before. I would have never slept then."

"Be nice, or I won't show you the rest of my sports bra collection."

"I was being serious. I don't mind a little cuteness now and then. But this is you. And I like you. Pure

Madison." He caught one puckered nipple between his teeth, the cotton providing a small barrier to the sting he knew she'd feel.

Her hands came to the back of his head, nails scratching his scalp through what little hair he had. God, he wished he had more for her to run her fingers through. She held him to her, then uttered a small, inventive curse when he let go long enough to move to the other breast and repeat the process.

One hand lifted the elastic over her first breast so he could thumb her nipple, roll it. She arched into him, her hips thrusting up against his thigh, helping herself along. Always impatient, he thought with a smile. But he was growing as impatient as her. Damn, she made him about as edgy as a teenager on his first big score. Where the hell was his control?

"Off. Off, off, off," she muttered as she ripped the sports bra over her head and flung it God knows where. He heard a small crash and figured that was either a lamp or a glass. Who cared? He was too mesmerized by the sight of her breasts, finally unbound, completely open to him. The elastic of the bra had left slight red lines on her skin, and he traced them with a finger, then his tongue. Madison shivered and he smiled. So he could do something right after all.

"Jeremy, I swear if you don't get your clothes off and get inside me in a minute or less, I'm going to lose my mind."

"That would be a serious pity." Because he was as bad as she was, he took a step off the bed to remove his clothes. Then he realized he was standing in his socks, not his boots. "Where the hell did my boots go?"

She grinned. "I took them off. You were passed out facedown on the bed. It looked uncomfortable, so I fixed it."

Such a small, insignificant little thing, but it made him warm inside that she cared enough to make the effort when she'd been exhausted herself. "Thanks." He stripped in record time, reminiscent of the OCS days when he'd had five minutes or less to shower. Effective stripping had been a lifesaver then. Just like now.

A quick reach into the nightstand produced protection, and he was ready to roll. Literally, figuratively, all of the above.

He crawled over, something under his skin warming further when she simply relaxed into the mattress and reached her arms up for him in welcome. It was quite a sight, one he would remember as long as he could. Hooking his right elbow under her left knee, he positioned himself and thrust in quickly, leaving them both breathless.

"Oh my God," she finally whispered.

With one leg angled up, the new depth he could reach was perfection. Rolling his hips clockwise, he smiled. "Yeah."

Savoring the closeness, the absolute feeling of completeness for another minute, he pulled back and thrust more carefully the second time, then a third. Until he developed a rhythm that built them up without pushing them over the edge.

Madison's jaw clenched. "You're holding back."

"Yeah." He didn't deny it. "Better that way."

"For who?"

"Us."

That word, with Madison, was more than he ever hoped to be able to say, even temporarily.

"Jeremy. Please, touch me." She pushed at his left shoulder, and he shifted until he could reach between them and find her swollen clit, brushing against it gently.

But it was enough, and she surged up against him as much as she could with one leg hooked around his arm. She cried out his name—another memory for when it was over—and pulled him along with her into his own climax.

~~~

Madison drew patterns down his arm, wondering how to keep the moment intimate. How to keep him from pulling away again. "You never got inked."

"Hmm? Ink?" He didn't move, didn't seem to breathe, he was so still. The sound came from the back of his throat. She traced up and over his Adam's apple with her finger, barely skimming the surface of his skin. He swallowed in response.

"I think you're like in the one percent of Marines without a single tattoo."

"Ah. Yeah." He cracked one eye open. "I came close, several times. Usually right after a deployment. Nothing like your boots hitting American soil after facing down war to make you feel invincible and want to record the moment with some permanent reminder."

"But you didn't."

He shrugged. "Never found anything I was willing to live with the rest of my life."

"Not even the EGA?"

The Eagle, Globe, and Anchor. Marine Corps

insignia. And a tattoo staple among jarheads. Some of the most common ink art, aside from the words "Semper Fi" in the Corps. Day in and out, she saw one form of artistic dedication to the military or another on the men and women she treated at the hospital.

After a moment of silence, she rolled onto his stomach so they were face to face, then kissed each of his arms. "Well, you look pretty good without all the decoration anyway, so I think you're okay."

"How sweet." He stroked a hand down her spine, and she melted into him almost automatically. What she wouldn't give to be able to stay like this forever. Or at least the next day or two straight. Eventually they'd have to leave the cave for sustenance, after all.

"Madison, you know this thing…" He drifted off.

She tilted her head up, but all she could see was his chin. "Are you looking for the word 'affair,' by any chance?"

He paused, then nodded. "That works. It's temporary. You know that, right?"

So you think. "Hmm," she said, burrowing closer, breathing in the clean scent of his skin.

"Because it wouldn't work out in the end, you know. You want to stay in the Navy, and I'm in the Marines, and that's just too much right there. Not to mention, I'm pretty sure Tim would skin me alive."

She rolled her eyes and propped herself up on her elbows to look down at him. "I'm a grown woman now. My brother doesn't control who I date."

He lifted a brow.

"Okay, so he's vocal," she conceded. "And he thinks he has some sort of say in it. And I appreciate his opinion… most of the time. But when push comes to shove, I'm the one calling the shots in my life. Dating and otherwise. Besides, you're his best friend. Would he be friends with you if you were a jerk?"

"I am a jerk," he said sardonically.

"No, you act like a jerk… sometimes. There's a difference. You're not actually a jerk."

"More fool you."

She pinched his arm and he yelped. "Stop saying that. Tim wouldn't care."

"So why haven't you told him you and I hooked up?"

"I hate that term."

"Why haven't you told him you and I are doing the—"

She clapped a hand over his mouth to stall any crude remarks he was about to make. It was a point he wanted to prove, she knew. Reducing what they had to the most basic, primitive form. A defense mechanism. But that didn't mean she had to enjoy it.

"How do you know I haven't told him we've been having an affair?" She stressed the word affair, voice tightening.

The corner of his mouth twitched.

"Okay, so I didn't. But I could. I would. I will."

Jeremy shook his head. "No you won't. Because this is the last night. So it doesn't matter. If you tell your brother now, he's going to think I'm using you for an easy lay because this isn't going anywhere. And then he'd kill me. And you don't want to be responsible for my death."

"Ha. Little does he know, you were the one playing hard to get." She jabbed him in the ribs and he gave a cough of surprise before rolling her under him, pinning her arms down at her sides. "I'm a big girl and I can take care of myself. He won't care, Jeremy."

"He will," Jeremy said flatly.

She sighed and realized she couldn't predict her brother's actions. Hell, a year ago she would have laughed if anyone told her he'd elope in Vegas with a woman he'd met an hour earlier... but that's what he did. She just couldn't say. "He might. But that's his problem."

"And it's my teeth he'll knock out, and your family relationship he'll screw up. Just let it go, Mad. We've had fun. We satisfied the curiosity."

"But we—"

"No." There was a cold finality to his voice that hadn't been there before. "Don't push."

He didn't have to tell her twice. Though her instinct was to plow on, to keep needling, digging, find out what the true root was, she knew the limit. Push harder and he'd break. So for now, she nodded and rested her head on his shoulder. "All right."

"This has to be it, you know. We can't keep sneaking and doing this. It'll only get harder."

"All right," she agreed easily, though it was a total lie. Any man who called just to have a napping buddy wasn't about to give in so quickly. He might convince himself he would. But she knew better.

———————

Veronica cruised into the apartment, in a great mood thanks to a good shift at work. If she kept this up, she'd be able to pay back the rest of the money she owed Skye and Tim for the car they helped her buy ahead of schedule. It wasn't much to begin with, and they'd begged her to accept it as a gift. But she couldn't. Not without feeling guilty. So she took the loan for the car—how else would she get around?—and was ready to pay it off as soon as possible.

Just one more step in the direction to total independence.

"Hey," Madison called from the built-in desk in the hallway. "How was work?"

"Good, thank you." She made a side trip to the kitchen to grab a cup of water. Much as she wanted to take one of Madison's bottles for convenience sake, Skye had given them the water pitcher with the filter and she would use it.

As she walked back to the hallway, intent on heading to her room for a quick nap before cracking open her textbooks, Madison waved her over.

"Come here. Dwayne, you've met Veronica, right?"

Dwayne? She glanced at the screen and saw, yes, Dwayne Robertson smiling at her. Or at least, she assumed he was smiling at her.

"I sure have, squirt. Hey there, Ronnie."

"Veronica," she corrected automatically, then winced at how uptight she sounded.

His grin widened. "Sure thing. How's kicks?"

"Kicks?" What in the world could that possibly mean?

"Kicks. Things. What's going on, in other words." He looked confused by her uncertainty. "Never heard that expression before?"

She waved it off, using one of her practiced excuses. "Sorry, I'm a…" What was that phrase Madison used all the time? "A little out of it. Long day at work."

He smiled and nodded understandingly. Momentary crisis averted.

Madison glanced at her cell phone sitting by the

keyboard. "I got a text from work asking me to come in an hour early."

Veronica glanced down and realized Madison was in her work scrubs. "That's unfortunate."

"No kidding. Murphy's Law rules around here. But D and I just got started talking, and I know he misses me so super much."

"Uh-huh." Dwayne made a face, and Madison returned the gesture with a big, exaggerated kiss. "Who wouldn't miss a squirt like you?"

"Don't call me that. And I'm going to leave you in Veronica's capable hands. I have to jet. Sorry, sweetie; we'll catch up again soon!" Before either of them could protest, Madison blew him a kiss through the screen, grabbed her cell phone and keys off the desk, and ran for the front door, slamming it behind her.

Veronica stared after her for a moment, then blinked. "That was fast."

"That was Madison."

"Right." She gripped the back of the chair Madison had just vacated. "Do you want me to let you go? I'm sure you would love to rest or something. I won't hold you to it." *Please say yes. Please say no.*

Why was she so conflicted? She hardly knew the man. No, she didn't know the man at all. A few conversations via Skype did not make her acquainted. She'd never even shaken his hand.

"I could always use a touch of home. Could you sit? I can't see your face where you're standing. Right now all I've got is a great shot of your, uh… shirt," he finished dully, then coughed. Even through the computer screen, she could see his face flush a little.

She looked down at her work shirt, all black, and wasn't entirely sure what was so embarrassing about it, but she sat down anyway. And immediately wanted to groan in satisfaction. "Oh, that feels good."

"Long day at work, you said?"

"Very. But satisfying. Of course, not as important a day as you probably had," she added quickly.

"A satisfying day is always important, no matter who gets it," he replied easily, stretching back with a yawn, his arms reaching up overhead. His olive shirt raised up just a little to expose his stomach, flat and tan, with a thin line of hair running down into the waistband of his shorts. Veronica's cheeks flushed, and she felt a little flutter in her own belly. Why did she constantly feel something strange when she spoke to this man?

"Are you safe out there?"

He shrugged. "Safe as you can get on a deployment, I'd say. I'm rarely even outside the wire. Outside the perimeter of camp," he clarified. "Not much sinister action going on in here."

"But that's good. I want you to be safe!" she blurted out.

He smiled. "Do you?"

"Well, yes. Of course." She looked away, his intense gaze making her uncomfortable. "I want everyone to be safe."

"Ah. Naturally." He settled back in his chair, the squeak of the metal heard even through the speakers. "So how are you getting along with Madison? She a good roommate?"

"She's great." Veronica relaxed, glad to be back on more even ground. "I couldn't ask for a better roommate.

Though she's not even here most of the time, it seems. Our schedules are so conflicting. But the place is nice. And I like having my own space."

"Right. So many Marines room together to save up on cash, and I can see the appeal of that. But when I'm home, I want my own area. I don't want to trip over three other guys to get my cereal in the morning."

She grinned at the mental image of a room full of Marines all in sleeping bags, like a slumber party. "Sort of like how you're living right now?"

He chuckled. "Luckily, with this deployment I have my own box." He stood and all she got was the image of his torso again. Then she heard a metallic ping and he sat down again. "Hear that?" When she nodded, he said, "That's my aluminum box. My own little dorm room. Just a little slice of privacy out here."

He tilted his head. "So when you're not at work or enjoying your own space, what are you doing?"

"Oh, reading. Hanging out with Madison or Skye and Tim. Or learning about the city, since I'm still so new." Understatement of the century, as Madison would say. She fiddled with the edge of her bag sitting on the floor by her chair.

"No guy?"

"Hmm? Guy? There's Tim. And Jeremy sometimes, when we all hang out together."

"No, I mean, no boyfriend?"

"Oh." There was that low buzz in her belly again. "Uh, no. No… boyfriend." That was on her list as well, just not quite yet.

He frowned. "Hard to believe a girl who looks like you, sweet as you are, doesn't have a guy waiting in the wings." Then his frown shifted, morphed into a slow smile that put her a little on edge. "Can't say I'm upset by hearing that, though."

Something gave her the instinct to run, and she gave in to it. "I think I need to go now."

"Now?" He checked his watch. "You just sat down."

"I know, I'm sorry. I just… I have so much to do today. I'm sorry." Before he could respond, she clicked the disconnect button, then felt like the worst sort of person. Who hung up on a deployed Marine because they asked a simple question?

She still had so far to go. And eventually she would need to make amends to Dwayne for her poor behavior. But not right now. Not while her hands were still shaking, just a little.

Chapter 15

JEREMY WAS FIVE KINDS OF FOOL. NO, TEN. INFINITE. There were no words to describe what a moron he was. But somehow, despite this rousing pep talk he repeated on loop, he ended up parked in Madison's parking lot anyway, calling her cell phone.

"Hello?"

"Wanna go for a ride?"

She laughed. "Is this like you asking me to come over to your place for a nap?"

"No." But he smiled at the memory. Napping... good. "I'm asking if you wanna go for a ride. As in on the bike."

"Oh! Sure. What's your ETA? How long do I have to change?"

"I'm downstairs."

"So negative five minutes. Check." She hung up without saying good-bye. He pocketed the cell and watched the parking lot. What he was looking for, he had no clue. But he scanned anyway, routinely. Just another thing he hated about this whole affair. The secrecy made him as jumpy as any deployment. He left his always-aware mentality back in the sandbox... but it seemed as though this whole thing was reviving it. Exhausting was the only way to put that.

"Hey."

He jerked a little, steadying the bike between his

legs. And taking a full look at the woman standing before him.

Black leather molded to her legs without a whisper between the material and her skin. A tight tank top skimmed over her breasts, barely covering her abdomen where the band of her pants stopped. And a leather jacket dangled from one arm, paused in the act of slipping it on.

"What?"

He shook his head. "Where'd this outfit come from?"

"Oh." She slipped the jacket on the other arm and shrugged her shoulders to settle it. "After our last ride, I just realized I might want to look more the part. Plus I know leather protects better in the case of a spill."

"True." But what she wasn't saying was that she'd assumed there would be more rides. Though he was here, so could he really fault her for it? "So how about a Saturday spin?"

"I can't think of a better way to spend my day off. Now, where's that ugly ass helmet?"

Uh, yeah. The other reason he knew he was a total goner. Reaching back, he retrieved the helmet.

And almost went deaf at her squeals.

"It's pink!" She grabbed the helmet from his hands and clutched it to her chest.

Point of fact, it wasn't actually pink, at least not completely. It was still mostly black. But he'd had the same bolt pattern painted on hers, only in a light pink color rather than his own silver.

"You bought me a pink helmet?"

"Yeah, well, you said the other one was ugly." She stared at him, eyes wide. He swiped one hand through the air. "Don't do that."

"Don't do what?"

"Don't look into it. Don't do that female analysis thing, okay? It's just a helmet."

"Okay," she said, nodding gravely. But he could see the sparkle of humor in her eyes. She popped it on and straddled behind him, wrapping her arms tightly around his waist. "Let's do this."

He backed up, revved the engine just a little—he was a guy, after all, so sue him—and drove out.

He knew exactly where he was heading, had a destination in mind. But she didn't know that, and he was enjoying the feel of her arms and legs squeezing around him with every turn. So he took the long way to the park where they'd first come.

Even on a Saturday, it was deserted. But there were nicer parks for kids to play at, so he wasn't surprised. The parking lot was the real draw this time. He slowed to a stop a good fifty yards away from the grass and waited for her to step off and remove her helmet.

"Why are you parking over here?"

He killed the engine and stepped off. "Thought maybe you'd want a turn."

"A turn for what?"

He motioned with his head to the motorcycle.

Again with the earsplitting shriek. "You'll let me drive it? Your baby?"

"It's not my baby," he grumbled.

"Coulda fooled me." She ran a hand reverently over the handlebars, and his skin tingled with the reminder of what those fingers felt like over his own body. "So that's why we're out here, in the empty lot."

"Always best to learn somewhere you can't kill anyone."

"I'm not that bad a driver."

"If you were, I wouldn't let you touch her."

"Her. See?" Madison gave a smug smile. "Told you this bike was your baby."

"Hush. You want to learn or not?"

She rolled her lips in as a show of her silence and nodded.

"Okay. So, this is the handlebar."

Madison groaned. But when he shot her a look, she widened her eyes innocently.

"This," he said again, patting the part of the bike, "is the handlebar."

"I can't believe you let me drive her!" Madison jumped down and spun around on the sidewalk in front of Jeremy's apartment building. "That was fantastic! I think I want one now."

Jeremy chuckled and shook his head. "Not so fast. You've got a long way to go before you're ready to handle one all on your own." But then he grinned. "Addicting though, isn't it?"

"Very!" She hopped up the first few steps toward his second-floor apartment before halting. He brought her back here without asking. Not that she was arguing... but what did that mean? Was he coming to accept their relationship? Or did he just want one more lay for the road?

No, that was too callous, even for Jeremy. Maybe he didn't even realize that he'd—

"Come on. Up you go." He gave her a playful slap on the butt and nudged her up the stairs.

Okay, so he realized. No problem for her. He unlocked the door and opened wide for her, taking her jacket and draping it over the arm of the couch.

"Grab a drink or something if you want. I'll be right back." He headed down the short hall and into the bathroom.

Madison grabbed a bottle of water—*sorry, Skye*—and sat down in his computer desk chair, swiveling around. Taking in the bare walls, the mismatched furniture. The complete disregard for anything aesthetically pleasing. It was almost like he tried hard to make the already unimpressive apartment seem worse off. And why?

Her elbow bumped the mouse and the screen, previously in sleep mode, came to life. Another word document. She saw the chapter heading, a new one from the last time, and read on without guilt.

"I'm going to change really fast," his voice called a moment later as he darted into the bedroom. Clearly he didn't see her, and lucky for it. Because she wasn't going to stop reading.

She scrolled, gasped softly, and quickly covered her mouth. No way did she want him busting in and stopping her now. It was good. Fantastic. When the end came two quick pages later, she found herself wondering how pissed he'd be if she searched for the other chapters on his computer. If he'd written more past this. There was no way this cliffhanger was the end.

This had to be his writing. She knew without a doubt. Jeremy's voice was stamped all over the page. His attitude, his thoughts, mannerisms… It was all him. And it was unbelievably amazing.

"Well?"

She jolted, then turned around, suddenly feeling more guilty for reading than she'd previously felt. "Uh… well what?"

He raised a brow. "Yeah, I've been standing here watching you read. Nice try, O'Shay."

She rolled her eyes. "Can you blame me?" She held one finger in the air. "I'd like to take this moment to point out that I wasn't snooping on purpose. It opened by accident when I bumped the mouse. I didn't mean to." When he said nothing, she burst out, "How the hell can I read that and not want to keep going? Do you know how good you are? Seriously, do you?"

He shrugged but wouldn't meet her eyes. He stared at the blank wall to the left of the desk, a flush creeping up his neck. "It's just something I play around with when I'm bored."

This was more than play. It was finely crafted, honed, edited, sweated over. Loved over. But she didn't point that out. "Have you considered trying to get published?"

"No." His voice was firm. "Writing isn't a career. It's just something to keep my mind off… other stuff. It's nothing. I could delete it and not care. I don't even know why I save it."

She stared a moment at the man who sounded so lost. "Liar," she said softly. "You love it, don't you?"

He said nothing.

Madison glanced around once more at the pathetic surroundings. "Is the reason you're saying that like the same reason you keep this place like this, when you could do so much better? Do you think you don't deserve to be happy about something?"

A muscle in Jeremy's jaw twitched.

"It's okay to love writing. I couldn't do it, but I think you really have a way with words. It's not harming anyone."

He scoffed at that but turned his face to hers. "It's not something I talk about. Okay?"

She nodded, knowing to push harder would be cruel. Despite his bluster, Jeremy's heart was tender and she knew that. "Sure. I won't say anything—"

"Thanks."

She held up a hand. "On one condition."

He watched her warily. "I'm afraid to ask."

She smiled. "Nothing so sinister as that. I just want to read the rest of it. If you'll let me. From beginning to end."

He sighed. "There is no end. For now. But the beginning is all there. If you want to read it sometime, that's fine."

Sensing he'd let down a very important, very serious wall, she stood and rewarded him with a hug and a kiss. "Thank you. That means a lot to me."

He grunted, but his arms came around her to squeeze.

They could do this. Little by little, she'd tackle the other walls he'd built up and she would tear them down. With or without his help.

Jeremy reached for the lamp on his nightstand, wondering what woke him up. As his hand contacted cool, empty sheets beside him, he sat up and stared around the bedroom. Where the hell did Madison go?

Then a ringing sound penetrated his sleep-fogged brain. Phone. Yes, where the hell was his phone? He rummaged through the items on his table and found it, flipping it open a second before it would kick to voice mail.

"Phillips."

"Jeremy. Third time I've called today. Where the hell have you been?"

"Dad?" Jeremy sat up, momentarily stunned. He rubbed his eyes and shook his head, wishing he hadn't answered the phone until he was more awake. "What's wrong?"

"Nothing, except my own son doesn't answer his father's phone calls."

Jeremy rolled his eyes and stretched, stepping out of the bed he and Madison had practically wrecked earlier. As he grabbed a pair of jeans from the floor and slid them on, he studied for any left behind clothing of hers. No sign of her in the bedroom. He stepped into the hall-way. Light was off in the bathroom, same in the kitchen and living room. "I didn't hear the phone ring."

"It's been a while since we talked. Not gonna call your old man to catch up?"

"You were just here. I didn't realize I had to check in with you regularly. I thought I was a grown-up." His tone was annoyed, bordering on rude, but this wasn't exactly his finest moment either. Where the hell was she? He searched, but her jacket was gone.

How the hell did she leave? He'd driven her over here, so she didn't have her car.

"I'm just worried about my son. I'm hoping my visit straightened your head out. Checking in to see if you've spoken to your monitor yet. Any clues on where he might send you next?"

"No, I haven't. And so therefore, no. No clues. You

keep asking, and nothing's changed." Ah, there. He picked up the piece of paper torn from one of his notebooks, covered in Madison's short, impatient handwriting.

Grabbed a cab. Needed at the hospital. Didn't want to wake you. Thanks for the lesson.

She'd signed a big letter M. And at the bottom, under that, so quickly scratched he almost couldn't read it, she'd added, *I'll miss you.*

His heart clenched just a little at the reminder. That their time was limited.

"Jeremy." His father's sharp tone cut through the mental wandering. "Are you paying attention?"

"Hmm? Yes, of course, sir. Could you repeat that last bit?" He sank down into the computer chair, staring at the note without really seeing anything.

"I said you needed to get your head out of your ass and into gear. This is your career we're talking about. Have you even looked into grad school? A master's is the ticket for promotion here on out, you know that."

"Not yet, sir." He turned the paper over in his hands, wishing he'd had a chance to say good-bye. "I'm not sure what I'd want to study. Still thinking about it."

"Stop thinking, start doing. You're a Comm guy. Get a degree in something communications related. Hell, get a master's degree in foozeball; it doesn't matter. Just don't waste any more time."

He set the note from Madison on his keyboard, bumping the enter key and flashing his screen to life. The blinking cursor at the end of his last sentence captured his attention, taunted him. Dared him.

"Maybe this isn't for me."

"Comm? It's a little late to change your MOS now,

son. You picked it, you've got ten good years in. It's a perfectly fine—"

"No, Dad. The Marines. Maybe I want to do something else."

A stunned silence hummed through the phone, and he immediately wanted to take it back.

"There is nothing else. You're a Marine. Just like me. This is what we do."

"Dad, I—"

"I know what you're going through," his father said, more calm now. "I went through it as well."

"You did?" That was the first Jeremy had ever heard of it. He would have sworn on a stack of Bibles his dad breathed the military, never wanted to do anything but.

"Sure did. I think most Marines go through this at one time or another. Perfectly natural. Usually came up around deployment time, or around a long exercise. I'd think how nice it might be to just be in one place for the rest of my life. Not move around so much. Have some stability."

It wasn't due to a deployment, but it was a start. "Right. It's not so much the moving around thing. There's more to it than that. Moving doesn't bother me. But—"

"But that was all just a mind game. Trick the mind played, only the weak would give in to it."

"It's not a trick of the mind, Dad." He had to see this through. See what he was up against for his own father's affections. See exactly what level of disownment he'd reach if he actually grabbed the balls enough to pick another track for his life. "It's something I've been thinking about for a long damn time."

"Well, stop thinking about it." He sighed. "Son, this

is a good life. It's job security, it's health care, it's pulling retirement pay at age forty-three."

He knew all that. Had been hearing all that since he was eight and told his dad he might want to be a cop or a firefighter or a circus performer.

"Family legacy is important to me. This family's legacy should be important to you too." His father's voice was quiet, almost emotional.

He sighed to himself. "Yes, sir."

His father cleared his throat. "So get a move on. Now isn't the time to go soft."

"Yes, sir." He stared at the cursor another minute after hanging the phone up. What he'd said to Madison was true. The opportunity to make a living from writing was rare. But that didn't mean he couldn't do something else he might enjoy while he tried, did it? Go back to school and get a masters in English. Teach. Or something.

No. He closed out of the document and flicked the screen off. He was a Marine. Just like his father. The man who hadn't given up on him, even when others might have. He wasn't about to give that up because of a dream that he'd never realize anyway.

Jeremy sat back in the chair and had the most odd feeling he'd disappointed someone, but he wasn't sure who yet.

—∿∿∿—

Skye stretched her arms up and over her head. "Having a girls' day was a perfect idea, Madison."

"We all work such weird schedules. It's not often all three of us have the entire day off together. Gotta take advantage when we can." Madison sat back in her own lounge chair, smug as she sipped some of the fruity con-coction they'd tossed together in the kitchen with what-ever juice they could find and a splash—or three—of vodka. "I think my drink needs an umbrella."

"They're wasteful," Skye replied with a tsk to her voice.

"I think they're pretty," Veronica said, sipping her beverage, made virgin at her own request. Then she glanced at Skye and added, "But of course wasteful."

Skye laughed. "You don't have to agree with me. I'm not going to toss you off my patio for it."

"This time," Madison added in an ominous tone, and cracked up at the look on Veronica's face.

"Right. Joke. Of course." Veronica caught on—finally—and stuck her tongue out at both of them, which only sent them all into another peal of laughter.

"How are things at Chez O'Shay-slash-Gibson these days?" Skye asked.

Veronica smiled widely. "Great! My own space is so nice."

Where in the world had this woman come from that she'd never had her own space before? Madison was dying to know but forced herself to keep to the no-questions-asked policy Skye had insisted on. "I like having a roommate, honestly. Living alone sucked. Too quiet."

"Dwayne said that after a deployment, the quiet of his own apartment was a welcome change," Veronica said thoughtfully, taking a sip of her drink.

Skye and Madison exchanged glances.

"You talked to him again?" Skye asked.

"She caught the tail end of my Skype with him before I got called in early. She picked up for me." When Skye stared at her, she shrugged. "What? I know he's feeling isolated out there, and she's going to meet him soon enough when he gets back. Might as well know a little about him now."

"He's nice, I think. But a little outlandish at the same time. He calls me Ronnie, even though he knows I don't like it." Veronica paused, then reached for a grape, her voice casual when she asked, "What is he like, here in person?"

"You've talked to him several times now, it seems." Skye set her drink down on the deck below her chair. "He's a teddy bear. Sweet and friendly."

"Country to the bone," Madison added dryly. "And almost brilliant when it comes to numbers. But he almost likes it when someone underestimates him because of the accent. He thinks it's funny, and keeps them off-balance, gives him the upper hand."

"Hmm." Veronica settled back in her chair, staring off into the distance. "I didn't really mind listening to his voice."

They were all silent for a moment before Skye asked, "So, Madison, are you seeing anyone?"

Madison choked a little on her punch. When Skye raised a brow, she waved it off. "Vodka down the wrong tube."

"Uh-huh." Not buying it, clearly, Skye rephrased the question. "You are seeing someone, right? I mean, you're busy all the time, even when you're not at work."

"That's true," Veronica—the traitor—put in. "You've been gone so much we barely see each other anymore at the apartment."

Madison took another sip to clear her throat and

stall for time. It'd been almost three weeks since she and Jeremy first went at each other like monkeys in isolation. But that really wasn't up for discussion. Though she trusted Skye to keep things confidential, and Veronica as well, she wasn't about to put them in the middle of her deception. Keeping something from them was bad enough. Asking her brother's wife to lie to him—even by omission—was crossing a line she wasn't comfortable with. "I'm just very... busy. With stuff."

"Hmm. So you're free to set up then? I think I met the perfect guy for you." Skye rotated to her side so she could see them better. "He's pretty tall, which I know you're not fond of, being as short as you are. But—"

"I'm not short," she bit off. "I'm vertically challenged."

"Whatever you say," Skye sang.

"Walking pair of stilts," Madison retorted, which only had Skye laughing again.

"He's cute though. And funny. He's—"

"No thanks." Madison waved a hand in the air to stop her sister-in-law's matchmaking efforts. "Not really interested."

"Oh. Pity." Skye sipped from her straw and rolled onto her back. "I guess Jeremy wouldn't really like it, anyway."

"Probably not," Madison agreed, then shut her eyes in disbelief. Had she seriously said that?

"Oh my Goddess!" Skye jumped up, heedless of her glass clinking to the deck floor, punch running over the wooden boards and dripping down between the cracks.

"Uh-oh. I'll go get a towel." Veronica excused herself quickly into the house through the sliding glass door.

"You are such a little sneak! You and Jeremy are doing the horizontal mambo! You're burning up the sheets! You're—"

Madison shushed her. "Quiet! Seriously, Skye, not another word."

Her sister-in-law's eyes widened, then her mouth clamped shut. But Madison knew she was dying, so she sighed and sat up, placing her own drink on the low table between her and Veronica's loungers. She hadn't planned to tell, but given she'd already figured it out, it might be better to set the record straight rather than let assumptions reign.

"You get the bare minimum. Yes, we are sort of seeing each other. No, it's not anything serious. No, it's not up for discussion. And yes, I'm sorry but you have to keep this from Tim."

Skye's excitement deflated like a balloon with the stopper pulled out. She sank to the chair, metal and plastic creaking. "Not serious? How is that possible? He's always serious."

"Not about this. Neither of us are. It's just… something fun." It hurt, admitting that out loud. Mostly because on her end it was a total lie. But Skye didn't need to know that.

Skye shook her head. "I am absolutely positive that's not the case for him. I know… something just tells me that he's holding back."

He is. He really is. But that wasn't the point. She stuck one finger in Skye's direction. "Not a word of this to my brother."

"You mean my husband?" she asked dryly.

"Him too. I mean it. I shouldn't have said anything.

I can't believe I let it slip to begin with." She side-eyed Skye. "Exactly how did you think to ask about Jeremy anyway?"

Skye gave a negligent shrug of her shoulder. "Just a hunch."

"Bullshit."

"Complete and total."

They both smiled, back on more even ground. Then Madison had to ask. "Does Tim suspect anything?"

Skye smirked. "He's male. Do they ever suspect anything?"

"No," they both said in unison.

The sliding glass door opened slowly. "Is it safe to come out now?" Veronica asked, towel in hand.

"Yeah." When she approached, Madison added, "You didn't have to go running off. I know you can keep a secret. The cat was already out of the bag anyway." It seemed half of Veronica's life was a secret. If anyone could keep something under wraps, it was this girl.

"Thanks. But it seemed like something between you two." She stepped over to hand the towel to Skye, who mopped up the spill. "You might want to run some water through the hose in a little bit so that's not sticky when it dries."

Skye sighed. "Probably. Tim's such a baby about messes. Goddess only knows why he married one."

They all laughed again, and Madison felt lighter than she had before.

Chapter 16

THE END. HOLY SHIT.

Jeremy stared at the computer. Was that it? Could he honestly have finished the entire thing? A whole book, front to back?

He read the final two words again.

Apparently.

Damn, that felt good. He cracked his back on the chair, rotated his neck to relieve some of the stiffness, and stood to stretch his legs. After a quick check to his cell phone, he called Tim.

"Hey, you texted?"

"Girls are all over at the house. I got done with some work stuff early and I'm under strict instructions not to pop the estrogen bubble until after dinner. Wanna shoot?"

Jeremy couldn't think of a better way to celebrate finishing up his work in progress. "Yeah. I'll meet you at the range in twenty?"

"Roger."

Jeremy was there in ten, having the advantage of living closer. He waited for Tim to drive up, then they headed in together. "Where's your case?" he asked.

"I'm going to rent a .45. Thinking about buying one; wanna see how it feels."

While Tim went through the process to rent the pistol, Jeremy set up in his assigned lane. They had the place to themselves for the moment. Mid-afternoon lull. As he clipped on the paper target, white with a black center, his mind floated back to the last time he'd been on range. With Madison in the lane next to him. The sight of her, legs spread, shoulders back, pistol steady in her small, delicate hands had him fighting against the fit of his jeans. Damn it. Now, of all times?

"What'd you bring?" Tim asked, walking in.

"Just my nine mil." He removed the gun from the case, checked the chamber, and ejected the clip, ready to load in the first round of casings. "So the girls are all over at your place, huh?" Did that sound casual enough?

"Skye, Veronica, and the squirt, yeah. I think after dinner they're going to go see a movie." Tim ejected his own clip and focused on loading.

He knew most of this already, as Madison had told him via a text she'd be busy all day. Just like a girlfriend would tell her boyfriend. Dammit. "Good day to get out of the house then, huh?"

"Right. I had paperwork anyway, so it was a good excuse to head in to work. But it's good to get out every so often. God knows I love my wife," he added, snapping the clip back in his pistol, "but the break is good."

He couldn't relate. It was like Madison was a fever in his blood, and he ran hotter, faster, brighter when she was nearby. If he could tuck her in his back pocket and keep her with him all day, he would.

And that was just the most dramatic, corny thing you've thought for quite some time. Which is saying something, Phillips. Pull your head out.

"Sort of wish they hadn't kicked me out though. Haven't seen Madison in weeks, it feels like. I got so used to seeing her regularly, and now it's like she's not around much, even when she's got time off." Tim looked up suddenly, gaze sharp. "Hey, you might know. Is she seeing someone?"

Jeremy bobbled the bullet in his hand, the metal rolling off the edge of the ledge and into the lane out of reach. He took a deep breath and tried to morph his face into a look of impassivity. "What?"

"Seeing someone. Dating. Going out, whatever." Tim loaded another bullet and looked back up. "She's just gone or busy so much now."

"Wouldn't she tell you if she was?"

Tim snorted. "I'm her brother. Knowing her, she'd hide it as long as she could so I wouldn't have a chance to warn the guy off."

"Warn him off?" From what?

"She's a handful." Tim grinned. "I figure any guy who gets caught by her deserves a fair warning what he's walking himself into. And who would know better what putting up with Madison is like than her brother?" He shrugged. "But if you don't know, then I'm back to square one."

Oh, he knew, all right. But like hell was he about to say anything right now. The man was armed and loaded, for Christ's sake.

Jeremy looked down and realized he'd only loaded in three of his sixteen bullets, naturally not including the one round he lost into the galley. After fitting his required eyewear and ear protectors on, he put the task in the front of his mind, loading the rest with quick efficiency and snapping his magazine back in and slingshotting back. He checked quickly to make sure Tim had his ear protectors on. Using the white dots at the tip of his barrel to center himself, he waited between breaths and squeezed gently.

The shot rang out, even through the protectors. In the black. He breathed and fired again, again, and again. Sixteen total before he was empty, ejected the magazine, and laid the gun down gently.

"As you go on, you're pulling down," Tim said loudly behind him. He glanced back to see his friend standing at the bench where they'd set down their bags.

"Did you even shoot?" he asked, removing the ear protectors and letting them hang around his neck.

"Nah. Got a text from Skye so I read it first."

Married people. Jesus. "You're here to shoot, Rambo."

Tim held up both hands in surrender, one still gripping the phone. "Hey, she was just letting me know the four of them were heading to an earlier movie and going out for dinner after, so we're in the clear if we want to head back to the house to eat by ourselves."

"We?"

"Told her I was with you."

"Ah." Something else clicked in his mind. "Four? I thought it was just Veronica, Skye, and Madison."

"Looks like Madison's friend, Matthew, is going to join up with them for the movie." Tim shrugged and dropped the phone back in his duffle bag. "More power to him. I certainly didn't want to see that one. Some chick flick I'd fall asleep during. Glad Skye's crossing it off her list without me."

Tim walked to his lane and started to settle back up, but Jeremy stayed at the bench.

Matthew. What the fuck? Had she invited him along? Did she think he wouldn't care?

Did he even have a right to care?

A small part of him whispered… *no*. He'd made it clear that a relationship—a real one, with being out in the open, making plans for the future, doing things like going to movies together and not sneaking around—wasn't in the cards. And she'd agreed.

Too fucking bad, a bigger part of him argued. Loudly. She'd made her choice, and she chose him. He wasn't seeing other women; why would she see another guy?

It's not exactly a candlelit dinner, the small, reasonable part of him reminded. *Just a group of people going to a movie.*

In a darkened theater, where nobody could see what other people were up to. Where every dude knows how to make wandering hands effective.

"Dude."

He whipped around to find Tim staring at him like he was an idiot. "What?"

Tim pointed to his own bright green ear protectors. "Wanna put those back on? I'm about to shoot here."

"Oh. Right." He slipped them on, then watched Tim test out the Ruger, firing eight shots succinctly and with near-perfect precision.

"Nice." He went back to his own lane and loaded the mag en route. Then he lined up and fired, knowing after the first shot he should step back and shake it off. But he kept firing, poorly, until he ran empty.

"That round was just plain shitty. And I say that with love," Tim commented from around the half-wall.

"Yeah. I can feel all that love." He ejected the mag and set the pistol down. Grabbing a handful of bullets, he started loading up again. Casually, he said,

"So, wanna head back to your place and order a pizza after this?"

Tim's head once more poked around the half-wall. "Yeah, sure. With Skye gone, it's not like I'll be making gourmet for myself."

"Sounds good. Maybe one of those movies I've been waiting to see will be streaming and we can watch."

"Deal. I'm going another round." Tim disappeared, and a moment later Jeremy could hear—almost feel— the faint *pop pop pop* of the .45 from the stall next to him. Another minute later, the door to the lobby opened and a group of guys walked in, heading to the far lanes past them.

So maybe dinner at Tim's place wasn't the best idea he'd had. But if he could get another glimpse of Madison and Matthew, judge how things were going there, it wouldn't hurt anything.

Satisfaction, pure and simple, hummed through his chest. He finished loading, pushed the magazine in, slingshot back, took aim, and hit dead center in the black.

―⁂―

Matthew's SUV pulled into the driveway of the town-house, only making it a few feet before he had to stop. Dread swirled in Madison's gut at the sight of the object in his way.

"That's Jeremy's truck," Skye said from the back-seat. "Huh. Tim didn't mention he was having Jeremy over." She reached forward and patted Matthew's shoulder. "Why don't you go ahead and park in the street and come in? We can all hang out."

Matthew shook his head. "That's a sweet offer, but I think I'm going to head on out."

"Please?" Veronica asked quietly from the other side of the backseat. "We're having a lot of fun. I'd hate for you to take off now."

Matthew glanced at Madison. She knew exactly what he was thinking. How the hell did he turn down such a sweet invitation? She shrugged, held out her hands in an *It's your choice, not mine* gesture, and hoped he understood he was under no obligation to stay.

Something new, a little different, and a little scary brightened his eyes. "Yeah, what the hell? I'll come in for a few." He backed out and pulled forward onto the curb next to the mailbox. "Not too long though. You ladies wore me out."

She took her time grabbing her bag and heading to the front door. Not because she wanted to avoid the scene that possibly awaited her inside, but more because—oh, hell. Who in God's name was she kidding? She totally wanted to avoid the scene.

"Hey, Skye." She reached in her satchel and grabbed her keys. "I think I'm—"

"Don't even think about it," Matthew said low in her ear, taking a firm grip on her upper arm. "You're going in with me. End of story."

Skye turned at the front door. "What?"

"I'm just warning I might not stay very long," she finished lamely. "I'm really tired too. But I'll come in for a bit."

Veronica and Skye pushed forward, Skye calling out Tim's name to let him know they were back. Madison waited until they rounded the corner of the entryway and whirled on him. "What the hell?" she hissed.

"You started this by inviting me over a few weeks ago, need I remind you?" He tapped the end of her nose with one finger. "So you can be a big girl and finish it."

"There's nothing to finish!" she growled. "It doesn't matter. I apologized for using you."

"Look," he said, one arm slung over her shoulder. "I'm your best friend. Right?"

"Right now? Not so sure," Madison mumbled.

"I'll pretend you agreed with me. That's my favorite. So when you and this lover boy finally make an official item of it, we're going to be meeting up a lot. It's just a fact. He needs to get used to seeing me around. Because I refuse to lose you to some Neanderthal who won't let you have male friends."

"That's not how he is," she protested. "It's just, I really don't want to do this right now."

"Too late," he said through clenched teeth as the front door swung wide open again and Veronica stood in the entryway, a confused look on her face.

"Are you guys not coming in?"

"Of course we are." Matthew abandoned Madison— nice best friend—and looped his arm through Veronica's, leading her back to the living room and leaving Madison to follow behind. "Have I told you how much I love your hair? So few women grow it out this long anymore. It's really unique."

Veronica flushed a little and smoothed one hand down her long braid. "Thank you."

Entering the living room, Madison took quick stock. The lights were off and the glare from the movie cast an eerie blue glow over the room. Tim sat in the armchair, Skye draped over his lap, her feet dangling over the arm of the chair. Matthew led Veronica to take up the couch. But no sign of Jeremy.

"Sit down, squirt. You're blocking the view." Tim motioned at her with one hand—the one not draped around his wife's midsection.

She jumped to the side, then realized some action movie was on. But still, no sign of Jeremy.

Do not ask. Do not ask. Do not—

"So, where's—"

"Hey."

She jumped again, this time straight up. "Jesus. Scare a few years off my life why doncha?" She held one hand to her beating heart, turning her head to look at Jeremy, who'd snuck in silently from the kitchen.

"Sorry. Thought it was obvious that's where I was. What with the kitchen light on and all that." He held out a bottle. "Beer?" he offered innocently, eyes full of amusement.

Ha. Right. Like she needed any more damage to her poor nerves. "No, thanks. I'm driving home soon."

"But you just got here."

"Jeremy. Hey. Good to see you again," Matthew called from the couch. She tried to make a face at him, imploring him to behave, but with Tim watching, there was no way to do that undetected.

Jeremy took a few steps and offered a hand to shake. "Yeah, same to you. How are things at the hospital?"

"Oh, crazy as always. Madison keeps me sane. Thank God for her." Matthew smiled at her, face as full of innocence as Jeremy's had been a minute ago.

What—were all the men in her life turning on her in one big joke?

"Uh-huh." Jeremy side-eyed her but said nothing more.

"Are you going to sit?" Matthew patted a cushion beside him. "We can scoot over, right, Veronica?"

"Sure," she said with a grin. Madison watched her friend blush just a little, and felt a tingling sense of dread. No, no. She was looking into it too much.

Madison started to walk toward the couch, but a jerk on her shirt had her plopping down in front of the coffee table on the floor, right next to Jeremy.

"Looks a little crowded over there already," he commented idly. "We'll hang down here."

"Oh, will we?" Madison asked sweetly.

"He's probably right. I don't mind having the couch to ourselves," Matthew said.

She narrowed her eyes at Matthew, who gave her a shit-eating grin back in response.

Madhouse. The place was a madhouse.

After a few more minutes and a little more theatrical bloodshed, Veronica squirmed a little. "I'm actually not great with these kinds of movies. They sort of make my stomach ache." She stood, shooting Matthew an apologetic grimace. "I'm sorry."

Matthew looked concerned. "No worries. I'm not a big action man myself. Why don't we grab some sodas and head out to the porch? Clear night to watch the stars."

"Sure," Veronica breathed and followed him out easily.

"Shit," Madison murmured.

"Jealous?" Jeremy asked, biting off the word like it tasted bad.

Madison rolled her eyes and started to stand. She couldn't, regardless of what it might look like, let Veronica dig herself too deep into a possible infatuation with Matthew. She knew what Veronica was seeing. Good-looking guy, easy on the eyes, a sweetheart with a charming smile. But despite Madison not knowing much about her past, she got the distinct impression that Veronica was more sheltered than she would like everyone to believe. More naive. And she feared the poor thing would hang her hopes on a man who hung all *his* hopes on the other team.

She turned to make her excuses to Tim and Skye, only to find them absorbed in each other. "Newlyweds," she said with a sigh and headed for the patio.

She slid the glass door open and walked out, praying she wouldn't have to step in between the two of them. Hoping Matthew realized the possible problem.

"And that's Cepheus." Veronica pointed up in the sky. When Matthew pointed as well, she grabbed his wrist and directed him a little to the left. "There. Now you've got it."

Madison froze. Veronica all but shied away from touching men. The fact that she felt so comfortable with Matthew could be nothing but bad, bad news.

"Hey, guys," she said, announcing her presence. She flopped down into another lounger and watched for some sign of anger or frustration from Veronica at crashing the intimate moment.

None there. Her roommate simply smiled. "Hi. I was showing Matthew the few constellations I know. Not many, I admit. Do you know some?"

Stars? Seriously? That's all they were up to? She

glanced quickly at Matthew, who seemed to be innocently staring up into space. "Uh, sure. Let's see, over there we've got Draco. And if you looked just a little behind us, you'd find—"

"Ursa Major." Jeremy's voice cut through the quiet night like a knife. He sat down at the edge of Madison's lounger and pushed her feet to give himself some more room. "But it's a little cloudy that way so you won't see it right now."

"Right," Madison said, then mouthed *what the hell are you doing?* toward him. He merely grinned, a wolfish action that made her want to shiver. Not at all a friendly face.

"I thought you were going to head home soon," Madison asked Matthew. Her friend raised a brow at her and she mumbled, "Well, that's what you said."

He rolled his eyes, shook his head, and said, "Hey, Veronica, would you mind grabbing us a couple of waters and maybe a blanket or two? It's going to get chillier out here and I don't want you to get cold. I'd go, but you used to live here so I'm sure you know where it all is."

"Oh. Sure, I'll go, no problem." Veronica stood.

Matthew gave her a pointed look. "Maybe you could help her, Mad."

"No, I'm not thirsty."

"Help her," he said again, more steel in his voice.

She wanted to argue, God did she ever. But she recognized that tone of voice and knew that there was a purpose to Matthew's order. So, in the trusting way of best friends, she nodded and followed Veronica inside, closing the glass door behind her.

—◇◇◇—

Jeremy watched Madison's back as it disappeared into the darkened townhouse.

"What are you playing at, Phillips?"

His head snapped back to Matthew. Taking his time, he shifted so he was sitting in the chair properly, with Matthew at his side. "I might ask you the same thing."

The other man sighed. "I was afraid you might make this difficult. Look, we went over this before, didn't we? I love Madison—"

A growl escaped Jeremy's throat, completely catching them both by surprise. Though Matthew smiled like it was funny.

"I thought so. You'll have to get used to that. She's my best friend, and she will always be my best friend. But I told you once I wouldn't go after her, and I meant it."

Jeremy absorbed that for a moment. "It's hard to believe someone who spends so much time with her wouldn't at least give it a try," he admitted finally.

"Maybe," Matthew said with a chuckle. "But she's missing a few assets I look for in a partner."

"Missing a few assets?" For some ungodly reason, Jeremy felt insulted by that thought. "What the hell is wrong with you? She's not missing anything."

"Except a Y chromosome," the other man answered easily, taking a sip of his soda and staring back up at the stars.

"Except a… oh." Cue the *I feel like a dipshit* music. "Uh-huh." He scratched his chin, wondering how to avoid the minefield he had just inadvertently stepped right into.

"Don't turn it into a big thing." Matthew waved a hand as if swiping a slate clean. Hopefully Jeremy's. "It is what it is; I am what I am. I don't make a big deal of it. If people want to bitch and moan about me being gay, so be it. But I don't think you're that kind of person."

"No, I'm not." And really, he wasn't. It was the surprise, the abrupt one-eighty, that his mind had to take to follow this new train of thought that was throwing him off.

Matthew nodded once. "Thought so. I don't talk about it, because it's nobody's business. But when I say Madison's safe with me... I mean it."

"Clearly." He settled back in the chair, feeling at once more relaxed and more ridiculous than he had in quite a while. "Sorry."

"It's nothing. Between us, if I ran that direction, I'd be giving you one hell of a fight for her. Not that it would be much of a fight, since I'd clearly kick your ass in a New York minute." He gave Jeremy a wink. "So count your blessings and don't be a dick."

"Nice advice." So simple, so easy. *Don't be a dick.*

He could try it on for size.

Madison watched as Veronica poured a glass of ice water for herself, then for Matthew. She turned and held up the pitcher. "Did you want one, Madison?"

"No thanks." She popped up to sit on the kitchen counter, smiling when Veronica shot her a disapproving look for sitting up there. "Sorry, Mommy. This is just how I do it."

"I know." She sighed and settled the pitcher back

in the fridge. She took a sip of her water and smiled. "Matthew is very nice."

Oh boy. Here we go. Her chest tightened in anticipation of the difficult conversation ahead. "Veronica, uh, look. I think we should have a quick chat about Matthew."

Veronica tilted her head expectantly, a blank look on her face. "Okay."

"I hope you aren't, uh, aiming for him."

Veronica tilted her head the other way, a line of confusion creasing her forehead.

"Matthew's not available. For you, I mean."

Veronica blinked.

"I mean, he's not really looking to date… a woman." Oh, this was so not going well.

Veronica's nose scrunched up. "I don't think I understand."

She took a deep breath and let it out again, heat creeping up her neck. "He's gay. Matthew, I mean."

"Oh. Well, yes. Of course." Veronica grabbed the second glass with her other hand. "Did you just find out?"

"What? No!" Good Lord.

"Did you think I didn't realize that?"

"Uh…" There was no safe way to answer that, so Madison stalled by twisting her hair back into a ponytail and securing it with the band she kept around her wrist.

"I think he's a lovely person, and very sweet. Though he did intimidate me a little at first. He's rather big, muscular. Now I know he's practically a kitten. I would like to hang out with him some more. But I'm not looking to date him," Veronica said slowly, like she was speaking to a child. "Honestly, Madison. I think your own preoccupation with love is making you a little crazy." With that, she turned on her heel and headed out the door. Just before she closed the glass behind her, she nodded toward the blankets they'd found and set on the kitchen table. "Bring those out with you." She shut the glass door with a snap.

"Yes, ma'am," Madison murmured, feeling distinctly like she'd been put in her place. Which she deserved.

She grabbed the set of blankets and headed outside.

Chapter 17

JEREMY WAITED LIKE A FREAKING TEENAGE GIRL BY his cell phone, hoping it would ring. He'd left Tim and Skye's place after the movie ended two hours earlier, sure that the others would be taking off soon after. And maybe they had. But so far, Madison hadn't called or texted.

And he sat around, waiting like an idiot for a call that wouldn't come.

So he instead turned to the forms sitting on his desk. A desk he had felt such triumph at that afternoon now felt like a millstone just waiting to hang itself around his neck. The simple form to fill out that would cement his next three years in the Corps. The papers felt like lead when he picked up the small folder. Dread settled low in his gut, just as it had the time before.

It's a good career. A fine way to make a living. Respectable. Honorable.

Oh holy shit. Had his inner monologue just sounded like his own father?

He let his head bang down on the desk, rattling the cup of pens and the mouse. Jesus. He'd slowly slipped into his own father's life. On purpose? Or out of sheer habit, unconsciously?

Did it really matter?

He stared once more at the folder. God, this wasn't what he wanted. But somehow, it still felt like what he needed. His father's obvious desire for Jeremy to follow in his footsteps. To honor his father's career with his own. Continue on the legacy.

And he owed it to his father. Right? The man could have dumped him on his grandparents permanently when his mother died. At times, Jeremy felt like that's what he wanted to do. That he would have, if Jeremy hadn't slipped so easily into his life. Claimed to want to be just like his father. Joined the Junior Marines, then Junior ROTC as soon as he could. Get an ROTC scholarship for college. Commission right after graduation. Just like his old man.

If that pride hadn't been there, would his father have kept him around? Maybe. More often than not, though, Jeremy had his doubts.

His phone rang and he knocked it off the desk in his haste to grab it. Breathing hard from relief, he answered.

"I'm sorry, must have the wrong number. I called Jeremy Phillips. This sounds more like the Creepy Stalker Hotline."

He calmed his breathing and tried again. "What's up, Mad?"

She paused. "I was just curious if you were busy."

The folder seemed to shift on his desk, though he knew that was stupid and impossible. It caught his eye, nonetheless. He shoved it back, under the keyboard. "Nope. Nothing going on."

"Right."

An awkward silence.

"Madison? Did you want something?"

She sighed. "Yeah. Are you going to let me have it?"

You can have anything you want. The answer almost flew out of his mouth. "Depends."

"I know we said to cool it and all. But I'm… "

What? Lonely? Missing him? Wanting more?

"Horny," she finished, a definite hint of humor in there.

"Uh-huh. Are you sure you didn't mean to dial one of those 1-900 numbers instead of the Creepy Stalker Hotline? Sounds more your thing."

She laughed, and his body tightened in response. He liked how she laughed, engaging her whole body. When she lay next to him, sweaty from another round of mind-blowing sex, she would laugh, and he could feel her whole body contracting with the force of it.

"No. I called the right number. I hope."

Those two words hung in the air like a promise. Or maybe like a curse.

Say nothing. Hang up. Don't keep doing this to yourself. To her. Don't.

"Wanna come over?"

"Yeah."

Idiot. He was a total idiot.

But at least this idiot was going to enjoy his night.

Madison curled up beside Jeremy, warm and content and completely ready to snooze. But she somehow knew that they needed to have The Talk soon. That their affair couldn't go on much longer without having a conversation about where things were honestly headed. A serious one. One that would lay down the gauntlet.

And if he didn't pick it up, then that would be the end of it. The final straw. No more hope for them. No more turning back, pretending it didn't happen. She wouldn't have the dreams of What Could Be with him any longer. Just the depressing memories of What Might Have Been.

"Jeremy."

He didn't make a sound.

She rubbed one foot up and down his calf. "Jeremy." Nothing.

She rolled over, sure he hadn't actually fallen asleep so fast. Two minutes ago, he'd been inside her, hard as a rock and still sweating from their intense round of lovemaking.

But when she peeked, his eyes were closed, lashes set so gently against his cheeks, breathing deep and even.

Okay. Maybe he could have fallen asleep.

So they'd have The Talk tomorrow. She snuggled back down beside him, head pillowed on his chest, one leg draped over his. His body heat seeping into her, keeping her warm despite the coolness of the night air around them.

They'd talk tomorrow. And if nothing else, she'd have one more night of uninterrupted sleep to remember.

———

Dwayne tossed his cover on the bed and sat down next to it, too tired to even contemplate bothering with his boots quite yet. Or maybe not bothering at all. Twenty-fucking-four hours without shut-eye made Dwayne a cranky boy. He could sleep for a week, if he only had the chance. And with the pain meds the doc gave him, he probably would. Those things were intended to knock a rhino back on its ass.

A faint buzzing sound penetrated his brain fog, but he shook it away. He was too tired for anything, even imagined distractions. He scrubbed one hand over his face.

The buzzing kept going, despite his willing it away. Not imagined then. He used his good arm to push off the bed and walk toward his computer, seeing an incoming call on Skype from Madison.

He almost turned the speakers off and ignored the call. Madison wouldn't care; he'd just explain it to her later. She knew the deal. Sleep came before all else, especially when healing.

But then he wondered…

No. She wouldn't. *Nice dream, big guy, but there's no way*.

But if it was…

Almost on autopilot, his hand shifted to the mouse and he clicked Answer.

Like his dream, Miss Veronica appeared on the screen. Holy hell, had he conjured her there?

"Hi," she said shyly, a questioning tilt to the end of the word.

He thumped down in his computer chair, the rusted metal shrieking in protest. "Hi."

She fiddled with the ends of her hair, the same long braid he'd always seen her with. The tail draped over her shoulder and onto the desk in front of her. "I thought you might still be in your room before work. I didn't know what time you…" She trailed off, squinted at the screen. "Is that a sling?"

He shrugged his good shoulder. "Yeah. Had myself a little misunderstanding."

"With what, a brick wall?"

She was getting feistier. He liked that. "Not quite."

More like an IED and his MRAP. The one fucking time his boots moved outside the wire and he gets hit with an explosive. Luck was not always on his side.

But she didn't need to know that bit. "It's just dislocated." Probably. "I don't even need the sling. But doc wants it stabilized."

"Oh, you poor thing. Should I let you go?"

"No. No, don't do that." Her soft, soothing voice was like a balm to his tired, frazzled nerves. He'd been awake all night, in and out of the infirmary, checking up on his Marines. Being checked on himself. The word *exhaustion* didn't begin to cover it. But the adrenaline in his system wouldn't let him contemplate hitting his rack. Not yet. The drugs would push him under, but the fog they created, the alternate version of true sleep, fucked with his brain.

"Well, can I…" She grew quiet, closed her eyes, and smiled. "Sorry, I was about to ask if I could help. But that's silly, isn't it? You're thousands of miles away. Not as if I could run over with a bowl of soup."

"This helps. Having something else to concentrate on." Which reminded him… "What brings you to call?" So far each conversation they'd had resulted from an accident or being in the right place at the right time. This was the first time she'd truly reached out and made contact on purpose. Which felt damn good.

She started playing with the ends of her braid again, fingers nervously plucking, pushing, and pulling at the strands. "I'm not sure. I sat down to do a little research on a paper and send an email. And then after that, I couldn't sleep." She paused. "It's late here, you know."

He smiled. "Yeah. I know."

"And then I saw the Skype button and I just—" She put her hair down and looked straight at him. "Promise you won't laugh?"

He crossed his heart with his good arm. "Promise."

Her nose scrunched up, as if still deciding whether to say it. But then she shook her head and said, "I just felt like maybe you might need to talk."

She had no clue how true that statement was. "I never mind a friendly face. Yours happens to be prettier than most."

She flushed, not just a faint blush of color across her cheeks, but a total flush that crept up her neck and straight past her cheeks into her hairline. "You say outrageous things on purpose, don't you?"

He'd called her pretty. On a scale of one to outrageous, that ranked pretty damn low, in his estimation. But she was clearly shy. "Just speaking the truth." He felt his eyes droop but fought to keep them open. "I might not be much of a conversation partner today, just so you know."

"You really should be sleeping, shouldn't you?" Concern and worry laced her voice. "I'll hang up now. You go on to bed."

"Can't sleep. Not quite yet. And I don't wanna take the meds they gave me. Knock me on my a—butt. Don't like 'em."

"Oh."

He gave her a lazy grin. "You could talk to me, though. I like the sound of your voice."

"You do?"

"Hmm. Yup. Tell me something."

"What do you want to know?"

For whatever reason, his video chats with Miss Veronica were becoming the highlight of his deployment. For damn sure, they were more entertaining than the last few first dates he'd been on. He wanted to know her inside and out. What made her tick, kept her motor running.

What revved her engine.

He shifted a little in his seat, fighting off an ill-timed—and surprising—erection.

"You look uncomfortable. Should you still be sitting up?"

"I'm good." That was the problem with nothing but your hand for company. Not nearly satisfying enough, and even the hint of something sexy had you harder than Kevlar. "Tell me something nobody else knows."

She nibbled on her bottom lip and glanced around her as if making sure nobody would overhear. Then she smiled a little, but this one seemed a little sad. "I didn't have many friends before I moved here."

That took him by surprise. "I find that hard to believe. Sweet thing like you, I'd think you were swimming in the deep end of the friend pool."

"Let's just say, I'm still learning how to doggy paddle." She grinned. "But Madison is the best. And Tim and Skye. Even Jeremy."

Jeremy. Something completely unwelcome and totally unexpected reared its ugly head deep in his gut. Something akin to jealousy. "Hanging out with Jeremy a lot, huh?"

She made a face and shook her head. "Mostly only with the group total. I think he didn't really want to accept me here at first. But he's getting friendlier."

Sounded like Jeremy. Slow to trust, cynical always. He relaxed a bit. "What do you girls do when you hang out?"

She lit up like a Christmas tree. "Oh, well, we go shopping. I never really realized how fun shopping was. And movies. I didn't know how much I was missing out on with movies. Madison is a total movie buff."

"Yeah. We usually watch all the new releases together when I'm there." He settled back farther in his chair. "Who were you emailing?"

"My aunt and uncle. Skye's parents." She grinned again. "I lived with them for a while before moving here."

Dwayne let her hop from one topic to the next, never slowing down. It was the most he'd ever heard her speak before, and he had a feeling she wasn't a real chatterbox on her own. So that she felt comfortable enough to keep talking with him was a little ego boost.

Slowly, his eyes started to close. He could still listen to her with shut eyes. His ears worked fine. And she didn't seem to mind. Miss Veronica kept on going like nothing was different.

And with her sweet voice in his mind, he slipped under and into the dreamless darkness that called to him.

———※———

Veronica watched as Dwayne slumped forward, settled, then started breathing more deeply. She watched his chest rise and fall in steady rhythm. She debated making a sound to wake him so she could encourage him to head to bed. But then the thought that she could startle him and have him fall off his chair made her rethink that plan. Though the angle didn't look entirely comfortable, she assumed if he started to get sore, he would wake up and shift over to his bed.

Maybe she should be insulted that her voice had put him to sleep. But she knew it wasn't boredom that slid him under, but a final sense of calmness. Of being able to relax enough for his brain to step back and give his body the chance to rest. Poor guy. Even while he joked and tried to look calm and in control, the signs of pain and discomfort had been written all over his face.

He was deep asleep, that much she knew. The deep rumbling snores couldn't be missed. But for some reason her finger hovered over the end call button rather than clicking it. She couldn't take her eyes off of him. And really, it was a safe, harmless way to investigate the male half of the species. Especially this one.

He was tall, that was easy to see, even from the computer screen. And his voice was something straight out of a movie, with his deep Southern drawl. She wondered where he'd grown up. What his life had been like before the Marines. What made him join the military in the first place. What he'd kiss like.

What he'd kiss like? She barely caught the laugh that rose up her throat by slapping a hand over her mouth. Watching his chest rise and fall for another few moments, she finally made herself end the call and close down the Skype program.

But while he intrigued her to no end, she knew he wasn't the one for her. Dating wasn't even a viable option right now. And when it was, it would be with a man who didn't intimidate her so much with his... well, his attractiveness, for starters. One who wouldn't completely blindside her with his charm, disarm her with his smile. One who wasn't completely out of her league in almost every respect.

She had to be reasonable, after all.

She shut the computer down, padded to her own room, and climbed in her own bed under the sheets she'd picked out herself. And after a quick round of prayers, she turned off the light and snuggled down, hugging a pillow to her chest.

But until the time came for her to be reasonable, Dwayne Robertson would make a lovely dream.

Madison rolled over and smacked her nose into a hard wall of warm muscle. She cracked one eye and found Jeremy looking right at her, looming over her, propped up on one elbow. The sheet covered his hips, barely. But the not-so-small bump under the fabric told her he was wide awake, in every way possible.

"Morning," she said.

He didn't answer.

She tried again. "Sleep well?"

He shook his head. "You hog the covers, you know."

"You hog the bed, so we're even." She was prepared to roll back the other way and grab another hour of sleep when he hooked one arm beneath her and tugged her to the center of the bed.

"I beg your pardon!" She slapped at him playfully when he pulled her shirt up and over her head. "This is not the wake-up call I ordered."

"You get what you get, and you'll like it." With zero finesse, he latched his mouth onto her breast and pulled deeply.

She moaned, arching into him. Gone was the playful, silly, laughing lovemaking from nights past. Something seemed to be driving him that wasn't humor-based. That wasn't built on fun, motivated on a good time. It was almost…

Desperate. That was the only word her mind could form when he came up for air shortly, moving to her other breast, his hand closing over the first, pulling and toying with her nipple.

"Jeremy. Slow down."

"Can't." He surged up, capturing her protesting mouth with his, sliding his tongue in, silencing all possible complaints or questions. Her hands automatically went to his hair, tunneling through for a good grip. His chest hair abraded her now-sensitive nipples, and she couldn't decide whether to rub against him or pull back from the sensation.

One knee nudged her thighs apart, settled there, pressing against her center. With every slight movement, he brushed against her and she felt a familiar twinge low in her belly. She pulled back from his mouth long enough to ask, "Are you trying to drive me crazy?"

"Is that what's happening?" he answered her question with one of his own. Damn, she hated when he did that. But his mouth was too busy to give a different answer, moving down her throat, down her sternum, over her ribs, down to the edge of the waistband of her shorts, tugging down harshly as he went.

Before she could even kick off the shorts from her left leg, he was back up, fitting himself to her and thrusting up. His face was a mask of someone she'd never met before. Impassive almost, if she didn't know better. Like her body could have belonged to anyone and it wouldn't have mattered. She cried out, not in pain but in a mixture of fullness and confusion. Where was Jeremy? Her Jeremy?

He slowed at her sound, then stopped. Breathing hard, completely still but for the in-and-out motion of his chest, she watched as some of the coolness left his eyes. His forehead came down to hers, sweaty and warm. And he pushed in again, slower this time, more controlled. More aware of her body, her reactions, her needs.

One hand reached between them, found her clit, and applied pressure and motion until she couldn't stop her own reaction. She moved with him, following his pattern until the point of no return came and went.

"Jeremy. Jer—I'm going to…"

She tightened around him, and when he leaned over and whispered, "Come," in her ear, she had no choice but to follow his command, muffling the worst of her scream into his shoulder as she felt his own release take him over.

———

He was a shit. A total piece of shit.

No, worse. What was worse than shit?

Jeremy Phillips. That's what.

He disengaged all limbs from Madison and pulled out, regretting the instant loss of warmth as he flopped onto his back.

"Mad, I'm sorry. I forgot…" He couldn't believe it. Never, not once in his adult life, had he ever forgotten protection. And with the one woman he wanted to protect the most, he fucked up.

Wasn't that just the way of it?

She turned her head and smiled lazily, hand coming up to smooth his hair back. "Condom? Yeah, I realized that about two seconds after you were in."

She knew and said nothing? "So we're good?"

"I'm on the pill, if you don't remember." When he looked at her funny, she laughed. "What did you think I was doing when I took a pill with breakfast all the times I've been over here? That wasn't a Flintstones vitamin, buddy."

"Oh. Okay." Suddenly he had a moment of stark disappointment, followed swiftly by horrified confusion. Disappointment? That he wouldn't get her pregnant? The girl he wasn't supposed to be seeing in the first place? Right. He could see how that convo would go with Tim.

So, uh, don't freak out but… your sister's knocked up. It's mine, but, really, no clue how that happened. Guess it jumped in there while we weren't looking.

Yeah. Better this way.

"That was the most amazing progression of facial expressions I've ever seen." Madison drew a finger from his forehead down his nose to tap his chin. "What's going on in there?"

"Nothing." He rolled over and sat on the edge of the bed, his back to her. Scrubbing one hand down his face, he stood and grabbed the closest pair of shorts available and stepped into them. Then he checked the clock. "It's really late. I was about to suggest breakfast, but lunch seems more appropriate."

He heard her sit up and tempted fate by turning around enough to see her. Her hair was a wreck, frizzy in places, flattened down in others. Her face was completely free of makeup, the way he really liked. And she clutched the sheets from his bed to her chest in some vague attempt at modesty.

All he wanted to do was rip his shorts back off, tear the sheet away, and start the day all over again, taking care with her this time. Doing it right. Not letting himself go like an animal.

"You don't have to be so upset, you know."

Her lips were moving, but the words weren't connecting in his brain.

She smiled. "I'm not upset. It's fine. This affair has two people in it, you know. I get what I want. You should get what you want and need too. You needed the release, you got it. There's no harm in that."

Ha. Right. "I'm not in the mood to leave the apartment. Do you want Chinese or pizza?"

Her brows knit together, but she didn't push further. "How about that sub place that delivers?"

"Done." Anything to keep from having the deep, meaningful conversation she was clearly looking to have. "You okay with splitting a sub with me?"

"Sounds good." She gingerly stepped out of bed, letting the sheet fall as she shivered when her bare feet hit the tile. "You could get a freaking rug or something for in here, Phillips."

"Don't go all Martha Stewart on me," he warned as he headed for his computer to look up the number and the online menu.

Chapter 18

"I'M TAKING A SHOWER," MADISON CALLED OUT AFTER Jeremy as he scrolled through the bookmarked sites of places to eat in town.

"Fine, fine." He found the number, called in an order, and paid by credit card over the phone. The sound of running water from the bathroom filled the small apartment. He grabbed two bottles of water and a couple of paper towels to double as napkins and set them on the poor excuse for a coffee table in preparation for their lunch's arrival.

And realized how homey and easy the whole thing was. Rolling out of bed on a lazy Sunday afternoon with nothing to do and nowhere to go... at least for now. Madison had work later that night. Ordering lunch in because neither wants to leave the house. Sharing a sandwich. Madison in his shower.

Something he could get used to. Way too easily.

Danger signs flashed in his mind just as the bathroom door opened. He heard some rustling in the bedroom area, then Madison appeared wearing a button-down shirt of his and, well, he wasn't quite sure if anything else was under it, since the shirt hung down to basically her knees.

She followed his gaze down the front of her body and back up, an amused grin on her face. "Sorry, I just wasn't really ready to put my own stuff back on right now. Do you mind?" She lifted one hand to run her fingers through damp hair, pressing the shirt tighter against her breasts. The outline of one puckered nipple showed clear through the light fabric. The hem rose up, tempting him to look and see if she had on shorts beneath, but he couldn't tell.

"What's on under there?" he asked hoarsely.

"Do you really want to know?" Her eyes twinkled with impish humor.

No. "Yes."

She sashayed a few steps forward, brushing by him with barely a touch, a whisper of feminine scent following in her wake. "That's a secret. Maybe you can find out later. Mind if I check my email really fast while we wait?"

He cleared his throat. "No, not at all." To get rid of the horrible, immature squeak his throat was threatening to make, he opened one of the bottles of water and chugged until he couldn't breathe, tanking down over half the bottle before he stopped. Clearing his throat again, he felt a little better.

"You coming down with something?" Madison asked over the click of keys. "Need me to take a look?"

"No. I'm good. Allergies or something," he lied, sinking down to the couch. He examined his living room one more time and saw, really saw it through Madison's eyes. Or, at least, what he assumed would be her eyes.

Sagging couch that the Goodwill wouldn't take as a donation. Nothing matching. The main focus of the room was his baby, the forty-two inch plasma flat-screen TV. The only piece of furniture worth a damn was the TV stand, and that's only because he refused to have his flat-screen resting on anything that might break and let it fall. But even it didn't match.

It looked like he didn't give a damn. And he hadn't, at least up to now. The rest of his life wasn't how he wanted it, so why should his apartment be any different? But why was it bothering him so much?

He caught another look at Madison from the corner of his eye and watched her cross one leg over the other, her dainty bare foot swinging to some unheard rhythm in her mind.

That's why. When it was just him, it didn't matter. When the guys came over—which wasn't often, because he didn't have much room—they understood. It was just a guy's place to crash. But seeing Madison among the furnishings that screamed *I don't give a shit* made him feel… incomplete somehow. Not that he had to rush out and Martha Stewart the place, like he'd said. But he was almost thirty-three years old. Was he not a little too old to be doing the college dorm look? The *whatever's free and easy to carry* style of the newly graduated, living on a shoestring budget crowd?

Yes. He was. And it didn't matter that Madison wouldn't be around to see the transformation. He was determined to set some shit straight. He deserved better. Nobody else would believe he deserved better if he didn't think so himself.

Holy shit. He deserved better. Why did that sound so foreign to him?

"Why haven't you signed these yet?"

He shook off the mental wanderings and squinted at the paper Madison held up. Then felt his blood turn cold.

His re-up papers.

Stalking over, he grabbed the paper from her hand, sliding the folder from her other hand and setting them back on top of his computer tower. "Leave those alone."

She stared at him, like trying to put together a puzzle piece. "I mean, I don't get why you haven't signed them yet. It's not that hard, right? You just put your name on the dotted line. The CO signed them more than a week ago, from the date under his signature."

"Leave it alone, Madison."

"Isn't that what you want to do? Stay in for the twenty?"

What you want to do... He spun on his heel and headed back for the water he'd abandoned. Suddenly the closed-off feeling in his throat was back.

"That's why you said we wouldn't work out long-term. Isn't it? Navy and Marine Corps, not matching up, hard to raise a family." She gave a hollow laugh. "Not taking into account the whole best friend's sister part, since I still think you're overexaggerating how Tim would react."

He uncapped the water, forcing his hand to relax before he crushed the plastic. "Stop."

She sat back, chair squeaking in protest. "I have to say, while I don't like it, your theory on why we wouldn't work out long-term? I understand it. I think if two people cared, they could make it work. But I do understand. The thing that gets me, though, is this was your choice. It was one of the big factors in why you were keeping me at a distance. Your career, the biggest thing in your life. And yet you still haven't signed the papers. It's not like there's any ceremony that goes along with it. You just sign, turn them back in. I've never even seen someone take them home before."

Tilting her head, she studied him. "You do want to stay in, don't you?"

"Madison." Her name was a plea to drop it. Not that she listened.

"Because if you don't, then I think you have a really good shot at making it as a writer."

"Stop!" He threw the now-empty plastic bottle against the wall next to the front door, startling even himself with the sharpness of his voice. "Just leave it the fuck alone." Hearing her voice the one dream he'd been secretly harboring for years, the one thing he'd never told anyone. Ever. The one thing he knew would never in a million years happen. It hurt. Hurt more than he realized it could, to hear someone else say it out loud. As if she'd opened up some long-forgotten, well-hidden old wound just to pour some acid in there and stitch him back up again.

Madison's wide eyes narrowed. In sympathy. No, in pity, dammit, which was worse. "Are you scared you couldn't make it work?"

"No. Because there's nothing to work. I'm a Marine. My father was a Marine. If I have kids, I'm sure the legacy will pass down from there." Marines, Marines everywhere.

"Whose dream is that?" she asked softly. "Is that what you'd really want? Consigning your kids to the same lack of choice that you had?"

"You don't know what the hell you're talking about."

"Do you think—"

"I'm taking a shower. If the delivery guy comes, just sign my name on the receipt. The tip is already included." Before she could say another word, he stormed into the bathroom—the one place in the apartment with a door that locked—and shut it, leaning his back against the scarred wood.

Goddamnit. She was going to leave, and he couldn't blame her. Who the fuck would want to stay after he all but let her have it for asking questions? Questions that ripped at his basic desires, made him think about things he had no right to dream about or feel. Dreams that, after he signed those papers Monday morning, would be all but dead.

So now he'd lost a little piece of his heart in two huge ways.

Madison stared sightlessly at the bathroom door, wanting to be aware if he came back out again. But no noise could be heard from the tiny room. No water running, no shower curtain being moved. Not even the sound of him kicking something. Nothing. It was almost frightening how still he had to be to achieve that silence.

Following his blowup, the eerie silence was deafening. Not to mention the blowup itself had been… unexpected. But at the same time, almost refreshing. Jeremy had always been the most calm of the three guys. The most placid, feathers rarely ruffled. She'd always looked at Jeremy through the theory of still waters running deep. But Madison had always sensed he needed to release something. That he held back for who knew what reason.

She swiveled back around and stared once more at the papers, now a little crinkled, sitting on the computer tower. She hadn't meant to pry, but they'd been right there. And she wasn't about to let that go unanswered. Those papers were so simple. Just a signature committing to another three years. No pomp or circumstance involved. People walked into the office, signed, and walked back out again.

So why was he taking so long to sign them if this was what he really wanted?

She had a distinct feeling the answer revolved around his father, this legacy he mentioned, rather than any actual desire to serve more than what he'd already put in.

The bathroom door opened and he stepped out but didn't glance her way, heading instead for the bedroom area. She started to head that direction, but a knock at the front door had her detouring.

"Can you grab that?" he asked.

"Yeah. I've got it." She snagged a pen from the desk to sign the receipt, then opened the door. "Hey, thanks for—oh, shit."

Tim's back was turned to the door, as if he was already heading down the steps. He turned slowly at the sound of her voice, eyes raking over her from head to toe.

In moments of high stress, Madison knew from working in the ER, the brain had the most amazing ability to move at warp speed but allow you to process the scene as if it were moving in slow motion. You could have several minutes' worth of thoughts in only a nanosecond worth of time.

Okay. This was not a disaster. It was already past noon. She was friends with Jeremy. She could have just stopped by to hang out and watch a movie and eat some lunch. No big deal.

But when Tim's face turned a rather unflattering shade of purple, she knew playing it off as a simple friendly visit was a no-go. The time of day might not have been a dead giveaway. But her appearance, that was another story. Her hair, still damp from the shower she'd taken, hung around her shoulders, already a little wavy as it air-dried. Her breasts, no bra in sight, were pressed against the fabric of Jeremy's button-down shirt, a shirt that was long enough to cover the clean pair of boxer shorts she'd tossed on, and no shoes, making her look completely naked under the shirt.

She crossed her arms over her chest—partly in annoyance and partly to hide her breasts. "What are you doing here?" she asked, accusation clear in her tone.

"What am I doing—what the fuck are you doing here?"

She gave it one last-ditch effort. "What, I'm not allowed to hang out with Jeremy?"

Tim stomped to the door, standing over her by a good eight inches. Damn, she wished she was wearing heels right about now. "Squirt, you're not dressed for a friendly game of chess and a movie, are you?"

"Don't call me that." She pushed at his chest. "And stop acting like this. It's none of your business why I'm here."

"I'm your brother. It's always my business."

"God, what is this? 1812? Jesus, Tim. Back off. My personal life is none of your—"

"You." Tim uttered the single syllable with such quiet, intense menace she took a quick step back in automatic response. Never before had she feared her brother, even when they were children and fought like cats and dogs. The tone of his voice, though, was something she'd never heard before. And she didn't like it.

But he wasn't looking at her. No. His eyes were focused over her right shoulder.

She turned to see Jeremy standing there, with khaki cargo shorts on but hands frozen on the third button of his own button-down shirt, the rest of the fabric open to reveal his chest.

Oh, boy.

Before she could react, Tim sidestepped her and was in the apartment. One fist clenched at his side, he pointed a shaking finger at Jeremy. "I'm seeing things. Right? She's not seriously here after spending the night. Is she?"

The question seemed to unlock Jeremy, and he finished the third button, disregarding the rest. "None of your business, O'Shay."

"Which O'Shay? Your best friend? Or the girl you're fucking?"

"Hey!" Madison shoved at his arm, but he didn't budge. "Go home."

"Watch yourself, Tim." Jeremy's voice dropped, taking on the same lethal edge that Tim's had. "Say whatever the fuck you want about me. Leave her out of it."

"Like you did?" Tim ran a hand over his hair. "My sister, dude. What the hell?"

"We didn't exactly plan—"

Jeremy couldn't finish the statement before Tim's fist plowed straight into his jaw and knocked Jeremy to the ground. Taken off guard, he sat stunned for a moment on the floor, then stood slowly. Tim shook his right hand out, and Madison could already see the reddened skin of her brother's hand, knew his knuckles had to be killing him. A jaw punch, bone meeting bone, was never a pleasant thing to feel… on either side.

"Oh my God, and it's come to this." Madison, accepting the fact there was nothing she could do to stop the insane, and completely moronic, male ritual of beating the shit out of each other, sat on the far end of the couch, arms still crossed over her chest, and mentally started triaging the possible injuries two very stupid males in a fistfight could develop.

"Broken hand," she murmured to herself. "Dislocated elbow. Bloody nose."

Jeremy stood slowly, carefully working his jaw back and forth. "You get one. And I deserved it. But next time I punch back."

"Broken jaw, black eye, cracked ribs…"

"Oh, now you're a big tough guy. What, so tough you couldn't tell me to my face you were sleeping with my little sister?"

"Younger," Jeremy said quietly.

"What?"

"Eyebrow gash, split lip, chipped teeth…"

"Madison," Jeremy said softly. "She's younger. Not little. In case you blinked and missed it, your sister's twenty-six years old. She knows her own fucking mind. God knows I've tried to change it for her more than once," he muttered at the end.

"Oh, a concussion!" Madison was almost relieved at the thought. At least that would end the damn thing, if one of them was unconscious.

"Knock it off, squirt!" Tim yelled at her.

"Don't yell at her," Jeremy shot back through clenched teeth. Though whether it was anger or pain from the punch that had him clenching, she wasn't sure.

Tim ignored that. "There I was, talking about some

guy I thought my sister was sneaking around with, venting to my supposed best friend, looking for an outsider's perspective. Meanwhile, you're the fucking guy. And you're not outside at all. You're right in the thick of things. Damn, dude."

"Need I remind you, when you brought all that shit up, you were holding a loaded weapon? I didn't feel it was the best time to break out the heart-to-heart confessions."

"I'm perfectly capable of being rational," her brother said through clenched teeth of his own. Which Madison knew had to be from anger, since *he* hadn't been punched in the jaw. Yet.

"I beg your pardon?" Madison asked from her perch on the couch. "What about this scenario screams rational to you?"

"You. Be quiet." Tim whirled to face her and shot her a look that likely had his junior Marines pissing in their pants. To her? That face stopped intimidating her when she was seven.

"Right. Forgot my lines. I'll just sit here and swoon at the first sight of blood. Oh *fiddle dee dee*." Madison punctuated the fake Southern accent with a one-fingered salute special for her brother.

Despite his best efforts, Jeremy's face split into a wide grin, then winced at the pain. "She's a total smart-ass, isn't she?"

"Always has been," her brother agreed. He glanced sideways at Jeremy. "You seriously put up with her? Voluntarily?"

"I'm still here," Madison sang out.

"Quiet," they both barked back in unison.

She opened her mouth on autopilot, ready to sass

them right back. She could give as well as receive. But then she snapped it shut again. If they were busy talking trash about her, then they weren't killing each other. While not her favorite option in the world, it did save them all a trip to the ER. She chose the path of least resistance and let them bond over mocking insults.

Jeremy walked to the fridge, reached in the freezer, and pulled out a frozen bag of veggies—one of those deals you could microwave right in the bag—and gingerly placed it over the bottom of his jaw.

Tim smirked. "Pussy."

"I'd rather avoid the swelling, to be honest. It didn't hurt. You punch like a girl."

"That's not what your ass said when it hit the floor."

Lord, but men had the most bizarre way of showing affection. Madison realized they weren't going to kill each other after all and took the opportunity to slip past Tim's back and into the bedroom area. This would be so much easier to face if she were properly dressed, including underwear.

"I saw that, squirt."

She froze, one hand gripping her shirt from the floor. Shit.

"We're not done."

"Bite me." She did some fancy maneuvering to pull her bra on under the oversized man's shirt, then her own shirt replaced Jeremy's. A quick change for her bottoms and she was at least decently attired for the inevitable awkward moment.

Peeking out, she couldn't see either Tim or Jeremy. Nor could she hear them. She tiptoed around the corner and gasped in surprise when she saw them sitting on the couch together, both gripping bottles of beer, staring at the blank flat-screen.

They looked zoned out, completely unaware of her presence anymore. Or even each other.

Men. Were. So. Bizarre.

"Should you really be drinking? It's like eleven in the morning."

Silence.

"Is everyone all right in here? Are my stellar skills as a nurse required?"

The joke didn't crack the tense air.

She took a step forward, intent on checking Jeremy's jaw. Not that she didn't think he could handle his own, but a possible broken jaw wasn't something to mess around with. Reaching out, her hand was almost to his chin when he grabbed her wrist.

"Go home, Madison."

"Just let me look at—"

"Go. Home." When she raised a brow at the condescending tone, he added a terse, "Please."

Looking between Jeremy and Tim, she shook her head and stepped back. "You know, men are completely illogical. Which is the nicest word I can come up with for what you two are acting like right now." When neither responded to her insult, she tossed her hands in the air. "Fine. I know when I'm not wanted."

"That's not it," Jeremy said quietly, enough to soften the blow of being removed from the whole situation like a child being kicked out of the room when Mommy and Daddy were arguing.

She huffed. "I'm going, I'm going." Slipping on her shoes, she grabbed her bag and slung it over her shoulder. With a quick glance to Tim, she ordered, "Do not kill him. I don't have that much money for bail, and Mom will just murder you afterward anyway." Then she walked out and shut the door behind her, not at all sure she should have left.

———

The clock over his desk ticked the time, each second louder than the last. One minute passed in silence. Then two. Seven minutes later, neither man had spoken and Jeremy started to wonder if he could completely escape the entire scenario without saying a word.

"She's my sister."

Damn. There went that idea. He took a swig of beer. "Yeah. I know."

"I've always protected her. Or, okay." Tim stopped to smile ruefully. "When I wasn't the one giving her shit like a big brother should, I was protecting her."

It sounded so easy, so simple, the love and affection of one sibling to another. Jeremy had nothing to base that on, so he just nodded.

"It's hard going from big brother, ultimate protector, and defender of her playground experience to…" He shrugged. "I don't even know. Just a friend, I guess."

"Still her brother," Jeremy said, taking another sip. The drink was growing warmer by the minute between his hands. The liquid rolled and sloshed in his empty stomach, making him regret the choice of beer over water. But his hands needed something to do. "She still wants you to be her brother. She loves you like crazy."

"I just need to dial back. Right. I'm starting to figure

that out," Tim said, self-deprecation painting every word. He sighed. "I just never want her to feel hurt. It's the same way I feel with Skye. Some asshole hurts my wife? I'd break him."

"Rightly so."

"Are you going to be that asshole with Madison? The guy who hurts her?" Tim asked. The *please don't be* was silent. But understood.

Jeremy thought long and hard about it. It would be easy to say no. That he'd warned her up front it was nothing, that the simple affair had zero strings attached. That he tried to avoid getting involved to begin with. That it was Madison who approached him, not the other way around. But was that all the truth? Could he not have tried harder to push her away? Couldn't he have done more, been more stern with his decision not to become involved?

Yeah. He could have. So in the end, he couldn't blame Mad, much as he'd love to not have any focused on himself. They both did a bang-up job fucking this one up.

Finally, he answered quietly, "I don't want to be."

Tim thought about that for a moment, then nodded. "I believe that. Now. How are you going to fix this?"

"There's nothing to fix. We're friends. We knew that walking in, we'll still know it walking out. The end." And what a way to go. Nothing said *this has been fun, but now it's over* quite like having the woman's brother knock him on his ass.

"So that's it? You were just in it for the easy goods?"

He snorted. "Please. You know your sister. Is there anything easy about that one?"

Tim tilted his head in acknowledgement, tapping his bottle against Jeremy's in agreement. "I've got twenty-six years of experience that says no. If there's a way to complicate a situation, Madison will find it and excel."

He let his head fall back, then stared at the popcorn ceiling. "I fucked up."

"Yup."

"This is a complete mess."

"Sure is."

"I could not have handled this worse."

"No way."

"Stop agreeing with me."

"Okay." Tim tipped the bottle, took a drink, and made a face, as if just now registering the taste. He rotated the bottle around, trying to read the label. "This tastes like piss. What the hell kind of beer is this, anyway?"

"Cheap." Jeremy grabbed both bottles and walked to the sink to dump them down. "Let's head out for a real drink."

"At what, eleven in the morning? On a Sunday?"

"Hell, why not? Aw, shit," he said, remembering his delivery. He checked the clock once more. "I had a sub being delivered... but that was supposed to be here like half an hour ago."

"Check your phone. Maybe they called."

Jeremy slid his phone out of his cargo shorts pocket and realized it was still on silent. He'd turned the ringer off the night before, not wanting anything to interrupt his time with Madison. "No voice mail. But a text."

He read the message and smiled, in spite of himself.

"What?" Tim asked.

"Madison ran into the delivery guy on her way to her car. She signed for it and took off." He looked up and grinned at Tim. "Your sister stole my lunch."

Chapter 19

"Okay. So let me get this straight. You're in the middle of a serious discussion with Jeremy. You're wearing his shirt and nothing else—"

"Boxers," Madison corrected Matthew. "I had on boxers under the shirt."

"You're really ruining the dramatic effect I'm trying to build here." Matthew sighed. "But it's not like anyone could see them though. Am I right?" When she nodded, he went on. "You answer the door, hair still wet from the shower, and it's your brother. Whom you've been keeping this torrid affair a secret from this entire time. He storms in, figures out what's going on, and defends your honor with a sucker punch to lover boy's jaw?"

Madison sprawled out on the couch in the break room, arranging her scrub top so it covered her stomach. "That about sums it up."

Matthew was silent for a moment. She finally dared to crack one eye open and check. And found him shaking his head as if in disbelief. "What?"

He sighed morosely. "I always miss the good stuff. Why didn't Jeremy defend your honor with a punch to my jaw?" He stood and found his reflection in the metal paper towel dispenser by the sink, rubbing his chin thoughtfully. "I might look pretty badass with a black eye, don't you think?"

"Shut up."

"What? It's like a telenovela! Right there in his living room. All that's missing is someone shouting 'Ay, caramba!' That's good gravy. You can't make this stuff up."

"I wish I was." She stared at the pockmarked ceiling tiles. "I'm supposed to be napping, you know. I took that extra shift to cover for Liz, thanks to her kid being sick. And you're distracting me."

"Oh please. Like you weren't dying to blab the whole story the minute you walked in. You all but bounced over to me."

"I did not bounce." Maybe just a little.

"Fine, then you pounced. Tigger-style."

"Does that really get the guys hot? You quoting Winnie the Pooh at them?"

Matthew flipped her off then pulled out his wallet and shuffled through until he found a dollar to feed into the soda machine, making a selection and pressing the button. After the plastic bottle rattled to the bottom, he cracked the top and took a sip. "Ah, better. Now, where was I? Oh. Right. So where does this leave you and lover boy?"

"For the seven hundred and forty-ninth time, stop calling him that. And I don't know. He's so intent on fulfilling his dad's bizarre legacy dream that he's not even remotely close to giving us a shot."

Matthew used one long-fingered hand to spin the cap on the scarred tabletop in the break room. "You can understand the legacy thing though, right? I mean, you're what, O'Shay generation number three in the military?"

"Four," she murmured. "And yes, I do get that. But the thing is... if this wasn't what Tim or I wanted, our parents would have been fine with it. There might have been some good-natured teasing, but at the end of the day if we were happy, that's what would have mattered most. It just so happened that both of our dreams coincided with our family's tradition of serving."

"Can you say the same for Jeremy's parents?"

"Parent. Just his father, from what I understand. I guess his mom was just never in the picture. He's never talked about her. And I don't know." She bit her lip. "But he's an adult. His dad lives on the other side of the country. He's been basically on his own since he left for college."

Matthew sighed. "Sometimes even independent adults struggle with how to break news of their lives to their parents. Remember when I said it took me three years to get up the nerve to come out to my parents?"

Madison gave him a side look. "Totally different."

"How?"

Good question.

Matthew took her silence as an invitation to continue. "My parents love me. My orientation was never brought up before. I had no reason to think they'd disown me. Not to mention, I'm an adult, completely independent from them both financially and emotionally, and they live three states away, thank the good Lord."

Madison snorted.

"Well, hey. I love my folks. But we all do better with a little distance. There was nothing standing in my way from telling them the truth and letting the chips fall where they may. But I held back."

"Because it was scary," she guessed.

"She gets it in one." Matthew rolled the soda between

his palms, little droplets of condensation flying from the bottle to the cheap laminate tabletop. "You never really know how a parent will react. And deep down inside, I think there will always be this little voice that encourages us to please our parents, no matter how old we are. You and I have it lucky. Our parents are pleased if we're happy, which makes being selfish and just doing whatever we want that much easier."

She smiled, mostly because she knew he wanted her to. But her brain was working a hundred miles a minute.

"I don't know the relationship he has with his dad. It sounds like you might not really know, either. Maybe that's something to investigate." He stood, capped the soda, and set it down on the floor by the couch where she could reach it. Leaning down, he brushed a kiss over her forehead. "Get some sleep. I'll tell the desk nurse to wake you in thirty."

"Thanks. Love you."

"Love you too, Mad."

Jeremy opened his work email early Monday morning, glad to be back in the swing of things. In his office, nobody could bother him about Madison, or writing, or his future. Nobody would tell him to make hard decisions… or at least not personal ones. And he could simply breathe and do his job without feeling the pressure breathing down his neck.

He quickly skimmed through two reports, one schedule update, and then hovered his mouse over an email from his father. The same father he hadn't called last week, like normal.

Time to bite the bullet. There goes my peaceful morning.

He clicked the email header, titled simply "My Son," and read quickly, hoping to treat it like ripping off a bandage.

Ten minutes later, he was on his third read-through when a knock came at the door. He held up a finger and finished the paragraph. Though why he couldn't stop going through the words time and time again, he wasn't sure. They weren't changing. Finally, he tore his eyes away to see Tim lounging in his doorway. "'Sup?"

Tim gave him an assessing once-over. "Little bruised, but not bad."

"Probably because you only grazed me. Your aim's off." Jeremy pushed back from the desk a little ways so he could prop his knee against the edge, leaning back in his chair. "That all you came for?"

"I promised Madison I'd make sure you weren't officially broken," he admitted before sitting down. "For some reason, she was worried I'd damaged your pretty face."

And two for two. Both subjects he would rather have avoided—Madison and his father—in a ten-minute span. Lucky day. "I'm fine." He worked his jaw a little, as if to prove to himself how fine he was. With a wince, he rubbed at the soreness below his ear. "Okay, a little tender. So I won't eat steak tonight. I'm good to go."

"Glad. You could use a refresher course in hand-to-hand combat, dude. I'm pretty sure I telegraphed that punch and you didn't even try to deflect or dodge."

"No. I didn't." He said it simply, looking his best friend in the eye. A moment later, Tim nodded.

"So that's the way of it. Figures."

"All you're doing is playing nursemaid then?"

Tim shrugged. "Blackwater needed to do some work in the system and his computer locked up so he's using mine. I made myself scarce. Not like I can do much without the system myself anyway right now."

Jeremy shuddered. "When's he outta here?"

"Few months. Should get word of the new CO sometime soon." Tim clapped hands over his knees and stood. "Guess I'll go wander around and pretend like I'm busy."

"Take some guys out for a combat lesson," Jeremy suggested. "Your right hook could use some work."

Tim flipped him off as he disappeared down the hallway.

Like a glutton for punishment, Jeremy waited to hear the bootsteps disappear and then opened his email back up to scan his father's message once more.

Though receiving an email wasn't at all shocking—his dad had a very firm grip on modern technology—it wasn't often that he used it to get in touch with his son. Seeing his father's words in print were almost more harsh than hearing them out loud.

Key phrases like "disappointed" and "concerned for you" jumped out at him. "Not what I expected from you," stung much more in black and white than he would have thought. Though the gem was "Thought you were my son," was the doozy of the day.

"Jesus, Dad," he murmured as he stared at the screen. "Twist the knife a little harder, why doncha?"

"What was that, Marine?"

The CO's unexpected voice had him jumping off the seat faster than a scalded cat. "Sir. Sorry, just… thinking. Out loud. To myself, I mean." He rubbed the back of his neck and wondered how many more times he would get to feel like a jackass today.

Quality over quantity.

"Hmm." Blackwater stared at the desk again, and Jeremy once more had that feeling that he wanted to gather everything up and hide it away from the man's sight. "Did you bring the re-up papers with you?"

Shit. "No, sir. I'm sorry, they're at home."

"Signed?" he asked, brow raised.

"No, sir. Not yet."

Blackwater shook his head. "It's not complicated. You sign your name twenty times a day on different forms. This is what you want. So simply sign them and bring them back. I'm not sure why I let you take them with you to begin with."

Because Jeremy had timed it perfectly to catch him when he knew they'd be interrupted. "Yes, sir. Of course. I apologize."

Blackwater nodded. "Well, good. Son, the Marine Corps needs men like you. Men I've trained to do their job to the utmost of their ability." As if bored with the conversation, he simply turned on his heel and left without a good-bye.

Men he trained. *Whiskey. Tango. Foxtrot.* Blackwater was a desk jockey, nothing more. He'd contributed less than lint to the entire battalion the entire time they'd been there. Jeremy could only hope the next man—or woman—they brought in would be more effective. More of a leader. More of someone they would respect enough to follow behind.

That man certainly wasn't Blackwater. Not that Jeremy was about to say that to anyone's face. Hell no. He might not enjoy his time in the Corps as much as the average Marine. But he still knew self-preservation when it bit him on the ass, and talking back to a superior officer— even an asshole one—was sort of frowned upon.

Jeremy sat once more, debating how to answer the email to his father. It'd been sent over the weekend, so at least two days ago. But he didn't have access to his email outside of work. Which his father knew. Odd that he didn't send it to his personal email, which he would have seen almost immediately.

Or was it fate? That big F-word that Skye always used. If he'd seen this email Saturday morning, would he still have been with Madison over the weekend?

And more importantly, did he deserve the email that was sent to him? Was he seriously a disappointment because he was taking his time to make life decisions? Because he wasn't sure what he wanted?

That much was a lie, anyway. He knew what he wanted… to write. But it was impractical. So he did what he should. His duty to his father. The man who stuck by him when he had every reason in the world to take off and leave him behind.

To make his father proud. Fuck. He scrubbed a hand over his face. What was he, seven?

None of it mattered anyway. He had the papers at home; all he had to do was sign them and he was done with it.

—⁓—

Madison approached Jeremy's apartment with a sense of dread. But she had to at least make sure he was okay, despite Tim's text that his jaw was fine and not at all injured like she'd worried. And to leave it alone and stop being a nurse.

Pardon her for caring.

Of course, Tim had also ended up sending her a text telling her he loved her and supported her in whatever she needed. So it was a little difficult to stay truly upset at the guy. No matter how hard she tried.

Now it was Jeremy's turn. He needed her support, and if it killed her, she would give it.

It just might. It really just might.

She knocked and waited. He didn't come to the door, so she knocked louder. His bike and truck were both in the parking lot. Of course, he could be taking a nap, but in that sham of an apartment, there was no way he couldn't hear—

The door creaked open, startling her. She took a step back and smiled. "Hey."

"Hi." He opened the door wide and swept open an arm in greeting. No hint to his mood at all. Damn the man and his ability to look completely and totally impassive.

She took a step in, then decided otherwise. "I have work in an hour. But I really don't wanna be inside any longer. I'll have twelve hours of indoors soon enough."

He was silent, then nodded. "I'll grab my keys. Meet me at the park."

She didn't have to ask which park. His. Or, as she'd started to think of it… theirs. She hopped down the stairs and into her car before he even came back outside. The extra ten minutes would help steady her. As she drove, she kept shaking out one hand, then the other. They were sticking to the steering wheel, palms slick with sweat she couldn't explain on the weather.

Nerves, moron. They're nerves.

She pulled in, a little surprised to see one other car parked in the lot. But after a quick glance, it appeared as though the dad with two kids were using the badly neglected soccer field to run around, avoiding the playground equipment completely. She surveyed, then decided to climb up the metal jungle gym a few levels and sit, letting her feet swing between two of the rails. The night air was getting cooler, and grateful she'd thought ahead, she zipped up the hoodie she'd tossed on over her scrub top. She heard Jeremy's motorcycle pull in and the engine cut off. Heard his boots crunch over the grass that always seemed to be three weeks overdue for a mowing. Felt the metal of the playground equipment vibrate under her butt just a little with his heavy steps as he climbed up to sit with her.

And they were silent. Together. As if in complete agreement that no words were necessary.

Finally, Madison's fidgety need for conversation overtook her. "Someone's finally using this place. Other than us, I mean." She pointed toward the trio on the soccer field.

"Yeah. Good for them."

Daring to glance Jeremy's way, she wished she hadn't. In his jeans, boots, and black leather jacket, sunglasses pushed up over his hair, smelling him so close by, feeling his heat, he was devastating to her senses.

She cleared her throat. "I've been thinking a lot about this whole thing."

He propped his elbows up on the lowest rung in front and waited, apparently content to be a spectator in the conversation rather than a participant.

So he wouldn't make it easy on her. Well, that was fine. "Tim's not as pissed as you thought he would be, is he?"

Jeremy grinned at that, then gave her a mock grimace and rubbed at his jaw. "I don't know. I think I'm lucky I've still got a full set of molars."

She nudged him with her shoulder. "Don't be a drama llama. He wasn't upset with you at work today, was he?"

"No. We had a beer yesterday, talked it out. I mean, he's not crazy about the secrets and sneaking and shit."

"Told you."

"But," he went on, ignoring her, "I think he's okay. Or, rather, he's pretending he knows nothing about it. Blind, deaf, and dumb." He shook his head, as if the thought that Tim could come to accept their dating was so unbelievable to him he struggled to wrap his mind around it.

"He's got a lot of practice with the dumb part," she said, mostly out of sibling-induced habit. As his sister, even without him there, it was her duty to give him some shit. But they both laughed. "So that's one hurdle down."

"Hurdle," he murmured. Not really a question, but she treated it as such.

"The list you gave me. Why things wouldn't work out."

One of the girls from the field shrieked when her father picked her up from behind and spun her in a circle. Jeremy's eyes tracked over to them and she watched as, finally, he let his guard down and showed some emotion. But her throat closed, and she wished she hadn't seen the stark longing in his eyes at the scene.

She cleared her throat a little and blinked furiously

before tears could even begin to form. "The thing is, I know you said you couldn't get involved with someone in the military. And I didn't really understand that part."

He watched her, eyes staring into hers. "My dad's a retired Marine. You know that much. But I don't really talk about my mom."

"I just thought she wasn't really in your life much."

"She's not. She died when I was really young."

"Oh, Jeremy. I'm sorry." Her heart broke for the little boy he'd been, not having the maternal comfort and love that she'd been so blessed to be brought up by. She reached out to put her hand on his arm, then pulled back, not sure what he needed. But he smiled a sad little smile and patted her knee.

"It was a long time ago. I can't even remember when it happened. I'm over it."

No, you're not. Oh, even a blind man could see he wasn't even remotely over it. And why should he be? Even if her mom died tomorrow—which she wouldn't, Madison thought fiercely—Madison would have had almost twenty-seven good years with her. Learned from her. Been guided by her. To lose all those opportunities for love and laughter and learning was a huge blow. One he might not even know he missed.

"So it was just me and Dad. He never remarried. But even though he was a single parent, he also didn't get out of the Corps. The moving part wasn't my favorite thing ever, but I survived it. Living on base, not a big deal. But when he was gone…" Jeremy shrugged. "He was all I had. The other kids, with their stay-at-home moms, or even moms that worked, it was like their world barely hit a blip. Sure, their dads were gone. But their moms were still there. Or vice versa. Mom was gone, but Dad was still home. There was a constant. That didn't change."

"What happened with you while your dad was gone?"

"I would move. Again. Go stay with my grandma. She was nice. But older. And it was hard with the constant coming and going. I was never in her life all the time, so she wasn't used to me. And I wasn't used to her."

Madison nodded. It wasn't something she could say she understood. How could she? Her mother had been the family's rock during deployments and long separations. They all leaned on her, even her father, when he was gone.

"So that sucked." He laughed harshly. "Understatement, I guess. But with all the times he was gone, I somehow just kept thinking, if he was proud of me, would he leave as often? The older I got, the more I realized it wasn't as if he was choosing to go. But the idea stuck. The habit of making him proud, of doing what I could to make him want to stick? Never went away."

"I know all about trying to make your parents proud." She rubbed his back in soothing circles, but he barely even moved. His body was still as stone.

"The fact is, if you have two military members who are parents, and they both get picked to deploy at the same time, then what? Or if they're put in different bases? They can't always guarantee you'd be stationed together. Additional separations. It's just not for me." He shook his head. "I couldn't willingly do that to a kid. It's not like I have to have some Suzy Homemaker or anything. But the dual military? It's like asking for something to go wrong. Tempting fate. I just… I can't."

"I can understand that much." She hated to say it, because it just gave him more ammo to use in keeping them apart. But it was the truth. She did see his point.

"So that's just something I've known. It's not so much that I don't want someone who works. That's her choice. But, you know…" His lip quirked, indicating he didn't feel it was necessary to finish.

She smiled sadly. "So that makes sense. And since I'm not getting out anytime soon…" No, that wasn't really accurate to say. It made it sound like she would leave when her current commitment was up. "I mean, this is it for me. I thought this would just pay for college, give me a few years' experience, give me something to sort of laugh at my dad with. And then I'd be done and find a nice job in the civilian world. Be a typical nurse who doesn't have to wear her dress uniform to meetings with her boss and take physical fitness tests twice a year. But I love it. I don't want out. I want to keep going in the Navy."

"And I want you to." One large hand covered her knee and squeezed affectionately. "You should stay in if you love it. So many people don't end up finding a career they love."

She nodded and tried to blink back tears once more, only this time she knew she'd fail. "That's not all I love, though."

His hand froze on her knee. He didn't turn to look at her, didn't acknowledge what she'd said at all. Just stared off into the distance, or as far as the distance went when there were overgrown trees blocking your view.

Something very small fizzled in her chest, like Pop Rocks, then burned down until she was cold. Well, she'd known this wouldn't be easy. Rubbing the heel of one hand over her breastbone, she cleared her throat. "Are you going to sign those papers for your monitor?"

His hand slid away, the last bit of warmth seeming to follow. He might as well have been wearing his sunglasses for all the better she could read his eyes.

"Because if that's what you want, then you should. I know you want to make your dad proud."

His head inched her way.

"I thought for about five minutes my dad would be disappointed in me for joining the Navy instead of the Marines."

"Which doesn't have a medical corps," Jeremy added dryly, finally speaking.

"Well, yeah. That would be the hitch there, wouldn't it?" She smiled a little. "But it was so short-lived. He teased me; so did Tim. But he knew it's what I wanted and so he was proud of me for going after what I needed. And if making your dad proud is what you need, then that's okay."

"Is it?"

Madison chewed on her answer a moment. It didn't seem like a rhetorical question. "I can't really answer that for you. I'm just saying, do what you need." Lord, that hurt. A pins and needles feeling started in her hands from clenching them into fists and she shook them out. "I want you to be happy." *Even if it kills me, be happy. Please, be happy.*

Otherwise, this pain was for nothing.

He nodded again, back to silence. Madison's cell phone chirped in her hoodie pocket. The alarm she'd set reminding her she had work in half an hour. Without looking, she reached in and pressed the side button that would silence the phone's alarm momentarily.

"I have to get going."

"Right. Work."

This, she hated. Maybe Jeremy was right from the beginning. They couldn't turn back now, and maybe it was better to have not known at all what it could have been.

Even as she thought it, she dismissed it. Knowing was infinitely better than playing *what if?* for the rest of her life. But what did he think?

She shifted and watched him closely. "So, we leave this all behind and start over. As if nothing happened?"

He nodded and continued nodding as if once he started, he lacked the ability to stop. "Sounds like a plan."

He was hurting as much as she was. Pair of freaking fools. Though she had no clue what the alternative was. She wasn't about to give up her career. And he wasn't going to let go of his need to please his father. Pasting on the brightest smile she could manage, she said, "Friends then. Back to good friends."

She stood and stretched her back a moment, but Jeremy didn't move. "You coming?"

"You go on ahead. Unless you need me to walk you to your car."

Madison scoffed and did a quick once-over. "I'm pretty sure I'll be safe making it the whole forty yards to my car. But thanks." He kept nodding like one of those bobbleheads on a dashboard. So she leaned over and brushed a kiss on his cheek. "Be happy," she whispered and took off at a run down the metal steps, over the grass, and all the way to her car.

Chapter 20

BE HAPPY.

Two short, simple words. For which there was no simple, short answer.

Jeremy turned a little, resting his back against the cool metal of the wall of the jungle gym and observed the family of three out on the soccer field. The younger girl, clad in jeans and a sweater with a puffy hat over her head, jumped on her father's back, laughing and holding on for dear life. Probably choking the breath out of her father, but he didn't seem to mind, if his own laughter was anything to go off of. The older girl, in track pants and a sweatshirt, dribbled the soccer ball between her legs, taunting her father by setting the ball near him, then snatching it away at the last moment.

Of course, he was likely letting her. But the point wasn't to win. The point was to spend time with his daughters. Quality time. Time to make them feel good about themselves and give them the security of knowing there was a man in their life who thought the world of them.

Jeremy wondered if those girls realized how lucky they were.

Quality times like those had been few and far between in his life. Partly from separations. And mostly because, well, his dad didn't "do" the bonding thing. Any important time together seemed to revolve around his father's military career, or planning Jeremy's.

And Jesus. Didn't that just explain a boatload of issues? He let his head bang back against the metal a few times. He didn't have to watch *Dr. Phil* to call this one.

The only question was… did his reasons for wanting to please his father matter, if he felt the compulsion all the same? And did they matter more than the fact that he'd clearly put his own happiness second?

Skye dropped her bag on their entry table and kicked her shoes off. "Hey, babe, are you home?" she called out.

"In the kitchen," Tim replied from deeper in the house. "And don't leave your shoes there," he added, as if he'd seen her with his own magical neat-freak X-ray vision.

"Mr. OCD strikes again," she mumbled with a smile and scooted them off to the side, out of the way. As she drifted through the townhouse, the most delicious smells permeated her sluggish mind. "Oh my Goddess, what is that? Are you cooking?" Rounding the corner, she reached the kitchen and found the answer for herself.

Tim stood at the stove, wooden spoon in hand, making a stir-fry. He shot her a smile over his shoulder. "Hey, baby. Hungry?"

"Starving." She walked over to him, wrapped her arms around his waist, and pressed one cheek to his warm back. "Working around food all day long when you don't have time to eat any of it is akin to torture."

"Tell that to the boys in SERE school. They'll give you the real definition of the word torture." He pointed to the side counter and a pile of veggies left on a cutting board. "Leftovers that I didn't need, if you want a snack to keep you from dying."

"Thanks." She really was hungry, but she stayed in position a moment longer. He was so warm, and she was so tired...

"Hey. Sleeping Beauty." Tim's shoulder blade shifted beneath her cheek and she snapped out of it. "Can you pass me two clean plates?" He waved a hand in the direction of the cabinet where she had stocked nice, reusable plates rather than the paper and plastic crap he'd been using until she moved in.

"Sure." Moving slowly, she reached up and grabbed one, passing it over her shoulder, repeating the process after he'd piled the first with food. "So when did you learn to make this? And why haven't we been putting this hidden talent to good use before now?"

"I figured you'd want something good after working so long today. Talked to Mom today; she walked me through it. Said it was one of the easier recipes, and a good meal to make both meat lovers and veggie lovers happy. I cook mine in a separate pan but use the same ingredients, just adding the strips of steak. Voila. Everyone happy, minus the fact that there's one extra pan to wash."

"I'll do it." She breathed in and made an appreciative sound at the spicy smell. Carrying their plates to the table along with a bottle of wine, she sank down and immediately propped her feet in her husband's lap. She watched his hands as he poured wine into two glasses. Damn sexy, watching strong hands like that cradle something as delicate as a wine glass. "So have you seen Madison this week?"

Tim grimaced and took a big bite of steak, which he took his sweet time chewing. Skye wasn't fooled.

Stalling tactics were a manager's bread and butter. She'd seen every trick in the book, and used plenty of them herself. Waiting with a patience she didn't often tap into, she eyed him while he chewed, swallowed, and took a sip of water. When her eyes didn't leave his, he rolled his own.

"Come on, honey. We're eating. Do I really have to think about my sister and Jeremy and their… issues?" He gave her a comical—if a little pathetic—sad face.

"You're not worried about it? About her? Or them? I haven't seen Jeremy either, but I'm thinking he's not doing so hot either."

Tim's face sobered. "He's been moody at work, more so than usual. Which is saying something, if you ask me. But I think he's trying to get with the 'everything's all right' program. They've got their story and they're sticking to it." He shrugged. "They're convinced they can return back to normal, just friends, hanging out with the crew, and life will resume as before."

Skye blew out a breath, shifting the hairs that abandoned ship from her ponytail and drooped around her face. "And so we're all just going to play the game of pretend? Act like they weren't an item? That's stupid."

"That's their choice," Tim said, more forcefully. "Don't even think about it."

Skye picked up her fork and studied her plate of food. Spearing a slice of bell pepper, she raised it to her lips before glancing his way. "Think about what?"

"Don't even think about it," he repeated.

"I'm not getting involved, I just—"

"Good." Stabbing at a piece of steak, he used it to point at her, as if trying to intimidate her with it. "Not our business. She's my sister. Your sister-in-law. But we need to stay out of it."

"Like you did when you punched Jeremy?"

"That was reactionary. And completely different." Obviously smug that he had an immediate answer for her, he took another bite of dinner.

"Different, my ass," she muttered around a mouth full of noodles.

"And what a nice ass it is," he said, grinning wolfishly at her.

"Cute, really cute. Let's stay on track."

"Let's not and say we did."

"More cuteness. You're full of it tonight." She pushed her plate forward a few inches. "I just want them to be happy. And if they could use a little help…" She shrugged. "Isn't that what friends are for?"

"No. Friends are for buying you a beer when you've had a shitty day, taking you shooting, hiding the body—"

"Not mine, I hope."

"Goes without saying." Tim picked up her hand and kissed her palm, thumb caressing the spot where his lips had touched for a moment. "Friends are not for managing your life. They're for standing out of the way and letting you make your own decisions, and making sure you don't hang yourself with them."

Skye sighed and settled back in her chair, the soothing feeling of his caress lulling her closer to exhaustion. "So we do nothing. Watch them both suffer."

"They're not suffering, drama queen. They're… reevaluating. It's what we in the military do after a blow. We step back, reassess, and find a new plan of attack."

"And if their plan doesn't include each other?"

"Then that's their call to make."

"Damn." Skye rolled her shoulders and stared at the empty plates and then toward the messy kitchen. "I promised to clean, didn't I?"

"You did."

She slowly smiled. "How about I use my powers of persuasion to distract you from that fact and let me leave it until morning?"

Tim raised a brow but stood and tugged her into his arms. "As your husband, I have the utmost confidence in your persuasive abilities. Let's go give it a shot."

———

Jeremy thumbed over the top of his pen, clicking the tip on and off repeatedly until even the noise bothered him. He set the pen down and watched it roll over the unsigned commitment papers. His time was up. Even he knew that. They couldn't wait forever for his answer. Time to man up and make a decision. He placed the tip of the pen on the signature line, then set it down.

Nah. Not right now. He rolled his chair back. Time to get out for some fresh air. He could man up after lunch.

Just as he was about to stand, Tim appeared in his doorway. "You've got a call."

Jeremy looked to his desk phone. No lines were lit. And why would Tim know that before him anyway? "Who?"

"Dwayne." Walking in without invitation—not that he needed one… the general rule between them was *mi oficina es su oficina*—Tim walked around the desk and used one booted foot to push his chair out of the way. Jeremy rolled for a good three seconds before he hit the back wall, clanging into the furnace with a jolt.

"Dude. Whiskey tango foxtrot?"

"You pulled this same shit on me when I was being a total jackass about Skye and our relationship."

"Marriage."

"Whatever. Turnabout's fair play and all that." A few keystrokes later and Dwayne's ugly mug popped up on screen. "We're here."

"I thought you said you were going to his office, but I don't hear him. Where's the little shit?" Dwayne drawled.

Rooted to the spot with confusion, Jeremy didn't budge. "What's going on?"

Tim rolled his eyes and grabbed the arm of his chair, yanking hard until he rammed against the desk with enough force to rattle the drawers. And a few teeth. "Hey!"

"Jesus, stop being a woman and get over here."

"Damn, dude. Stop jerking me around." Jeremy pushed back a little, childish as it might have been.

"There he is. Now I hear that idiot." Dwayne leaned back, hissed out a breath, and settled a little more comfortably in his chair. "Now. Tell Uncle Dwayne all your problems."

Jeremy flipped off the computer screen.

"He can't see that; you don't have a webcam," Tim reminded him.

"Flipped me off, didn't he?" Dwayne asked, eyes lit with amusement.

"Yup."

Dwayne chuckled, completely unphased. "Amateur stuff, bro. Now, do you wanna tell me what's the deal with Madison?"

Jeremy glanced at Tim's deceptively lazy posture,

leaning back against his desk like the answer didn't matter at all to him. "Not really."

"Let me rephrase the question. Tell me about Madison."

"That's not a question."

"You city boys and all your fancy English grammar," Dwayne drawled harder, sounding like a caricature of an old-fashioned Southern gentleman. Though he'd be the first to admit… he was no gentleman.

"Bite me." Jeremy breathed deeply. "There's nothing to tell. And how do you know any of this crap anyway?"

"I've got eyes, dude."

"Not in Cali you don't. In case you missed the landscape, you're in the sandbox."

Dwayne was quiet for a moment, then shrugged. "Veronica told me bits and pieces. Skye avoided telling me anything. And Madison should never play poker. 'Cause when I asked her about it, the face said it all, even though she kept mum too."

"You talked to Madison? When? Recently? How did she sound?"

"Nothing to tell, hmm?" Tim murmured.

"Yeah. He's lying like a cheap rug, O'Shay."

Jeremy watched as Dwayne shifted in his seat, a grimace crossing his face. He struggled to check it, though, the lines across his brow and bracketing his mouth easing quickly into that familiar smirk once again. "What's wrong with you? I know the furniture over there blows, but that's the second time you've made that stupid face."

He shook his head. "Still sore from the IED hit. I'm fine, just not taking it as easy as I probably should."

Just the mention of an IED had ice sliding into Jeremy's gut. He did a quick once-over of his friend, heart surging fast before he could calm it down with a silent pep talk. He was fine. Talking, joking. A little sore. But fine. Damn, these were the parts he really hated about this life.

"You're punishing yourself is more like it," Tim put in, arms crossed over his chest. "You're supposed to be resting. You would have healed fully a week ago if you weren't dragging your ass around the FOB like a madman trying to make up for something that wasn't your fault."

"Yeah, well, sometimes you don't have that choice. I was in charge, so the blame falls to me. That's how it works."

"Not with shit like this. You know that." Tim shook his head, despite the fact that Dwayne couldn't see. "You can't take the blame if the route clearance missed the IED. It happened. You all came back. Let it go."

"Yeah, well, I don't—wait. Why are we arguing about this? We're supposed to be kicking his ass, not mine." Dwayne pointed directly at Jeremy, though how he could have known which direction to point toward, Jeremy had no clue.

"I'm not supposed to kick anyone's ass. I'm supposed to stay out of it," Tim said mildly.

Jeremy gave him an *are you shitting me?* look. "This? This is what you call staying out of it?"

Tim raised his hands, palms out. "On this I am merely a messenger. The vessel, if you will. Dwayne wanted to talk to you, so I had to do his dirty work."

"Uh-huh." He turned back to the screen. "So talk, big guy."

Dwayne folded and unfolded his arms, clearly trying

to find the most comfortable position possible, each new possibility met with a scowl. After a moment, he gave up. "Madison's as good as my sister."

"Oh boy, another brother," Jeremy muttered.

"Shut it. I can't see you, but I can hear you, dipstick. I get that you tried to avoid her. Hell, I think we all saw how the two of you were doing your best to avoid each other."

"I didn't." Tim shifted against the desk.

"You had blood relation blinders on," Dwayne said with a wave of dismissal. To Jeremy, he continued, "I know you wouldn't use her for a quick fling. You respect her too much. Not to mention, Tim would kill you. And after he was done killing you, I'd kick you. So that's why I can deduce that when you did eventually get involved with her, you couldn't say no. Quick flings are easy to get into, but they're also easy to walk away from. This was Madison. And you couldn't start something easy with her. Because walking away would suck donkey balls."

Jeremy grimaced. "Your southern fried colloquialisms are astounding."

Dwayne grinned. "Thanks. So clearly, you feel more for her than you wanted to admit. Am I right?"

Jeremy glanced between the screen and Tim, debating his options. Declaring himself to a computer monitor was not really how he saw this whole thing ending in his mind. But hey, roll with the punches. "Yeah."

"Good." Dwayne looked smug. "So what's the holdup?"

"The holdup is he's got to make the choice himself," Tim chimed in. "So don't pressure him. Nobody wants to be with someone who doesn't want them back."

"I never said I didn't want to be with Madison," Jeremy bit off, then regretted it. Dwayne suddenly wasn't the only smug-looking bastard. "I hate you both right now."

"We're your favorites and you know it." Dwayne's smile only grew.

Jeremy did the only thing he could think of. Deflect. Turning to Tim, he asked, "Does this not seem a little familiar to you?"

"Hmm?" Tim picked up the pen he'd been playing with before and started clicking it.

"The whole meeting in the office bit, outflanking someone with Skype? International ass-kicking? We did this a few months ago. With you. About Skye."

Tim mocked thinking hard. "Oh. Right, right. You did, didn't you? And, oddly enough… it worked. Didn't it?"

Well, he just painted his own ass into a corner. Tim chuckled, knowing that hadn't worked out quite like he'd wanted it to.

Dwayne leaned in, the squeaky chair's metallic whine grating on Jer's eardrums even through the speakers. "Get what you need to get in your life together. Don't leave this thread hanging. There are important things in life… and then there's this. Too important to rank. Don't blow it."

Don't blow it. Always easier said than done. Jeremy nodded silently, but he realized it really could be that easy. That simple.

"Sorry, D. I hate to do this, but I've got stuff to do."

Far from looking annoyed or offended, Dwayne just grinned and waved. Jeremy took that as a sign and clicked to end the call.

"Uh, dude. I wasn't done talking to him," Tim said.

"You're done now. Out. I've got shit to do."

"What could be more important than... oh. Oh. Right." Tim smiled a little as he looked Jeremy in the eye. "I'll be in my office if you need me."

"Thanks."

———— ∿∿∿ ————

Two hours later, Jeremy let himself into his apartment. He'd busted his ass to get his work done for the day, delegating a few things he normally did himself and deciding what could be put off until the next day. He wanted to be home for the next part of his plan. Needed to be home.

Checking the clock, he knew that thanks to the time difference, his father would be getting home soon. It was a little early, but his nerves were on the edge of frayed and he needed to shore this up. Now. Taking a chance, he dialed his father's home number.

"Hello?"

Fate. It had to be. Maybe Skye was onto something with all her Fate talk. "Hey, Dad."

"Jeremy. What's wrong?"

"Wrong?" He sank down on the couch and rubbed his forehead between his thumb and finger. "Why would you say that?"

"You usually call on the weekend. It's a Thursday."

"Maybe I just wanted to hear your voice."

Silence.

So his dad's bullshit meter was up and running. Fine. "Okay then. I called to give you the news."

His dad grunted. "Finally signed the damn papers.

Took you long enough. So, did your monitor give you an idea where you're headed next?"

"No. Dad, you mis—"

"Well, that'll come soon enough. You've been there three years now. I'm sure you don't want to leave your buddies, since they got there after you did but—"

"Dad."

"I'm trying to give you some good advice here, son. Pipe down and take it."

"*Dad.*"

His father humphed. "What?"

Jeremy breathed in and out. "I didn't sign the papers."

A beat of silence passed. Then, "What?"

"I didn't sign—"

"Jesus, Mary, and Joseph. Son, you can't screw around with your career like this. I know you're hitting some sort of roadblock. But the longer you take to simply acknowledge to your monitor you're staying in, the less seriously they're going to take you. Nobody wants someone who can't make up their mind. Just sign the damn papers. Deal with whatever crisis you think you're going through later. Sign the damn papers."

"I'm not signing them. I told them I was getting out."

If he hadn't heard his father's breath catch, he would have thought he'd hung up. The silence, as they say, was deafening.

Cue the cartoon crickets.

"Dad?"

"This isn't amusing." His father's voice was low, menacing. It was the voice Jeremy always remembered being scared of as a kid. More than the yelling, more than the screaming. If his father used the low, hushed, almost whispered voice, it was time to hide. "This is your career. Our legacy. And you're going to blow it? For what? Tell me what is so goddamn important that you're walking away from a damn good career and a reputation the Phillips men have fought to uphold."

"I've served. I served ten years. Honorably. Three tours in Afghanistan." *I've been a damn good son.* "Why does that mean nothing?"

"It's not what we do. We retire. We are lifers."

"So what if I'm not?" The question was met with complete silence. With each passing second, each moment his father had to make a fresh start with his son and chose not to, it became easier to say what was on his mind. "I'm not a lifer. I didn't want to be a lifer when I joined. And I don't want to now. The only thing I can think of that would be worse than staying in for another ten years would be losing the two things I want more than anything else because I couldn't get my head out of my ass long enough to realize I was living another person's dream, and they didn't even appreciate me for it."

"Don't speak like that to me. Don't you dare speak like that to me." Something slammed in the background, and Jeremy could easily see his father pounding a fist on a table, rattling coasters. "I raised you by myself. I did what I could for you. Showed you how good the Corps could be for a man. What a good life it provided."

"And I'm grateful. But Dad, how far do you expect that to go? You want me to repay you for keeping your own son around by doing what you want for the rest of my life? I'm a man, not a kid anymore. Would you seriously respect someone who couldn't make their own decisions and had their father do all the thinking for them?"

"That's not what this is!" his father roared. Jeremy pulled the phone back a few inches and waited for the echo to die down.

"That's exactly what this is. I can't apologize for it. I'm sad you're upset about this, instead of hearing that my career was making me miserable." God. It was all clicking into place now. Why hadn't he been able to do this years ago? Why had he re-upped three years ago when he had the chance to get out?

Maybe because you wouldn't have met up with Madison again.

Right. That. Oddly enough, the voice in his head sounded nothing like his, and very much like Skye's. There was something to be said for Skye's Fate theory.

"Misery is temporary. And if you'd…" His father trailed off slowly, but thanks to his heavy breathing Jeremy knew he was still there. "You said you didn't want to lose the two things you want more than anything else."

Had he?

"What are they?"

Well, in for a penny, in for a pound. "My writing. And Madison O'Shay."

"Writing?" His father chuckled. "Writing. Writing… what? Books?"

"Yes," Jeremy ground out through his teeth.

His father laughed a little harder. "And Madison O'Shay. That's… that's the…" He sucked in a breath around belly-deep laughs. "That's the Navy nurse. Sister of your friend Tim. The lifer?"

"That's correct."

No longer able to hold back, his dad burst into laughter.

Jeremy gave him two minutes before barking, "You done yet?"

Winding down, a few stray laughs escaping, his father admitted he was.

"Well, thanks. Your support means the world to me." Every word oozed sarcasm.

"Can't say I expected this. And I'll have to tell you, I'm not okay with it." Back to his gruff self, not a chuckle in sight, he went on. "This isn't the plan we laid out. You don't toss away plans because of a distraction."

"They're not distractions. They're what I want. And they're what I'm going to have." *If Madison is still willing to have me*. "If you've got a problem with that, then…" Then what?

"Then what?" his father asked, almost as a threat.

"Then that's all I have to say, I guess. I hope eventually you'll change your mind. Call me when you do."

He hung up amidst his father's protests. But he gave it another moment, waiting to see if his father called back, before closing the phone completely.

So there it was. The official final straw. Jeremy walked over to his desk calendar and flipped a few months ahead. Taking into account the six weeks it would take before paperwork and other bureaucratic crap would be filed, and then adding on his terminal leave, he had a good four months left before he was actually out from under the military's wing. In theory, anyway. He'd get a more exact date later.

Plenty of time to follow up on the leads he received constantly from corporate recruiters to contract jobs to fellow Marines who'd gotten out recently and loved their jobs.

He jiggled the mouse a little and smiled when the screen of his computer came to life. Writing was his passion. And until he could make it a living, he'd find another job. No problem. But he'd always write. And hopefully it would start paying off soon.

But in the meantime, he had a girl to win.

Chapter 21

"YOU WANT A WATER?" MATTHEW CALLED FROM his kitchen.

Madison dropped down on one end of his couch. "Sure." Her voice cracked a little, and she scowled into the empty room. She had to shake this. Clenching and unclenching her fists, she looked around the room for a distraction. And found herself realizing that even when in another man's apartment, she couldn't stop thinking of Jeremy.

Matthew's home was the polar opposite of Jeremy's place. Open, airy, decorated perfectly with little personal touches here and there. A painting, a picture frame, a bowl full of interesting pebbles. Of course, Madison knew her friend hadn't done any of it himself. An old boyfriend chose the décor and did the hard work. Matthew just paid for the furniture and was glad to have the decision out of his hand.

Matthew walked back to the couch in his apartment and sank down at the other end, completely opposite from Madison. She smiled and shook her head.

"You don't have to give me space. I'm not mad at you."

"I know. I just wanted some room so I could stretch out my legs." With that, he plopped his feet down by her butt on the cushion. "There. That's better. Now. Tell Matthew all your problems." He handed her a bottle of water.

Madison cracked the top open and took a drink,

hoping the water would wash down the tears that crawled up her throat every time she thought about it. "That could take weeks. We don't have that kind of time."

"Right, this is true. But we have until our shift in a few hours." Matthew reached over and grabbed the leg of her jeans and hauled her around until she faced him, her own feet draped over his thighs, her back pressed against the arm of the couch. "And since we can't guarantee a good time to talk in the ER, let's go ahead and talk now."

Madison shuddered at the reminder of being back at the ER again. "Don't remind me. It'll be bad enough when we get there." She thought for a moment, tapping the bottle cap against her chin. "I think I might see about working my way in to surgery. I think that's where I belong."

"Really? Not full-time OB?" Matthew reached and snatched the bottle from her to take a sip of his own. "Color me shocked." He raised a brow. "And won't that be like asking for more deployments?"

"More? I haven't even gone once yet. Not that I'm dying to," she added when his brow only raised further. "My number just hasn't been called, as they say. But if that's the result, well, so be it. If I'm happy with my job, then that's what matters. I didn't exactly join the military under false pretenses, thinking it would be a cakewalk. I figured I'd go over to play in the sandbox eventually."

"And are you?"

"Am I what?" She gave up on her water and grabbed a magazine off his coffee table, mostly to have something to occupy her twitchy hands.

"Happy."

"Hmm. That's a hard one. I like my job. No, love. I love my job. I have my family, my friends. A new place to myself—minus Veronica, of course, but I chose her, so clearly I wanted her—and so what's left?" She glanced down at the magazine and saw the picture of some new Hollywood couple staring back at her with glowing smiles and eyes full of love, as if nothing could stand between them and eternal devotion. She mentally scoffed at them. *Don't you have a lot to learn?* She opened to the table of contents, where she wouldn't have to look at them.

"Oh, I don't know. Maybe a mysterious, brooding Marine who looks at you like you're his everything and you have the power to devastate him with one careless word?"

Madison's hand froze mid-page turn, and she narrowed her eyes. "Drama much? Stop DVRing *General Hospital*. It's not good for your psyche."

"Fine. But simply using his name is so much less of a punch. Jeremy. What's left is Jeremy."

"Jeremy's a friend." She held up the magazine and pointed. "What the hell is this?"

"It's a bandage dress."

"A what?" She glanced again at the glazed-eyed starlet in the dress so tight it made her look fat. Which was a little odd, since she probably weighed ninety-two pounds soaking wet.

He sighed in exasperation. "A dress that wraps around like a bandage. It's super-tight, and as you can tell, it's not always flattering, depending on the cut. Now stop stalling." He ripped the magazine from her hand and tossed it over his shoulder.

"It's nothing." She raised her hands over her head and stretched her back. "We agreed it wasn't going to last. I knew that going in. So I don't exactly have room to complain."

"I must say, that's very grown-up." He set the bottle on the coffee table. "Much more mature than I could ever be."

"That's because you have the maturity of a fifth-grader," she said wisely.

"Do not."

"Do too."

Matthew laughed. "And I'm the only fifth-grader here?"

Despite her poor mood, Madison smiled. "I'm rubber and you're glue."

"Quite frankly, I'm glad you're over the whole thing. Since that's the case, I have something else to talk to you about."

"Hmm?"

"There's this guy..."

She smiled and patted his leg. "Tell Madison all about him," she said, playing on his earlier words.

Matthew threw a pillow at her. "Not for me. For you."

"Me?" She was stunned. And not really in a good way.

"Sure. He's a friend from high school and now conveniently lives pretty close by. He's cute—for which you know I'm actually a reliable source on that—was always a good guy in high school. Athletic, but not a meathead. Actually, he was a golfer, if I remember correctly..."

"Matthew." She couldn't breathe very well.

"Shh, you'll get your turn in a minute. Anyway, he does something with computers right now. Goes from company to company helping them shore up against hackers and things like that. Security stuff. Pretty intense, but seems like it's a good, solid job."

"Matthew," she tried again, a bit louder. Why did her stomach hurt all of a sudden? And that ringing in her ears… Was she developing tinnitus?

"Oh!" Matthew clapped his hands and rubbed them together, an unholy gleam in his eyes. "Let's go get my laptop and Facebook stalk him. I'm friends with the guy. Total access to his pictures and profile."

"No." Madison pressed a hand to her stomach. Definitely feeling ill.

"You're right. Why move off the couch when we're comfortable right where we are?" He dug in his jeans pocket to pull out his phone. "I've got the Facebook app. I'll do it here. You just wait, give me a minute and I'll—Ow!" He jerked one leg back, rubbing along his shin. "What the hell?"

She sighed. "If you'd let me get a word in edgewise then I wouldn't have to pinch you."

"That wasn't a pinch. You pulled leg hair." He grimaced and rubbed harder. "Exactly why do women get waxed again?"

"For reasons you'll never know." Madison sat back. "I'm not interested in Boy Wonder you have stashed in your friend list."

"Any reason why not?"

She bit her lip. "No."

"Liar."

"Prove it."

"And back to fifth grade we go." He grabbed the water bottle and took another sip before passing it to her. "Look, if the guy means that much to you, then fight."

"I tried."

"Fight harder. Break out the big guns. Cry if you need to."

"Tears are the big guns?" she asked skeptically.

"Yeah, sure. Girls are great criers. Beg. Leave your pride at the door and weep at his feet. Show him the pain."

Madison pointed the capped bottle at him. "Okay, one? Completely offensive that just because I'm a girl, you think I can cry on command."

"Can't you?"

"Yes. Comes standard issue with every pair of ovaries. Not the point."

Matthew smirked.

"Two? I'm not leaving my pride behind. If I wanted to do that, I'd quit the military myself. And I'm not about to give it up for a man." Even the man she loved. "So, we're back to square one."

Matthew shrugged. "Was worth a shot. So is there a plan B?"

Madison nodded. "Of course there's a plan B. There's always a plan B. Plan B is to stick to my guns. Keep my chin up and hope eventually…" Suddenly, as if a dam broke unexpectedly, her lip quivered and she pulled her legs up tightly against her chest. Through a shuddery breath, she finished, "And hope eventually it stops hurting so much."

"Oh, baby. Come here." Matthew sat up straight and pulled her across his lap, legs draped over his thighs, her head on his shoulder. Long arms went around her, and for a moment, while her tears soaked the cotton of his T-shirt, she could believe that this was all she needed. Friendship. Platonic love and commitment.

As she sniffled, she said, "We should just move in together and spend the rest of our lives with each other. Like Will and Grace, but without that awkward part where they tried to have a baby together."

Matthew smoothed a hand down her hair, briskly rubbing over her upper arm. "That's very thoughtful of you, sweetie, but I've got a man on the hook and I'm close to reeling him in. That might make for very uncomfortable cuddle sessions."

Damn. That didn't work out either. Would none of the men in her life cooperate? "Guess I'll just have to toughen up. I'm in the military, after all."

"Oh please. You don't have to be tough to be in the military. They let me in, after all."

"No, they didn't," she said with a reluctant smile. "You're a civilian nurse."

"Hmm. I guess I have to say they have excellent taste then."

She laughed, partly because it was funny and partly because he wanted her to. "You always manage to make me feel better. Thanks, Will."

"You're welcome, Grace."

A few quiet moments passed by.

"So, are you going to go out and buy a red curly wig now? Ouch! Stop doing that! I can't have bald patches on my legs. Tony is going to think I'm weird!"

Madison smiled into his shirt. Men. Such babies.

Once more.

No.

It won't hurt anything.

Absolutely not.

But maybe if I just…

Veronica sighed, hating the feeling of indecision pressing against her chest. Her finger hovered over the mouse like a trigger, hesitant to pull back. The past ten minutes had been a continuous argument with herself over whether she should use Skype to call Dwayne.

On the one hand, she'd done it once before, and he seemed to appreciate the gesture. He'd been nice, and he'd needed the support. Not to mention, she'd enjoyed herself as well.

On the other hand, she had nothing to tell him. Nothing to share. No messages from friends to pass on. No true excuse for making the call.

But she still wanted to. Like an addict, she'd become used to their chats, infrequent though they were. And for some reason, she simply felt the overwhelming desire to call him again. On purpose. Once more, like she had before.

It was so forward of her. One time could be excused as a silly lark. Or an accident. But twice was intentional. And not at all her style. If she even had style…

Huh.

If she left her previous life behind because she didn't care for how things were going, and this was the opposite of what the former Veronica would have done… didn't that mean it was the perfect thing for the new Veronica to do?

She shook her head. That barely made sense even in her own mind. Time for action, no more thinking.

Her nerves tingled with some strange, hypersensitive mixture of excitement and anticipation. Or maybe they were responding to her sweating palms out of sheer terror. Just like she'd felt the first time she dialed him. But he'd appreciated it, that much he'd said. He wanted to hear from friends. It helped. He swore it did.

Before she could click, her cell phone rang. She jumped, falling sideways out of the chair and landing on her shoulder with a jarring thump.

"Ow." That hurt. Her pride as much as her body. She gave herself a moment to make sure she wasn't truly injured, then moved slowly to a kneeling position so she could grab her phone from the top of the computer tower. "Hello?"

"Hey, it's me. I wanted to—are you okay?" Madison's voice shifted instantly from casual friend calling to intense nurse diagnosing.

"I'm fine. Just made a fool out of myself falling from my chair when the phone startled me." Not normally something she would share. But with Madison, she always felt so safe being open and honest. With most things, anyway.

Madison hissed in a breath through her teeth. "Ouch. You okay? Everything moving the way it should?"

"Yes, I'm fine. Thank you. You were saying before?"

"Ah, sure. Just warning you that I wouldn't be home like normal, so don't worry. I've got errands and things to run. Since I'm usually walking in and we cross paths at breakfast, I didn't want you to worry."

"I appreciate the consideration. Thanks. Good luck with your errands."

Veronica wasn't fooled. As she hung up the phone and climbed back into the chair, she said a quick prayer for Madison's heart. Her poor roommate was nearly sick with sadness, though she tried her best to hide it by being unbelievably busy. Never sitting still for more than a minute, as if she was afraid the silence and loneliness would cause her to break.

On one level, Veronica could relate to wanting to stay busy so thoughts wouldn't overtake you. On another, she'd never been in love before. That was a fate she had yet to run into.

And oddly, that last thought seemed to bring her full circle, to the call she was about to—or not about to—place.

He said he needed friends. Calling to say hello when you have a moment is simply a kind gesture. He won't think anything more of it. She would simply tell him she was bored—or maybe desperate for a distraction from homework—and thought to say hello. That sounded casual enough, didn't it? And as long as her face didn't flame red like it normally did when she was lying through her teeth, then she could get away with it.

On second thought… She reached over and turned off one of the two desk lamps, darkening the hallway a little more. There. Less light meant he couldn't see her flush.

Finally, she reached for the mouse and quickly clicked on the call button, screwing her eyes shut in disbelief she'd actually done so.

The first ring was like a twist to her belly. The second pounded through her head. After five rings, she realized he wasn't going to answer. On the sixth, she told herself to hang up. By the ninth, she managed to click the end button.

Staring at the once-again blank screen, she knew this was her sign. For once, they weren't going to cross paths. She'd tempted it one too many times. A man like Dwayne was too busy to sit around and chat with someone like her. Someone he'd never even met before. It was time to give up and stop hovering around the computer in case he happened to be calling. Time to let go of her surprise pen pal.

Time to move on.

She hesitated only a moment before shutting the computer down completely and walking to her room.

Chapter 22

HE'S NOT COMING, SO STOP WATCHING THE DOOR.

"Madison?"

"Hmm?"

Skye stared at her for a moment, then waved a hand in front of her face. "I was asking about how soon we'll have details on when D gets back from Afghanistan."

"You were?"

Both Skye and Veronica stared at her for a moment. Then Veronica quietly asked, "Do you want to talk about Jeremy?"

"Finally!" Skye tossed her hands in the air, flipping her pen over the back of the couch in the process. "I thought you'd never ask!"

Veronica made a face. "Why did I have to be the one to ask?"

"Because I'm not allowed to," Skye grumbled, then pointed at Veronica. "But Madison can stand witness that you started it." She turned back to Madison. "So spill."

"There's nothing to say." She played with the edge of the rug she was sitting on, not wanting to make eye contact. She really did suck at this whole lying thing. The entire last week, she'd been trying so hard to act as if nothing was wrong. The biggest lie of all.

"If you miss him, isn't there something you can do about it?"

Veronica's soft question made her smile. "You're

sweet. But no, nothing I can really do about it. What are my options? Chase him down the street and beat him with a whiffle ball bat until he caves?"

Skye snorted. "I'd hold him down for you."

"Always good to know who your friends are." Madison smiled a moment at the image, but the smile didn't hold. "He's made up his mind as far as what's important. Everyone should have a chance to do that. He's made up his mind, so that's that. I just want some time to work through it on my own. If that's all right with you, oh Zen one." She gave Skye a pointed look.

She sniffed. "Natural female curiosity is not the same thing as not being Zen. Just so you know. Now, back to the topic at hand, which is D's homecoming party, and the aforementioned timeline of events."

"Oh. Right." Madison stared down at her notebook, though she already knew the answer wasn't going to be there. "That's Tim's thing. He'd have more accurate information than I ever would. I'm just in it for the food."

"You're planning a homecoming party specifically to get to pick out the food?" Veronica tilted her head to the side, braid falling over her shoulder, looking like a confused cocker spaniel with long floppy ears.

"Sort of. I'm in it to make sure all of Dwayne's favorite food is here. It's his party, and he's been eating the slop they call food in the chow hall and the dirt they call MREs for the last seven months."

Veronica held up a hand. "MREs? Translation, please?"

"Meal, Ready-to-Eat. The pre-packed, dehydrated food that you mix with water and is supposedly edible. If the world went into nuclear war tomorrow, the only things that would survive are cockroaches and cases of

MREs. The man will be starving for food. Real food. He should get to eat something other than what the Veggie Queen would pick out."

Skye rolled her eyes. "I'm perfectly capable of realizing that other people eat meat on a regular basis. I work in a restaurant, after all. I don't switch out all the steaks for blocks of tofu, thank you very much."

"No, thank *you*," Madison replied. "But you know D. I just wanted to check and see that he'd have what he wants."

"Which is?" Veronica asked.

"Beer. Pretzels. Nuts. Chips and non-vegan dip. Pigs in a blanket. Some version of recently dead animal grilling outside. And stop making that face, Mrs. O'Shay."

Skye stuck her tongue out. "It's still Ms. McDermott, if you please." Her eyes sort of glazed over in that weird dreamy way she had. "But I'm considering changing it."

"Why?" Veronica bit into a baby carrot. "You said you liked your name and didn't want to change it."

"I do like my own name. I just think maybe…" Snapping back to her practical self—well, at least more practical than a moment ago—Skye waved it off. "Not important right now. Back to the party. How much time, truly, do you think we would have to plan once we get word they're on their way?"

Madison lifted one shoulder. "A week, two days, two hours. It all varies."

Skye groaned.

"Haven't you learned the rule about schedules yet?" Madison teased.

"There is no schedule," both she and Skye said together. Madison continued, "The good thing is that all this stuff is really easy to store. So if he's delayed a day or two, no big deal."

"You have a point." Skye leaned around, grabbed her pen from behind the chair, and scribbled furiously over her notepad.

Madison settled down for a moment, then pointed a carrot stick at Veronica. "Why did you ask to come along, again? You don't even know Dwayne."

Veronica's eyes widened and she looked around the room. "Well, I mean, he's your friend. And Skye's. And I've spoken to him… a few times… on, you know…" Her voice slowly grew quieter with each sentence until it was almost a whisper.

"Stop interrogating her, Madison," Skye said without looking up from her notepad.

"Not interrogating. Just asking."

"I'm fine," Veronica insisted.

"Take your bad mood out on a punching bag," Skye continued.

The door leading from the garage opened and Tim stepped into the townhouse. "Afternoon, ladies."

"Oh look. Here comes one now," Madison said with false cheer. Veronica snorted behind her, poorly disguising a laugh with a cough.

Tim froze mid-step and glanced behind him. "Here comes what?"

"Nothing. Ignore your sister." Finally ready to put down her pen, Skye stood and gave her confused husband a kiss on the cheek. "Glad you're home. I could use your input for the homecoming party for Dwayne."

"A party?" Tim shook his head. "I don't remember anything about a party."

"I just decided to have one. He'll have been gone longer than we anticipated, and so I think he deserves to have a little fun. It's just a casual get-together. Nothing big."

Tim put on his fake pout. "I don't recall getting a party the last time I came back from deployment."

"For one thing, you weren't married," Madison pointed out. "So your wife, queen of the get-together here, wasn't around."

"I was married the last time," Tim corrected.

"You didn't even make it out of the country."

"It counts."

Skye stepped between them "Fine, then you got a 'Hey, remember that girl you married? Congrats, here's your wife' party. Which is just like a homecoming party, only better." Skye grabbed the front of his shirt to yank him in for a longer kiss. "Now stop playing sibling squabble and be the charming, helpful man I know you are." With a playful slap on his thigh, she nudged him into the armchair.

"Charming? You really have her fooled." Madison ducked the carrot he threw at her.

"Anyway," Skye put in forcefully. "I'm going over timelines now. But as Madison pointed out, we can simply be prepared with most of this stuff since it's easy to store. Which alleviates my mind. Can we keep some of it at your place?"

"Fine with me if it's fine with Veronica." She grabbed a piece of celery slathered with peanut butter.

"Of course, no problem." Veronica nodded.

"I know Jeremy's worthless when it comes to food storage, given his fridge is the size of a stamp. But do you think he can be counted on for heavy lifting when the time comes? Setting up tables and moving furniture around?"

Tim shrugged. "He's been busy lately. Even I haven't seen him much in the last week."

"What is he up to?" Skye asked.

"It's none of my business."

"But if you would just—"

"Skye."

There was that tone. The voice no sister could forget. The one that said *I love you more than anything, but if you don't back off things will not go well.*

And for once, it wasn't directed at her. Huh. Funny how things change.

Skye sat on the corner, silently glaring at her husband, but said nothing more.

It was then Madison realized the whole room was quietly holding their breath, as if waiting for her to burst into tears and run out of the room at the mere mention of Jeremy in casual conversation.

"It's fine, guys. Seriously. Stop tiptoeing around the subject. We're all friends. We'll be in the same place at the same time. You don't have to stop talking about him."

"We just want you to be okay," Veronica said.

Yeah. Me too.

Five kinds of fool. No, six. Maybe seven. As the minutes ticked by, Jeremy began to feel more and more foolish, standing outside of the staff parking lot in the middle of the night. Like some creepy stalker. He'd be lucky if nobody called security and reported a weird guy nervously pacing in the shadows.

"Come on, Matthew," he muttered. "Do your part."

Ten more minutes passed before he heard the side door open and close. Which meant a whole lot of nothing, since he'd heard that door open multiple times in the last ninety minutes that he'd been out there, and false alarms, every one of them.

But this time, the glorious sound of Madison's voice assured him his time was near.

"Matthew, why are you walking so damn fast? We have a full hour break. And exactly how did you work it that we had our break together again?"

"Switching things around. I just wanted to hang out; I miss you. Now come on, slugabed."

"I'm not in bed. And—hey! Matthew, slow down!" He watched from a distance as Matthew reached back and grabbed her hand, tugging a little to get her moving. She planted her heels and refused to move. Of course, Matthew was bigger, by a large margin, and pulled her along like a child's toy.

Matthew looked around the lot, quite obviously looking for him. "We've got something to do. That's all."

"Something to—no. You promised me food. If that something isn't food, I'm going to be seriously pissed."

Jeremy hoped not. Taking a deep breath, he stepped under the warm glow of the parking lot light and waited for Madison to notice. But Matthew was the one who saw him first.

"Dude. Finally. You could have given me warning she'd put up a fight."

"I figured you would know better than anyone how Madison handles being pushed around." Jeremy held out a hand, shaking Matthew's. "Thanks, man."

Squeezing a little in silent warning, Matthew stared him down. But Jeremy didn't blink, only nodded a fraction of an inch. Enough to give Matthew the encouragement to step back and kiss Madison on the cheek.

"I'll see you inside when your break's over. If you're running behind, I'll cover."

Madison stood in the darkened lot, mouth gaping open. "You two were in on this together?"

Matthew nodded, completely unapologetic. "He called. I didn't go to him. Now close that mouth, fly-trap." With a tap on her chin, he sauntered away.

"Love you too," she called dryly after Matthew. Then she turned to stare at him, arms crossed over her chest. Anger? Or hurt?

Neither one was a great option. Worse would be a combination of the two.

"So what's the deal, Phillips? I don't have that long of a break."

The unspoken *I don't want to waste it on you* wasn't missed. He smiled. "I hope this won't take up too much of your time then. I needed to talk to you, and you're always busy."

"How would you know?" she shot back. "I haven't seen you in two weeks."

"I've been driving by your place, hoping to catch you when Veronica wasn't there."

"Oh." Her arms dropped to her sides. "So what's so important?"

He rocked back on his heels. It hadn't seemed real at first, hadn't seemed true. But saying it out loud to her... It was the first time someone's opinion of his choice mattered so much he couldn't breathe for the nerves battling inside his chest. "I'm done."

She raised a brow. "I thought we both were."

Oh, God, he was messing this up. "With the Marine Corps," he clarified. Waiting as the look of understanding—then shock—passed over her face, he smiled quietly. "Yeah. I know. I think I probably had the same look on my face when it hit me." Hands in his pockets, he dared to take a step toward her. Counted it as a good sign when she didn't counter with a step back. "I realized that people go into the military for too many reasons to count. And it doesn't matter what that reason is, as long as they're okay with it. But I wasn't."

She blinked, but astonishment still covered her face.

"I was trying to make amends for some wrong I thought I committed, just by existing. Live up to some standard that my father had no right to place on me. Which was easy enough, when I didn't know what I wanted for myself. Good enough career, decent paying job. Met my two best friends because of it." He breathed out and went for gold. "Met the woman I love because of it."

She blinked again, the shock on her face being replaced with something better. Something warmer, encouraging.

"But those weren't good enough reasons to dedicate myself to this career. Not when I wasn't happy. So I'm out. Well, not immediately. Paperwork and terminal leave take a while. But I've got a contractor job lined up. Which isn't my ultimate goal either. But I need to work, and there's no serious commitment or extensive travel involved."

"What about you and your dad?" she asked.

Jeremy shrugged. "Broken, but not shattered. Time will help. I just couldn't keep living his dream and ignoring two things that are way more important."

"What are they?" she asked in a whisper, barely heard over a car several lanes away pulling in to park.

"The important things? One is writing. I finished the book, completely. Still needs work, but hitting the end made me realize it wasn't just a fluke, something to get out of my system. I loved it. I was dying to start all over again with a new idea. But I have to be practical; I can't live on whatever writing pays alone... if the book ever even sells." His lips quirked. "That's too many maybes for me. But a nine-to-five helps."

"And the other?"

He gave her a knowing smile. "I thought that was obvious. No? Maybe I shouldn't be surprised, since I kind of botched shit up with us before."

"Kind of?" Madison placed her hands on her hips, starting to resemble the spitfire he knew and loved.

"Okay, totally. I screwed up. But I'm male. It's in our DNA to screw up. Just like it's in the female DNA to forgive us our transgressions. So, you have to forgive me."

"Have to, huh?" Taking a few steps forward, she stopped just in front of him. "Go ahead and spell it out for me. What's the other important thing?"

"You. You're the important thing. I love you. I've loved you longer than I ever wanted to admit, because it was terrifying to acknowledge that and know it would never go anywhere. But we can. I know you are set on staying in the Navy. If it's what you want, I will be there for you one hundred percent."

One corner of her lips tilted up. "You won't feel bit-ter, following me around when I change duty stations? Waiting back here if I deploy?"

"Please. Will I get to do this whenever I want to?" Taking a chance, he reached around her back, hauled her to him, and kissed her until he had to catch his own breath.

She arched her back and looked up at him. "Anytime you want."

"Then I'm good." He kissed her again, not caring when a group of chatty nurses who hovered by the side door for a smoke break giggled.

Madison wrapped her arms around him, breaking off the kiss and burying her face in his shirt. "I missed you."

"Missed you too, Mad." Careful to not ruin her work-required bun, his fingers caressed the back of her neck. "Are you going to say it back?"

"Say what back?" she asked, laughter in her voice. He squeezed her nape a little and she squealed. "Okay, okay!" She looked back up at him. "I love you."

He kissed her again, gently, fleetingly. "I love you too." God, it felt good to say it out loud.

"You don't expect me to move into that hellhole of an apartment, do you? Not even a woman's touch could salvage that place."

He chuckled. "No, I don't. We'll talk about it later."

"Later?" she asked hopefully.

"Much later. Far as I'm concerned, we've got a for-ever's worth of later."

"Sounds good to me."

From *The Officer Says "I Do,"* available now
from Sourcebooks Casablanca

Chapter 1

TIMOTHY O'SHAY WAS POSITIVE OF ONE THING.

He would be dragging his friends' drunken asses out
of a ditch before morning if things progressed the same
way the rest of the night.

"Twenty!" Dwayne crooned next to him. Whenever
D drank, his southern accent only became thicker until
it was all twang. If someone wasn't careful, they could
easily take Dwayne for an idiot. Big mistake.

"Twenty-one. Sorry, sir," the blackjack dealer said
in a monotone voice before sweeping a crestfallen
Dwayne's chips away.

Somewhere else in the casino, a siren alerted to a slot
machine winner. The sound seemed to rub the loss in
Dwayne's face as he scowled more.

"You're going to lose everything you have on the last
night in Vegas," Jeremy warned. Not drunk, but plenty
buzzed, he seemed to be slowly working his way toward
the hammered side of life.

Since Tim had zero intention of using his last night
of pre-deployment leave on babysitting their drunk
asses—again—he shoved Dwayne until he tumbled out
of the chair. "Grab some food to soak up the keg in your
stomach. I'm not hauling you around by your shirt collar
for what's left of leave."

Tim loved his friends like brothers. Meeting them in The Basic School was the best thing that had happened to him, to all of them. But often their fondness for free-for-all fun led to more problems than good times. Tim's tendency toward moderation and keeping a cool head kept them out of hot water more than once.

"Tim, let me borrow a few more bucks."

"And watch you lose my cash as fast as you lost yours? Hell no." Tim made another modest bet and watched as he broke even with the dealer. Unlike Dwayne and Jeremy, Tim was about to leave Vegas with the exact amount of cash he entered it with. Moderate play and moderate drinking ensured he never played too deep.

Moderate. The story of his life. Hard to shake the "play it safe" feeling when your entire life in the Marines consisted of just that. But then again, if he wasn't willing to play nanny to the two boobs he came with, they'd all be knee-deep in shit.

"Bet your own cash, then. It's our last night," Jeremy reminded him as he doubled down on his next hand.

"I am betting my money, Jer. And I'm doing just fine without a drunken Statler and Waldorf in my ear."

"Statler and who?" Dwayne asked.

"The Muppet hecklers, you idiot," Jeremy shot back.

"Both of you knock it off," Tim started. "I'm not going to—"

He cut off, turning his head to follow a woman who passed behind the table, headed toward the slots. She was tall, her head high, and she floated more than walked. A thick mass of chestnut curls rioted down her back, almost covering her bare shoulders.

"Tim. Earth to Timmy." Jeremy waved a hand in front of his face.

Tim slapped it away and snapped, "What?"

"You're daydreaming and the dealer's waiting."

"Oh, sure. Right." Trying to find the brunette again, he shoved some chips out in front without counting. Jeremy whistled and Dwayne muttered a curse, but he didn't take his eyes away from the hunt. She must have slipped down an aisle of slots.

And why did he care? One woman, one night. In the end it amounted to nothing.

"Congratulations, sir."

"Holy shit," Jeremy breathed next to him.

Dwayne slapped his shoulder. "That was some playing, bro."

Huh? Tim looked down and saw that instead of his normal modest bets, he'd shoved almost three hundred dollars in for the hand. And won.

Holy shit indeed. He could have lost three hundred dollars and never even realized it. A cocktail waitress bent over to hand Dwayne the whiskey he'd ordered. Tim grabbed the glass first and tossed the drink back. The burn down his throat only ignited the adrenaline that was blazing low in his gut.

One shot wouldn't kill him. He wouldn't lose control from one shot.

"Do it again," Dwayne encouraged. His friend was starting to sound less sloppy, more like his normal good ole country boy self.

"Are you crazy?" Tim asked. "I could have lost that entire thing!" And why, when the thought should have been a cold wake-up call, did the fear thrill him, just a little?

"That's why it's called gambling," Jeremy pointed out. "Don't be a pussy. Do it again."

"You two are nuts."

Jeremy grabbed his wrist in a tight grip. "If you lose, I'll pay you back every penny," he muttered in a low voice.

"What the hell has gotten into you?" Tim started to scrape his chips into the palm of his hand. Maybe he could catch up with the hot brunette before she got too far away. Playing all or nothing wasn't his style. Never had been. Measured risks made him a good officer and kept his ass out of trouble.

"Place your bets, gentlemen," the dealer intoned over the clang of another winning alarm bell somewhere in the slots section. Where his anonymous woman had disappeared to. Where he was heading.

"You have spent the entire trip playing nanny. And don't pretend you haven't."

"Someone has to," Tim grumbled. And yeah, it grated just a little that even if he wanted to have fun, it wouldn't be possible. Not with his two friends always being the first to sign up for Party Mascot.

"And we love you for it. But it just occurred to me that while you're babysitting, you're not having as much fun." Jeremy took the glass of Jack and Coke and pushed it in front. When Tim stared at him, he motioned to the glass. Tim took a sip, then a gulp.

"Place your bets." The request was more forceful.

"Hold on," Jeremy shot back, then faced Tim. "Do this. You're my best friend. You need to live. For one fucking night, stop thinking about what can go wrong. We have seven months in Afghanistan to worry about that. Have fun and let go. Don't be a pussy; just go for it."

Let go. It sounded like heaven. And really, if Jeremy was going to pay him back, was it really that much of a risk? For one night, he could act a fool like his friends normally did and worry about the consequences later.

He took all of one second to debate. He stole Dwayne's shot of tequila, ignoring Dwayne's protests, and tossed it back, adding to the burn of whiskey. Then he shoved his pile of chips forward.

"All in."

Acknowledgments

Another book, another set of acknowledgments. These things always scare me, as I worry about forgetting people. So to you, those I forget and regret not listing, you are first. Thank you, for whatever you have done to help me get to this point! I'm sure you know who you are.

My family, you are all amazing. Your support is rivaled by none, and a writer (or a woman) could not be more lucky.

My husband must get an extra-special nod in here for taking me to the gun range and showing me how to shoot a pistol. The man has the patience of a saint. (Also? It turns out I'm not a terrible shot. Just so you know…)

My critique group, you are all a bunch of angels. And my critique partner in crime, Keri Ford, thank you for helping me put my best foot forward.

Emmanuelle, you're unbelievable. And to the team at Sourcebooks, from cover art to promo to my editor Deb… you guys have been wonderful.

Lastly, as always, all mistakes are mine and mine alone. I'm pretty sure there shouldn't be any. I ordered them all removed. But, you know, just in case…

About the Author

Jeanette Murray is a contemporary romance author who spends her days surrounded by hunky alpha heroes… at least in her mind. In real life, she's a one-hero kind of woman, married to her own real-life Marine. When she's not chasing her daughter or their lovable-but-stupid Goldendoodle around the house, she's deep in her own fictional world, building another love story. As a military wife, she would tell you where she lives… but by the time you read this, she'll have already moved. To see what Jeanette is up to next, visit www.jeanettemurray.com.

SEALed with a Promise

by Mary Margret Daughtridge

~~~

Navy SEAL Caleb Delaude is as deadly as he is charming

Professor Emmie Caddington's quiet intelligence and quirky personality intrigue him. When he discovers that her personal connections can get him close to the man he's vowed to kill, will their budding relationship be nothing more than a means to revenge…or is she the key to his salvation?

~~~

Praise for SEALed with a Promise:

"This story delivers in a huge way." —*RT Book Reviews*

"A wonderful story that will have readers experiencing a whirlwind of emotions and culminating with an awesome scene that will have your pulse pounding." —*Romance Junkies*

"What an incredibly powerful book! I laughed and sniffled, was turned on and turned inside out." —*Queue My Review*

For more Mary Margret Daughtridge, visit:

www.sourcebooks.com